Enflamed

by R.M. Prioleau

Book 2 of *The Pyromancer Trilogy*

Cover art by Sarah Ellerton.
Aransiya Map by R.M. Prioleau.
Edited by Misti Wolanski.

First Printing: November 2012.
First Paperback Edition: November 2012.

ISBN: 978-0-983-77191-3

An image of the orb appeared before Kaijin in the thin air. The creature held up Kaijin's necklace. "This necklace's powers sent you here while your body slept. You have been asleep for precisely two and one-third mortal cycles."

Kaijin looked at the objects and gasped. The orb was grey and hazy. He focused on the necklace and, panicked, patted his chest. *It's gone!* His eyes widened. "That's mine! Why would the necklace save me?"

The creature held the necklace aloft and teasingly swung the charm like a pendulum. "Because the Master is not yet finished with you."

"Master?" Kaijin scrunched his brow. "I don't understand. What master?"

"The Master is He to whom you have vowed your soul."

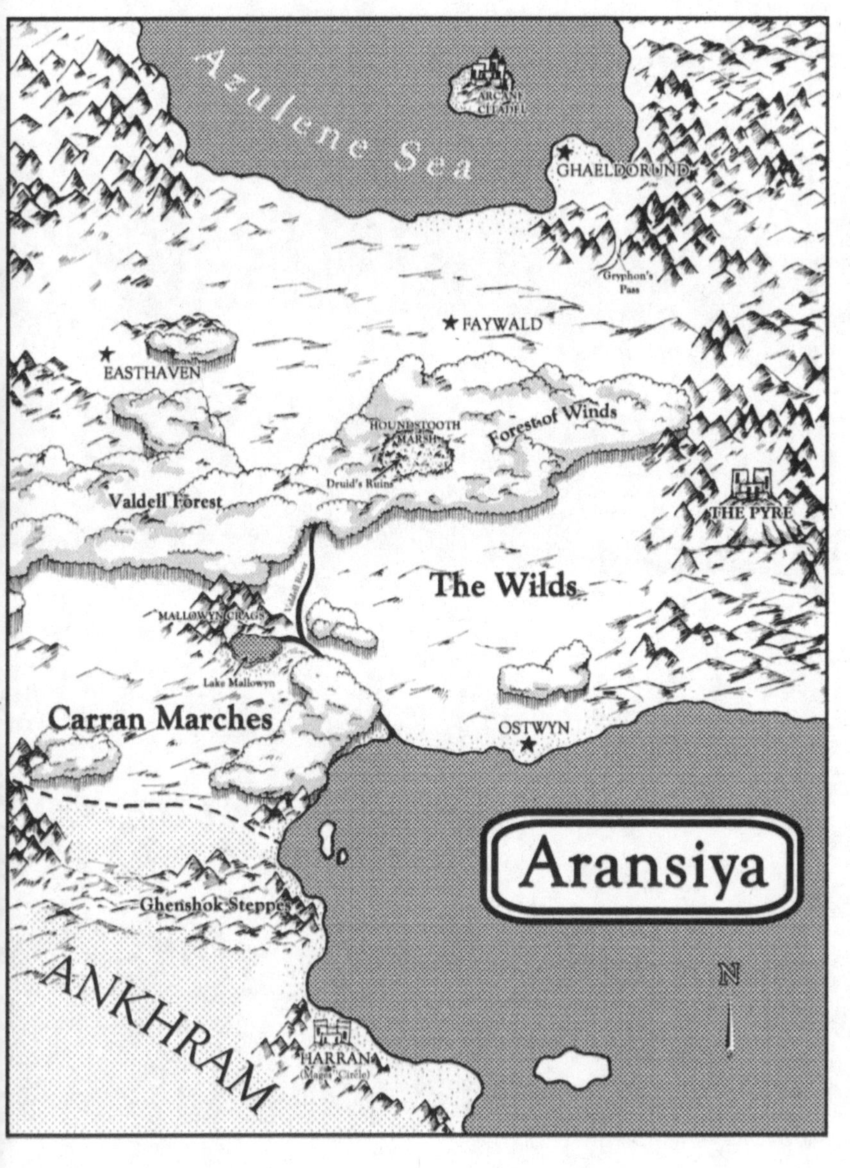

Azulene Sea
ARCANE CITADEL
GHAELDORUND
Gryphon's Pass
FAYWALD
EASTHAVEN
HOUNDSTOOTH MARSH
Forest of Winds
Druid's Ruins
Valdell Forest
THE PYRE
Valdell River
The Wilds
MALLOWYN CRAGS
Lake Mallowyn
Carran Marches
OSTWYN
Aransiya
Ghenshok Steppes
ANKHRAM
HARRANA
(Mage's Circle)
N

I

The orange-hued skies began to darken, and Kaijin walked alone, speaking to the presence he couldn't see. "I am yours," he murmured through dry, cracked lips, tasting blood. He slowly raised his eyes to observe the stretch of wilderness and the dirt road he had been traveling for only the gods knew how long.

He heard faint whispers in his mind, resembling the sound of crackling flames: *"You belong to me, Kaijin Sora."*

Kaijin smiled, listening to the unknown entity. "I belong . . ." How long had it been since he felt acceptance?

"The boy's smart, but he has no common sense," his father had often said.

"There's nothing wrong with him, Ramon," his mother would argue. "He's just . . . different."

His younger brother, Rorick, had often given him odd looks, saying, "You're strange, Kaijin."

Kaijin shifted his gaze toward the ground. No one understood him—or perhaps they were simply afraid of him. Fate had an interesting way of contending with fear. An entire city was destroyed as a result.

The city.

Easthaven. The name rang through his ears. The more he dwelled on it, the more his mind was flooded with memories, both old and new. His eyes burned, unable to shed another tear. The screams of the dying, the sights, the smells—he'd forgotten none of that fateful day of judgment.

Kaijin blinked when he realized his mind was wandering again. "They didn't have to die," he muttered.

"You think they were all innocent?" the fiery voice asked in his mind.

"No," he replied aloud, shaking his head. "Not everyone was guilty. Not everyone had to die."

"Death is not fickle. The lands have been purified."

He chewed his bottom lip, staring at his travel-dirty hands. "Then why does the blood of so many innocents remain?"

"Ignorance is not innocence."

Before Kaijin could respond, he heard high-pitched screeching from above. Miele, his familiar—a furry, brown fruit bat—fluttered happily in the sky. Other creatures began emerging from their habitats, and soon the eerie sounds of night filled Kaijin's ears.

Where am I going? When he received no response from the flames in his mind, he asked aloud, "Why do you continue tormenting me with your damned riddles?"

"You chose to serve me, and serve me you shall," the flames replied. *"The debt you owe has yet to be repaid."*

Kaijin frowned. "I think I have paid off that debt from the suffering you've put me through. Why are you doing this? Who are you? Why won't you face me, coward?"

The sizzling sounds of the flames tickled Kaijin's ears. *"You belong to me in more ways than your mortal mind can begin to comprehend. . . ."*

Kaijin stopped in his tracks. His stomach twisted anxiously. On the road ahead, several armed men loitered amongst the remains of a broken cart. The air seemed to stiffen, and the shadows of approaching night danced eerily about the area.

The vagabonds spotted Kaijin and fell silent. One man emerged from the group and approached. The remaining light cast shadows over the stranger's pockmarked face as he carefully assessed Kaijin's unkempt condition.

The stranger's lips curled into a light smirk. "Well, now, what do we have here? Bit late to be out alone on an evenin' stroll like this."

Kaijin met the man's gaze and scowled. "I'm rather tired, sir. I've traveled a long way and am in no mood for your senseless banter."

"Oho! A little cocky, aren't you, jack?" The man crossed his arms. "And just where'd you come from?"

"Easthaven."

The man raised an eyebrow and then acknowledged his comrades. "'Ey, Durant! Might wan' take a look at this one!"

Moments, later, a path was cleared from the group, and another man came forth. Torn, bloody leather armor covered Durant's brawny frame. Two short swords were strapped to his back. He stood before Kaijin and studied him briefly. "What's going on, Lander?" he asked his comrade.

"Easthaven, Boss!" Lander replied, wide-eyed. "This jack's sayin' he's from Easthaven!" He looked at Kaijin. "You *did* say 'Easthaven', right?"

Kaijin frowned. "Did I stutter?"

"Impossible," Durant said. "Easthaven's gone. Destroyed by the gravers almost a month ago."

"You sure it was gravers, Boss?" Lander interjected. "Thought someone said it was—"

"—Gravers!" Durant reiterated, shooting a glare at the other man. "I don't believe in all that finger-wigglin' shite those gullies keep raggin' about." He returned his attention to Kaijin. "This road was plagued with slaggers up until a few days ago, though. Thought we picked everyone clean. Looks like we missed one."

Kaijin blinked at the bandits' strange dialect, but he understood their threat well enough.

The air grew tense. He looked from Durant to Lander—who had vanished. Unnerved by the man's sudden disappearance, Kaijin refocused on Durant. "Please . . . just let me pass. I don't want any trouble. . . ."

Durant snorted and gestured to the rest of his band who began closing in. "Trouble? There's no trouble here unless you're intendin' to start some." His gaze hardened. "You see, we've had almost half the city of Easthaven comin' to town. Faywald's practically overflowin' with slaggers, now. The city's going to need some funds to be able to accommodate everyone. Your contributions would be . . . most helpful." He grinned.

Kaijin's left eye twitched as he attempted to stave off the rage fueled by Durant's threats. "I've no money. I've nothing of value. Let me pass."

"Hogwash." Durant's gaze bore into Kaijin. "What kind of heartless bastard are you, to not want to help all those poor, displaced jacks, marys and scamps?"

Kaijin's arms were restrained from behind. He gasped and attempted to pull away, but the grip on him was too tight. Kaijin peered over his shoulder spotted Lander, smirking wickedly back at him. Black, smoky mist dissipated from around the vagabond.

"As I was sayin'," Durant continued, stepping forward. "I'm sure you've plenty to donate to the cause." He pinched one of Kaijin's gold-plastered earlobes and gave it a firm tug.

Kaijin winced. Except for his necklace, all his gold jewelry had melted into his skin in what had happened in Easthaven.

Durant whistled as he appraised the gold with his eyes. "This is easily worth two hundred right here—enough to feed many mouths." He yanked Kaijin's earlobe so hard, some of the skin ripped off with the gold.

Kaijin let out a terrified scream of pain. Another vagabond approached and delivered a hard punch to his gut, silencing Kaijin's cries. Kaijin's eyes burned. His ears numbed from pain. He smelled blood he was certain was his own. A bitter, coppery taste lingered in his mouth.

Durant ripped the gold from Kaijin's other ear, and then tore the globs that remained of his rings from his fingers. "Hey, I'm being gentle here, you know." Durant laughed. "It would've not hurt at all, if you'd cooperated before. Now, what else do you ha—"

Miele dove at Durant's face then took off again, leaving behind bloody bite marks in one of his eyes. She soared back into the night sky and disappeared.

Panic and confusion swept over the group of men as Durant cried out, holding his face. Blood poured from his left eye and seeped between his fingers.

"Boss! You're bleedin'!" one of the vagabonds shouted.

"No shite!" Durant bellowed, his voice muffled by his hands. "What in the bloody hells bit me? Gods! I can't see! I think . . . I think I'm blind!"

Some of the men scrambled to tend to their leader, but he shoved them aside. Blood dotted the ground around him.

"Search this jack, then chalk him afterwards," Durant ordered. He turned and then stumbled down the road. "I'm goin' back to town to find a warder."

Kaijin felt a twinge in his mind and winced. He frantically scanned the skies. He concentrated through the pain in his body to find Miele's whereabouts. Sensing her preparing to give Durant another round of attacks, Kaijin told her mentally, *"No, Miele. Get away from here. There are far too many of these ruffians. I don't want you hurt. Go hide, and don't come out until I tell you."*

Miele's silhouette fluttered to a nearby tree, where she remained.

Someone pulled Kaijin backwards. The men around him disappeared and then reappeared from the shadows. In unison, they drew their weapons, the steel of the blades reflecting the light of the rising moon.

"Stop!" *Why are they advancing?* "I told you! I have nothing!"

Lander pinned Kaijin to the ground on his back. Four men pointed their blades at Kaijin's throat. One of the men took Lander's spot while Lander began rummaging through Kaijin's haversack.

"Now, let's see what we have here. . . ." Lander pulled out Kaijin's weathered spellbook, which locked with a metal clasp. Lander scrutinized the book, running his fingers along the raised crevices of runes, glyphs and tiny gems embellishing its cover.

"No! Don't touch my spellbook!" Kaijin cried weakly.

"What kind of book is that?" one of the vagabonds asked.

Ignoring them both, Lander attempted to unsecure the metal clasp, but it wouldn't budge—the *lock* spell made sure of that.

Lander finally shook his head in puzzlement. "Hells if I know. But it looks like something that'll fetch some good coin." He tossed the book aside and emptied the container. A sealed jar and a well-kept silver dagger spilled out. He took a moment to examine the dagger's blade and then sheathed it in his boot. "Not worth shite, but one can't have too many shivs around, eh?" He opened the jar, and then snorted at what he discovered inside. "What in the bloody hells are these things? Sugar sticks?" Frustrated, he threw the jar to the ground.

Kaijin struggled against the men's grip as Lander picked up the book again. He felt his golden amulet slip out from beneath his robes. The symbol, shaped like a flame, pulsated a warm, soothing heat against his chest in time with his heartbeat.

The smile on Lander's face brightened. "Now *there's* the shiny we've been lookin' for!" He reached for the charm.

Kaijin's breathing became ragged. "No, don't! Don't touch it!"

Lander's fingertips barely touched the golden surface, and something sizzled. "Ow!" He yanked his hand back and nursed the tiny burn wound. "Now, if that isn't the strangest shite I've ever seen . . ."

"No. . . ." Kaijin's voice weakened. His mind was jumbled, and he felt dizzy. Soon, the men's voices around him began growing fainter in his ears. He knew this sensation, and he felt unable to stop it.

Lander thoroughly examined the necklace, then grabbed it, gritting his teeth.

Too weak to resist, Kaijin blacked out for a moment. He began to come to when he heard Lander cry out in pain, followed by several sets of feet trampling closer. Kaijin quickly opened his eyes and spied Lander holding his hand, which was burned to the bone. The other men scrambled about in a panic. Watching Lander suffer brought a smile to Kaijin's lips.

The unknown presence spoke to Kaijin's mind again. *"Such insolence will not go unpunished."*

A soothing warmth filled Kaijin's body, and he felt himself lose his will. He closed his eyes briefly, succumbing to the unknown force that possessed his body. When he reopened them, the world around him was painted red. He stared at the group of men.

Tightening their grips on their weapons, the vagabonds began slowly backing away from Kaijin and Lander.

Lander gawked at Kaijin. "Who—What in the—"

"Looks like finger-wigglin' to me!" one man shouted.

"Them finger-wigglers are dangerous!" another said.

"The boss don't believe the slaggers' rumors about a finger-wiggler destroying Easthaven."

"Hogwash! Ain't no finger-wiggler doing that shite. Pretty sure it was gravers."

"Get your facts straight, jack. It was neither."

"Hey! I know finger-wigglin' when I see it."

Lander whipped his head around to face his comrades. He shouted, "Enough! This jack's just some punk who wishes he was like them Ghaeldorund finger-wigglers. Now, someone help me get this damned necklace off him."

One of the men broke from the group and approached cautiously, keeping his wary gaze on Kaijin.

Kaijin's ears perked. *"They seek to destroy you, Kaijin Sora,"* the voice in his mind said, eclipsing the men's voices surrounding him. *"They seek to destroy . . . us."*

Everything went red. Something took over Kaijin's body so fast that it left him confused. He opened his mouth to utter a chant, but a ball of fire was already evoked in his hands. Against his will, Kaijin felt himself launch the fireball toward the group of vagabonds.

A few men caught in the blast screamed as their bodies caught on fire. The others scrambled out of the way, cowered, and ran.

Lander watched his comrades flee and was about to do the same. He looked back at Kaijin, trembling, his shaking hands clutching the spellbook. "H–hey, who—What . . . what *are* you?"

The pulsating heat from the charm intensified, increasing in tempo. Kaijin stood and faced the cowering man. He clenched his fists, which began to burn in whitefire. He took a step, and the fire encompassed his entire body.

Lander stepped backwards. "D–don't hurt me!" he begged, nearly stumbling over his own feet.

Kaijin's eyes narrowed. One of his fists raised, preparing to unleash another fiery attack.

The sight of the intensifying flames seemed more than enough for Lander to turn and sprint down the road. "I'm not ready to die!" he screamed, dropping the spellbook as he ran. The dagger also slipped from his boot.

Rage still filled Kaijin, even after the commotion ceased. He stared at the burned corpses of the three unfortunate vagabonds and soon felt the sensation in his body subside. "No . . . not again. . . ." he muttered.

He took a deep breath, and his vision returned to normal. The corpses had been rendered unrecognizable by the raging flames. Kaijin turned his head away from the sight. He staggered to his discarded spellbook and sank to his knees before it. He pulled it to him and brushed off the dirt that had found its way inside the cover's raised metallic crevices as he allowed his mind to refocus on his present state.

Kaijin turned his face to the sky. *"Come, Miele,"* he said in his mind.

Miele's high-pitched screeching came moments later. She leapt from her leafy hiding spot and fluttered to him.

Kaijin smiled briefly to her, then returned his spellbook to his haversack. "That was . . . unfortunate," he said to her aloud. "I'm just glad you're safe, Miele. And my spellbook . . ."

Miele responded with several happy shrieks and then fluttered around his head.

Kaijin arose and gathered the dagger and discarded jar, salvaging as many of the spilled honeysticks as he could. He presented one to Miele before securing the rest.

"Here, Miele. You were very brave, to do what you did. You protected your master! Such courage deserves a fitting reward."

Miele dove toward her favorite treat. With her tiny maw opened wide, she plucked the honeystick from his hand and settled on his shoulder to savor it happily.

Kaijin felt a newfound strength fill him as Miele's excited energy amplified. It was strength he needed to resume his trek along the stretch of winding road eastward, unknowing of where his journey would take him.

II

The late evening shadows cast a faint outline of a city in the distance. Kaijin slowed his steps and looked ahead. *How long have I been traveling?* The sight of the city toyed with his senses. He could already taste the warm meals and feel the soft beds. Living out in the wilderness for weeks had proved brutal on his body, and he wanted nothing more than to live a simple life again. But he already suspected things would not come easily—not if that fiery spirit in his mind had anything to do with it.

Kaijin urged his exhausted body forward. Two guards posted outside the gates spotted him and watched as he trudged past. One of the guards moved to assist Kaijin but was promptly stopped by his fellow soldier.

"Stop helping every damnable refugee that comes through here," the other guard scolded.

"Sorry, sir. He looked too weak to walk. I just wanted to—"

"Use that strength to help keep order around here. All these refugees are liable to cause trouble."

"Yes, sir. . . ."

Kaijin glanced sidelong at the two men before making his way into the city. Looking above, Kaijin noticed Miele flutter over the gates, entering the city unnoticed.

Once he was inside, she swooped back down to follow him.

The city appeared considerably smaller than Easthaven; however, it was just as crowded. Refugees young and old filled the streets and alleys. But even amid the despair hanging heavily in the air, streamers, ribbons and other decorations adorned some of the buildings, creating colorful paths toward the town square. Flashy posters embellished the walls near the city gates, advertising an upcoming event.

Tired, Kaijin spied an inn nearby, and relief spread through his body like a wave. As he dragged his exhausted and beaten body to the door, he heard murmuring around him and noticed some refugees and resident passersby cast curious glances his way. Candles flickered in the windows of the inn, emanating a welcoming glow.

Before entering, Kaijin looked to the sky. He felt Miele's presence nearby but could only make out the faint outline of her small body against the black night sky. *"I doubt they will allow you inside. Enjoy the evening, but don't stray too far from the inn."* Miele screeched softly in response, and he watched her silhouette flutter to the side of the inn, where a blossoming moonflower vine grew. Kaijin smiled slightly, feeling her contentment.

Kaijin stumbled through the door and slumped over at the counter. The inn was quiet inside, with very few patrons milling about at that late hour. The smell of stale ale and spoiled apples lingered heavily in the air.

"Welcome to the Bottomless Cauldron," a portly man greeted him in a husky voice. "What'll it be tonight?" He paused, looked down his nose at Kaijin and scowled. "Hells! Not another one."

Kaijin lifted his gaze. "Sir?"

"I thought all you damned refugees stopped coming days ago!"

"How do you know I'm a refugee?"

The man crossed his thick arms. "Seen enough of 'em to know what they look like . . ." The man's bushy peppered-blonde mustache lifted slightly, revealing his sneer. "And smell like. And don't even think about asking for a room. Did you not see all those people sleeping on the streets on your way in here? Every inn in town's been filled beyond capacity—including mine. I suggest you find a nice li'l corner to sleep in like the rest of 'em."

Kaijin heaved a sigh. "Please, sir. I'll do anything for a room. I'll work and pay it off, if I must. Please. I just want to sleep in a bed."

"You and half this city. Look, I told you—I've nothing available. Now, unless you intend to buy a meal or a drink . . ."

A meal sounded nice, but a good night's rest sounded even better. It was getting harder to stay awake the more he thought about a cozy room. Out of desperation, Kaijin dumped the contents of his haversack—his spellbook, dagger and the honeystick jar—onto the counter. "If it is gold you want, I will give you all that I own."

"What did I just—" The innkeeper paused as Kaijin turned the bag inside out.

Kaijin couldn't find a single coin. He felt for his jewelry—checked his bloody, skinless earlobes and his hands for any gold the vagabonds might have missed. They were likewise barren.

"No," Kaijin muttered, "I could've sworn I had . . ."

The innkeeper frowned. "Wait a minute." He pointed to the book. "Those symbols—I've seen those kinds of things before from those pompous Ghaeldorund folk that often come around here." He narrowed his eyes at Kaijin. "You're one of those . . . *mages*, aren't you?"

Kaijin paused and then met the man's gaze. "Is that a problem?"

The innkeeper growled and shoved the book off the counter. "Mages are nothing but trouble. Get out of my inn. Hells, get out of Faywald! We don't need Ghaeldorund's corruption spreading here."

Kaijin knelt to retrieve his spellbook. He regarded the innkeeper again, raising his brow curiously. "What are you talking about, sir?"

"Everyone knows Easthaven was destroyed by mages. It's obvious the mages came from Ghaeldorund. Buncha wicked, vile monsters, they are! Now get the hells out of here, and don't come back!"

Kaijin swallowed. Disturbing images flashed in his mind—the frightened innocents, the undead, the chaos. His master's voice, speaking a single name: *Xavorin.*

Has news of Xavorin's misdeeds caused all of Aransiya to despise mages?

"*Xavorin didn't destroy Easthaven. You did,*" responded the fiery voice in his mind.

Kaijin gritted his teeth. *No!*

He cast a wary gaze around the rest of the inn. The lingering patrons had looked up from their drinks and toward the two of them. Frowning, Kaijin turned back to the innkeeper. "I'm sorry for disturbing you, sir. I will leave." He hastily stuffed his items back into the haversack, then left.

Standing outside the inn, Kaijin surveyed the crowded streets and occupied alleys. "Hells if I'm leaving now," he muttered bitterly. "I can barely keep my eyes open." He heard horses nearby. Following the sounds, Kaijin walked east from the inn back toward the main entrance. Across from the gates, a trail of hay stopped before a small stable. Kaijin spied three horses in their stalls.

He carefully looked around, ensuring he wasn't being watched or followed. He heard Miele flutter overhead and saw her make her way into a small opening in the gable. He hustled to the stable and quietly opened the gate.

The horses' ears flicked his way. They turned their heads and acknowledged Kaijin's presence by snorting at him.

Kaijin's heart anxiously pounded. He took a deep breath to calm his nerves. He crept toward one of the horse's stalls, placed his finger to his lips, and whispered, "Shh. . . . It's okay." *Gods, what am I doing, trying to calm these animals?*

To his surprise and relief, the mare turned her attention elsewhere. The horses in the adjacent stalls followed suit.

Kaijin entered one of the empty stalls and plopped down on the small nest of hay inside. He lay on his back and stared up at the shadows among the stable's rafters, where he spied Miele hanging from one of the wooden beams. The dim lights from outside reflected eerily off her large, ochre eyes as she stared at him intently.

"It's not the luxury of an inn, but at least it's better than sleeping on the hard cobblestone streets. I really need to rest, now. Go out and play. Alert me if there's trouble."

Miele responded with a series of soft, high-pitched screeches and then promptly flew out of the gable.

After she left, Kaijin tucked himself into a fetal position, clutched his haversack, and listened to the sounds of night. His necklace pulsated warmth, a soothing sensation against his chest, and soon he was lulled to sleep.

*   *   *

Miele embraced the shadows of night, encircling the stables from above. Her keen nose detected the pleasantly sweet fragrance of the moonflowers' nectar she had feasted on earlier, and she perked up. However, her attention was drawn to the sounds of scuffling below. She spied a tiny figure walking near the stable and toward the Bottomless Cauldron. She swooped down, clung to the wooden beams above the stable's entrance, and scrutinized the stranger more closely.

The newcomer, a male, appeared to be a small child. Shadows concealed his face and traced the outline of his lean frame. Walking with a skip in his step, he whistled a hearty tune as he counted a handful of coins. One of the coins slipped from his hand and rolled underneath the stable gate.

"Soddin' 'ells!" he grumbled. He rushed to the gate as fast as his little legs could go before the coin rolled out of his sight.

Miele watched the coin roll down the stable's aisle before settling to a stop beside one of the stalls. The pinging sound of the silver piece roused a nearby horse, and one of its ears turned backwards.

The stranger swore under his breath. "Why does it always gotta be one?" His ears suddenly perked and he immediately took refuge behind a stack of unopened crates sitting beside the stables. Two guards walked past, making their way toward the Bottomless Cauldron while they chatted. When they were gone, the small, shadowy figure re-emerged and opened the stable gate.

Miele watched the stranger crawl on all fours down the aisle in search of the lone coin. He ran his hand along the ground.

"Aha! Found you," he muttered quietly, locating the coin next to a hay bale. He scooped up the coin and placed it in a pouch tied to his belt.

The horse nearby turned its head and snorted at him. Its tail swished back and forth.

The small figure tilted his head back, gazing up at the towering unsettled hackney in awe. Barely standing as high as its gaskin, the stranger held up both hands in surrender. "'Ey, now, I was just leavin'. No need to get your 'orse'airs in a foddle."

The horse shook its head and gave another snort in response.

As the stranger turned to leave, he craned his head toward the adjacent stall, where Kaijin huddled atop a small bed of hay, snoring lightly. The stranger slinked into the stall to get a closer look.

He blinked in surprise. "A man?"

He reached out to touch Kaijin's face, but his hand drifted downward, toward the haversack, where the top of

Kaijin's spellbook peeked out. The stranger tilted his head. "Ey, now. What do we 'ave 'ere?" He nervously licked his top lip and reached for the book.

Miele screeched and flew down from the beams, diving toward the intruder. She plunged tiny fangs into the ruddy flesh of his pointed ear.

"Ow!"

* * *

A sound woke Kaijin, who instinctively tightened his fingers around his haversack. He opened his eyes to discover a small male.

The pointy ears were enough for Kaijin to realize that the stranger wasn't exactly human. His straight, ebony hair was braided in several spots and tied back in a single topknot. Light battle scars marred his young, sideburned face, and a single, prominent scar extended across the bridge of his nose.

"Ahh! I'm bein' attacked!" the creature cried out. He dove into the nearest hay pile and hid.

Kaijin looked at Miele just as she returned to the rafters. He stood and approached the hay. "What are you doing?" he demanded, prodding the top of the trembling mound with his finger.

There was a moment of silence before the small creature's topknot poked from the top of the hay. His head slowly appeared as he rose and he gazed at Kaijin with wide, fear-filled eyes. "Is it gone?" he asked in a trembling voice, muffled somewhat from the hay. His large eyes turned left and right, as though anticipating another surprise attack.

Kaijin arched his eyebrow. "Is *what* gone?"

"That 'orrible, man-eatin' bat! 'Ow could you not see such a thing? Look! I got th' scars to prove it, I do!" The stranger bent over his injured ear, revealing two tiny bite marks on the tip.

Kaijin studied the marks, then chuckled softly. "Miele is no man-eating bat," he assured. "She is my familiar. She likes eating fruit and sweet things—like honeysticks."

The creature scrunched his face. "'Oneysticks?"

"Yes." Kaijin retrieved the jar from his haversack and pulled out a treat.

"Oh! *'Oneysticks!* Kinda like *nyrium-tegos*."

"What?"

"It's a popular treat amongst brownie children. *Nyrium-tegos* are made from sweetberry nectar. Very tasty, indeed!" The stranger licked his lips. "Ah, brings back memories of Mum givin' me one before bed every night."

Before Kaijin could respond, Miele screeched. She swooped down, snatched the honeystick from his hand, and returned to the rafters.

"'Ey, now! Get that soddin' thing away from me!" the stranger sank back into the hay.

Kaijin smiled as he watched Miele hang from one of the wooden beams and began feasting on her treat. "Don't worry. She would rather eat her honeystick. She is a fruit bat."

"Fruit bat, vegetable bat—does it matter? She's soddin' dangerous! She bit me, she did!"

"She probably thought you were trying to harm me, so she attacked—and perhaps she had every reason to. Who are you? Rather, *what* are you?"

The stranger gawked at Kaijin. "What? Never seen a brownie before? Well I sure as 'ells seen plenty of 'umans.

This place is swarmin' with 'em—'umans, I mean. Did you 'ear about all those refugees comin' from Easthaven? Soddin' shame, it is. . . ."

Kaijin opened his mouth to respond, but the brownie continued talking.

"Oh! Th' name's Nester. Also known as 'Nimble' Nester Two-Blades. An' you are?"

Kaijin exhaled once Nester finally stopped. "I'm, ah . . . Kaijin. Sora. Also known as Kaijin."

"Kaijin! Good to meet you!" Nester relaxed a bit, his attention no longer focused on locating Miele. He emerged from the hay and picked out the strands from his hair and long sideburns. Standing before Kaijin, Nester's head barely reached his waist. "What were you doin' all 'oled up in 'ere for?"

Kaijin sighed. "I was tired and needed a place to sleep."

"Well th' stables ain't no place for winkin'—'less you like th' smell of 'orse piss." His eyes focused on Kaijin's haversack. "'Ey, that was a . . . a nice book you 'ad in there. . . ."

Miele shrieked a message to Kaijin in his mind. *"He did that, did he?"* Kaijin replied through the link. He shot a cool gaze at Nester and said aloud, "It is, isn't it? Some ruffians tried to steal it from me, too. I dare ask what kind of bold fool you are to attempt to steal from someone who is far bigger than you?"

Nester huffed and puffed out his chest, making his leather jerkin appear smaller on him. "'Ey! I may be short, but that don't mean I don't get around. 'Sides, your book looked interestin'."

"There's nothing interesting about this book, I assure you," Kaijin said flatly. "If it's gold you want, I have none. Those ruffians beat you to it."

"Pah! These peepers know value when they see it." Nester deflated his chest and picked out another stray piece of hay from beneath his jerkin. "Are you lookin' to sell it? 'Ow 'bout we . . . ah . . . split th' profits, aye?"

"What!" Kaijin's eyes widened. "My spellbook is *not* for sale!"

Nester's jaw dropped. "S–spellbook?"

Kaijin pursed his lips and quickly averted his gaze from him. "Yes, I'm a mage," he muttered in a low, bitter tone. "Apparently, people like me aren't allowed in this city."

"Well, it ain't like that. There're lotsa superstitious sods 'round 'ere—more than ever now after th' news of what 'appened to Easthaven. You know that Ghaeldorund's only a three-day walk north from 'ere, aye? Everyone around 'ere says a fiddler from that city came an' destroyed Easthaven. Can you believe it? One soddin' fiddler destroyin' a 'uge city like that?"

"'Fiddler'?" Kaijin chewed on his bottom lip. "If you mean a mage, then yes, I can believe it."

"Poor sods are scared, as you can imagine. They don't want th' same thing to 'appen to Faywald. Everyone says fiddlin' is dangerous—'ells, *fiddlers* are dangerous! They got every soddin' right to be afraid if a fiddler can destroy a whole city."

"Magic is only as dangerous as the wielder." Kaijin's mouth turned bitter.

"Well I sure 'ope th' evil fiddler's been stopped. I sure wouldn't like to be th' unfortunate bloke to meet 'im."

Nester's words stung. *Did I really cause this?* "Yes, well . . . I'm just a man trying to survive like the rest of the refugees here. I'm not looking for trouble."

"You're not just a simple bloke. You're a simple bloke who knows a bit of fiddlin'. Say! You can 'elp me, y'know!"

"Me? Help you?" Kaijin blinked. *How absurd!* "I'm a mage, remember? I'm 'dangerous'. How can I possibly help you?"

"Pah! I never said I believed in all that soddin' rubbish." Nester waved his hand dismissively. "'Umans tend to take things out of proportion, y'know? Buncha cowardly blokes, some of them are. But a scared 'uman means 'is peepers ain't watchin' 'is coin purse none too closely, if y'know what I mean." He gave a gap-toothed smile.

Kaijin frowned. "You take pleasure in stealing?"

Nester gasped and looked overly surprised. *Probably acting.* "'Pleasure'? Nay, Kaijin. Who do you think I am? Some kinda poor street bloke lookin' for a 'andout? I've got a bit more dignity than that." He proudly thumbed himself in the chest. "Th' way I see it is, if all these soddin' refugees are just sittin' on th' streets with pockets full o' gold and not spendin' it, then what's th' point in 'avin' it in th' first place? That's where I come in. I 'elp 'em spend th' money they're not spendin', see?"

Kaijin crossed his arms, eying him coolly. "I fail to understand your logic."

"That's 'cause you're a 'uman." Nester tapped his finger against his temple. "It's a known fact that brownies got th' sharpest wits."

"I see. . . ."

"As for th' 'elp, well, I'm runnin' out o' funds here, y'know? Th' soddin' innkeeper at th' Cask an' Iron thought it'd be nice to raise th' prices of th' rooms a few days ago when all th' refugees came floodin' into town. And on top of all that, th' sod wants all th' inn patrons to pay *three days* in advance! 'E's gonna kick me out soon, I know it! Can you believe it? Anyway, I prigged—er—*did favors* around town but I'm still short—er, not literally. Well, I *am* short, but I didn't mean it like that. . . ."

"Whatever shady business you're doing, you can count me out. Why don't you ask some of those ruffians who tried to rob me, instead?"

"Pfft! No, they'll just get all th' good stuff and leave me th' scraps—or try an' prig 'em off me if they're good enough. But you, Kaijin—you're a fiddler! The first fiddler I've seen around 'ere who actually talked to me! Not like some o' those other arrogant, pompous sods from Ghaeldorund and beyond. 'Sides, if we 'appen to get in a pinch, then you can show off your *'dangerous'* fiddlin' skills, aye?"

"Magic is *not* a toy, nor should it be misused."

"Never said that, mate, though it must be fun to make li'l sparklies come outta your 'ands, aye?"

Kaijin rolled his eyes.

Nester tapped his chin. ". . . Tellya what. If you 'elp me, I'll share my room at th' Cask an' Iron. Other than that soddin' annoyin' innkeeper, th' place's got comfy rooms, good food an' drinks, an' cute, tall women." He chuckled. "So, do we 'ave a deal or what?"

Kaijin paused to consider his options. He was beginning to smell horse piss on himself, which reminded him of the dreary conditions he'd endured. He looked at Nester, who bore a childlike, mischievous grin on his face.

"I don't know if I should trust him, Miele. What do you think?"

Miele responded with a soft screech and a single flap of her wings.

A surge of excitement filled Kaijin's mind, and he cracked a smile. *"Yes, I know you'll keep me safe. You're a good bat."* He regarded Nester again and his smile quickly faded. "All right. I'll help you earn some coin. But no thievery, you hear?"

Nester's face brightened, and he clapped his hands together once, startling the horses. "Wonderful! Well, then! Let's be off. Th' Cask an' Iron is in th' northern part of town—quite ritzy, I might add. I'll tell you all about my li'l project when we get there." He turned and walked out of the stables, with a happy skip to his steps.

* * *

Entering the Cask and Iron, Kaijin was overwhelmed by the scents of various types of wines and strong incense. The windows were decorated with colorful, cascading draperies, while plush, exotic rugs covered the wooden floor. Dim light from the sparse candles placed throughout the quiet, empty main room created an atmosphere so calm, it made Kaijin yawn sleepily.

"Looks like th' innkeeper stepped out," Nester whispered to Kaijin as they made their way to the stairs. "Good riddance, I say. Let's hurry upstairs before—"

A door creaked shut behind them.

A set of footsteps padded across the wood floors from the backroom. A thin, middle-aged man poked his head through the doorway. He bore a deep scowl on his angular face as he regarded Nester and Kaijin with dark brown eyes.

Nester sighed as the man approached.

Kaijin studied the innkeeper's immaculate attire. The sleeves of his tunic were trimmed in silver. A matching silver buckle molded in the shape of an abstract design accented the belt he wore around his small waist. His white pants were clean and crisp, devoid of a single speck of dirt.

"You think I not forget?" the innkeeper said to the brownie, placing his bronze hands on his hips. His voice rolled in a thick, exotic accent.

"'Ey, I'm paid up for three more days, yet!" Nester retorted. "Don't go 'oundin' *me* 'bout payin'!"

The innkeeper bent down and prodded his finger in Nester's chest. "Your type are sticky-fingered cheats. I have my eye on you."

Nester slapped the man's hand away, glaring. "And 'your type' are a buncha greedy sods!"

The innkeeper stood and regarded Kaijin. "Do not trust these little people, sir. They pick your pockets faster than you blink!"

Kaijin nodded absently, remaining silent. He tried to place the man's strange yet familiar-seeming dialect.

"All right," Nester grumbled. "If you're done patronizin' us, can we be off to bed, now?"

"He pay?" The man thumbed at Kaijin.

Nester groaned and rubbed his hands over his face. "Soddin' 'ells! Fine!" He grabbed five silver pieces from his coin pouch and presented it to the innkeeper forcefully. "'Ere!"

The innkeeper took the coins, carefully counted them and then looked at Nester. "I charge you double for trying to sneak him in."

Nester's eyes widened. "What!"

"Excuse me," Kaijin said finally. "I don't mean to cause any trouble here. I will find someplace else to sleep for the night. Please give Nester back his money. I will leave." He headed for the door.

"Oy! Wait!" Nester rushed after Kaijin and grabbed a handful of his robes. "I still need you, Kaijin! A deal's a deal, y'know! I'll grit my teeth an' bear 'avin' to lose th' money if it means a greater treasure awaitin' at th' end, aye?" He glared at the innkeeper from over his shoulder. "I can't stand you Ankhram sods!"

Kaijin paused, reaching for the door handle to go outside.

The innkeeper huffed. "It is called business, little man. I can easily throw you out of my inn."

"Try as you will. You'll have to catch me, first!" Nester jeered.

Kaijin quirked his eyebrow at the innkeeper. "Ankhram? You are from Ankhram?"

The man's eyes turned to Kaijin. "Yes, and contrary to what the little man says, I am quite reputable, as is anyone from Ankhram. We are a noble race."

Kaijin moved away from the door. "How interesting. My mother—she was from Ankhram. . . . At least, that was what my father once told me when I was a boy."

The man's thick, jet-black beard shifted slightly upward as he made a wide smile. "Ah, then you would understand, yes? It is not often I meet travelers from the old country. Most are traders."

"My father was a trader," Kaijin said. "My mother stayed at home and took care of my brother and me." He paused, feeling a lump forming in his throat as he remembered his family.

"Ankhram is very far from here. You have come a long way. How wonderful it is to speak to a fellow brother."

"Well, actually, I'm not—ow!" Kaijin glared at Nester.

Nester innocently glanced toward the ceiling, then regarded Kaijin. "Oh! Sorry, mate—did I step on your foot? Didn't see it there. Silly me."

The innkeeper looked between the two, then approached Kaijin, handing him the silver pieces. "I will be lenient just this once because of this pleasant conversation. But business is business, and you will need to pay next time. But I will give you . . . special rate." His gaze briefly shifted to Nester. "Your price still remains, little man."

Nester puffed out his chest. "'Ey, now! If it wasn't for me bringin' Kaijin here, you wouldn't be chewin' gums with your 'fellow brother'!" He swiped the silver pieces from Kaijin's hand.

The innkeeper made a sour face. "Perhaps you have point. Fine. In three days, you pay, and not a day later."

Nester smiled wide. "That's fine with me! Come on, Kaijin."

Before Kaijin could speak, Nester grabbed his hand and pulled him upstairs.

* * *

Nester clicked open the last door down the short hallway and shuffled into the room. "Ah, 'ere we are."

Kaijin peered inside. The tiny room was furnished for a single occupant—a stripped, wooden bunk; an engraved armoire that sat against the wall across from it; a small desk atop which several parchments were strewn; and a washtub in one corner. A makeshift hammock crafted from the linen bedding was strung in another corner next the room's only window, which sat on the far wall. The ends of the hammock were nailed haphazardly to the adjacent drab walls.

"You're paying double for this?" Kaijin asked, stepping into the room.

"Aye, can you believe it? 'E's robbin' me blind, I tell you! But what can I do? If I don't play by 'is rules, 'e'll kick me out. An' there ain't no other place to stay in this city. Anyway, I don't mind th' room so much. Th' bed's too soft for my tastes, though. You can 'ave it."

Kaijin beamed at the sight of the bed. "Thank you, Nester. You don't know how grateful I am to be able to finally sleep in a bed again."

"Sure I do." Nester chuckled. He wriggled out of his leather jerkin, kicked off his boots, and then climbed into his hammock. "The more I think about it, the more I realize we're not that different from one another, y'know?" After making himself comfortable, he pulled the woolen blanket over him.

"I doubt that." Kaijin wandered over to the corner and peered at the washtub, which was half-filled with water.

Nester propped his hands behind his head and watched him. "It's simple, really. No one likes me 'cause they think all brownies are nothin' but priggers and lowlifes. Well, it ain't true, y'know. We actually got a spot of dignity in our 'earts. I don't like 'urtin' people—well unless they intend to 'urt me first. Anyway, 'umans are stubborn. I'd just be wastin' my breath tryin' to convince 'em I'm not a bad person. As for you? Well, no one likes you 'cause you're a fiddler—and fiddlers are s'posedly dangerous. No one likes us, mate—we're outcasts! Ain't that a soddin' shame? . . . Oh, th' water got changed this mornin'."

Kaijin peered at his reflection in the water. His short, thick red hair stuck up haphazardly like wildfire. His tanned face had lost its boyish charm and good looks— replaced with a weathered, tired face that looked haunted. *Damn, how did I let myself get like this?*

He began taking off his once-flamboyant noble robes, which were dirtied and frayed at the hems from the many days' travel. Keeping his back to Nester, Kaijin glanced over his shoulder. "So what's this 'help' you need from me?"

Nester rocked himself in the hammock as he thought. "Well, you see, contrary to what you've probably 'eard about me, I'm an explorer—an . . . an obtainer of rare antiquities. Aye, that's it. My Uncle Nickle's a merchant, you see, but th' poor sod's gettin' on in years. 'E wants me to take over th' family business, but I ain't got nothin' valuable to sell. So, I'm 'opin' to find a trinket or two to get th' business started again."

Kaijin scoffed. "By stealing?"

"Nay! I ain't a prigger—I'm an *explorer!*"

"I fail to see the difference in your words."

"I swear on my pa's grave I ain't priggin' no one for somethin' like this! It's too easy to do that, anyway. Uncle Nickle ran 'is business sellin' stuff 'e found on 'is adventures. Well, 'e did have fast fingers, too, but 'e really loved th' thrill of explorin'. Anyway, priggin' ain't bad if no one knows you're doin' it—that's what my pa used to say."

Kaijin's head was starting to throb. He rubbed his temples. "Look, just get to the point, will you?"

"Well, I was gonna do some explorin' outside o' town," Nester said. "There's this place about a day's travel southwest that I've been wantin' to visit since I came to Faywald a week ago. Some ruins are supposedly there that were once used by th' foresty blokes a long, long time ago."

Kaijin was about to get into the tub when he paused. "What's so special about some ruins?"

"Th' foresty blokes are an odd bunch, they are, but I've 'eard they sometimes tend to 'oard a few trinkets. That's where you come in. I need you to 'elp me search th' ruins and 'opefully find somethin' worthwhile."

"Forget it. I'm not a thief, and I don't intend to pillage some ruins in the middle of nowhere."

"'*Explorer*'!" Nester corrected. "We're doin' *explorin'*! Besides, you said you'd 'elp. A deal's a deal, aye?" He rolled on his side and closed his eyes. "Now, I'm gonna catch me a few winks. Tomorrow's a big day, y'know. We're gonna find us some treas—ah, that is, find somethin' amazin' in those ruins for my Uncle Nickle's business, aye!"

Kaijin sighed and got into the tub. Letting the cool water settle over him, Kaijin half-listened to the brownie's ramblings and began meditating on the day's events, instead. He stared down at the partially submerged charm hanging around his neck. Steam rose from the fire symbol, which glowed faintly, its light reflecting beautifully off the water's surface. The charm felt warm against his skin, and soon the water warmed to a soothing temperature. He sighed. *How is it that I've been spared from death for this long?*

"You will never understand me, Kaijin Sora," the fiery voice responded.

"Like hells I won't," Kaijin said aloud, frowning.

"Eh? You say somethin', mate?"

Kaijin blinked, pulled from his trance. He looked up at Nester, who was gazing at him sleepily. "N–No, sorry, I was just thinking to myself."

"Well think quieter, will you?" Nester rolled back over and closed his eyes.

Kaijin resumed his bath. He sensed Miele's presence nearby. He spied the faint flutter of shadows outside the window. *"I'm fine, Miele,"* he assured her. *"Go play. Enjoy the night. But stay near the inn."* He felt a pleasant pang in his mind moments later, and the shadows were gone.

After a relaxing bath, Kaijin washed his dirty clothes in the tub and hung them out the window to dry. Afterwards, he finally lay on the bed, not caring that it was stripped of its linens. The featherbed cradled him, and the charm around his neck maintained a steady heat as it pulsated against his chest, soothing his body. He immediately fell asleep despite the memories that still haunted him.

III

R ise an' shine, mate!" Nester's strident voice broke Kaijin's peaceful respite.

As Kaijin slowly opened his eyes, he was momentarily blinded by the morning sunlight. His eyes adjusted, and he gazed upon the brownie's grinning face.

"C'mon." Nester leaned over the bed, watching him. "We'll never get out there at this rate. Oy! Get up, will you?"

Kaijin groaned, shaking off the remainder of sleep. He rolled onto his back and stared up at the ceiling. He felt the steady warmth of his necklace pressed against his bare chest.

"That's a mighty fine necklace you got there." Nester sounded awed. "Quite a beauty. It looks just like fire. I feel as though I've seen somethin' like that somewhere before. . . ."

Kaijin glimpsed Nester's hand extending toward the charm and promptly grabbed the brownie's hand. He muttered sleepily, "It's just a worthless trinket. Nothing someone like you would find interest in, I'm certain." He shoved Nester's hand away.

Nester's belly groaned, interrupting his response. "We'll continue this later. I'm starvin'! Y'know, th' innkeeper's wife makes th' finest poached eggs this side of Aransiya 'as ever seen!" He went to his side of the room, slipped on his jerkin and belt pouches, grabbed his satchel, and bolted out the door.

After Nester left, Kaijin slid out of bed and retrieved his clean, dry clothes from the windowsill. As he got dressed, he sensed Miele's presence nearby. He peered out the window. The cool, crisp morning air kissed his face. He rubbed his damaged earlobes, which itched as they began to heal. The sensation triggered memories of the previous day's incident.

Miele flew inside and landed atop his haversack on the floor. Screeching happily, she nudged her tiny nose against the leather flap.

Smiling, Kaijin approached her and knelt down. *"Hungry, are you?"* He retrieved the honeystick jar from the bag, opened it, and pulled out a single treat. He stroked her tawny fur while he watched her savor the honeystick. *"You're making me hungry, now. Why don't you enjoy your snack outside?"* He returned to the window, and Miele followed, carrying the honeystick in her mouth. She flew outside and up toward the inn's rooftop. Kaijin put on his shoes, grabbed his haversack and headed downstairs for breakfast.

He maneuvered through the crowded inn, looking for a place to sit. He spotted Nester, who sat alone in a corner at a large round table. Kaijin shuffled over and took an empty seat adjacent to him. Kaijin arched his eyebrow, noticing the numerous dishes on the table and the sheer amount of food that piled each of them.

Nester stuffed a poached egg into his mouth. His cheeks bulged as he chewed.

"Don't tell me you're really going to eat all this." Kaijin gestured to the untouched dishes.

Nester swallowed. "An' why not? Y'think just 'cause I'm small, my appetite's gotta be, too?"

"Well . . . yes, actually."

Nester waved him off. "Bah! You 'umans an' your soddin' stereotypes. S'gonna be a long trip y'know. I may not 'ave another meal like this for a few days, yet!"

Kaijin shook his head at him. *This was a bad idea.* He quickly gestured to one of the passing serving wenches. "One bowl of apple porridge, please. And some cinnamon tea with honey."

Nester wolfed down another egg, then picked up a piece of rye toast. "Apple porridge? This is one of th' few places in Faywald that offer th' grandest meals, an' all you get is soddin' porridge?"

Kaijin blinked. "What's wrong with porridge?"

"It's commoner food. If you're gonna stay in a place like this, you gotta act like th' ritzy blokes."

"Strange. No one told me that." Kaijin skeptically eyed the brownie.

"You 'aven't been around ritzy blokes much, I take it."

"No, I haven't. And I've always liked apple porridge since I was a boy."

Nester's eyebrows raised in surprise. "Aye? Well you don't look like a boy to me. It's 'igh time you start eatin' like a man!"

"Look, Nester. Don't criticize my eating habits."

"Why? You criticized mine. Gotta make things even, y'know."

Kaijin rolled his eyes.

Nester smirked at him mischievously, then began smearing globs of honey on the toast.

Silence lingered between them as Kaijin leaned his elbows on the table and watched the rest of the patrons. Compared to those folk, he looked like the refugees on the streets.

The serving wench returned and set a bowl of steaming porridge and a small cup of tea before Kaijin.

Kaijin eyed his meal before dipping his spoon into the porridge and stirring in the sliced apples that sat atop the mix. It smelled heavenly, sparking memories of home. He took a modest taste from his spoon. It was rather bland—nothing like how his mother used to make it. There was no cinnamon, and the apples did not complement the overall taste of the porridge like he'd expected. He ate it anyway, taking Nester's advice that it might be the only meal he would have for a while.

Nester finished his meal, then whistled at a serving wench to take the empty dishes away. He gave the shapely woman a small pat on her rear, and she giggled. He winked back at her.

Kaijin paused midbite. "Really, Nester?"

The brownie grinned. "Ah, I love comin' to this place. Th' women 'ere think I'm cute, y'know? Well, they speak th' truth. Th' innkeeper could learn a thing or two from 'em, y'know."

"Cute? They think you're cute?"

"Aye! I'm a regular ladies' man, y'know."

"I find that hard to believe."

Nester laughed. "Well, believe it." He scrutinized Kaijin. "You sound like you've 'ad a good plenty of women yourself."

Kaijin quickly resumed eating.

Nester gaped. "Wha—? You mean you ain't 'ad a woman before?"

"Of course I have. I just . . . don't like to talk about it." Kaijin felt his face warm. He didn't have to look up to know that Nester was most likely smirking at him.

"If I ain't 'eard th' biggest crock o'shite this side of Faywald . . ."

Exasperated, Kaijin let go of his spoon. It clanked loudly against the edge of his bowl. "Can we talk about something else, please?" He glared at Nester.

"Aye, aye. Of course." Nester waved him off. "It ain't bad that you ain't 'ad a woman before—well, not so bad, anyway."

Kaijin sighed and slowly took a bite, changing the subject, himself. "I suppose I should thank you for providing me with accommodations and a meal. I will find a way to repay you."

"You can start by 'elpin' me." Nester rummaged into one of his belt pouches and pulled out a tiny, folded piece of parchment. He began opening it up slowly, piece by piece. It took several minutes, but by the time he finished, almost the entire table accommodated a large, crude map of Aransiya, forcing Kaijin to move his meal. "See there?" Nester pointed to a particular spot. "A few blokes I was chewin' gums with said th' ruins lie somewhere in 'Oundstooth Marsh."

Kaijin finished eating and then scrutinized the map. The writings and etchings were in a language unfamiliar to him, but he could still discern where certain places were. He noticed some scribbles around Easthaven, but a big 'X' crossed through the entire area.

He scanned the northern lands, tracing the mountains and the sea. He recalled only a handful of times he had ever seen a cartographic overview of his home country. Nester's map didn't detail Ghaeldorund or the Citadel, which lay north on a small island in the Azulene Sea. The southern portion of the map was rather bare—perhaps unexplored—but a familiar symbol in the southeastern mountain region caught Kaijin's attention. The flame resembled the very one he wore around his neck. He blinked and clutched his charm through his robe. "What's that fire symbol over there?"

Nester dismissively waved his hand. "Oh, that? That's some strange place. Accidentally stumbled across it, I did. It was 'igh in th' mountains. I was looking for a place to stay when I saw that . . . that . . . *castle-lookin'* place from miles away! It's an aurorium, I think. Th' warders there seemed to really like fire. I mean, they're soddin' obsessed with it! Everywhere you look, there's fire burnin' somethin'. Even th' warders were dressed all fire-y. They didn't let me in, unfortunately. Said I was 'walkin' on 'oly grounds.' Really, how can anythin' be "oly' there? Everything's all burnt up! Anyway, ah . . . Why do y'ask?"

Kaijin pulled his necklace out of his robe, revealing the fiery charm.

Nester's eyes widened in awe. "Wow! It's even shinier than before! You sure you don't wanna sell it? Don't you realize 'ow much coin we could get for that, mate?"

Kaijin glowered at him. "It is *not* for sale."

Nester sighed and rolled his eyes. "Oh, all right. If it means that much to you, then . . . . Say, now I remember where I've seen that symbol before! One of the warders wore somethin' similar. A real fire-lovin' bloke, 'e was! He shooed me off before I could ask 'im anything about it, though." He cocked his head to the side. "You like fire, too, Kaijin?"

At the unexpected question, Kaijin found himself glancing around at the other patrons, hoping none were eavesdropping on their conversation. "I . . . well . . ." His gaze shifted to Nester, and he leaned over, lowering his voice. "Look, it's not easy, you know? People think I'm . . . strange."

"Strange? You?" Nester chortled.

"Shh!" Kaijin winced and scanned the room again. Nobody seemed to be listening, and Nester was the first person to scoff at the idea that Kaijin was odd. Maybe it wasn't all that unusual to a brownie. "People think I'm strange because I like playing with fire. Now, keep your voice down about it, will you?"

Nester leaned in and whispered, "Well that *is* kinda strange, y'know. Playing with fire an' all that. Doesn't it 'urt?"

"No . . . . Not anymore, anyway."

"Wha—? You mean, you can play with fire and not burn yourself?"

Kaijin nodded and smiled faintly. "Don't get me wrong. I'm not ashamed of my passion for fire, but it's bad enough I'm a mage in this town. I'd rather keep all of this a secret."

A wide grin stretched from ear to pointed ear. Nester nodded quickly, then he refolded his map into a neat, tiny square. "Oh, I get it. Well, don't worry, mate. Your secret's safe with me! I won't be chewin' gums with no one about your fiery fetishes."

Kaijin cringed.

* * *

After breakfast, Kaijin and Nester shuffled through the city's morning bustle, snaking their way toward the southern gates. Miele flew above them, concealed high in the sky. Passing the plaza, Kaijin spied colorful streamers draping across trees and between buildings. Large, colorful banners hung from the second and third story windows of some of the buildings. Men were pitching tents and hauling tables, crates, and sealed barrels, while others were painting signs.

"Oh!" Nester exclaimed, startling Kaijin behind him. "'Ow could I've forgotten 'bout th' summer festival? It starts in three days. Let's hurry to th' ruins so we can be back in time for th' festivities. I love me some good fun, I do!" He hastened his walk.

Kaijin made a sour face and took longer strides to keep up with the brownie. He heard children laughing nearby and slowed. Six small children huddled around what appeared to be a large rock. Several adults stood nearby, looking horrified.

A boy climbed atop the rock and sat, chortling at a little girl standing at the rock's base.

"Me next, Big Brother!" She jumped up and down. "I wanna climb next!"

Kaijin halted and watched the children. He smiled at the boyhood memory of playing with his brother. *What I wouldn't give to see you again, Rorick.* His smile slowly faded.

"'Ey! What gives, mate? We don't 'ave all day y'know!" Nester called, retracing his steps to return to Kaijin's side.

Kaijin blinked. "I, ah . . . sorry. My mind was elsewhere."

"I'll say!" Nester huffed, crossing his arms.

"All right, come on. Let's—" *Wait . . . Did that rock just move?*

The boy atop the 'rock' laughed harder. He flailed his arms about as he began sliding backwards but was suddenly caught by another large mass that looked like an arm. The 'rock' shifted and became a massive, male human-like figure that slowly rose to his feet. He reached up and scooted the boy onto his broad shoulder. Barefoot and wearing only a pair of dark blue silken trousers and a grey silk sash, the towering stranger was built like a bull, with rippling muscles of his exposed chest and arms. His skin shimmered a silvery hue in the morning sun. His brown, silver-tipped hair was trimmed short, revealing the many piercings that adorned both ears. He smiled at the children, revealing a set of long, sharp canines.

Kaijin's jaw dropped. "Will you look at that, Nester!" he whispered, pointing.

Nester rubbed his eyes twice in disbelief. "Tell me I'm dreamin', mate. Or is that the biggest bloke I've ever seen?"

"He's hideous! And the children aren't even afraid!"

"Now ain't that somethin'. An' 'ere you are, shunned from th' world for bein' a fire-lover and a fiddler."

Kaijin frowned. "It doesn't make sense. What makes him more special?"

"Hmm . . . Maybe it's 'cause 'e's actin' like a child, himself, aye? Look!"

The creature happily swayed the little boy back and forth in the air, laughing with the rest of the children. After setting the boy down, he picked up the next child and began again. Soon, one of the adults mustered enough courage to get the attention of one of the guards. The guard hustled over and separated the children from the hulking stranger. After sending the disappointed children back to their parents, the guard began scolding the stranger.

"We've told you before, Aidan. Leave the children alone. Their parents are wary of you."

Aidan looked down to the guard, his silver, cat-like eyes full of disappointment. "Aidan meant no harm. Aidan went for walk in town and children started following. They asked Aidan to play with them." His voice was deep and gruff, but sincere.

The guard shook his head. "I'm sorry, Aidan, but if this keeps happening, then we will have to ask you to leave Faywald."

Aidan sighed. "Yes, Aidan understands. . . ."

Nester exchanged glances with Kaijin. Finally, the brownie piped, "'E's a big one, mate. 'E'll be perfect!"

Kaijin winced at Nester's shrill voice. "Perfect for what?"

"A big bloke like that could make our job even easier—and *faster!* 'E'll be able to move 'eavy stuff and discover somethin' we may overlook."

"You can't be serious, Nester! We don't even know who—or *what*—he is!"

"Sure we do. 'Is name is Aidan, right? At least, that's what 'e kept saying. As for *what* 'e is . . . well, 'e looks like a 'uman to me."

"He's too tall to be a human. He's probably as tall as two humans put together! And I've never seen a human that big with *that* many muscles. . . ."

"Well, 'e can't be all that bad, aye? I mean, they allowed 'im in th' city, after all. An' he was playin' with *children* for soddin' sake!" He paused and then frowned. "I just had a thought. 'E might be a little too soft for us after all. . . ."

Kaijin's initial fear of Aidan was turning to curiosity, and he no longer paid attention to Nester's ramblings. *Maybe I should ask him how he got accepted here.*

". . . So I'm thinkin' it might not be a good idea to ask 'im to join us after all, 'cause . . ." Nester trailed off as Kaijin passed him and cautiously approached the hulking creature.

As Kaijin drew closer, he took in every detail of Aidan's strange features—from his slit-pupiled silver eyes to his clawed hands, which Aidan had begun rewrapping with a long, dirty strip of cloth. When Kaijin was but several steps away, he saw the creature briefly glance over his shoulder. After knotting the hand wraps securely, Aidan faced Kaijin, whose height barely reached above the middle of the creature's chest.

Kaijin met his gaze and quickly averted his eyes. "Ah . . . Excuse me, sir. I, ah . . . couldn't help but notice how well you, ah, handle children. Yes, that's it."

Aidan raised a thin dark brown eyebrow.

Nester suddenly said from behind Kaijin, "What Kaijin's . . . ah . . . tryin' to say is that 'e was wonderin' 'ow such a big, scary bloke gets to walk freely around th' city like this." He smiled nervously. "Not that we think you're scary-lookin' or anythin'. Ah, p–please don't 'urt us!"

Aidan's gaze hardened, and he shook his head, waving his clawed hand dismissively. "Aidan does not like violence."

Such a heavy accent and awkward speech. He's definitely not local. . . . And now I know for certain he can't be human.

"Oh! Neither do I!" Nester chirped, clutching a handful of Kaijin's robe.

Frowning, Kaijin slapped Nester's hand away. "Enough, Nester. If he wanted to hurt us, he would have done so already."

Nester rubbed his hand. "Maybe you're right. I guess some introductions are in order, aye?" The brownie's unhappy expression quickly faded, and he held his hand out in greetings for Aidan. "Aidan, wasn't it? I'm Nester. Also known as 'Nimble' Nester Two-Blades. This 'ere's my mate, Kaijin. Did y'know 'e's a fire-lovin' fiddler?"

Kaijin reeled. He clapped his hand over Nester's mouth while his eyes darted around the area for any passersby. "Must you tell the world I'm a mage?" he snapped in a low whisper. "You said you'd keep quiet about all this!"

Nester glared at Kaijin, grabbed his hand and pried it from his mouth. "'Ey, if someone like Aidan can walk around 'ere, why can't you?"

"Maybe because he's not a mage?" Kaijin eyed Aidan once more. "What say you? Are you adept with magic?"

Aidan scratched the side of his head thoughtfully. "Aidan does not think he knows magic."

"Either you know magic or you don't," Kaijin said.

Aidan simply shrugged.

"Say, Aidan," Nester broke in. "'Ow 'bout you join us on a little trip, aye? Could be fun. It doesn't matter if you're a fiddler or not. You'd still be useful enough to . . . ah . . . to keep us company! Aye, that's it!"

Aidan looked at the both of them and thought for a moment. "A trip? Aidan does enjoy nice walks. When Aidan was little boy, Master once told him that walking is nice time to relax and be one with nature."

Nester's face brightened. "So you'll come with us?"

"Yes, why not? Aidan can use exercise."

"Great! Let's get going, then!" Nester strode off.

Kaijin watched the brownie depart, then waited for Aidan to follow before picking up the rear. Miele swooped down to rest on his shoulder.

Before long, the three of them left through the southern gates and traveled along a beaten path that snaked through the countryside. Kaijin maintained a modest distance from Aidan, keeping his head lowered as he walked along, but he caught a close glimpse of silvery skin, rippling muscles, and two small nubs protruding from the upper back.

IV

The first hour went by, silent and uneventful, as Aidan, Nester, and Kaijin followed the road to the southwest. With Nester leading the way, they kept a brisk pace. Aidan's slow but long strides matched the brownie's quick gait. Aidan took in his surroundings as he walked, admiring nature's splendors.

It wasn't until he noticed Kaijin out of the corner of his eye, staring at him intently, that Aidan finally acknowledged him. He glanced to the bat resting on Kaijin's shoulder, her wings wrapped partially around her. She tucked her head in her body just enough to shield the light from her eyes. It seemed odd for such a creature to be domesticated, and Aidan wondered how Kaijin first obtained her. He'd not seen bats that close except in books.

Kaijin continued staring, and Aidan's interest in the bat waned. "What? Is something on Aidan's face?"

The red-haired man quickly turned his head, looking straight ahead. "Well . . . ah . . . no. I've just not seen someone so . . . *different* as you before."

Aidan scratched the side of his head. "'Different'? What do you mean 'different'?"

"Surely, you're not human—you can't possibly be. I mean, look at you—you're huge! And look at your hands—or should I say, *claws*. And I've never seen a human with silver skin before. . . ." He leaned closer to Aidan, studying his arm. ". . . Silver *scaly* skin, that is. . . ." He stared at Aidan's face. "And your eyes . . . they look a lot like Sable's."

Aidan furrowed his brow. "Who is Sable?"

"She is a cat."

"But Aidan is not cat."

"No, you're not. So what exactly *are* you?"

"It's obvious what 'e is," Nester interjected, not looking behind him. He walked several steps ahead of them, his hands clasped behind his head, his pointed ears twitching. "'E's a terrabeast!"

Kaijin blinked. "What!"

Aidan scratched his head. "Terrabeast?"

"Nasty gruesome things, they are." Nester stopped walking and spun around. "My grandpa, Nepp, almost got eaten by one! They got an endless appetite, they do. That's why they're so soddin' 'uge, y'know. Anyway, Grandpa Nepp, who was a great bard of 'is time, managed to sing th' gruesome creature to sleep. Then, 'e fled out that cave faster than a scared deer, 'e did!"

Kaijin grimaced. "That sounds . . . rather disturbing."

"Oh, don't worry, mate. Grandpa Nepp said terrabeasts are rare creatures that live deep, deep underground. They 'ate th' sunlight more than vampires do."

"Aidan likes sunlight," Aidan said.

Nester rolled his eyes and sighed. "All right, all right. No need to get all technical. So you're not a terrabeast, then—you're a *'alf* terrabeast!"

Kaijin crossed his arms. "He's no terrabeast."

"Oh no? Then what is 'e?" Nester mimicked the mage's gesture.

Kaijin gazed at Aidan. "I don't really know. Don't you have a family, Aidan?"

Aidan deflated. He continued walking, brushing past the two, his gaze wandering off to the plush fields of the scenic countryside. "Master told Aidan story one day. Aidan's home city was in civil war when Aidan was little boy. Master met strange woman who was trying to get Aidan to safety. She was about to become captured by officials, and Master tried to save her. But she told him to take Aidan instead, so he did. He fled city and brought him to White Lotus monastery. Master never knew what happened to her—whether she was alive or dead. He believes she might have been relative of Aidan's—like mother . . . or sister. . . ."

Nester contorted his face. "'Seestor'?"

Kaijin chuckled. "I think he means 'sister'."

Aidan looked at them, bemused. "That is what Aidan said!"

"Nevermind." Kaijin waved his hand dismissively. "So you have no recollections of your origins whatsoever?"

Aidan shrugged. "Aidan lived with Master and White Lotus monks all his life. That is only family Aidan ever knew."

"But surely, they are not your *real* family, no?"

"Well, that all depends," Nester broke in. "What if th' White Lotus monks were really terrabeasts in disguise?"

Kaijin groaned. "Not this again!"

Aidan shook his head. "Aidan is pretty sure monks were all human. Even Master was human."

"Well, it was worth a try, at least," Nester said, shrugging.

Aidan looked at Kaijin more seriously. "Does it trouble you that Aidan looks so strange to you?"

Kaijin bowed his head. He chewed on his bottom lip. Finally, he met Aidan's gaze again. "Yes. Yes, it does, actually. I want to know why the city does not fear you. Hells, why do the children not fear you? You can easily kill a man with one of those fists of yours!"

Aidan grimaced. "No, Aidan does not like violence."

"'Ave you ever killed a man before, Aidan?" Nester asked.

"Violence solves nothing. It only ends up in someone getting hurt." To Aidan's relief, his dodge satisfied Kaijin and Nester.

"I find it insulting," Kaijin said with a huff. "Strange, intimidating, outlandish creatures are allowed in Faywald, but human mages who come in peace are not? Do the guards even know what you are?"

Aidan shrugged.

"You seem very nonchalant about this," Kaijin continued. "Don't you have enemies?"

Aidan shrugged again. "Aidan would like to get along with everyone and live in peace. Sometimes worst enemies become best friends."

"True, but—"

"'Ey, Kaijin," Nester interrupted. "'Ave you ever stopped to think that maybe Aidan's just a seriously deformed 'uman?"

Kaijin raised his eyebrow at the thought. "Perhaps. You may be right. Though, Aidan looks like something that would defy even the laws of nature."

Aidan tapped his chin in thought. "Aidan recalled monks once saying he was different from normal child because when he was four years old he was already almost as tall as Master. And, well . . . Aidan never stopped growing. . . ."

Kaijin gasped. "Don't tell me you're *still* growing!"

Aidan chuckled softly. "No, no. Aidan thinks he is done growing. He has been same size for long time."

In unison, Kaijin and Nester exhaled deep sighs.

Aidan turned back around and continued walking, hiding his smile. Their curiosity amused him; he usually got such questions from children rather than adults. But even he wasn't sure of his origins—something he hoped to learn as he journeyed.

* * *

Their brisk walk continued well into evening. Nester strayed from the main road and led Kaijin and Aidan along a scenic path, which snaked through a forest of towering black walnut trees. Along the narrow trail, patches of brightly colored wildflowers grew.

"This is quite a walk," Aidan said, "but it is very relaxing. Thank you for letting Aidan come along."

Nester looked back and beamed at the giant, mischief hinting his eyes. "No problem, mate! It's fun walkin' together, aye?"

"Why, yes, it is, actually. Makes Aidan feel young again."

"Young?" Kaijin blinked. He couldn't spot a single wrinkle on Aidan's scaly face. "Just how old are you, anyway, Aidan?"

"Yeah," Nester added. "If I wasn't mistaken, you were playin' with children in th' city earlier."

Aidan smiled blissfully. "Ah, yes, the children. Aidan loves children. They are not afraid of him like adults are." He acknowledged Kaijin's question. "Aidan does not know how old he is . . . . Fifteen? Twenty-five?" He shrugged. "Whatever age, Aidan always feels like little boy again when he plays with children."

It was Kaijin's turn to smile. "You did look like you were having fun back there. I hope one day you will be able to learn about yourself."

"If Aidan is meant to know, then, in due time, Aidan will know."

The changed scenery around them drew Kaijin's attention from Aidan. No more did the colorful wildflowers carpet the landscape. The air grew humid and the skies darkened to shades of grey. His foot sank deeper into the spongy earth with each step he took. He wasn't certain how long they had been walking, but they had clearly traveled a great distance. The road appeared less beaten than earlier. In following Nester's lead, Kaijin hadn't noticed when they strayed from the main road.

Tall oak trees stretched toward the grey skies. Signs of life were scarce, save for the occasional bird and the light buzzing of insects. He felt Miele stir, and he looked to his shoulder. Miele untucked her head from her wing and surveyed the landscape.

Nester halted and retrieved his map. He easily unfolded the oversized parchment and made certain it didn't touch the ground. He studied the map carefully. "We'll be at those ruins in no time. It's about an 'our's walk, I think—" He paused and held the map high above his head and pulled his feet out of mud with a gasp just before they were completely submerged. "Yuck! We're in th' marsh, all right."

Aidan grimaced and looked down. The soft mud squished beneath his bare feet and between his toes. "Aidan hopes we are not lost. . . ." He lifted his head slightly and sniffed the air. His nose wrinkled in disgust.

Sensing the creature's tension, Kaijin glanced sidelong at him. "Something wrong, Aidan?"

"Blood," Aidan said absently. His head turned, and his silver eyes narrowed, as if he had seen something off in the distance.

Nester's pointed ears twitched. "Did you 'ear that?" He quickly refolded his map.

Kaijin noticed Aidan's muscles tense and bulge, prompting his own senses to rise. He followed Aidan's gaze and spotted a cluster of shadows off the muddy path. The slight shift in movement only lasted a split second before the area became calm again. Furrowing his brow in confusion, Kaijin regarded the giant again. "What is it, Aidan?"

Slowly, Aidan slid his foot to the side until he had discreetly set himself into a defensive posture. "We are not alone," he said quietly.

Kaijin opened his mouth to speak and felt a sharp pain in his mind. Shrieking frantically, Miele leapt from his shoulder and soared into the air, above the treetops. Kaijin clenched his fist and concentrated on a spell, ready to unleash it at the first signs of trouble.

Nester backtracked until he bumped into Aidan's thigh, like a fly colliding with a tree trunk. He flicked his wrists, and two twin daggers appeared in his hands from unseen sheaths. He nervously spun the weapons around.

The wind whistled lightly.

Several guttural voices cut through the evening.

Kaijin listened closely to the crude unfamiliar language. *What?* He made a face. "What in the hells is that?"

Aidan furrowed his brow. "Sounds like heated conversation. Though, Aidan could be wrong."

A creature leapt from the underbrush and faced the group, yelling a string of sharp phrases in its native tongue. The creature was rubbery, lanky, gruesome, and human-like, standing almost the same height as Aidan. Its moldy, green face was distinctly angular. Two ears, pointed and looking as though something had chewed on them—with tufts of scraggly obsidian-colored hair sticking out—complemented the creature's oblong, drooping nose and wide, blood-spattered mouth, from which sickly green, acidic-looking drool oozed. Warts and fungus covered its skin, making the creature seem nearly one with the dank marshlands. It assessed the group briefly before resting its yellow eyes on Aidan.

Aidan tensed and muttered, "What manner of creature is—"

"*Troll!*" Nester blurted.

The brownie's outburst startled Kaijin enough to release his spell, flashing bright light in the troll's eyes; it reeled in pain.

While the troll was momentarily disoriented, Aidan rushed forward and grappled the creature, digging his claws into its skin. The troll howled in pain and attempted to hurl its attacker off, but Aidan didn't budge. The troll spat corrosive saliva into Aidan's eyes.

He let go, holding his face. "Gah! It burns!"

"Aidan!" Nester pushed past him, glaring at the troll. Using both daggers, Nester simultaneously sliced through the troll's leg and across its midsection. Globs of greenish, curdled blood poured out of the wounds—but only briefly. The wounds immediately began to mend. Nester widened his eyes. "This ain't good, mate—not good at all!"

Three more trolls emerged from the shadows and encircled the group, snarling and drooling on the muddy ground.

Kaijin glanced at each of the towering monsters. "*Flamm annul!*" A ring of white fire appeared, encircling Kaijin, Nester, and Aidan. "Keep back!" he yelled at the monsters.

The trolls cringed and kept their distance from the flames, but showed no signs of leaving. The intense bright flames slowly transitioned to a steady, flickering, amber hue.

"What is happening?" Aidan exclaimed, rubbing some of the liquid substance from his eyes. He spotted the roaring flames and winced. "Kaijin! Nester!" He reached out, feeling for his comrades.

Kaijin rushed over, grabbed Aidan's hand, and tugged him toward the center of the fiery circle. "Stay right here."

"We can't keep this up, Kaijin!" Nester called over his shoulder. "We need to get rid of these soddin' things fast before even more come!"

Kaijin glared at Nester. "Do you have any suggestions?"

Nester twirled his blades, eyeing each creature. "I remember Grandpa Nepp encountered a troll once. Nasty bugger, it was. Wasn't nearly as big as these things, though. Said he managed to kill th' thing, but I forgot 'ow."

Kaijin rolled his eyes. "Well that doesn't help, now does it?"

"Let Aidan handle it," Aidan said.

Both Kaijin and Nester looked at him.

Aidan rubbed his eyes again and tried to open them further. He advanced slowly toward the snarling creatures.

"Aidan! Wait!" Kaijin called. He grabbed Aidan's burly arm, but Aidan broke his grip with a quick flex.

The trolls eagerly awaited Aidan on the other side of the fire ring. Their claws extended, the monsters appeared ready to pounce on him like a pack of hungry wolves.

Aidan stopped at the edge of the ring before the creatures. After a moment, he closed his eyes again, took a deep breath, and barreled through the scorching heat, parts of his leathery skin catching fire. He collided with the cluster of trolls, who also caught some of the blaze.

Kaijin watched in awe as Aidan blindly fought each of the creatures with his bare hands, clawing at them, ripping through rubbery flesh and hurling them into the ring of fire. The monsters howled in pain. Panic resounded in the creatures' guttural voices as they frantically searched for a means of escape.

The creatures scrambled about, seemingly oblivious to everything but Aidan. Nester smirked at Kaijin as he twirled his blades. "Looks like Aidan's made it easy for us, now, eh? Look at them! They're runnin' around like they just seen a ghost!"

Kaijin observed the monsters more closely. The scorch wounds on their skin didn't appear to be healing. Moreover, the monsters seemed terrified of the flames around them. The phenomenon sparked a memory of his own childhood, during those endless days and nights of study under his master's watchful eye. He had learned about many types of creatures—both the very strange and not so strange, the rare and common—and how the concept of magic affected and influenced them. *Yes, of course. How could I possibly forget?*

His lips curled into a smile as he realized what he needed to do. "No, they don't like fire too much, do they?"

Nester cackled. "*Now* I remember! Grandpa Nepp tossed 'is torch at th' troll, and th' thing burned up like paper, it did! It was so scared o' th' fire, it ran around in circles 'til it dropped dead. That's when Grandpa Nepp ran like th' 'ells."

Kaijin nodded to Nester and smirked. "Open them up a bit."

Nester twirled his blades again. While the four trolls were disoriented, Nester charged at them and began slashing new wounds across their bodies quicker than they realized what had happened. Globs of green liquid oozed out of the wounds and mixed with the mud.

Their wounds began mending again, and Nester gave a quick nod to Kaijin.

The air seemed to waver around Kaijin, as if he were a furnace. The tempo of his pulsating necklace increased, keeping pace with his racing heartbeat. Soon, his entire body erupted in flames.

From the dark recesses of Kaijin's mind, a soothing voice broke through the maelstrom and directed his fury. *"Obliterate them."*

He remembered the undead, overtaking Easthaven—then the aftermath of the chaos, that destructive inferno. Kaijin cracked a smile.

A fireball materialized in Kaijin's hands, and he hurled it toward the trolls, sending them fleeing and snarling in panic. They didn't get very far before they collapsed, one by one, in the mud. A wall of flames burst over the heaps of fallen creatures and devoured their bodies hungrily, leaving behind ashen remains.

Just as quickly as Kaijin felt the fantastic sensation, it subsided, leaving him feeling somewhat content—satisfied. He smiled faintly at the destruction. The fiery magic dissipated, as did the ring of fire. He looked down at his own hands, which emitted faint traces of white smoke.

He exhaled slowly and looked to his comrades.

Aidan groaned and rolled over on his back. "Kaijin? Nester?"

Nester ran over to Aidan, dodging smoldering remains of troll in the mud along the way. "Aidan! They're gone!" He tugged at Aidan's arm, beckoning him to stand. "Kaijin burned them to a crisp, 'e did! You should've seen it!"

Aidan slowly stood to his feet. He stared blankly toward Nester.

"Aidan? How are you feeling?" Kaijin approached them.

Aidan's eyes flickered. His pupils were dilated, and the corneas were devoid of their silver tint. He turned toward

Kaijin and reached out to him. "You look like blurry blob."

Kaijin frowned. "We're in the middle of a marsh. It will be a long walk back to town to try and find help."

"What!" Nester exclaimed. "We can't go back now! We just got 'ere! We still got some ruins to check, remember?"

Kaijin glared at the brownie. "Aidan won't be of any help if he can't see a damn thing!"

"Well, uh . . ." Nester thought a moment. "'E can just stand there an' look all intimidatin' so no one'll bother us, aye?"

Kaijin rolled his eyes.

"Don't worry," Aidan said. "Aidan will manage as best he can."

"I *knew* this was going to be a bad idea," Kaijin muttered. He reached for Aidan's massive, clawed hand. "Take my hand, at least. I will help lead you through the marsh."

Aidan nodded and gently clasped Kaijin's hand. With Nester leading the way, the three of them resumed their walk through the muddy trail.

Aidan's claws scraped Kaijin's skin, and Kaijin cringed. Beneath the remains of Aidan's torn handwraps, Kaijin spied many callouses. And yet, there was a certain gentleness about those hands. *He really is a man of peace.*

Kaijin's silent musings were interrupted by an excited Nester. "That was th' most amazin' thing I'd ever seen, mate! No *wonder* th' people in Faywald say fiddlers are dangerous!"

"Let's not get into that again, Nester," Kaijin warned.

"You gotta teach me that trick sometime! I know a few sods who need a good burnin', I do! Maybe teach Aidan that trick, too! We'll be unstoppable, I tell you! Not to mention, filthy, soddin' rich!"

Kaijin groaned.

V

The group emerged from the veil of underbrush to view a stretch of wetland blanketed with a thick mist. Broken columns and stone structures of various shapes and sizes, placed in a crude circle, littered the area. Mold and ivy covered the majority of the structures, affirming that the site remained undisturbed. Tiny fireflies swarmed in slow circles, creating an eerie dim illumination that penetrated the mist.

"What a serene place," Kaijin whispered under his breath.

Nester's ears perked, and he snorted. "'Serene'? This place is spookier than my Aunt Netta when she wears that ridiculous orange ruffled dress she got for 'er birthday three years ago!"

Kaijin chuckled.

A small figure moved amongst the ruins. He squinted. Of a human shape, the figure walked the perimeter of the ruins, stopping briefly at each structure.

He nudged Nester. "Hey, looks like someone else is here."

Nester followed Kaijin's gaze and cringed. "Told you this place is spooky, mate! That looks like a ghost over there, it does!"

"Shouldn't we see who or what it is before we start searching?"

"Ah . . . Ah . . . . All right. I'll be right behind you!"

Aidan sniffed the air, then tilted his head curiously. "Honeysuckle?"

Kaijin furrowed his brow at the giant. "Excuse me?"

"Those flowers always smell so nice," Aidan said absently. "Where are we?"

"We're at th' ruins," Nester replied. "I assure you, mate: There ain't no flowers around 'ere."

A brief passing breeze carried the wetlands' moldy, mildew odor. Kaijin wrinkled his nose. "Yuck! Nester is right."

Aidan shook his head. "No, Aidan is certain he smells honeysuckle. It is Aidan's favorite flower." He released Kaijin's hand and wandered ahead.

Kaijin watched Aidan a moment before following. "Aidan, are you mad? You can't see! Where are you going?" He halted when he realized the direction Aidan was walking.

The figure stopped and turned toward them. Kaijin heard a soft female voice utter a string of phrases and saw a flash of white light emit from her hands. Shining it at Aidan, she yelled, "Stay back!"

Kaijin and Nester saw the light from afar and shielded their eyes. The flash dissipated moments later.

"Oy! Where'd those spots come from?" Nester grumbled, swatting at the air. He stumbled around and ran into the back of Kaijin.

"Oof!" The spell's dazzling effects subsided, and Kaijin rubbed his eyes. "What was that?"

Aidan stopped in his tracks and gazed at the source of the light, seemingly unfazed. "What are you doing here, miss?" he asked politely.

The woman was taken aback. "Who are you . . .?"

Aidan smiled, bearing his canines. "Well, we are not trolls," he joked. "We are just out for nice walk."

She warily regarded Kaijin and Nester as they slowly approached.

Kaijin fixated on the strange woman. Her tall, lithe body—perfectly proportioned—accentuated her graceful movements and soft voice. Silken snow-white hair cascaded down her back. While her pale face appeared young, he spotted a maturity in her sapphire eyes, which made it difficult to determine her age. Her flowing silver-trimmed blue robes were branded across the skirt with Celestra's symbol: a rose intertwining a silhouette of a Dragon's head. Over the robes, she wore a chainmail top and a tabard that was marked with the same symbol. A short, steel-flanged mace was secured at her side.

The woman's nervous expression slowly softened to one of amusement as she acknowledged Kaijin's inadvertent gawking. "Forgive me. I was not expecting to find anyone out here."

Nester's eyes widened, and his jaw dropped. "Neither were we. . . ."

She studied Aidan for a moment. Frowning, she reached out and touched his face. "Your eyes are badly injured, sir. Please, allow me."

Aidan opened his mouth and froze as soon as the woman laid her hands upon his cheeks.

Kaijin gasped. "What—what are you doing to him? Stop that, now!"

"Wait!" Nester tugged at Kaijin's sleeve. "I think she's a warder, aye? She wears Celestra's symbol, after all."

"Yes, but . . ." Kaijin bit his bottom lip, reluctantly restraining himself from stopping her.

Brushing her thumbs over Aidan's eyes, she lowered her head. "*Goddess of Exodus, may his afflictions be mended and his sight returned to once again view the beautiful world you have created.*"

Her voice was like an angel's.

Aidan's muscles relaxed, and his eyelids fluttered, his blank stare gone. He whipped his head around and gasped. "Wha—? Aidan can see! Aidan can see again!"

The woman withdrew her hands from his face and stood back, smiling. "Praise be to the goddess."

"Amazing," Kaijin said as he exhaled.

"How did you get injured, sir?" the woman asked Aidan. "Did something attack you?"

"Terrible, it was!" Nester broke in. "We got attacked by trolls, we did! One of them tried to eat Aidan's face!"

Her eyebrow arched at the brownie. "Truly? Well, I must say, your companion, here, is certainly as big as a troll—or two."

Nester laughed. "Aidan's the size of a troll with the mind the size of a li'l child's!"

She regarded everyone in turn. "So you are all in acquaintance with each other, I gather?"

"Certainly!" Nester nodded, beaming. "We're as close-knit as those comfy li'l blankets my mum used to make!"

She chuckled and then offered a humble bow of her head. "Well, then. Pleased to meet you all. My name is

Zarya. I am a traveling priestess of our great and mighty goddess, Celestra."

Kaijin couldn't help but smile at her. *What a beautiful name.* "My name is Kaijin." He gestured to his other companions. "This is Nester, and that is Aidan."

Zarya's gaze focused on Kaijin. "Goodness, Kaijin. Your ears . . ."

"I—" Kaijin blinked in surprise, not expecting her comment. "Yes, well . . . ah . . . I was robbed yesterday."

The priestess frowned. "That's unfortunate. I'm sorry."

"It's all right. I'm still alive, aren't I?" He chuckled.

Zarya approached him slowly and extended her hands. "Please, allow me."

"W—wait. I—" Kaijin froze, unsure what to do. He looked to Nester frantically.

The brownie returned a wide, mischievous grin and a thumbs-up gesture.

Kaijin swallowed once and turned back to Zarya. "It's . . . not going to hurt, I hope."

She laughed. "Not at all. Just be still." She placed her hands over his ears and began chanting softly.

Her soothing voice almost lulled Kaijin to sleep. Her touch was unbelievably soft and warm, and he couldn't stop smiling. She emanated a sense of peace and assurance. He studied her face. He couldn't spot a single flaw about her. Such perfection seemed unnatural, almost jarring to him, but he couldn't doubt the reality of what he saw before him.

When she finished, she released him. "It is done."

Kaijin ran his hands along his ears, shocked. The pain was gone. The skin was mended like new, with nary a scratch nor blemish to be felt. "Amazing," he whispered, looking at her. "Thank you."

Zarya nodded politely. "It was my pleasure, Kaijin."

Aidan rubbed his eyes again. "Aidan is also eternally grateful for what you have done."

Zarya smiled at the giant. "It wasn't me, Aidan. It was the power of our wonderful goddess."

The talk of the gods made Kaijin cringe. There were too many questions unanswered—too many memories he would have preferred forgotten. He decided to shift the subject of the conversation. "What brings you out here, Zarya?"

Kaijin's distraction seemed unnoticed by the priestess, who regarded him thoughtfully. "I happened upon this place by accident during my travels southward to Ostwyn. These ruins seemed intriguing, so I decided to have a look." She approached one of the stone structures and slid her hand along its surface. "Judging by the markings on some of them, they appear to be of druidic origin. I thought it might be interesting to search for some clues about the druidic deities and perhaps learn more about them."

Kaijin approached another ruin. The porous surface felt rough as he brushed his hand over the grooves of etched runes and glyphs.

Nester rubbed his hands together. "Well, now that you're 'ere, you can 'elp us look for things, aye?"

Zarya lifted an eyebrow. "Look for what?"

What else but things to fill his pockets with? Kaijin rolled his eyes and whispered, "He wants to look for treasure."

Zarya curled her lip with utter disgust.

Nester crossed his arms. "'Ey, now! Don't go chewin' gums with every soddin' person about what we're doing!"

"It's the truth, Nester, and you know it." Kaijin glowered at him. *And I'm only joining you on this trifling journey in order to pay off a debt.*

Zarya put her hands on her hips. "This place is not to be desecrated. What if it's a druidic graveyard? The dead should be left in peace."

Aidan glanced at Zarya. "Aidan agrees."

"It's no graveyard, I tell you!" Nester piped up, flailing his arms about. "If it was, we'd be seeing ghosties and all th' li'l things that go bump in th' night, aye?" He looked up at Zarya. "No need to get your robes all foddled, beautiful. These are just a buncha old ruins left behind by th' foresty blokes." He scanned the ground and picked up a piece of stone. "See?"

"Let's just forget about it, Nester. We won't find anything out—" Kaijin paused, spying a bright light flash from the corner of his eye. He turned and saw a small object beneath one of the fallen, crumbling columns.

"What is it, mate?" Nester asked excitedly.

Kaijin approached the object and knelt down. He brushed aside strangely warm stray dirt and debris. His eyes widened at the deep orange hue of the sphere, its surface smooth. *So beautiful.*

Nester peered over Kaijin's shoulder. Aidan and Zarya joined them.

Nester gasped. "Wow! Will you look at that!"

Kaijin held his hand over the object, startled by the intense heat that radiated from it. The heat was soothing—very similar to his own necklace. He touched the glass surface and left his hand there for a few moments, until he heard a soft sizzling sound and felt small tingling sensations flow through his hand and up his arm. Kaijin took the object. He cradled the sphere in both hands and examined it closely.

"It's even more amazin' up close!" Nester exclaimed.

"It looks like a glass orb," Zarya said. "Perhaps it's a druidic artifact of sorts?"

The swirling orange and yellow within the center of the orb fascinated Kaijin. They transitioned into variations of fiery hues. "I sense magic," he said absently. "Actual arcane power." Closing his eyes, he felt such great, unspeakable power in his hand. He clenched his fingers around the orb. The voices of his companions sounded distant, but clear.

"Woah! You're glowin', mate!" Nester exclaimed.

Kaijin opened his eyes. The air around him wavered as if from a furnace. A dim light encompassed him.

Zarya gawked. "Amazing, Kaijin. Are you, perhaps, a druid?"

Kaijin slowly shook his head, not taking his gaze off the orb.

"Quite a find, ain't it?" Nester asked. "Think of 'ow much we could get for that!"

There was a moment of silence, and then Zarya said, "You should put it back, Kaijin."

Kaijin remained fixated on the orb and didn't respond.

"Nay!" Nester exclaimed. "We found it fair an' square, we did!"

"You are stealing!" Zarya retorted.

"Who knows 'ow long that thing's been sittin' there, all clotted with dirt, like? It's rightfully ours for th' takin', it is!"

A low, somewhat animalistic growl came from Aidan. "Is that *trinket* what you have been looking for, Nester?"

After a brief pause, Nester piped, "Ah . . . aye . . . aye, that's right. That's th' *exact* thing I've been lookin' for, now that you mention it. Uncle Nickle would be all grateful to 'ave such a nice li'l trinket like that, 'e would! Let me 'ave it, Kaijin. I'll tuck it someplace safe."

Kaijin shook off his trance and looked at Nester. The brownie had his hand extended to him, a wide, gap-toothed smile plastered on his mischievous face. Ignoring the gesture, Kaijin settled his gaze on Zarya. "There's something very familiar about this orb when I hold it."

"Familiar?" Zarya asked. "What do you mean?"

Kaijin thought a moment. "Something . . . something about it makes me feel compelled to keep it close to me—to protect it. It's as if it's calling to me—as though it belongs to me. I can't explain."

"But is it wise for us to take it from this place? What if it's cursed?"

"No . . . It's . . . It's warm. I feel like it belongs to me."

Zarya lifted an eyebrow.

"'Ey now!" Nester broke in, reaching for the orb. "Why don't we see if someone in town can identify it, aye?" His gloved fingers touched the sphere, and he yanked his hand away. "Ouch! That smarts!"

Kaijin eyed Nester, who had pulled off his glove and began sucking his wounded fingers. "Did it burn you?" he asked the brownie.

"Sure did!" Nester showed him the wounds. He cast a glance at Zarya. "Think you can fix this, beautiful?"

Giving the brownie a half smile, Zarya reached into one of her belt pouches and retrieved a small roll of white bandages. After unraveling a modest amount, she quickly wrapped Nester's minor wounds and then returned the roll to her pouch. "There."

Nester looked at his newly wrapped fingers and frowned. "Aw, that's it? Just a couple of soddin' bandages?"

"The bandages are spidersilk. Your fingers will be good as new in a few hours," Zarya explained. "Have patience." She turned to Kaijin. "This is all very strange. Does the orb not burn you, too?"

Kaijin regarded her, confused. "No, and I don't understand why this thing burned Nester. It's like it has a mind of its own!"

"That's puttin' it mildly, mate," Nester said.

Aidan held his clawed hand out to Kaijin and said, "Give to Aidan."

Kaijin clutched the orb more tightly. "I . . ."

"This just looks like simple trinket with pretty colors. Aidan thinks Nester is exaggerating. Now, give to Aidan."

"'*Exaggeratin*'?" Nester blinked. "You call *this* 'exaggeratin'?" He showed Aidan his bandaged fingers. "That thing nearly burned my fingers off, it did!"

Kaijin pursed his lips. Slowly, he held the orb out for Aidan to take. His hands began to shake as he fought against the urge to keep the sphere close, to keep it safe.

Aidan snatched the orb from Kaijin's hands. Seconds later, however, the creature's eyes widened, and he let the orb drop. Hissing, he shook his hands, which were burned almost to the bone.

Kaijin's eyes followed the orb as soon as it fell from Aidan's hands. He dove for the object, landed hard on his stomach, and caught it before it hit the ground.

"By the goddess!" Zarya exclaimed. She rushed to tend to Aidan's injury.

"Good catch, mate!" Nester said to Kaijin. He looked at Aidan. "Are you all right?"

Another snake-like hiss escaped Aidan's lips. Once they were healed, he examined his hands again. "Yes, yes, Aidan is fine. But why is Kaijin the only one who can touch that thing?"

All heads turned to Kaijin.

Kaijin got up from the mud, his clothes and face smeared. "How in the hells am I supposed to know?" He wiped the excess mess from his eyes as best he could.

"Maybe you really *are* a druid, Kaijin." Zarya said.

Kaijin shook his head firmly, flinging more mud off his face. "No, I assure you, I'm not. I know absolutely nothing of the druidic arts. Look, why don't we just find someone that might give us some insight on what this thing is?"

Zarya sighed. "I still do not think we should take that from here."

"Well nothin' bad's 'appened to us yet, 'as it, beautiful?" Nester asked.

"Nothing except those nasty burns you and Aidan received?" Zarya responded.

"Aidan might suggest consulting Celestran aurorium in Faywald about it," Aidan broke in.

Nester blinked. "Wait! We can't leave! We 'aven't even finished explorin' the rest of th' place, yet!"

Zarya frowned. "You have done enough in desecrating these grounds with your thieving. What Kaijin is holding may very well be cursed."

"If it is cursed, then . . . then I will take that chance." *It's too intriguing to ignore.*

Zarya looked at him in disbelief.

Aidan huffed. "Enough trinkets. Enough exploring. Aidan would rather rest. It is late."

Nester stamped his foot. "Nay! We came all this way, and—Oy! Put me down!"

Aidan had grabbed Nester by the back of his jerkin collar and lifted him off his feet. He raised the brownie to eye-level and scowled. "We are leaving. Now."

Both Kaijin and Zarya gazed at the creature, wide-eyed.

Nester's face paled. "Ah . . . Ah . . . Aye! Of course. W–whatever you say. I think leavin's a great idea. I was only jestin' before, y'know?" He gave a nervous laugh. "All in good fun, aye? Uh, p–please don't 'urt me!"

Unamused, Aidan set the brownie down and pointed. "Lead us out of this marsh."

Color returned to Nester's face as he took a moment to catch his breath. He scrambled ahead to lead the group.

Aidan beckoned Kaijin and Zarya to follow with a slight tilt of his head.

After exchanging a glance, Kaijin and Zarya proceeded to follow Nester without protest. As Kaijin tucked the orb in his haversack, the voice in his mind said, *"Kaijin Sora . . . my greatest treasure."*

VI

འཉཇ

After leaving the swamp, Kaijin, Nester, Zarya, and Aidan rested for the night, camping out in the woods not too far off the main road. The following morning, they set off again and arrived in Faywald's vicinity by midday.

When they were within view of the city gates, Nester sprinted ahead of the others, rushing past the guards and disappearing into the city. Miele hovered high above, trailing Nester. She soared over the gates and was soon out of sight.

"Did he forget that I'm the one carrying the orb?" Kaijin muttered aloud.

Zarya chuckled. "Looks like something else has caught his attention, instead."

"The festival begins tonight," Aidan said absently. His gaze drifted toward the lush countryside.

"Oh, yes, I forgot," Kaijin said. "Nester did make mention of that. Well, hopefully, he'll be distracted long enough for me to finish my business and leave."

"Where are you going next?" Zarya asked.

Kaijin thought for a moment, then shrugged. "I don't know, yet, but I hope I will get some direction, soon." *Very soon.*

* * *

Nester arrived at the plaza and skidded to a halt. The place was heavily decorated and lighted from the colorful lanterns hanging from overhead lines. The booths, however, were devoid of customers. He deflated.

"You're a few hours early," a man's voice said from behind him.

Nester jumped, then spun around. He gazed up at an armored guard, and his eyes widened in shock. "I didn't do it! I swear on my pa's grave, I didn't!"

The guard scoffed. "Oh, it's you, Nester. Look, the festival won't begin for another hour, so find something else to keep your grubby little hands preoccupied—and that *doesn't* mean thieving!"

Nester was about to speak out in protest when he spied his other companions in the distance. He brushed past the guard and ran to meet them. "Looks like there won't be any festival yet."

"Lovely." Kaijin rolled his eyes. "Whatever will you do in the meantime?"

Nester grinned. "I'll just be taggin' along for a little while longer—at least long enough to find out what in th' soddin' 'ells that shiny is."

Kaijin sighed. "I was afraid you'd say that."

* * *

The front doors of the Celestran aurorium slowly creaked open, allowing the outside light to pour into the stone-covered interior of the main atrium.

Kaijin breathed in the cool, crisp air, lightly scented with honeysuckle. He welcomed the pleasant aroma, after the stench of the fetid marsh.

Nester sniffed the air. "You smell that?"

Zarya inhaled deeply and smiled. "It is honeysuckle. It represents the goddess's sweet fragrance."

"Aye, but . . ." Nester's gaze shifted sidelong to Aidan, who appeared lost in thought.

"Come." Zarya beckoned as she made her way down the red-and-gold carpet of the center aisle.

Gold shimmered on the high ceilings from the midday light that poured in from the stained glass windows. Two winding staircases on opposite ends of the room led up to two higher stories, where bookshelves in open lofts could be seen from the ground floor. Several robed clergymen and women walked about, toting books and stacks of parchment. Two rows of five pews stretched down the middle of the atrium, leading to an exquisite grand altar trimmed in gold and silver. Statues of dragons and beautiful, nude women posed with swords were placed throughout the hall, adding to the regal atmosphere.

At the base of the altar knelt an elderly, white-robed priest. His head was lowered in prayer as he tended to a middle-aged man who also knelt, holding his left arm as if in pain. Standing next to them was a young, robed boy, who held a small golden dish.

Kaijin, Nester, and Aidan quietly shuffled down the aisle, following Zarya. When they were midway, Zarya held her arm out in front of them, barring them from continuing.

"Wait," she whispered. "We mustn't disturb him whilst he is convening with the goddess."

Kaijin watched the two men a moment. "It's fascinating that he is able to heal that man by praying to the goddess."

Zarya nodded. "The goddess is the source of our powers, Kaijin. If we are not faithful to Her, then we are powerless."

"Oh, so if I stub my toe or somethin', all I gotta do is say a few nice things about th' goddess, and it'll be all better?" Nester asked in a whisper. "'Ow convenient!"

Kaijin groaned. "I don't think it works like that, Nester."

Zarya shot them both a glare. "Enough, you two. Be quiet, and watch."

The priest placed his hands on the man's injured arm. A faint blue glow emanated, trailing up the man's arm to encompass his entire body. The man winced before relaxing. The priest looked at him and smiled. "The goddess has answered this day, Ulric."

Ulric opened his eyes and lightly touched his arm where the injury was. He smiled. "The pain is gone! Thank you, Honored Father. I can finally go back to work."

The priest shook his head. "Don't thank me. It is She who has brought you healing. Go now. Walk in Her steps."

Ulric lowered his head reverently. He placed a small donation of coins in the dish, then backed away from the altar.

"Oy! Watch it!" Nester exclaimed as the man nearly backed into him.

Ulric jumped in surprise and looked over his shoulder. "Oh! Excuse me, sir!"

Nester crossed his arms, frowning. "Right, just be careful next time, aye?"

Ulric did a double take and quickly left without another word. Kaijin and the others advanced to the altar.

The priest smiled in greeting, assessing each of them. His gaze rested on Zarya the longest. "Yes? May I help you?"

Zarya stepped forward and lowered her head. "Greetings, Honored Father. My name is Zarya, an aspiring priestess of our beloved goddess, Celestra. This is Kaijin, Aidan, and Nester." She gestured to each.

"'Ello, Your Majesty!" Nester said with a broad smile and a wave.

Kaijin nudged the brownie and muttered, "He's not a king, you fool!"

Nester frowned. "Well 'ow in th' soddin' 'ells do you properly address a 'igh-rankin' warder, then?"

"I think 'sir' would suffice."

Nester scoffed. "That's too bland, y'know? I would think someone who talks to gods an' things would want somethin' a little fancier than that, aye?"

Kaijin rolled his eyes.

"Nester, you're not being facetious, are you?" Zarya put her hands on her hips.

Nester made an exaggerated gasp. "What? Me? Of course not! Why would I do such a thing, beautiful? I meant every word, I did! I really *am* impressed by all the wardin'."

"Nester . . ." Zarya began.

Grinning, the brownie pulled the bandages off his fingers and showed off his unscathed fingertips to everyone. "Look! I'm all better, see? I should be bowin' down to your amazin' skills, too, beautiful!"

Zarya frowned. "Don't mock—"

"It is all right." The priest smiled at the two.

Zarya and Nester looked at him.

"I appreciate your willingness to humble yourself within these walls, Nester," the priest continued, "but such fancy titles are not necessary toward the clergymen. We are simply mediators."

"Indeed," Zarya said. She cast a hard stare at Nester before acknowledging the priest again. "If we may have a moment of your time . . . ?"

The priest nodded once. "Of course, my dear."

Zarya gestured to Kaijin while she continued. "During our trip in Houndstooth Marsh, we discovered a very mysterious and intriguing artifact hidden in the ruins there."

Kaijin pulled the warm, shining orb out from his haversack and presented it to the priest.

"You bet, it was mysterious!" Nester exclaimed, his eyes widening in excitement. "As an *explorer*, I think that's th' most amazin' thing I've ever seen! It's so amazin' that I don't even know what in th' soddin' 'ells it is, but it's amazin', I tell you!"

While Nester continued rambling, Aidan went up behind him and put his hand over his face, leaving just enough space for Nester to breathe.

Nester's muffled voice became agitated. He attempted—futilely—to pry Aidan's massive leathery hand away.

Aidan nodded for Zarya to continue.

The priest briefly scrutinized the orb and then turned to the boy beside him. "Get Geoffrey and Rose, quickly," he ordered.

The young acolyte nodded, rushed toward the east transept, and bounded up the stairs to the library. Moments later, the boy returned with two more robed clergy—a middle-aged man and woman.

"Is everything all right, Elder?" Geoffrey called as he approached, looking concerned.

The elder nodded and beckoned them over. "Please, come see this."

Geoffrey and Rose acknowledged Kaijin and his group. The orb, with its swirling fire inside, drew their attention.

"They say they found it in Houndstooth Marsh," the elder said.

Rose blinked and then looked at Kaijin. "Truly?"

"Houndstooth Marsh?" Geoffrey repeated. "That's the druids' ruins, is it not, Elder?"

The elder priest nodded. "Indeed, it has been abandoned for hundreds of years."

Zarya nodded. "Do either of you know what it might be?"

Geoffrey rubbed his chin. "It's certainly druidic in nature, but that's about the extent of my knowledge of it. However . . ." He stepped forward and reached out for the orb. The heat emanating from it increased. He winced and yanked his hands back.

Everyone gasped.

Rose asked, "Are you all right?"

Geoffrey shook off his startlement. "Y–yes. I am fine."

The elder looked at Kaijin, who still held the orb. "I am rather curious that this orb has not harmed you while you hold it, young man."

Kaijin swallowed. *I can't tell him anything. He won't understand.* "Ah . . . I . . . I don't know, either, sir."

"While I do not sense the presence of the goddess within this artifact," the elder continued, "I do sense something . . . something beyond the simple element of fire inside. This is something powerful, young man."

Kaijin quirked his brow and then looked at the rest of his comrades.

Aidan finally released Nester and gestured for him to shush.

Nester regarded the giant sourly and crossed his arms.

"Is the orb cursed, elder?" Zarya asked.

"No," the elder replied. "That, I am certain."

"Could the power inside it be divine flames?"

"Yes, perhaps. But such a phenomenon eludes me."

"It's as if the essences of the world are infused in this one artifact," Rose mused aloud.

Essences of the world? Magical essences, I wonder?

"There's probably magic inside, too," Geoffrey said, nodding. "Not that any of us would know that for certain."

Kaijin chewed his bottom lip, watching Geoffrey. *Gods, don't let him suspect me of anything!*

"It would be worth the effort in finding out," the elder said. "Kaijin, I think you should try consulting the mages in Ghaeldorund. They may be able to provide further clues."

Kaijin blinked. "But with all due respect, sir, Ghaeldorund is a magocratic city. Does that not trouble you?" *Is he unaware that mages are despised around here?*

The elder's white eyebrow rose. "Trouble me? Of course not. Though we are well aware of the fear of mages and the city's problems, the aurorium does not take sides in these affairs."

Kaijin nodded slowly. "So, you're saying the aurorium would provide a safe haven for mages?"

"The aurorium is a safe haven to all—so long as peace is maintained within."

"Soddin' 'ells! So, we gotta travel all th' way north to that city? It's a three-day journey, y'know!"

A journey I'm willing to travel in order to learn the truth, Nester. "If I want to find out what it is, then I must."

Nester crossed his arms and huffed. "Well, you're a fiddler—why can't you just figure it out, aye?"

Kaijin paled. *That damned idiot!* "Nester! I told you not to—"

Rose and Geoffrey raised their eyebrows in surprise. They looked to the elder, who held up his hand dismissively.

"Do not be troubled, young man," the elder said to Kaijin. "You have come to us peacefully. The aurorium does not judge an individual based on others' actions."

Kaijin exhaled in relief. "Thank you. I've not come to cause trouble, and I hope my presence here does not do so."

"It is not wise to stay in Faywald longer than needed," Geoffrey said. "But of course, the aurorium is open to all, so you are free to stay here for as long as you wish."

"Thank you, but I will have to politely decline." Kaijin tucked the orb back into his haversack. "I will take your advice and head to Ghaeldorund. I want to know more about this artifact."

"As do I," Zarya said, nodding.

"And to think, she wanted us to leave it behind," Nester muttered to Kaijin.

Zarya whipped her head around, her long white hair swishing across her face. She scowled at Nester. "Yes, well, I realized I might have misjudged you all. For that, I apologize. From what the priests have said, this artifact sounds like a gift left by the gods. It may very well be the key to unlocking the many questions I have about the nature of the gods and perhaps bring me one step closer to completing another tier of my clerical studies."

Nester then turned to Aidan, who was eying the interior decorations. "You've been awfully quiet there, mate."

When Aidan didn't respond, Nester nudged him in the thigh. "You're gonna come with us too, aye? It's a long trip—we're bound to run into trouble along th' way."

Aidan's gaze shifted to the brownie.

Nester looked at him expectantly. "Well? Is that an 'aye' or 'nay'?"

"Leave him alone, Nester." *You've caused enough trouble as it is.* Kaijin turned back to the elder, Rose, and Geoffrey. "Thank you for your time and information."

The elder nodded and smiled. "May Celestra's protection be bestowed upon you and your companions."

Zarya, Kaijin, and Aidan reverently bowed their heads. The sounds of the festivities beginning outside could be heard, and Kaijin glanced toward Nester, who grinned and bolted for the door, not looking back.

VII

७४ॐ४ॐ

Faywald became a lively, colorful city of celebration as soon as night fell. Streamers, flowers, and pennants streamed from the rooftops and entwined on corners throughout the city, bringing a warm and inviting atmosphere to even the gloomiest of places.

The main part of the festival took place in the central plaza. Tents and vendors' booths overflowing with food, handmade trinkets, exotic silks and linens, books, and other various items lined the plaza's perimeter, while throngs of people converged in the center.

Kaijin, Zarya, and Aidan walked briskly through the colorful streets. Nester, who had sprinted ahead of them, stopped short in front of the plaza. He spun around; his mouth hung open, and his eyes grew wide at the melting pot of people partaking in a seemingly endless variety of activities. Children bobbed for apples, played ball, wrestled, and raced through the crowds in a dizzying swirl of color and motion. The adults that weren't perusing the merchants' wares played games of chance, visited the nearby taverns, or wandered the area, observing the festivities. Local street entertainers displayed their array of talents and their performances drew clusters of enthusiastic gawkers.

"Amazing, is it not, Nester?"

Nester jumped as Zarya spoke from behind him. He quickly slurped up the tiny stream of drool escaping from his mouth.

"What is city celebrating, anyway?" Aidan asked.

"The summer festival is a long-standing tradition, started by the barony several generations ago. It is a time of peace and unity—at least, that is what I have been told. It does seem rather exciting, though. We might as well have a little fun before the long trip tomorrow, yes?"

Nester beamed. "I like th' way you think, beautiful. That's probably th' best idea I've 'eard all day!"

Ignoring the others, Kaijin stared off into the crowd and toward the vendors' booths. Amongst the bustle, he spied a book vendor like the ones he had frequented back in Easthaven. He swallowed a small lump in his throat. *I wonder if I'll run into Master Jarial out here.* He doubted it, but his stomach tied in knots.

"Kaijin?" Zarya called, her voice filled with concern.

Kaijin snapped out of his trance and shot her a nervous smile. "Uh, yes, it's nice," he said distractedly, turning to leave. "Say, I think I'm going to have a look at that book vendor over there."

After a few moments' silence, Zarya asked shyly, "Do . . . do you mind if I join you?"

Kaijin stopped and glanced over his shoulder, not expecting the question. He looked to Nester, who smirked at Aidan, nudging him in the thigh.

Zarya clasped her hands behind her back and dropped her gaze to the ground, a blush coloring her cheeks. "To . . . to look at books, I mean."

Kaijin ignored Nester's snicker. "Well, sure, if you wish. Though I don't know how entertaining you will find it."

Zarya lifted her head, her expression brightening. "Well, I do like to read, too, you know." She walked past the group and toward the bookstall.

Kaijin gaped after her, admiring her graceful movements. *Beautiful* and *likes books?*

"Well I'll be an orc's mum." Nester came up beside Kaijin, wearing a wide, gap-toothed grin. "So you're not so clueless, after all."

Kaijin blinked. "What?"

"I saw th' way you looked at 'er—gettin' all tongue-foddled an' all."

Kaijin bristled. "I don't know what you're talking about."

"She's pretty, she is—maybe a little *too* pretty, though. I'd be careful, mate. You know th' saying, 'Things aren't always what they seem'?"

"It's not like that, Nester. She's an acquaintance—like you and Aidan."

Nester rolled his eyes. "Oy! Are you really so daft, Kaijin? She likes you, she does. Even *I* can see that. An' I'm no expert on 'uman love!" He turned to Aidan. "You can talk some sense into 'im, can't you, Aidan? Or at least *beat* it into 'im, aye?"

Aidan looked from Kaijin to Nester and then shook his head. "Aidan knows when to mind his own business." He pushed past them and walked toward a large crowd standing away from the plaza's main bustle. The people were gathered in a large circle, watching something in the center. Screams and cheers erupted sporadically.

Nester crossed his arms and frowned. "Aidan's no 'elp, Kaijin. Why in th' soddin' 'ells did we decide to let 'im join us again?"

"It was your idea," Kaijin said simply. "Now, if you'll excuse me." He followed Zarya before Nester had a chance to retort.

* * *

Aidan stood behind the edge of the large gathering, his arms crossed as he peered over many heads, toward the center of the ring. A portly man, sporting a wide, excited grin and a flamboyant merchant outfit, spoke loudly enough to be even more obvious than Aidan. "Who's going to be next to challenge Hugo the Mauler? Try your luck! Test your strength! Do you have what it takes?"

The crowd responded with yells, claps, and cheers.

Adjacent to the crowd was a small booth, where a line of people formed. One by one, each person slid money pouches to the attendant, who took it and then scribbled something in his book. Aidan saw several smaller groups of people escorting battered, broken men away from the festival.

"I can't feel my leg!" one of the leaving men cried.

"Hold on," one of the escorts said. "We're getting you to a healer."

"That Hugo's a maniac!" another injured man complained.

Aidan felt something tap him on the side of his thigh. Glancing down, he saw Nester standing beside him.

"Looks like it's just you an' me, mate," the brownie said. He craned his head to try to peer through the throng of people. "'Ey, what's goin' on?"

Aidan turned his attention to the middle of the gathering. "Aidan is not sure."

". . . And three hundred gold to the winner!" the portly man announced.

Nester blinked. "What was that about three 'undred gold?" he asked Aidan.

Aidan shrugged. "Does it matter?"

"What do you mean, 'Does it matter?' We could use that gold!" He jumped, trying to get a better view. "I can't see a soddin' thing!" He knelt and peered among the many pairs of legs.

The sea of people parted as the announcer began addressing prospective competitors. "Who will be our next challenger?" He looked left and right, his grin never leaving his face. He suddenly turned toward Aidan.

Aidan met the man's gaze.

"What's goin' on, mate?" Nester asked Aidan.

"You there!" The announcer pointed at Aidan.

A hush fell as the crowd turned. Dozens of pairs of eyes widened.

Nester struggled back to his feet, his expression contorted with confusion and frustration.

Aidan uncrossed his arms. He swallowed once, feeling the uncomfortable tension in the air. *Why is everyone staring like that?*

The announcer approached Aidan, topping off at just above Aidan's waist. "My good man . . ." He examined Aidan's features more closely. "You look like someone who can give these people the show of the year. Show off that power! That strength! That size!"

Aidan shook his head. "No, thank you. Aidan is quite fine."

Several people in the crowd snickered.

The announcer reached up and patted one of Aidan's bulging, rock-solid biceps. "A big man like you? Modest? Come, now. These people want a show!" He turned to address the people. "Don't you all want a show?"

The crowd responded with cheers.

Aidan yanked his arm away. "No, Aidan does not like violence."

A wave of laughter swept through the crowd.

Nester glanced from the announcer to Aidan in disbelief. He grabbed a handful of Aidan's trousers and tugged him aside. "I wanna talk to you, mate."

Aidan looked down at the brownie's feeble attempts at budging him. He finally walked on his own, following Nester's lead.

"'Scuse us a moment." Nester said to the announcer as they walked by.

The smile faded from the announcer's face.

The crowd began impatiently chanting, louder and louder.

Nester led Aidan away from the crowd and waved his finger up at him as he spoke. "See 'ere, Aidan. We're goin' on a long trip tomorrow. We could use that money, y'know? Ghaeldorund ain't exactly a thrifty city. There's a reason why that place is among th' most prestigious cities in Aransiya—no, th' *world!*" He paused and then grumbled, "Damn pompous fiddlers. . . ."

Aidan remained silent. He found Nester's 'seriousness' slightly amusing.

Nester cleared his throat. "Ah, anyway, so, 'ere's th' deal. You fight, you win th' money, and we can survive comfortably in Ghaeldorund, no problem!"

Aidan shook his head. "What is point of fighting? What is point of hurting someone for gold?"

Nester groaned. "Oy! 'E didn't say you 'ad to *'urt* no one. Just make it entertaining, aye? C'mon, mate. It'll be fun. Just a friendly sparrin' match, that's all."

Aidan scratched his chin. "Well . . . all right. Aidan will have fun—so long as no one gets hurt."

Nester's smile brightened, and he clapped his hands together. "Really? Great! All right, you get ready to fi—I mean, 'ave some fun. I'll let that loud bloke know, aye?"

Before Aidan could respond, Nester had already run off into the crowd. Aidan's gaze trailed toward the open center of the ring, where he spied patches of dirt, grass, and cobblestone. The spectators waited attentively for the event to begin. A man, clad in extravagant silver breastplate, stood not far from Aidan, watching the crowd. The silver scales of his armor glistened in the light. The man's gaze briefly locked with Aidan's, before narrowing and returning to the center of the ring.

The crowd parted as Aidan slowly made his way to the center to meet with Nester and the announcer.

The smile returned to the announcer's face. "Ladies and gentlemen! Aidan has accepted the challenge! He will be the next to face Hugo the Mauler in a no-holds-barred fight to victory!"

The crowd erupted in cheers.

Moments later, a burly man stepped forward into the ring. His body was as solid as Aidan's, but he was a whole foot shorter. He wore a confident expression on his face as he casually cracked his knuckles. "I can take him." He snatched a full tankard, sloshing with ale from a nearby spectator, chugged the contents within a few gulps, and then slammed the empty tankard to the ground. He roared like an animal, which also further riled the crowd.

"I wouldn't expect anything less out of you, Hugo," the announcer commented with a smirk. He addressed the rest of the crowd. "Without further ado, let the fight begin!"

Nester looked Hugo up and down and smirked. "Pah! There ain't enough luck in th' world for you to beat Aidan 'ere!"

Hugo glowered at Nester and raised his hand, as though about to slap him.

"Eep!" Eyes wide, Nester scrambled out of the ring. He yelled over his shoulder, "Knock 'is soddin' 'ead off, Aidan!"

Aidan stared at his opponent, ignoring Nester's words. He respectfully bowed to Hugo and extended his fist as a show of good sportsmanship. "An honor to meet you, sir." He cracked a small smile, awaiting Hugo to bump fists.

Hugo scrutinized Aidan up and down, and then snorted. "What in the bloody hells are you? No, I don't think I want to know." He stepped back into a defensive posture.

Aidan's smile faded, and he lowered his fist. He spotted Nester at the ring's exterior, wandering aimlessly about the crowd. The brownie casually approached an unaware spectator, quickly glanced about, and carefully untied a small hanging pouch from the man's belt. Nester snatched the pouch and skittered away, disappearing in the crowd.

Aidan gawked. *Did he just—?* Frowning, he looked around for the announcer. "Sir! Sir! Aidan requests that—" He caught sight of Hugo's fist coming toward the side of his face and leaned back to dodge the blow. Hugo missed wildly, and his momentum sent him flying forward. He tripped over Aidan's solid body, rebounded, and fell flat on his face with a loud grunt.

The crowd was in an uproar.

Aidan gasped and rushed to the fallen man. "Aidan is sorry! Are you all right?"

But Hugo remained out cold.

Aidan knelt down beside Hugo and shook him, attempting to rouse him.

Nester broke through the crowd and ran over to Aidan. One of his belt pouches was fatter, nearly sagging off his hip. "That was amazin', Aidan! You beat 'im without even liftin' a finger!" He gasped. "That means we win the 300 gold, aye?" He smiled broadly and slapped Aidan on the back. "Good on ya!"

Aidan scowled at the brownie. "This man is hurt, and all you can think about is money?"

"Ah, 'e's not 'urt. 'E's just . . . ah . . . takin' a nap, that's all." Nester climbed atop Hugo's broad chest and slapped him across the face a few times. Nester seemed to be enjoying it, by the way his lips crept into a smile despite his twisting them.

Hugo groaned.

"See?" Nester pointed. "Good as new!"

Aidan opened his mouth to protest, then winced as the announcer's blaring voice resounded over the crowd.

"And there you have it, ladies and gentlemen! Hugo has fallen in less than a minute's time! Aidan has won the three hundred gold prize!"

A mixed reaction of cheers and boos swept through the crowd.

The announcer approached Aidan, smiling. "Now that you've defeated the champion, why not make things a little more interesting, hm? What say you increase your earnings to four hundred?"

Nester's eyes bulged. "*Four 'undred gold?*"

Aidan stood up and waved his hand to the announcer. "No! Aidan does not want to fight anymore. Aidan does not want anyone else hurt!"

The announcer leaned over and muttered, "You're doing great, Aidan. Keep it up."

"But—!"

"Aidan agrees!" Nester exclaimed, getting the announcer's attention. "Didn't you 'ear 'im?"

The announcer looked confused. "He—he did?" His attention locked on Nester, who smiled and gave a few quick nods in agreement. "Oh! Yes! He did! He *did!*"

Aidan glared at Nester and then turned to the announcer. "No! Aidan did not—"

"Ladies and gentlemen!" the announcer continued. "Aidan has agreed to put forth his earnings into an even *larger* purse! Four hundred gold is the new prize! Who will be the first contender to challenge him?"

Another man stepped into the ring and said, "I will accept the challenge. My name is Caiyn." He ripped off his tunic and tossed it into the crowd. The rippling muscles in his bare chest and arms were more toned than Hugo's, and he was taller and leaner. However, Caiyn's height barely reached the middle of Aidan's chest. After observing Aidan carefully, Caiyn stepped back into a fighting stance.

Aidan's head tilted to the side, studying his opponent's movements. *That stance is familiar. Light weight on the front foot, hands open, body angled ninety degrees . . . He will most likely favor his feet.* He briefly reviewed his training as a youth, when his master had introduced him to the many arts of fighting.

"Caiyn has agreed to challenge the reigning champion, Aidan!" The announcer bellowed. "Place your bets, everyone!"

Cheers of anticipation surged through the crowd, and people began scrambling to the betting booth. A few people patted themselves in a frenzy, realizing their money pouches were gone.

"I've been robbed!" One of the spectators cried. But the man's voice was soon drowned out by the crowd's murmurings. Aidan watched as the man joined a small group of spectators who had also apparently been robbed and scoured the sea of people in search of the thief.

Frowning, Aidan scanned the crowd for Nester, but the brownie was nowhere to be found.

When the last bet was taken, the announcer addressed everyone again. "And now, without further ado, may the best man win!" He quickly shuffled out of the ring.

Aidan bowed and extended his fist, hoping Caiyn, whom he sensed was more of a seasoned fighter than Hugo, would return the honorable gesture. "It is an honor, sir. Aidan will be careful this time and make sure no one gets hurt."

To Aidan's relief, Caiyn understood his gesture and bumped his fist. "Never underestimate your opponent,

Aidan," he said, then returned to his stance. The fight commenced. Caiyn shifted the weight on his foot and sprang forward through the air, aiming a side-kick toward Aidan's lower ribs.

Aidan sidestepped before Caiyn's foot made contact.

Appearing surprised, Caiyn tumbled to the ground, then rolled back toward Aidan to recover his attack. Aidan peered over his shoulder at Caiyn, who attempted to drop him with a back-sweep. Caiyn's leg impacted the back of Aidan's, and a loud snap was heard.

Caiyn let out an earsplitting cry of pain. A hush drew over the spectators as he collapsed to the ground, holding his ankle.

Aidan gasped. He spun around and knelt down to tend to the injured man. "Aidan is sorry! Aidan is sorry! Stay still! Aidan will get you to healer!" Picking Caiyn up, Aidan looked around frantically for the nearest aurorium.

"Put him down," a gruff voice ordered, breaking the shocked silence of the crowd.

Startled, Aidan looked toward the voice. It was the armored man he had seen earlier. He approached Aidan. Like everyone else, Aidan easily towered over the armored man, but Aidan's size didn't appear to intimidate him.

The man crossed his arms and looked at Aidan expectantly. "I said, 'Put him down.'"

A bitter taste came to Aidan's mouth. Something about the armored man bothered him. He carefully set Caiyn down and backed away.

The armored man smiled and then nodded toward an unseen person within the crowd. Moments later, another armored man emerged. He approached, hefted Caiyn's body, and carried him off.

After his comrade left, the man turned back to Aidan. "My name is Gaston, and I will gladly take up the challenge."

Aidan gaped. He tried to protest, but no sound came. He felt small nudging on his side.

"Did you 'ear that, mate? This bloke wants to challenge you! Give 'im a good one, an' we'll be soddin rich after this!"

Aidan glared at Nester. "No! No more fighting! No more violence! Too many people got hurt today! Aidan is tired!"

Gaston stroked his thin black beard in thought and then smirked at Aidan. "Entertain me, creature. Entertain us all. It's amazing that someone like you has been spared from death."

Aidan met Gaston's gaze. "Aidan does not cause trouble, so people do not bother him."

"Surely not. They know better than to wrestle with a *half-breed*." He paused and scrutinized Aidan more closely. "That *is* what you are, I presume."

Soft mutterings swept over the crowd. Even the announcer looked stunned.

"Soddin' 'ells, Aidan! You're gonna just stand there an' let 'im insult you like that?"

Aidan shook his head at Nester. "Aidan does not know what this man is talking about." He faced Gaston and then sighed heavily. "If it means Aidan can get some food and warm bed afterwards, then fine—Aidan will entertain."

"That's it, mate! Knock th' sense outta 'im!" Nester quickly scrambled out of the ring and disappeared in the crowd.

"Wonderful." Gaston grinned and stepped backwards, beckoning Aidan to make the first advance.

Anticipatory cheers erupted from the crowd, and people started placing bets.

Aidan regarded the man, attempting to assess his movements, but Gaston's cool demeanor was difficult to figure out. *What is it about him that's unnerving me?* Aidan wondered. *That armor, perhaps, or . . .* He paused and sniffed at him. Gaston reeked of blood, though Aidan saw none on his attire. Though it made him feel awkward, Aidan didn't bother attempting to bow formally to him; Gaston seemed ready to prove a point.

Gaston circled him slowly, the smirk remaining fixed on his weathered face. "Come, Aidan. Your audience awaits."

Aidan sighed. He reluctantly threw himself toward Gaston, to grapple with him.

Gaston stood as still as a statue as Aidan approached. When Aidan was mere footsteps away, Gaston turned his body slightly and braced for impact. Aidan's mass moved Gaston a few steps, but Gaston's armored body otherwise stayed firm. Aidan prepared to bear-hug Gaston, but Gaston surprised him with a gauntleted fist to the solar plexus.

Aidan grunted, and his body folded. Gaston came at him again, aiming another punch at Aidan's lowered head, but Aidan leaned back just as the punch brushed past his chin. Aidan countered by grabbing Gaston's arm and attempted to sweep him off his feet. Gaston, his arm still locked in Aidan's grip, spun backwards and elbowed Aidan hard in his side. Aidan gasped, feeling one of his ribs crack, and collapsed.

He landed on his back with a loud thump. The ground trembled.

The crowd roared.

Nester's jaw dropped. "That's not fair! 'E cheated, 'e did!"

Gaston stood over Aidan, planting his scale-armored boot upon Aidan's chest. He glowered down. "You disappoint me, Aidan. I was hoping to make this a worthwhile fight." Gaston pressed his foot harder into Aidan's chest.

Aidan stared up at the man and then coughed briefly. He eyed the scales on the man's foot. The armor appeared rough—like actual scales—despite their metallic shine. He stared at his own arm, similarly scaled—only the ones on Gaston's armor were much larger.

"What's wrong, Aidan?" Gaston jeered, smiling with amusement. "You look rather confused about something."

Aidan snorted. The scent of blood, underlined by a sweetness, grew stronger. Strength rekindled in his body. Sadness and rage welled in his mind. Aidan somehow recognized the scent from long ago, but could not recall where. He wrinkled his nose.

In a single motion, Aidan heaved up, tossing Gaston onto his back, knocking the wind out of the man. Pinning Gaston to the ground, Aidan stared into his eyes. All around them, the crowd cheered.

Gaston stared back at Aidan, smiling weakly and huffing, out of breath. "What . . . are you waiting for? Finish me . . . off."

"No," Aidan said promptly. "No more violence."

Gaston scoffed, "What does your kind know about pacifism? Look at you. You're a savage. Born with power you know nothing about. And bred to destroy."

A low growl rumbled in Aidan's throat. He glared at Gaston, baring his fangs slightly. "No. Aidan is done with this. All of this. There is no need for violence. Someone always gets hurt."

Unfazed, Gaston continued looking at him. "Sometimes violence is needed."

"Now is not time. Aidan is hungry. And tired."

"Then go. Run like the scared little boy that you are. It sounds like the crowd has been entertained enough by our little scuffle, anyway." The announcer returned to the ring, and Gaston turned his head.

"Aidan has successfully pinned Gaston in submission!" the announcer declared to the cheering crowd. "Ladies and gentlemen, Aidan prevails once again!"

Another deafening cheer arose, and the crowd began chanting Aidan's name.

Aidan pushed himself off Gaston and stood back, frowning and watching him a moment. Ignoring the chants, Aidan turned and hastily left the ring. The crowd made a path for him as he walked.

The announcer suddenly ran in front of him, holding out a filled pouch heavy with coin and yelling, "Wait! Wait! Wait! You forgot to claim your prize!"

Aidan shook his head and brushed past the man. "Aidan does not want."

"But—but this money is rightfully yours! You won the competition! Four hundred gold was the prize!"

Aidan stopped and looked back over his shoulder. "Then donate it to orphanage. The children will eat good for long time."

The announcer gawked at him. "Ah . . . o–okay then? I guess we will donate it to—"

"'Old on there!" Nester tugged at the announcer's tunic, and the man looked down. "I'm Aidan's manager, y'know," Nester continued. "I look after 'im an' all that. Aidan obviously got bumped in th' 'ead that last round, so 'is judgment's a little off. I'll just go ahead an' 'andle th' prize money for you, if you don't mind."

The announcer shooed Nester away. "Off with you! The money will be donated to the orphanage as per the winner's wishes, and that's final!"

The cheers had died down, and the crowd began to disperse.

Rubbing his pained ribs, Aidan quickly made his way out of the plaza.

"Aidan! 'Ow could you just up and reject a 'uge sum of money like that?" Nester had caught up with Aidan walking alongside him, trying to keep up with his long-legged gait.

Aidan kept silent.

"Now we won't 'ave enough money for our trip to Ghaeldorund!" Nester fingered some coins in one of his belt pouches. "Well, at least *I* managed to make a li'l 'ere an' there. And I'm sure as 'ells ain't givin' you a single soddin' piece! Th' kids are richer than us! Can you believe that?"

Aidan kept his eyes focused ahead as he made his way toward the nearest inn.

"I've never seen a more stupid bloke than you, Aidan," Nester continued. "'Ow could you . . ."

Aidan stopped listening. Gaston had unnerved him. That bitter taste never left his mouth, and those mixed scents of something bloody and pleasant were etched in his mind.

VIII

∽✦∽

K aijin couldn't stop grinning as he perused booth after booth of books. For the first time in a long time, he felt at peace with himself. Flipping through an assortment of tomes pertaining to the gods— more particularly, Ignis, the Firelord—Kaijin noticed Zarya out of the corner of his eye. She simply stared at him while he read in silence.

"How interesting," she said at last.

He stopped reading and looked up. "What?"

Zarya smiled. "Someone like yourself being so avidly curious about the gods." She lowered her voice. "Are you looking to become a Ignan cleric?"

"No," Kaijin replied. "I simply wish to further expand my knowledge about the god, whom I've grown to revere." He returned the books to their stacks and then sighed. He turned away from the stall and walked away, his head lowered. He could remember Easthaven's vast marketplace and the endless rows of vendors' booths that had lined the streets. Kaijin could still feel the same enthusiasm he had felt as a boy, walking with his father amongst the throng of shoppers. He could smell the aged books from some of the booths, and he could hear his father's scolding voice after Kaijin had wandered off alone to explore some of the bookstalls. Kaijin choked back tears the longer he dwelled on his past.

"Kaijin?" he heard Zarya call out softly.

Turning, Kaijin saw the priestess run to him, carrying two books. "You forgot these."

Kaijin blinked, realizing the books were the two he had been browsing through the longest. "You . . . you bought these for me?"

A hint of pink flushed her cheeks. "Well, you looked like you really wanted these in particular. . . ."

Kaijin swallowed a small lump in his throat. He slowly reached out and accepted the books from her. A warm, pleasant feeling, came over him, and he smiled. "Th— thank you. . . ."

Zarya beamed and nodded.

After placing the books into his haversack, Kaijin continued his walk. Zarya joined him.

"How did you come to know the Firelord?" she inquired.

Kaijin took a deep breath, his smile remaining. "I first discovered Him from a book my former master once gave me when I was five." He paused to reminisce. "But despite how long I've known Him, I feel as though there is still much more to learn—that I am still so new to His ways."

"Most Ignan followers travel the world, spreading the ways of the Firelord. Ignis believes in purity, strength, overcoming one's enemy and not showing fear. And yet, there is an even deeper meaning."

"Deeper? What do you mean?" He'd studied the magical side to the Firelord, but not the clerical, and her words piqued his curiosity.

"It is difficult for me to explain in a way that you would understand."

"I would like to try."

Zarya paused and rubbed her chin. "It is not something that can be explained in *words,* exactly, but rather *felt.* And that is something only possible for a cleric who is properly attuned to their god."

Kaijin frowned, his gaze idly following the passersby. He headed away from the large crowds and found an empty bench near one of the taverns that overlooked the entire festival from afar. He sat and sighed.

Zarya sat beside him. "Kaijin? Is something wrong?"

He looked at her, her soft, angelic voice soothing his nerves. He felt a brief pang in his head and looked to the sky just in time to see Miele happily fluttering overhead, visiting the rooftops. He turned back to Zarya and lowered his voice enough for only her ears. "My former master once said my magic was somehow . . . *tainted* by a divine power." *I think that was his way of saying I am cursed.*

One of Zarya's thin, white eyebrows rose. "Your magic? Tainted?"

Kaijin nodded. "I don't know what that means, but that is why I am here. I wish to learn more about myself."

"A mage whose powers are influenced by a god—now *that's* an interesting concept." She chuckled softly. "Perhaps it may not be so farfetched, but I'm quite sure that it's rarely seen and experienced. It could very well be a blessing from your god—or a curse."

"I do hope for the former rather than the latter." Kaijin smiled weakly. "Sometimes I hear things—voices. It's like the Firelord speaks to me."

"What does the Firelord say?" Zarya tilted her head to the side, curious.

"He says many things." Kaijin shifted uncomfortably. "Such as—" He suddenly stopped as he spied an aged man who had been standing by watching the festival turn and began walking in their direction. Bright yellow robes showed beneath his light chain shirt. A symbol of a flame was emblazoned on the tabard, matching the designs woven along the bottom hem of his robe. As he drew closer, Kaijin noticed burns and scorch marks on his hands. *A cleric of Ignis.*

The cleric passed them, heading toward the tavern beside them.

"Kaijin." Zarya nudged him. "He looks like—"

"Yes. . . he is," Kaijin said absently, following the stranger with his gaze.

The stranger opened the door and then paused. He turned his head sharply their way, his ebony ponytail whipping behind him.

Kaijin met the man's gaze, and swallowed nervously. *I . . . I can't believe it. This has to be a dream.* His gaze fell back to the symbol on the tabard.

The stranger's eyes narrowed at Kaijin. His hand slowly fell away from the door handle, and he approached them.

Kaijin gasped. *Oh gods,* now *what do I do?* "Zarya, he's coming this way," he whispered. "What should I say?"

Zarya smiled reassuringly. "Don't worry, Kaijin."

The stranger stood before them, assessing them both but focusing on Kaijin. "Greetings, Brother."

"Ah—" Kaijin was lost for words.

"Greetings, sir," Zarya broke in. Kaijin was relieved that she decided to speak in his stead. "We couldn't help but admire your . . . attire. May I assume you are of the Ignan clergy?"

The stranger's thick, black eyebrows rose. "Indeed, m'lady. I am a servant of the Firelord. Are you looking for guidance?"

An actual cleric of the Firelord! Kaijin stared at the man in awe. His tanned face was rough and weathered, as though he had traveled much. Kaijin humbly bowed his head.

Zarya shook her head, then spoke in a soft, polite tone, "I am not, sir, with all due respect to the Firelord. My name is Zarya. I am an apprentice of the Celestran clergy and on a journey of my own. This is my friend, Kaijin. Like you, he is also a . . . a servant of the Flame."

The stranger nodded politely to the priestess and then stroked his trim, grey-streaked beard. His attention returned to Kaijin.

Kaijin exhaled, finally mustering the courage to speak. "I . . . I seek guidance, sir. I wish to learn more about myself, my abilities—and my god. I'm . . . not a cleric, however. . . ."

The stranger dismissively waved his hand. "One does not need to be a cleric to learn about Him. Have you ever heard of the Pyre?"

Kaijin quirked his brow. "No, sir, I have not."

Zarya looked thoughtful. "The Pyre. . . . Is that not a formal name for the Ignan aurorium?"

"Nay, m'lady." The stranger turned to Kaijin. "Far to the southeast, there is a place high in the mountains known as the Pyre. It is one of the few holy landmarks in the world dedicated to the Firelord."

Kaijin brightened. *A place dedicated to the Firelord? A place where there are others like me?* "Oh, thank you, for the information, sir!" He glanced at Zarya. "That is where I'm going to head next."

Zarya blinked. "Wait, Kaijin. What about the orb?"

"Orb?" With sharp curiosity, the stranger's gaze bounced from Kaijin to Zarya.

"Ah . . ." Kaijin glanced around cautiously, but he saw no eavesdroppers. He reached into his haversack and cradled the orb in his hand, but he hesitated to reveal it to the stranger. Kaijin eyed him warily, then looked at Zarya.

The priestess closed her eyes. When she opened them again, she stared blankly at the stranger. Her eyes glowed a moment before returning to their normal sapphire hue. She turned to Kaijin and nodded once. "It's all right, Kaijin. He means no ill intent."

Kaijin regarded the priestess with newfound curiosity. *How does she know that?*

The stranger frowned at her. "I am a servant of the Flame, m'lady. I would not dare bring harm to a fellow brother. While your cautiousness is understandable, casting a detection spell on me was unnecessary."

Zarya bowed her head. "Forgive me, sir. I meant no offense."

"Brother Kaijin." The priest turned to him. "What is it you have there?"

Grasping the orb, Kaijin took a deep breath and slowly pulled it out of the haversack.

The priest gazed upon the artifact. The magical flames within swirled and flickered in a beautiful display. He gasped, his eyes widening in amazement. "By the gods! Where did you find that?"

"The druids' ruins in Houndstooth Marsh," Kaijin replied. "Do you know what it is, sir?"

The priest stared into the orb with intense scrutiny. He whispered reverently, "His beautiful flames are contained within." He extended his hand but stopped before his fingertips touched it. He yanked his hand back and winced. "You hold the essence . . . the essence of . . ."

The priest's stare had gone blank, as if hypnotized. Kaijin promptly returned the orb to his bag and secured it. "It's been doing that to me, too."

As soon as the orb was concealed, the priest snapped out of his trance. He rubbed his eyes and refocused on Kaijin. "Ah . . . Y—young man, that artifact should be taken to the Pyre immediately. The grand cleric there would know exactly what it is and what must be done with it. Make haste. The power you hold must not fall into the wrong hands."

Kaijin gulped and regarded Zarya.

She stared back at Kaijin, saying nothing.

"I would gladly accompany you on your journey," the priest continued. "However, I have duties of my own. Head southeast toward the mountains. You will soon spot plumes of smoke in the sky arising from the offerings to the eternal flames in the sacred brazier. Let the smoke guide you to the Pyre."

"Thank you, sir!" Kaijin beamed.

The priest nodded once, then turned away. "Safe travels, Brother Kaijin, and to you, as well, m'lady Zarya. May His holy flames burn strong in you both."

Kaijin bowed his head graciously, accepting the blessing. After the priest disappeared into the tavern, Kaijin turned to Zarya, his smile remaining.

IX

❧

our! *'Undred! Gold!" Is he as daft as he is big?*
Silver-lined tapestries, exotic rugs, and other extravagant décor embellished the interior of the Prancing Dragon Inn, which overflowed with patrons that made the place boisterous and merry. The air was thick with the smell of ale and steamed meat. Dozens of serving wenches hustled to and from the kitchen and bar, carrying trays of food and tankards sloshing with drinks.

Scowling bitterly, Nester sat across from Aidan and watched him wolf down a meal fit for seven people. On the table sat two tureens filled with thick, meaty stew; a large serving platter of smoked pork trimmed with mixed vegetables; a voluminous tankard brimming with mead; and two unused dishes. "'Ow can you think about eatin' at a time like this?" Nester whined.

Aidan took a long sip of mead, casting Nester a blank look over the brim of his tankard.

"We could've been rich, Aidan!" Nester wailed.

Sighing, Aidan lowered his drink and looked at the tankard's contents. "Aidan wishes they had almond milk here. This drink has strange taste."

Nester rolled his eyes. "It's called 'mead', Aidan. Don't tell me you've never drunk mead before."

Aidan shook his head. "Aidan has always loved almond milk since he was little boy."

Nester closed his eyes and carefully banged his forehead on the table, exasperated. "'Oy! Well you ain't a li'l boy anymore, Aidan!" He looked up at him. "Speakin' of li'l boys . . . we could've 'ad th' *world*, if you 'adn't 'ave given it all away to a bunch of soddin' kids! *Kids*, Aidan! Do you realize what you've done? A bunch of kids ain't gonna change th' world—*we* are!"

Aidan casually stirred the stew with a large wooden serving spoon. "Children do not need to starve. They are the future." Aidan offered a portion to him.

Nester blinked. "Listen to yourself! What's wrong with you?" He paused, looked at the spoonful of stew, and promptly shook his head. "Soddin' 'ells! For th' fifth time already, I told you I can't eat another bite. What're you tryin' to do? Make me explode? I think I ate myself deeper into depression realizin' 'ow much gold we lost today."

Aidan smiled. "Money is not everything, you know. We have food. We have shelter. We have good health. Is that not enough?" He stuck the spoon back into the stew then pulled the tureen in front of himself.

"Arrgh! You're impossible, Aidan! There's no gettin' through that thick, scaly 'ead o'yours!" Nester slumped down with his elbows on the table, and grumbled curses under his breath. He focused on what was going on in the rest of the inn.

* * *

The inn's front door swung open, and Kaijin and Zarya entered. They wove their way through the throngs of boisterous patrons.

"Most people in town recommend visiting this place during the festival," Zarya said to Kaijin over the noise. "I've heard they have good wine here, too."

He spotted Aidan sitting near the rear of the inn and pointed. "Hey, look, over there."

"Looks like they had the right idea." Zarya smiled. "Come on. Let's go sit with them."

Nester looked toward them as they made their way to the table. He quickly got up from his chair and ran to meet them. "Kaijin! Zarya! Am I glad to see you two! Please talk some sense into Aidan, 'ere! I think 'e's really lost it this time!" He grabbed Zarya's hand and tugged her over to the table.

Zarya followed Nester and stopped before Aidan, who, seemingly oblivious to their presence, was finishing off some stew from one of the tureens and then began working on the other. She yanked her hand away and regarded Nester curiously. "What are you going on about now, Nester? What did Aidan do?"

Nester remained standing and gestured for her and Kaijin to sit. "Oh, it started out great, aye! Aidan was challenged to a friendly li'l competition. First prize started at three 'undred gold! Aidan did great, 'e did. Gave 'is first opponent a good wallop in th' noggin, and *wham!* Sent th' poor sod flyin' an' landin' flat on 'is face!" Nester punched exaggeratingly at an invisible opponent. "Then, 'e went an' crippled 'is second opponent with a kick in th' leg.

Crack! Poor sod 'ad to get carried out." He kicked, and his foot impacted the bottom of the table. "Ouch!"

Aidan nearly choked on his mead. He glowered and slammed the tankard on the table.

Nester cringed, holding his foot as he hopped up and down. "I think I broke my big toe, I did!" he cried.

"You'll live." Zarya sternly eyed the brownie.

Nester cast the priestess a pleading look, but she seemed unfazed. He sighed in defeat and slowly let go of his foot. Afterwards, he stood on both feet, then hopped up and down and grinned. "'Ey! It's not broken no more! You 'ealed it! Thanks, beautiful!"

Zarya rolled her eyes.

"So, Nester," Kaijin said. "Why are you upset with Aidan? From your story, it sounds like he won the competition. Isn't that a good thing?"

Nester stared at Kaijin, wide-eyed. "Why am I upset? Why am I so soddin' *upset?* It's cause *this* big oaf gave *all* that money away—to a bunch of soddin' *kids!* We ended up winnin' four 'undred gold after th' competition was all over, an' Aidan decides to give it away to some soddin' orphanage!"

Kaijin blinked. *What?*

Aidan resumed slurping his stew, not appearing to pay the brownie any mind.

"So, let me get this straight, Nester." Zarya narrowed her eyes. "You are upset at Aidan for doing charitable work?"

Nester shook his head. "It wasn't 'charitable work', beautiful. It was foolish! We could've used that money for our travels, y'know. Ghaeldorund is an expensive city to survive in." He pointed a thumb at Aidan. "Now, thanks to *this* bloke, we won't be gettin' very far."

Aidan raised the entire tureen and slurped the remaining stew as if it were just a small soup bowl.

"Soddin' 'ells!" Nester gawked. "I can't believe you just ate all that by yourself!"

Zarya looked at Aidan and then the remaining food on the table. "By the goddess! Is all this Aidan's?"

"Aye," Nester replied. "We were on our way 'ere when we ran into this ritzy bloke who was so impressed with Aidan's performance at th' competition that 'e treated 'im to a free room and luxurious meal. A good twenty golds' worth of accommodations, mind you!"

"Twenty!" Zarya exclaimed, her eyes widening.

"That's a lot of food," Kaijin said.

Nester nodded firmly. "Aye. You two 'ungry? There's certainly plenty for everyone. In fact, 'ere! Please eat so Aidan will stop pesterin' me about it." He pushed the two unused plates in front of Kaijin and Zarya, spooned out two hefty portions of vegetables from the platter and placed two thick-cut slices of pork on top.

Zarya chuckled. "I can't believe that *you're* annoyed for a change, Nester."

Nester bristled. "I ain't annoyed. I'm just . . . uh, full . . . and . . . very upset. Aye, that's right. Upset at what Aidan did with all that gold."

Kaijin took a moment to eye and smell the delectable meal before looking back at the brownie. "No sense in crying foul about it now, Nester. I know you have your *methods* of obtaining more gold—methods I'd rather not get myself involved in. And I'm actually quite surprised that *you're* full. I've seen you eat before."

"Aye, well . . ." Nester returned to his seat. "Even I 'ave my limits. Aidan 'asn't stopped eatin'! I swear, 'e's got th' belly of a *Dragon!*"

Aidan rubbed his belly and let out a heavy, thunderous belch. Several nearby patrons looked his way, startled.

Kaijin stared at the giant. "Gods be damned, Aidan!"

"My thoughts exactly," Nester said.

Zarya grimaced. "Pardon you, Aidan."

Aidan smiled sheepishly at her as he refilled his tankard with mead. Then he pulled the entire pork platter toward himself. He skewered a hunk of meat with the carving fork and watched the juices dribble into the surrounding vegetables.

Nester sighed, shook his head, and regarded Kaijin and Zarya once more. "Anyway, there ain't no sense in goin' to Ghaeldorund at this rate. We don't got th' means to survive in a place like that. No sense in askin' those pompous fiddlers about that artifact. They just want more gold to fill their greedy big pockets, they do!"

"Look who's talking." Zarya coolly eyed Nester. She picked a chopped carrot off her plate and daintily nibbled it.

Nester huffed and stiffened in his seat.

"Well," Kaijin said, "I don't plan anymore on going to Ghaeldorund." He paused to take a small bite of pork. His eyes briefly lit up in surprise as the meat practically melted on his tongue. *Wow! I've not tasted anything so succulent before.* He took another, larger bite. *This is almost as good as Mother's cooking!*

Nester blinked. "What? You mean you know a better place to go to figure out what that thing is?"

Kaijin reluctantly paused his eating. "Yes. Zarya and I met someone earlier—an Ignan priest. He told us about a place called the Pyre and advised that we visit the grand cleric there. There is fire in this orb, of this I am certain. If anyone would know more about this thing, the Ignans at the Pyre would."

Nester looked thoughtful. "'Ey, that's not a bad idea. I mean, it makes sense, really. So, 'ow do we get to this place?"

"He said it's to the southeast, in the mountains." He blinked. "That fire symbol on your map, Nester—it must be there."

"Aye?" Nester fumbled through his pouches, pulled out his map, and began to carefully unfold it. He laid the oversized parchment out on an empty spot on the table and studied it closely. "Are you sure 'e meant that place?"

"Quite." Kaijin pointed to the fiery symbol.

Nester frowned. "What else did 'e say?"

"Well, he mentioned that you could see smoke billowing in the distance."

"Ah, th' ones that come from th' braziers sittin' on th' roof of th' place?"

Kaijin nodded.

"Soddin' 'ells! We'll just be wastin' our time goin' there. Th' warders won't talk to you. They'll just say you're 'walkin' on 'oly grounds' and shoo you off like they did me."

"But Kaijin reveres the Firelord," Zarya said. "Would they really turn him away?"

Nester glanced at Kaijin and then turned back to the map. "I don't know. . . . They might. Kaijin's not a warder, after all."

"I think it is worth a try, at least," Kaijin said. "After all, as you said, Nester, we don't have the means to survive in Ghaeldorund." He gave the brownie a halfhearted smile.

Nester grumbled sourly. "Well . . . All right." He refolded the map, stuffed it back into his pouch, and then looked across the table to Aidan. "Are you done yet?"

Aidan wolfed down the last few hunks of meat and slices of vegetables. He then swilled the rest of his mead, pushed the empty tankard aside and patted the subtle bulge in his gut. He suppressed another burp, wiped his mouth with the back of his hand. Zarya crossed her arms and frowned, and he stopped and lowered his hand.

Nester rubbed his eyes. "I can't believe it. Not a single bit of food left!"

Kaijin chuckled. "Well, that explains his size, at least." *Among other things.* "So, do we all agree to set out for the Pyre tomorrow?"

Nester made a sour face. "Ah, I guess we ain't got a choice, at this point."

Zarya nodded. "I will follow."

"All right." Kaijin nodded. He shifted his attention to the giant. "We're leaving early tomorrow, Aidan. Would you like to join us, as well?"

Aidan thought for a moment. "Aidan does not care about some simple marsh trinket, but . . . Aidan will consider joining. He has many unanswered questions of his own."

* * *

Aidan remained awake late that evening, long after his comrades and other festival-goers had retired. Though he had been gifted a free room for the night, he felt himself unable to stay. The cool night air and the hard, cobblestone streets seemed more appealing to him than a warm bed.

Senseless fighting deserved no reward. Aidan had been reluctant to accept the lavish meal, but his hunger had overcome his willpower.

He left the Prancing Dragon Inn and enjoyed the peacefulness of the city in the festival's aftermath. He leaned against the wall of the inn but winced when he felt the small, hard nubs in his back pressing against it. They often itched, and accidentally agitating them tended to cause him sharp pains. He shifted slightly to the side to take the pressure off his upper back. He idly scanned the dirty, debris-ridden streets that were devoid of the hundreds of people that had filled the plaza only hours before.

"Ah! Aren't you the one called . . . Aidan?" asked a youthful voice.

Aidan discovered an adolescent young man standing before him, staring in awe. The young man's clothes were torn to rags; his skin was mottled with dirt, as was his tawny, unkempt hair.

The youth smiled brightly. "It *is* you! The champion of the contest. I can't believe I had the great honor of watching you fight!"

Aidan frowned. "Aidan is no champion."

"What do you mean? All the children here love you! You're their hero—and mine, too."

"What is your name, boy?"

"It's Carver, and it's such an honor to know you."

Aidan pushed himself off the wall and scrutinized him. "Carver, when Aidan was little boy, his master once told him, 'There is no honor in senseless violence. It is easy to hurt people, but hard to help people.'"

Carver lowered his head. "I . . . I'm sorry, sir, I didn't mean . . . I just . . . I admire your strength and the way you move. I want to be like you. How did you get so strong?"

Aidan chuckled. "Aidan ate good and worked hard—very hard."

"Really?"

"Yes, but strength comes in all forms." Aidan pointed to one of his own bulging biceps. "This . . . will never be as strong as *this*." He tapped the side of his head.

Carver furrowed his brow. "What does that mean?"

"Mind is stronger than body."

"O–oh, I think I understand. . . . So what is the sense of having a strong body if you don't like to use it?"

Aidan shrugged. "Aidan uses his strength when needed—not because he can." He spotted faint, shadowy movement in the corner of his eye. Curious, Aidan stared at the night sky. It was empty, but he heard the batting of small wings and exhaled slowly. *Oh, it must be Kaijin's little pet bat.*

He heard a crow caw in the distance. His brow furrowed slightly. *A crow? This late at night? Must be my imagination.*

"Is something wrong?" Carver asked.

Aidan turned back to the young man and shook his head. "No, Aidan is just hearing and seeing things. He is tired. It has been long day."

Carver nodded once. He smiled again and flexed his arms. "So, do you think I have what it takes to be strong like you?"

The boy's thin, malnourished frame made Aidan grimace. "Aidan thinks you should eat something. You are practically skin and bone."

"That would be nice, wouldn't it?" Carver chuckled weakly. "I don't have money, though—and I don't intend to beg for it, either."

"You should go back to orphanage with the other children. The streets are no place for you."

"The orphanage won't let me in. I'm too old. Fifteen."

Aidan pondered a moment and then gestured toward the inn. "Go stay in Aidan's room, then. You will get free meal tomorrow."

Carver blinked. "W-what? But, I couldn't do that. What about you? Where will you sleep?"

"Aidan feels better sleeping outside. Now, go. Get key from innkeeper. The room is upstairs, second door on right." Aidan cast a stern gaze when the boy opened his mouth to protest.

Carver bolted into the inn, yelling over his shoulder, "Th—thank you, sir! Oh, thank you! You are not only a hero, but the most generous person I've ever met!"

Once the boy was gone, Aidan returned to the wall and resumed his thoughts. His eyes trailed back to the spot where he had seen movement earlier, but all was peaceful. Somehow, though, he still had a faint feeling that he was being watched. He slid down to the dirty ground and drew his knees to his chest. From where he sat, he had a good view of the empty plaza. He couldn't stop dwelling on Gaston's words. *A 'savage', he called me. And what was this 'power' he kept talking about?*

After what seemed like hours, Aidan's eyelids drooped. He huddled into a more comfortable position and finally drifted off to sleep.

* * *

As Carver ascended the final stair to the inn's second floor, he realized he wasn't alone. He scanned the darkened hallway, and his ears rang from the absolute silence. After a while, however, he shook off the paranoid feeling and quietly crept to the second door on his right. He slid the small iron key into the lock but didn't turn it. Perhaps some trace of the paranoia remained, because he pressed his ear to the door and listened carefully, instead. He heard nothing in the room beyond, and he turned the key. To his surprise, the door was already unlocked. He slowly eased the door open a crack and peered inside.

"Hello?" Carver called timidly. Moonlight poured in from the open window, creating shadows that danced about the floor and ceiling. When Carver received no response, he entered. As he did, a black crow flew through the window. Carver stopped in his tracks, watching in shock as the crow perched itself atop the bed's footboard.

The crow tilted its head, scrutinizing Carver, and then it hopped to the floor. It suddenly began to grow in size, taking the shape and likeness of a male human. Shadows flared over the skirts of the man's long, flowing garb as he crept into the dim light. He glanced briefly at Carver before turning his attention to the doorway.

Carver rubbed his eyes. *Did I just see that?* He had an uneasy feeling in his gut, and he shuffled back slowly. "Ah, I—I am sorry. I must be in the wrong room." He backed away until he hit something solid.

"No, my boy," a male voice commanded.

Carver heard the door shut behind him, and he turned around. He paled, staring upon a looming silhouette of an armored figure. "P–please forgive me, sir. I didn't mean to intrude. I will leave now."

"No." The man held up his gauntleted hand and nodded to the shadowy figure behind Carver.

Carver heard soft mutterings and saw a small flicker of firelight. The shadow-clad figure stood before them, holding a candle. Its warm, flickering glow lit the stranger's bearded, haggard face. He met Carver's gaze and cast a grim smile. Then he turned and proceeded to light the remaining candles around the room.

"That's much better. Thank you, Raban," the armor-clad man said. "After all, how are we to conduct business in the dark, hmm?"

Carver stared at the two men. His eyes settled on the larger, armored one, whose regal aura intrigued him. He relaxed a bit. "Wh–who are you? What—what do you want with me?"

The armored man removed his gauntlets. "I would like to present you with an offer. You're a young lad with ambition. Yet, you have fallen short of those goals."

Carver tilted his head. "I don't understand. . . ."

"You have not seen what it's like to earn the respect of the world. And you consult with . . . lesser beings to find your way. Creatures like Aidan are incapable of taking you far."

Carver smiled. "Oh! You saw me talking with Aidan? He's really generous. Do you know him as well, sir?" Carver paused and scrutinized the man closely. "Wait a minute. I think I know you. From the fight, yes? Gaston, wasn't it?"

Gaston nodded once and smirked. "I see my efforts have been admirable to some."

"You were amazing to stand up to someone like Aidan. He beat you pretty quick. . . ."

Gaston scoffed. "I think not. I let him win. It was all for entertainment, anyway. If I truly wanted to hurt him, I would have."

"I don't know, sir. Aidan's pretty strong."

Raban snickered lightly.

Gaston bristled and shot a piercing gaze at him, and Raban's expression quickly went stone again.

"I don't need to prove anything to you, boy," Gaston continued in a sour tone. "But I warn you to stay away from Aidan. His kind is a danger to society. He will prey upon your naïveté and use it to destroy you."

Carver blinked, confused. *But Aidan is too nice and generous to hurt anyone . . . isn't he?* "No, he helped me. How could he possibly be dangerous?"

"Of course. He's only masking his true intentions by 'helping' you. His kind are masters of deception. Do not trust him. This is your final warning. I've spoken to the guards, and they are already wary of him and in the process of throwing him out of the city. However, they are being cautious in their efforts, to avoid drawing too much attention to the situation. The last thing the city needs is mass panic. Aidan may have . . . *friends*—others of his kind. My group is still in the process of seeking them out while the guards are busy doing their duties."

Carver chewed his bottom lip. *He* was *mighty quick to help me.* "Maybe I *have* been too quick to trust. I've been desperate to get off the streets; it might end up biting me in the ass one of these days. Thank you for telling me about this, sir."

Gaston nodded. "I would like to offer you an opportunity to make something of yourself. To show the world your strength."

Carver tapped his chin. "Work? You mean, I won't have to scrap for coin anymore?"

"Of course not. You will be among brothers and sisters fighting for a worthy cause, cleansing the world of its evils and being revered as a hero. And in the end, you will find riches beyond your wildest dreams." Gaston approached Carver and studied him. "Tell me your name."

"It's Carver."

"Carver, have you heard about the terrible tragedy that befell the town of Easthaven a few weeks ago?"

Carver blinked. *What an odd, yet disturbing question to ask.* "Who hasn't heard of that? I can't believe such a horrible thing happened! That's why Faywald's filled with refugees. I heard some mages from Ghaeldorund were responsible for it all."

Gaston chucked. "Yes, of course, everyone blames the mages. But it is not so."

"It wasn't the mages? Then, who? I heard the city was engulfed in flames and practically burned everything to the ground."

"Indeed, it was. However, the mages are not to blame—not this time." Gaston looked at Carver closely. "The city was destroyed by a Dragon."

Carver gaped and paled. "A . . . a *Dragon?* How can you be so certain?"

"Because, in my many years of experience, I've studied the nature of the Dragons. I visited Easthaven—or what was left of it—just recently, and discovered several clues that led me to believe that its destruction was the work of a Dragon."

"But Dragons are supposed to be the guardians of the world, aren't they?"

"Yes, if you believe all that Celestran drivel." Gaston scowled. "The Dragons have been known to flaunt their powers and control lesser creatures—including humans. I have seen it for myself. And it is up to people like us to ensure that they do not take over."

"But why would a Dragon destroy a whole city?"

"The motives of Dragons are as erratic as the gods themselves. We may never know. All we can do is prepare."

Carver frowned. "I hope Faywald is not next."

"It doesn't have to be." Gaston smiled again, and he extended his hand to Carver. "Will you join us?"

X

ॐ

Why Ignis, Kaijin?"

Kaijin broke from his thoughts and regarded Nester, who walked ahead of him. The group—including Aidan, who had eventually made up his mind—had walked since early that morning, trekking southward back through the Forest of Winds.

"Why not?" Kaijin asked the brownie.

"Most 'umans I know follow Celestra, not a god of fire." Nester shrugged. "Celestra's th' creator an' all that."

Aidan scoffed. "Aidan thinks to each his own."

Nester glanced over his shoulder toward the giant, who brought up the rear. "Let me guess. Your master told you that when you were a little boy, too, right?"

Aidan frowned. "No. It is what Aidan believes. There would be less violence in the world if people were more tolerant toward one another."

"Does my faith trouble you, Nester?" Kaijin asked.

Nester whipped his head back around. "Nay! I was only curious. Sometimes, I think you're deeper in your faith than some of th' warders! Even *I* know that fiddlers don't get their powers from th' gods."

Kaijin sighed. "I follow Ignis because ever since I was young, I've had a fondness for fire. One day, I was given a book about the gods, where I learned that there was a god of fire. Since then, every time I look at a flame, I try to see if I can find Ignis inside."

Zarya smiled. "But Ignis *is* fire, Kaijin. You are already looking at Him, yes?"

Kaijin stared at the ground. "Yes, perhaps. But part of me senses there is something more to find within a burning flame. I always envisioned the image of Ignis to be something beyond its surface." He smiled slightly. "Something indescribable. Something—" He halted, nearly tripping over Nester.

The brownie stood stock-still, his eyes focused on the road ahead. His fingers twitched at his sides.

"Nester?" Zarya looked curiously at him.

"Shh!" Nester said, placing a finger to his lips. His ears twitched. "I 'ear voices nearby."

Aidan walked a few paces ahead of the group and sniffed the air. He slowly scanned the area.

Kaijin felt his comrades' tension, as well as a slight shift in the air. He looked to the skies and mentally called to Miele. Within moments, the bat fluttered from the treetops and circled the area, letting out soft, high-pitched shrieks in her nervousness.

He waited a few uneventful moments before calling to his companions. "Come on, everyone. Let's keep moving."

They proceeded along the road for several minutes but soon slowed again.

Nester's ears perked. "Someone's 'ere." He eyed the underbrush. "I think we're bein' watched."

Kaijin briefly acknowledged the brownie, but something else caught his attention ahead. Thick plumes of smoke billowed from a large object. Intrigued, he slowly approached.

"Kaijin!" Zarya yelled.

Kaijin ignored her and entered the clearing, drawn by the smoke. He found what appeared to be the smoldering remains of wood, metal, and debris.

Something glinted beneath a splintered piece of wood. Curious, he pushed the piece of wood aside with his foot and uncovered an old, silver locket. He picked it up and closely examined it. Etched on the cover was an arcane rune that meant 'storm'.

Before he could study it further, he felt a sharp ping in his mind. He saw Miele flying above him, flapping frantically before disappearing into the treetops. Kaijin stuffed the locket in his haversack, then heard the nearby bushes rustle and froze.

He looked to his group. Zarya and Nester approached him, tensed, scanning the area around them. Aidan remained where he stood with his head tilted back, focused on the treetops.

"Show yourselves!" Aidan yelled.

Several dark-clad figures flitted through the trees before concealing themselves in the shadows once more. Two others leapt from the bushes and landed before Aidan.

Aidan narrowed his eyes at the two strangers, leather-armored young human men. They slowly drew their longswords from their belt sheaths.

Aidan scowled. "Let us pass."

The elder of the two men stepped forward, scrutinizing the giant. "You . . . whatever you are . . . are trespassing. Turn around and leave." He paused and acknowledged Kaijin, Zarya, and Nester. "That goes for the rest of you, too."

Another man emerged from the underbrush and aimed a nocked arrow at Kaijin. "Get away from there."

Kaijin blinked, startled by the man's sudden appearance. He clutched his haversack close to his body with one hand and balled his other hand into a fist, as he prepared to utter the spell that was forming on the tip of his tongue.

"'Ey, now!" Nester stood between Aidan and the two strangers in front of them. "No need for all this, y'know? We were just passin' through, aye!"

The two men sneered at the brownie.

"Besides, I'd not get Aidan, 'ere, mad if I were you," Nester continued. "I've seen this 'ulkin' bloke in action. 'E's 'arder than my Aunt Netta's cakes!"

Aidan frowned. "Nester!"

"Enough!" the elder man snapped. "This is your last warning. Turn back now, or—"

A clicking sound came from the trees, catching Kaijin's attention. He kept the canopy in view from the corner of his eye while he slowly backtracked to rejoin the rest of his comrades. The archer near him followed closely, the point of his arrow trained unerringly at Kaijin.

"No," Aidan said, stretching out his hand. "No violence."

"Please!" Zarya shouted, looking at the men pleadingly. "Why are you doing this? We mean no harm. Please let us through."

The elder man huffed. "We obey no one. Go back to town with the rest of the refugees, or find another route."

"But we're not refugees," Zarya said. "We do not know any other route through this forest. We will not be a bother if you just let us through."

The elder man raised his hand. "You've been warned."

At the gesture, Kaijin turned his full attention to the treetops. He heard the twang and whistles of crossbows firing and suddenly felt himself tackled to the ground by Aidan.

"Get down!" the giant exclaimed, shielding everyone from the incoming blows with his body.

Nester yelped from beneath the large creature. "Don't crush me, mate! I ain't ready to die yet!"

All Kaijin could see was Aidan's broad, bare chest, covered in tiny, almost invisible, silver scales. Being pinned beneath Aidan's body, Kaijin felt helpless. He wriggled weakly, trying to free himself, but Aidan's recumbent bulk was too heavy.

"Aidan!" he cried, his voice muffled by the bulk. "What are you doing? Get off us!"

Aidan winced and grunted, his face paling and contorting with pain. His breathing became ragged.

Zarya lay on her back, staring up at Aidan, petrified. "What have you done?"

When the attack ceased, Aidan rolled off his comrades, stood up slowly, and faced his attackers. He turned away from his companions, revealing rivulets of blood running from dozens of crossbow wounds.

Kaijin, Zarya, and Nester scrambled to their feet. They gasped at the sight of Aidan's back.

"By the goddess!" Zarya exclaimed. "Aidan!" She rushed toward the fray, withdrawing her mace. Glaring at the three visible attackers, she ordered, "Stand down! He is hurt! Haven't you ruffians done enough?"

While the priestess attempted to reason with the brigands near her, Kaijin heard leaves rustle and the ratchet of crossbows being reloaded. He looked sidelong at Nester, whose ears twitched nervously.

"More of 'em," he muttered to Kaijin, his gaze focused elsewhere. "This ain't good, mate." He pulled four darts—two in each hand—out from his leather jerkin and scanned the trees.

Kaijin heard another sound, and he glimpsed a shadowy figure moving about the branches. Nester flung two darts at the figure. They hit their target, and the figure collapsed from the hiding spot.

The fallen figure grunted, and the crossbow dropped. The man's leather-clad body hung limp from the branches, which bent beneath his weight. The trees rustled as other figures scrambled to fill the gap left by their companion's fall.

Kaijin watched Nester dispatch two more hidden brigands from the trees with the remaining darts. One of them fell and hit the ground with a loud thump. Soon, the treetops were still, empty of the archers.

Kaijin rushed to Zarya, who called forth a translucent force shield around them both just as a flail of arrows came at them from the three men. Four more men emerged from behind the cart, weapons aimed at his group.

"Deal with these insolent fools," ordered the fiery voice in Kaijin's mind.

Kaijin licked his lips and concentrated, recalling one of his spells. The world turned a wavering orange hue, and the air around him began to shimmer. He felt the pulsating heat of his necklace as he uttered, "*Flammvallum!*" Flames erupted from Kaijin's hands, leapt to the ground, and created a blazing wall around the four brigands, halting them before they got far from the cart. The heat and brightness intensified, and they recoiled in unison.

"Woa! Woa! That smarts!" Nester exclaimed, scrambling backwards and shielding his eyes.

Amid the chaos, the three brigands by Zarya attacked. Sparks showered as a sword blade clashed between one of the flanges of her iron mace, and the sword's heavy impact nearly dropped her to her knees. Steel flashed as two more blades came at her. As she raised her mace against the second wave of attacks, Aidan shoved her away. She stumbled but regained her footing.

Grunting in pain, Aidan absorbed the brunt of the attacks on his thick skin. Blood oozed from the crossbow wounds, but he remained on his feet, swaying. "Enough. Enough fighting. . . ."

The three men wheeled and swung their swords at Aidan. He fell to one knee, attempting to dodge the incoming blows. The steel blades glanced off his silver skin and clashed together.

Aidan struggled back to his feet and threw himself at the group of men, knocking them to their backs and pinning them to the ground, weapons dropped. He crushed them with his weight, and the men cried out helplessly.

"No more," Aidan groaned.

The flames danced as Kaijin guided them with a subtle move of his hand, entrapping his four opponents in a burning prison. He relished the sounds of the men's screams.

"Do not disappoint me," the fiery voice told him.

Kaijin clenched his fist, and the flames intensified. Slowly, he began to slip into the heart of the fire, losing himself within. The ravaging flames swirled in a firestorm of chaos as if it attained a mind of its own.

"Kaijin! Stop it!"

Zarya's voice sounded distant to Kaijin's ears. His necklace pulsated more strongly as his rage intensified.

"Enough!" Aidan growled.

Out of the corner of his eye, Kaijin saw Aidan stand and approach him. When Aidan was mere footsteps away, the flames' heat intensified in reaction to his presence. Aidan halted, and Kaijin resumed his torment of the brigands, realizing the giant was no longer a threat. Kaijin manipulated the flames, stoking them, relishing the screams of the four men as the fire consumed them.

The flames soon extinguished on their own, and Kaijin collapsed to his knees. He took a deep breath, inhaling the ash and smoke that lingered in the air, and he coughed. His red-orange-hued vision soon subsided. He felt groggy, as though he had been roused from a dream.

The three remaining brigands—archers that had been trapped beneath Aidan—rolled around in pain. Slowly, they clambered to their feet, one by one. They surveyed the destruction around them and exchanged worried glances.

"Let's get out of here!" Holding his midsection, one turned and hobbled off into the forest.

Another injured brigand watched his comrade leave before taking a last look at the smoldering, ash-filled clearing, littered with the charred corpses of his fallen cronies. Frowning, he turned to his other living companion. "Come on!"

Together, the two men hobbled into the forest, following after their comrade.

Kaijin had an empty, yet satisfied feeling inside. The others in his group all stared at him in awe and horror.

Nester's mouth hung open. His eyes bulged as though they were about to pop out of his head. "Th–That was—"

"—Terrible!" Zarya finished. "No one had to die here!"

Aidan grunted and slumped to the ground. "That is why . . . Aidan does not like violence. . . . Someone always . . . gets hurt."

"You mean someone like you?" Nester pointed at Aidan's bloodied, injured body.

Zarya rushed to Aidan and began tending to his injuries. "Aidan, I can't believe you did that. What were you thinking? You could have died as well!"

He closed his eyes. "Aidan tried . . . to protect . . ."

"Shh. Don't speak. Stay still, now." Zarya chanted and prayed, and a blue glow encompassed her hands. The energy traveled to Aidan's body, blanketing him. He cringed, let out a small yelp of pain, and then relaxed.

The blood and visible wounds on his body disappeared. The crossbow bolts fell out of his back and onto the ground, leaving only small traces of his blood on the blades.

Zarya concluded her prayer, and the glowing energy ceased. She assessed his condition for a moment before standing. "That was very courageous of you to risk your life for us like that, Aidan. Thank you."

Aidan smiled at her and bowed his head. "It was least Aidan could do."

"Such bravery must not be forgotten." She placed her hand atop his head. "May Celestra's blessings protect you and Her strength flow through you." Zarya's hand emitted a soft, white glow. The light encompassed Aidan a few moments before absorbing into his body.

Aidan stood. He stretched and flexed his chest and arms. "Aidan feels great now!" He beamed. "Like he can run for days!"

Zarya smiled at him. "Praise be to the goddess."

"Aidan is grateful for your help." He bowed again, this time, more deeply.

Kaijin looked to the corpses before him, and his heart wrenched. The sight caused grueling memories of Easthaven's destruction to flood his mind. *No, not again. I didn't do this,* he told himself, trying desperately to push aside the disturbing images of his dead family's corpses. *I didn't kill them.*

Zarya approached one of the corpses, knelt down, and prayed over it. Kaijin turned to Nester and then to Aidan.

Aidan's brow scrunched while his gaze followed the priestess go from one corpse to the next, bowing her head in prayer.

Nester tugged at Aidan's silken trousers. "Why's she prayin' over dead folk for—and ones that tried to kill us, to boot?"

Aidan tilted his head to the side. "Aidan does not know, but we should not disturb her."

"Well it sounds like nothin' but gibberish to me. Not like when she 'eals us."

"Perhaps it is special language clerics use. Or her native tongue from her homeland."

After concluding her prayers, Zarya resumed following the forest path. She brushed past Kaijin, Aidan, and Nester, then stopped a short distance ahead of them and glanced over her shoulder. "Let's get going, please," she said sharply and continued walking.

Kaijin exchanged glances with Aidan and Nester, and the three of them followed the priestess.

Silence lingered for only a few minutes before Nester asked, "So, ah, should I be askin' why you're goin' around prayin' over corpses, beautiful?"

Zarya didn't stop walking. "I prayed that the goddess may take them peacefully. Please, let's not speak on it again."

"All right." Nester stroked his chin, and then looked sidelong at Kaijin. "I must say, mate, that was quite amazin' what you did back there."

"Nester!" Zarya stopped, spun on her heels and glared at the brownie.

Nester returned the stare. "What? I ain't say nothin' 'bout your infatuation with th' dead." He turned back to Kaijin, a smile creeping upon his face. "So 'ow'd you get so soddin' powerful, eh?"

Kaijin sighed. "I don't want to talk about this, Nester."

"Say, y'know, all that fire an' screamin' an' bodies burnin'—it's almost like 'ow some of th' refugees described Easthaven. Kinda frightenin' coincidence, aye?"

Kaijin paled. "Yeah, really frightening."

"So, ah, anyway. Will you, at least, show me some of those fiery tricks, then?" the brownie persisted. "That can be kinda useful, y'know!"

"'*Useful*'?" Zarya folded her arms. "He used magic to kill those men, and he almost killed all of us in the process!" Her eyes narrowed at Kaijin. "Now I understand why mages are so feared and vilified around here."

A sharp pain twisted Kaijin's gut. A bitter taste rose in his mouth, and his breathing faltered. The world spun around him. *Am I really hearing this from her?* He glared at Zarya and spoke in a low tone. "I thought Celestran clerics do not take sides?"

"We do not, but there is no denying what I saw with my own eyes—what we *all* saw. You lost control."

"No! It was not my fault!" Kaijin felt his blood boil. For a moment, the image of Zarya reddened. He blinked, and the red cleared.

Zarya's expression hardened. She shook her head and whispered, "You are a *monster!*"

Kaijin's left eye twitched. *What did she call me?*

"*She is like all the rest,*" the fiery voice in his mind said.

Kaijin gritted his teeth. "*Yes,*" he responded mentally, "*like all the rest.*" The image of Zarya began to blur. Clenching his fists, he took a step to her. "You ungrateful wench," he growled in a voice that seemed to shift from his own. "I should have let them kill you."

Zarya stood her ground, apparently unfazed. She slapped him across the cheek hard enough to snap Kaijin's head to the side. He recoiled, his cheek stinging and burning.

"*Punish her,*" the fiery voice commanded in Kaijin's mind.

Kaijin narrowed his eyes, feeling them crackle with warm magical energy. He raised his glowing fist and felt Aidan's leathery hand grab it.

"Enough!" the giant boomed. He grabbed Kaijin's other arm and dragged him away from Zarya. "No more violence." He glowered at Zarya. "From *either* of you!"

Kaijin and Zarya glared at each other.

"We have come this far together," Aidan continued, "and we will remain together until we reach destination." Looking at Kaijin and Zarya in turn, he added in a sharp tone, "Does Aidan make himself clear?" The anger in his voice amplified his already-intimidating physical features, and no one seemed to dare argue with him.

Aidan released Kaijin. He pointed ahead and ordered, "Now, let us continue."

*   *   *

Kaijin trailed several paces behind Zarya, and Aidan walked only a few steps behind him. Nester led the way as the majority of their travel passed in silence.

Kaijin stared blankly at Zarya's back. He was no longer charmed by her beauty, and he bore his gaze into her like daggers. *She dared call me a 'monster'.* The word stung every fiber of his being every time he heard it.

"Am I really a monster because I use magic, Miele?" She responded with a series of audible shrieks, and warmth eclipsed the bitterness. He smiled, but only briefly, before he heard Aidan's breathing behind him. Kaijin walked to one side of the path to allow the giant to pass. When he didn't, however, Kaijin glanced over his shoulder at him.

Scowling, Aidan walked uncomfortably close to Kaijin.

Kaijin felt trapped. He wanted to run. He wanted to destroy the world. He hated feeling so helpless. He clenched his teeth, staving off the urge to lash out at his comrades.

The rage confused him. Miele reacted to his distress by swooping down and resting on his shoulder. She rubbed her furry body against him and screeched softly. Kaijin frowned. *"They don't understand, Miele. They'll never understand."*

XI

ॐ

Shades of grey surrounded Kaijin.

His companions were gone. The ground was blanketed in a thick mist, obscuring his feet. The air was soft and warm, yet filled with tension. "Nester!" Kaijin's voice was muffled in the endless void. "Aidan? Zarya? Miele? Where are you?"

His calls went unanswered.

Kaijin took a deep breath and clutched the fiery charm around his neck. *Am I dead? How did this happen?* He held his haversack a moment before opening it and pulling out the orb. The artifact was ice cold to the touch, and it had lost its beautiful luster and mesmerizing colors. Instead, it had turned black.

"No," Kaijin muttered, "This can't be happening!" The sound of footsteps behind him broke his thoughts, and he stuffed the lifeless orb back into his haversack and turned around.

"Kaijin," said a woman's voice—his mother's.

Her voice was filled with love and compassion. Kaijin could smell her scent—apples, cinnamon, pinewood—reminders of home.

There was age in her dark eyes, though her bronze skin was hardly wrinkled. Flowing locks of auburn hair, streaked with grey, framed her strong, angular features, and the frayed edges of her flowing white gown rippled in the passing wind. A gentle, loving smile graced her full lips.

Kaijin blinked once. "M . . . *Mother*?"

She took his hand. "Kaijin, I love you."

Kaijin's teeth gripped his bottom lip. He felt his eyes burning. "Mother, how did you get here? Am I dead? Please, Mother. Please tell me I've not gone mad."

She shook her head slowly and smiled. "I am here, Kaijin." She pulled him in to a warm embrace.

Kaijin froze in her arms. He knew her scent, felt the softness of her bosom and the warmth and love she always emanated. "It's been so long," he mumbled, holding back the burning tears that threatened to fall from his eyes. "I can't believe you're alive! I thought . . . I thought . . . Where's Father and Rorick? Are they here, too?"

She abruptly pulled away from the embrace, frowning.

Kaijin tilted his head, alarmed by the sudden change. "What's wrong, Mother?"

She held up her hands, which shook, dripping blood.

Kaijin gasped. "Mother! You're hurt!"

"Why?" she whispered. "Kaijin, how could you . . . ."

"What? What are you talking abou—" He felt something warm and sticky on his own hands. A coppery scent stung his senses. He slowly dropped his gaze, and he gasped. "*Blood?* H–how can this be? What has happened?" He looked to his mother, frantic.

"I never wanted . . . to believe your father," she said weakly. "He said you were . . . misguided—a mentally strange child. There's . . . there's nothing wrong with you. . . . I just wish . . . you would . . . stop playing with fire. . . ." She gave a death rattle, and her body collapsed to the ground.

Kaijin gaped. Memories of his mother's death flooded his mind. "Mother!" he yelled, rushing to her side. "Mother! Please, wake up! Please, don't leave me again!"

But there was no response.

Grey smoke began to rise from her body, and Kaijin heard the greedy crackling of fire. The smell seared his nostrils, and the flames devouring her became visible. The heat intensified as the fire consumed her body—but strangely, as the flesh melted away from the bones beneath, Kaijin smelled not flesh, but burning pine.

Confused and frightened, Kaijin cried out to his mother again and again, until his grief finally spent. He collapsed atop his mother's smoldering corpse.

* * *

Kaijin awoke in a cold sweat, gasping for air. He found himself staring at a grey, starless sky, where he heard Miele's light shrieking and fluttering of her wings.

"Can't sleep, aye?"

Kaijin flinched in surprise, then turned toward Nester, who was sprawled out comfortably across the fire from him, sorting a small pile of gold and silver pieces. The campfire crackled and popped softly as it consumed the last of the pinewood.

Nester peered at Kaijin over the top of the dancing flames and grinned.

Kaijin rubbed the sleep from his eyes. Aidan lay to his left, curled up like a large cat, sleeping soundly with his head pillowed on his enormous hands. Zarya lay huddled alone beneath a willow tree outside of the flickering ring of firelight. She slept upright, her head leaning against the trunk.

"You've a few 'ours yet before th' sun comes up," Nester continued. "Might as well get some more winks in. I'm on watch, now, so you'll be safe, I guarantee! Nothin' gets past these peepers!"

Kaijin frowned. He couldn't remember the last time he had trouble sleeping, and when he did, he usually knew why. That night, however, felt different, and Kaijin was left bewildered. "I think I had a bad dream," he said slowly.

Nester chuckled, placing a gold piece atop one of the stacks in front of him. "Bad dream? I'll tell you what gives me bad dreams—watchin' my Aunt Netta and Aunt Nini sing!" He rolled his eyes. "First, they always gotta dress up in these gaudy pink dresses an' do their 'air in this crazy style that looks like a bird's nest. Then comes th' singin'! Neither of them can carry a tune if it 'ad 'andles! They both sound like they're chokin' on frogs, they do. Why, one time, they sang this song that nearly . . ."

Ignoring the brownie's gabble, Kaijin focused on Zarya. His scowl returned as he recalled the day's events. *How can someone so peaceful—so beautiful—be so spiteful?* His gaze shifted to the campfire. *Maybe Nester was right. I should be more careful. Things aren't what they seem.*

Nester stirred the fire with a stick as he hummed a merry tune to himself.

The flames blazed up for a moment, entrancing Kaijin, and he lost himself in thoughts about his nightmare. The campfire gave a pop of pine pitch before dying down again. Kaijin blinked from his trance, and then he sighed. *I'm not a murderer.*

"No, you are worse than a murderer," said a voice from the flames to Kaijin's mind. *"You are a mage."*

Kaijin clenched his teeth and tore his gaze from the campfire. He retrieved the orb from his haversack and examined it. Its color and beauty had returned—if, indeed, they had ever left—and it once again felt warm in his hands. Mesmerized by the swirling flames under its glassy surface, Kaijin wondered, *How does such a simple object hold such awesome power?*

"Better keep that thing 'idden," Nester said suddenly, snapping Kaijin out of his reverie. "If we ever run into bandits and th' like, you'd best believe that'll be th' first thing they'll prig."

"I'm not worried, Nester." Kaijin shook his head. "They will be in for a rude awakening when the orb ends up burning their fingers off."

Nester smirked, adding two more gold pieces to another stack. "'Ey! I like that, I do! Th' sods'll think twice about messin' with us, aye?"

"I'd prefer that no one touches it, though." Kaijin ran his thumbs along the orb's smooth, transparent shell.

Nester's smirk faded. "'Ey, now, you're not plannin' on keepin' that thing for yourself, are you? It belongs to both of us, remember?"

Kaijin tensed at the brownie's words. "Right." He reluctantly stuffed the orb back into the haversack.

"You gave us quite a scare, earlier, you did, mate."

Kaijin sighed. "Must we talk about that?"

"But it was amazin', it was! Your eyes started glowin' all fiery orange, and you 'ad all this flare burnin' around you like you were possessed or somethin'! Didn't it 'urt?"

"Nester—"

"Oh, an' that poor Zarya! 'Ow could you almost 'it 'er like that?"

Nester's question took Kaijin by surprise. He frowned. "Well . . . what does it matter? She should not have said those things."

Nester scowled in return. "What kind of man are you, to wanna 'it a lady? And a pretty one, at that?"

"She wasn't acting very 'ladylike' to me, saying what she said and doing what she did. She obviously has no clue about me."

"And you, obviously, 'ave no clue about women."

"What in the hells do you know about women?"

"More 'n you, apparently."

Kaijin huffed. "I've got my dignity. I'm not going to stand there and let her tell lies about me. She's liable to get me killed. She knows I'm a mage. What's stopping her from turning me in?"

Nester shook his head. "She won't do that."

"You sound so sure of yourself," Kaijin said flatly.

"Trust me, mate." Nester smiled reassuringly and then added some silver pieces to one of the stacks.

Kaijin's hard gaze drifted to the priestess. "She called me a monster."

"Eh." The brownie shrugged. "Sometimes people say things they don't really mean."

"I think she meant every word."

"Look, think positive, will ya? I think she was just . . . a wee bit flustered after all that fiddlin' you showed off earlier."

"But I'm a mage, Nester."

"And a soddin' good one, at that!"

"Why should I even be concerned about what she thinks?"

Nester groaned. "Oy! For soddin' sake! 'Ow daft can you be, Kaijin?"

Kaijin looked at him blankly and kept silent.

Nester shook his head. "Bah. Never mind. You'll figure it out one of these days—I 'ope." He paused to add the remaining gold and silver pieces to the stacks. "Thirty-nine gold and twenty-four silver." He whistled. "Not too bad."

"Where did you get all that from?"

Nester gave a nervous laugh. "Ah, well, y'see, I was doin' some, ah, *charitable work* of my own back in Faywald. No 'arm done, aye!"

"You *stole* all that?"

"Nay!" Nester promptly looked around and then lowered his voice. "What did I tell you before? It ain't considered priggin' if no one sees you do it. An' I assure you, mate—no one saw me do nothin'."

Kaijin crossed his arms, unconvinced.

"Oh, by the way, this is our li'l secret, aye?" Nester added. "Zarya wouldn't understand. And Aidan . . ."

Nester's expression turned sour. "Knowin' 'im, 'e'll make me donate it to some soddin' orphanage or somethin'. I worked too 'ard to get all this. Besides, th' kids got enough money as it is! So, ah, you can keep secrets, right, Kaijin?"

"Are you sure you really want to tell me your secrets, Nester?" Kaijin said. "I'm a mage—apparently I can't be trusted."

"'Ogwash. You an' I've been through a lot together in this short time. You ain't gave me any reason to not trust you."

Strangely enough, the brownie's words brought a small sense of comfort to Kaijin. Uncrossing his arms, Kaijin managed a weak smile. "All right. My lips are sealed."

Nester beamed. "Great! See? You an' I were destined to be together, we were!"

Kaijin cringed. "I think not. And I would advise you to put all that away before—"

As if Nester was reading his thoughts, the brownie scooped up his stacks of coins and carefully and quickly placed them in his pouch. With that small bit of reassurance, Kaijin shifted himself more comfortably in his spot, closed his eyes, and drifted back to sleep.

XII

⚭

Omari snaked his way down a brush-tangled path. He did not wish to recall the perilous encounter he had survived only hours before, but he still heard the screams of his convoy, saw the flash of blades drawn from the shadows, smelled the blood. He squinted at the night sky, hoping to locate Celestra's Tear between the clouds, to determine his direction. But the gods did not favor him, and he continued walking blindly through the forest. He was alone, but he was confident enough in his powers that he was not completely helpless—not yet, anyway.

A trilling sound interrupted his train of thought, and he smiled to the presence keeping to the shadows beside him.

"No, Percival, we are not lost. I know exactly where we are going."

Less-excited trills responded nervously.

"What? Confound it, I am your master. How dare you doubt my sense of direction!" Omari felt the weight of Percival's body, and then Percival's tiny claws clung to

Omari's robes as the weasel effortlessly climbed him and settled on his shoulder. Percival wrapped his long, slender tail around the back of Omari's neck, and he softly trilled.

The vibrations tickled Omari's shoulder, and he flinched. *"After all we went through earlier, and you are worried about whether or not I am going the right way?"*

A passing wind whistled between the trees, echoing ghostly sounds. Omari halted to listen. "Confounded forest," he grumbled. An uneasy coldness in the air brushed over his face, causing a brief shiver to travel down his spine.

Clutching a handful of his robes closer to his body, Omari took another step and stumbled. Percival's claws grazed his skin as the weasel held on for dear life. Something sharp tugged the bottom of his robes, and he heard the sounds of cloth ripping.

"Confound it!" Omari looked behind him. He couldn't see the ground in the darkness. He grasped his long, thin quarterstaff and pulled it from the leather thong that kept it secured to his back. The weapon lay lightly in Omari's hands, and he used it to poke at the unseen hazard. The solid object was rounded, with a rough surface. He thumped at the thing and heard a hollow sound. *Nothing but a small log.*

Percival trilled nervously and loosened his claws from Omari's robes.

Omari was just continuing his trek when he felt something smacking at his lower shin. He realized his sandal latchet had come undone. As he knelt down to re-tie it, he heard faint splashes of water nearby. Relief spread through him as he realized he had found a possible path to civilization.

Percival, with his nose raised and twitching, scented the air, hopped off Omari's shoulder, and scampered ahead.

Omari continued, following the sounds while he used his staff to locate small hazards along the path. As the rushing of the stream grew louder, Omari walked faster, until he came up to a large clearing, through which a stream raced. Soft, white light reflected off the water's surface. Omari looked up and saw portions of the quarter-moon struggling to break from the clouds. Kneeling at the bank, Omari peered at the water. In the dim light, he could barely make out his own wavering reflection. He was tired from the day's non-stop travel. He dipped his hands into the cold stream and drank.

Percival slunk to the water's edge and sat beside Omari. The moonlight reflected a dull shine on his tawny fur. He briefly scanned the water with beady eyes, and then his head snapped to the side, as though he heard something. He quickly skittered away from the bank and disappeared in a nearby patch of bramble.

Omari flinched as he heard a high-pitched shrill. "Percival! What is going—" He stopped in mid-sentence, watching the weasel emerge from the tangled brush, carrying a small, dead mouse in his mouth. He lay beside Omari with the carcass and hungrily tore into it.

Omari made a face. "*Ugh, must you eat that thing in front of me? I swear, for as long as we have been together, I have yet to get used to your eating habits.*"

Percival glanced up from his half-eaten meal and sniffed, focused on something beyond the stream.

The weasel's sudden movement startled Omari. He watched his familiar zip across rocks to the other side of the stream and bolt off into a curtain of underbrush. Omari blinked and quickly stood. *"Percival! Where did you go?"* He felt a soothing sensation ease his mind in response. Percival wasn't far, and Omari attuned himself to his familiar's location by focusing on his thoughts.

Percival stood atop a grassy hill that sat beyond the veil of underbrush. The hill dropped slightly, and a small precipice extended from it, overlooking a forest ravine below.

He crawled down to the precipice and approached its edge carefully. Standing upright on his hind legs, he surveyed the ravine. He focused on a small flicker of firelight, and he detected the scent of burning wood. He trilled excitedly.

Withdrawing from Percival's mind, Omari took a nervous breath. Then, trying desperately to keep his gaze focused ahead, he carefully hopped from rock to rock across the stream and tracked Percival through the patches of shadows until he eventually found his furry friend. Omari approached cautiously as he scanned the dark lands around them. He, too, eventually spied the faint, flickering firelight below. *"We should be careful. They may be the same bandits that attacked us earlier."*

Percival hissed and irritably arched his back. He cast a quick glance at Omari before edging over the precipice.

Omari ran to the edge. He watched Percival navigate down the rocky cliff face with ease. *"You waste no time wanting to get your revenge, do you?"* Omari smirked at him, then secured his staff to his back. *"All right. Let us make sure they never harm innocent people again."*

He reached into his belt pouch and fished for the tiny vial of featherfall potion. After uncorking it with his thumb, he quickly downed the vial's colorless, tasteless liquid, and then began easing himself over the cliff. He looked down and saw nothing but shadows, with faint spots of moonlight dotting the landscape.

Grunting, Omari dug his hands into the rocky wall and held on. His heart sank. *Gods, maybe this was not such a good idea.* Sweat beaded in his palms, and his grasp slipped from the rocks. He fell, and his heart dropped into his gut.

The fall slowed until his body felt weightless. During the descent, Omari plucked Percival from the rock face and tucked him close to his body.

Upon finally landing at the bottom of the cliff, Omari felt plush grass beneath his feet. The land smelled rich from the fresh scents of the flora wafting in the cool, crisp air. Percival wriggled in his arms. Smiling, Omari knelt and set his companion free. He trailed the weasel and concentrated, becoming one with him once again.

Percival scampered toward the campsite, sniffing the air and listening as he drew closer. He studied three sleeping individuals—a large male silver creature, a woman, and a red-haired man—sprawled out around the small camp. His eyes rested on the largest being, who appeared to be the most dangerous of the three.

"*Be careful,*" Omari said in Percival's mind. "*They look powerful—especially the scaly one.*"

Percival responded with an empathic wave of assurance into Omari's mind. Keeping a cautious distance from the three strangers, Percival went from one to another, slyly scouring their belongings. He paused upon approaching the last of them—the red-haired one. This young man slept clutching a leather container in his hands. Hesitation and curiosity stirred in Percival, sensing something strange emanating from within the bag. Keeping his body low to the ground, Percival began pawing at the bag.

Omari gasped. *"Percival! Stop that! What are you trying to do? Wake him up?"*

Percival let out a soft whine, then responded with another soothing, empathic wave. He continued his pawing and eventually released a tarnished locket.

"Is that—" *So these people must be associated with those bandits we dealt with.*

Percival proceeded to retrieve the locket when a small glass object rolled out of the bag.

It stopped with a sharp clank against a small rock. Fearful of the orb's unfamiliarity, Percival left the locket and quickly returned to Omari.

Withdrawing to his own mind again, Omari slowly crept toward the locket. The orb, which had rolled near him, caught his attention. The locket temporarily forgotten, Omari knelt before the orb and watched its fires swirl within. The continuous dance of the magical flames intrigued him. Heat emanated from the orb, making him hesitant to touch it. *Such alluring magic,* he thought. Suddenly, something small whizzed past his ear, and he felt the breeze on his cheek as it passed his face. Jerking alert, the orb forgotten, Omari saw a tiny throwing knife lodged in a tree trunk near him.

"I'd get away from that, if I were you," a voice warned from behind him.

Omari whirled around and saw a short, rough-looking fellow—a brownie, most likely—with another throwing knife ready in his hand.

Percival trilled irritably, baring his sharp canines. He arched his long slender back.

"Back away nice an' easy," the brownie said, appearing unintimidated by the weasel. "Or next time, I won't miss."

Where did he *come from?* Grasping his quarterstaff, Omari stepped back in a defensive position. He narrowed his eyes, which crackled with small electrical sparks. He remembered the locket. "You have something that belongs to me," he said to the brownie. "And we have some unfinished business."

The brownie scowled. "Fiddler." He backed away, taking aim.

Electrical energy channeled through Omari's staff, and he sent streaks of lightning surging toward the brownie, who cried out as all four of his limbs were given a strong electric jolt.

Dropping his knives, the brownie fell limply to the ground, twitching from the aftershocks.

The commotion roused the three sleeping individuals. The large silver creature sprang to his feet and rushed Omari with surprising speed for his massive size.

"Stop! Leave him alone!" the giant shouted.

Weary but maintaining his composure, Omari stood his ground and aimed his staff at the giant. *They all will pay for stealing her locket. And it is time I exact revenge for what their band of lowlifes did to my comrades.* "You—all of you confounded bandits will not harm another innocent person again!" He felt a sharp pang in his mind, and out of the corner of his eye, he saw Percival scrambling away from him. Tension emanated from the weasel's body, and he abruptly sat up on his hind legs, his elongated body erect and his dark, beady eyes following a moving silhouette in the sky. Percival scampered away into the shadows as if something had struck him.

The woman's attention was immediately drawn to Omari. "Bandits? There must be a mistake. Who are you? What are you doing in our camp?"

Omari clenched his jaw. "Your cronies took something valuable from me. I will have it back!"

The woman was about to reply, when the brownie let out another groan. She turned, rushed to his aid and began chanting softly.

The red-haired man heaved himself to his feet and stood groggily, swaying about. He placed his fingers over his temples and rubbed them, and he grimaced.

"Kaijin, watch out!" the woman called to the red-haired man.

Omari felt sudden pain, and he called out to Percival but received no answer. As he was about to try again, the silver giant lunged at him, clawed hands extended to grapple.

Omari stood his ground, terrified inside. Desperately, he brought his staff upward and down toward the creature's head, then immediately swooped it to his legs, attempting a sweep.

The creature side-stepped away from the first attack, then smoothly slid back to Omari's inside on the second, crowding him. The creature slammed Omari with his body. The weight knocked Omari backwards; he stumbled and landed on his back.

He crawled back to his feet. He clenched his fist in front of his face, and as he spied the woman, the giant, and red-haried man closing in on him, he chanted his reserve spell. "*Specul imagi!*" His form multiplied into nine identical semi-transparent images of himself. The images all rushed at the giant.

He began wrestling with the images, which tackled him and struck at him. Though the attacks literally went right through him, he stumbled and fell, still flailing at the ghostly images even as they began to fade.

The red-haired man ran toward the fray, his hands encompassed with a bright, fiery glow. He extented his hands toward the remaining duplicates. "*Flarago!*"

A sudden flash of light caused Omari to drop his staff and shield his eyes. When the brunt of the spell subsided, he slowly uncovered his eyes and grunted, disoriented. He was tackled to the ground, and someone—light, compared to the giant, but still strong—held him down.

After blinking the dancing after-images from his eyes, Omari found himself gazing up at the red-haired mage— he presumed it was Kaijin—who glowered at him. Kaijin smelled of burned wood and brimstone, and Omari could sense a strange power from within him—something he'd not felt before in another mage.

Kaijin grabbed Omari's throat and dug his thumbs into his neck. Kaijin's hands were uncomfortably hot against Omari's own cold skin, and the sensation made Omari flinch and gag. He grabbed Kaijin's hand but was unable to pry off his strong grip. All he could do was stare helplessly up at Kaijin.

The longer he gazed deep into Kaijin's brown eyes, the more Omari felt something strangely familiar about him. *No. I have never met this man before in my life.* With his mind too scattered to ponder it further, Omari reluctantly held both of his hands up in surrender.

"Who are you? Answer me, now!" Kaijin growled, shaking him.

Omari choked, unable to breathe.

"Kaijin!" the woman barked. "Stop! Get off him!"

"Why, Zarya?" Kaijin asked. "Why should you be so concerned? He is a mage like me. We're monsters, remember?"

Omari fluttered his eyelids. The images around him became a blur.

"'Ey, now," the brownie said. "That's no way to talk to a lady. Where are your manners, mate?"

"Shove off, Nester!" Kaijin snapped. The direction of his voice then turned back to Omari. "You have three seconds to explain yourself, or—"

Kaijin's weight left Omari.

"No more violence, Kaijin," the silver giant said gruffly.

"Argh! Release me this instant, Aidan!"

The blurred images came into focus. Kaijin struggled against the giant's grip, but Aidan grabbed both of his arms and restrained him.

Omari gasped for air, frantically eying everyone. Terror and confusion swept through him, and he finally croaked out hoarsely, "All right! Confound it, I yield!" He rubbed his neck.

All eyes turned toward him.

Omari rubbed his temples, his mind still reeling from the chaos. "My name is Omari. I am a traveler."

Kaijin ceased his tussle with Aidan and studied Omari. "I'm Kaijin. I daresay that you are dressed rather lavishly to be a simple traveler."

Omari huffed and locked his gaze on Kaijin. "I am a student of the Citadel in Ghaeldorund."

Kaijin blinked. "The Citadel?"

"Ghaeldorund?" Nester exclaimed.

Omari slightly raised his nose at them. "Yes, is that a problem?"

"No, of course not," Kaijin replied. "I did not realize students of the Citadel were allowed to travel so far."

"I have my reasons for my travel."

Aidan released Kaijin and approached Omari, scrutinizing him. "What were you doing, intruding on our camp?"

Omari curled his lip at the giant and crossed his arms. "I was simply looking for a place to rest when I discovered your camp. I thought you were all part of the same group of raiders that attacked me before. After all, you *did* have the very locket that they stole from me."

"Locket?" Nester looked intrigued.

"Yes. *My* locket." Omari glowered at him. "That means it does not belong to you, brownie."

"Don't get your robes all foddled. I ain't got nothin' like that. And if I did, I wouldn't be tellin' *you* about it."

Omari fumed. "Liar!" He pointed to the discarded locket near Kaijin's bag.

Nester blinked. "Wha—! Where in th' soddin' 'ells did *that* come from? I ain't prig it!" He looked flabbergasted. "Kaijin, did . . . did *you* prig it without me knowin'? *No one* prigs without me knowin'!"

Omari turned a stern gaze on Kaijin.

Some thief you must be, then, Kaijin thought, amused, then shook his head. "You were busy looking for bandits, remember? Besides, I found it beneath some debris. It looked like it was discarded. I had no idea—"

"Give it to me," Omari ordered. "Now."

Kaijin raised an eyebrow.

"Nay!" Nester crossed his arms, scowling at Omari. "'Ow do we know it's *really* yours?"

Omari balled his fists. He kept his eyes on Kaijin. "It is silver. Tarnished from age. On the cover is etched a rune: 'storm'. Now give it to me."

Nester looked to Kaijin for confirmation.

Kaijin hesitated, then retrieved the locket. He handed it back to Omari. "There."

"Now that *that's* settled," Zarya said, "would you mind telling me why in Celestra's name you were traveling *alone* looking for bandits?"

"That was not my sole purpose," Omari replied. He deflated a little, as his rage ebbed. "And I was not always alone. The Citadel assigned me a small escort of four guards. No sooner did we enter the Forest of Winds than were we attacked by a group of bandits. They burned our cart and killed everyone else. I barely escaped with my life, thanks to my invisibility spell."

Nester stroked his sideburns. "I wonder if those were th' same blokes we 'ad a scuffle with earlier, aye?"

Omari scowled at the brownie. "What?"

"Rude buggers, they were. Started shootin' at us for no soddin' reason. Poor Aidan 'ad a back full o'bolts, 'e did."

"Well, I certainly hope you killed every last one of them!"

"Yes." Kaijin shot a cool and slightly sinister gaze at Zarya. "They got what they deserved."

Zarya shook her head slowly.

"No one deserves death," Aidan said.

"Tell that to the bastards who killed my escorts," Omari said flatly. "I do not understand your sense of pacifism, creature. I find it rather . . . disturbing."

"That's just 'ow 'e is," Nester said. "You learn to get used to it."

Omari returned his attention to Kaijin. "So who are the rest of these people, Kaijin?"

Kaijin gestured to each of his comrades. "That's Aidan, Nester,"—Kaijin paused a moment, before continuing in a more bitter tone—". . . and *that one* is Zarya."

Zarya's face flushed.

Kaijin turned his nose up at her and scowled.

Omari looked between the two and then stroked his chin. "What an interesting group you all are."

Aidan shrugged. "We have all met in these past few days." Aidan shot Nester a glare as he opened his mouth to respond, and the brownie promptly closed it again. "Where were you headed, exactly?" Aidan asked Omari.

"To the Mallowyn Crags," Omari replied. "I have been searching for a road that travels west, but I think all I have ended up doing was getting lost. Those raiders killed the only scout in my caravan. I have been wandering alone for almost a day now."

Nester's pointed ears perked up. "Mallowyn Crags? I know of that place. My Uncle Nickle used to tell me stories of 'is adventures there. Sounds like quite a place, it does. 'E told me about th' amazin' view you can see from th' tallest point."

Omari scoffed at Nester. "Yes, well, I have official business there. I am to find and speak to the Dragon."

Kaijin, Nester and Zarya gasped.

"Soddin 'ells!" Nester exclaimed.

Kaijin blinked. "A Dragon? Are you serious?"

Zarya scrutinized Omari. "Are you speaking the truth?"

Aidan crossed his arms and kept silent.

Omari snorted at the group's reaction. *I cannot believe I have to waste my precious time trying to convince these idiots.* Before he could respond, he heard a squelch in the nearby underbrush. Percival leapt from the tall grass and zipped past him. A small fruit bat zoomed behind the weasel, nipping at his tail.

Ow! Omari grabbed his head, feeling his companion's pain. He heard a deafening, high-pitched shriek in his mind. He let go of his head and gripped his quarterstaff. Energy surged from his hands into the staff, charging it with an electric shimmer.

Kaijin lunged at Omari. "No!"

Omari glanced up, jarred by the sudden interruption. He glared at Kaijin. "What the—?"

"Miele!" Kaijin yelled to the bat. "Stop! Come here, now!"

The bat ceased its chase and fluttered over to Kaijin and rested on his shoulder. Percival took refuge between Omari's ankles. Miele shrieked happily, proclaiming her small victory over the frightened weasel.

With the jarring sensation in his mind eased, Omari was able to focus again.

Zarya requested, "Omari, please tell us more about this Dragon."

"I would rather not. My business with the Dragon is my own. Now, if you will all excuse me, I must find a place to sleep—"

As he turned, he felt a firm hand on his shoulder. He could hear deep breathing from behind him. He shivered and whipped his head around.

"Stay here with us." Aidan nodded politely.

Omari cast a half sneer at the giant and managed to tug himself out of his surprisingly gentle hold. "No. We are on separate journeys."

"Aidan does not think it is wise for anyone to be out alone at this hour. There is strength in numbers, after all."

Omari sighed and looked at the others.

Nester nodded once. "Aye, Aidan's right. There's plenty o' room to get some winks 'round 'ere. Just don't go snoopin' 'round our things again, eh?" He looked at the giant. "By the way, Aidan, it's your turn to take th' last watch."

Aidan nodded and sat under the willow tree.

Zarya cast an apprehensive gaze at Omari. "I suppose . . . it will be all right."

Kaijin crossed his arms, his eyebrow raising at the priestess. "He almost tried to kill us!"

"I am far more willing to forgive someone who has seen the error in their ways. Now. I will not have this conversation with you anymore. Good night." She stormed away.

Kaijin watched her and sneered.

Omari looked curiously at them. "Did I miss something?"

"No." Kaijin shook his head at Omari. "Nothing at all."

Omari smirked at Kaijin. *That is a crock of shite.*

* * *

Kaijin placed his hands behind his head and stared at the cloudy night sky, unable to sleep. He occasionally heard Miele's soft, playful shrieks in the sky. His mind wandered from the day's events to what his future journeys would hold. He turned his head and stared at Omari across the cooling embers of the campfire's remains. While everyone else rested, Omari was reading his spellbook. A small glow of light emitted from his hand, which hovered over the pages.

Something furry tickled Kaijin's hand. Startled, he sat up and discovered Percival sniffing at him. The weasel trilled apprehensively at the sudden movement.

Kaijin exhaled a relieved sigh. "Oh, it's only you." Smiling, he rubbed Percival's back. Never had he seen such a species of weasel with such coarse fur and a tail nearly longer than its body, and it intrigued him. "You're a sly little fellow, aren't you?"

Percival chirped and then scampered to Omari, climbing up his back and settling on his shoulders.

Omari glanced up from his book to the weasel, and then to Kaijin.

"You have such an interesting familiar, Omari," Kaijin said.

Omari stroked Percival under the chin. "Percival is a long-tailed sand weasel. He and I have been inseparable since I was a child. I daresay your familiar is just as strange."

Kaijin smiled. "Miele is a fruit bat."

"Yes, I can see that. Though she is rather small for a fruit bat."

"Yes, odd, I know. She seemed much bigger when I first met her, back when I was a boy. It's as if I kept growing and she stayed the same size. Or maybe she shrank...."

Omari chuckled. "She did not shrink. You grew. She did not. It is normal. Do not ask me why. It is the nature of some familiars."

"Very strange."

"Perhaps the magical bonds between a familiar and its master have something to do with its growth. I really do not know. It is a mystery that even the masters have not been able to unravel. Why are you worried, anyway? Do you not realize how big fruit bats are? Miele certainly would not be able to sit on your shoulder as she does now." Omari grinned, revealing a perfect set of white teeth.

Kaijin took a moment to scrutinize Omari's appearance by the glow of the reading light. He looked slightly older than Kaijin, but not by much—a few years, perhaps. Omari was lean and athletic in build. His angular features and especially his slightly slanted eyes and high cheekbones reminded Kaijin of his mother. A string of black tattoos ran from the left side of Omari's hairless head down his left cheek to his jawline. He was dressed extravagantly, in long, flowing turquoise robes emblazoned with abstract designs along the hem. A symbol, which Kaijin didn't recognize, was embroidered prominently on the sides of the garment's shoulders. Omari emanated a strong odor of ozone, as though he'd been struck by lightning. The smell wasn't too overwhelming, however, and Kaijin was soon able to ignore it.

Omari closed his spellbook and laid it aside. He dismissed the light, then ran his hands over his face and rubbed his eyes sleepily.

"So, why are you *really* looking for a Dragon, anyway?" Kaijin asked.

Omari paused and looked between his fingers at Kaijin, then dropped his hands from his face. "That is none of your business, Kaijin."

"Something tells me you'll be walking right into trouble."

Omari sneered. "And what is it to you? Why in the confounded hells would you care?"

"I don't." Kaijin shrugged lightly. "I'm just curious about what a Dragon would want with you."

Omari grumbled. He fished in his bag, pulled out a small handful of rations, and held it out in front of Percival.

Kaijin briefly bounced his gaze from Omari to Percival, who happily nibbled on the nuts and dried fruit, then fixed his gaze on Omari, awaiting his response.

Their eyes met, and Omari frowned. "I see you will not stop pestering me about it until I tell you. If you really must know, I need to have my staff enchanted by the Dragon that lives atop one of the peaks of the Mallowyn Crags."

"Truly?" Kaijin blinked. *What an adventure that must be.* "That sounds very . . . perilous."

"It has been, thus far, but I feel as though I am very close. In order to be deemed a full-fledged mage at the Citadel, one must undergo a series of tests—for example, tests of strength, skill, perseverance, and wisdom, among many others."

Kaijin nodded slowly. *I wonder if a Dragon would know about the orb?* "Why must you do this alone? And why a Dragon?"

Omari rolled his eyes and huffed. "Because that is what the masters instructed! I must do this alone if I am to pass my test." He raised his nose at Kaijin. "But someone like *you* would not understand that."

"Someone like me?"

"Someone who is not a student of the Citadel."

"Surely, they didn't mean for you to venture across these hazardous lands alone. That's why they sent escorts with you, yes?"

Omari opened his mouth then quickly closed it, retracting his initial reply. "Well . . . yes. What is your point?"

Kaijin thought a moment. It was a sound plan. A Dragon with all its wisdom would be the perfect one to consult. Besides, who on Exodus would not, in their lifetime, want to meet one of the goddess's greatest creations? "Perhaps we should travel together."

"You hardly even know me, Kaijin."

"Does it matter?"

Omari thought for a moment. "No, I suppose not."

XIII

❦

Aidan watched the first signs of dawn peek over the horizon and realized he had only a few minutes left before his watch was over. With no further incidents happening during the night, he took the opportunity to get a few extra winks of sleep. He nestled beneath the willow tree, the only spot around camp he found remotely comfortable, and closed his eyes.

His brief nap no sooner began than it was interrupted by Nester's unintelligible muttering. Aidan opened his eyes and spotted the brownie in the branches above.

Nester's pointed ears twitched as he huddled on a sturdy branch, sleeping soundly despite his position. The morning light touched his eyes, and he shifted to his side, moving his face away from the light, mumbling incoherently. His ears twitched again as he groaned and turned on to his back, sending leaves fluttering toward the ground.

Aidan swatted away the shower of willow leaves that tickled his tough skin. He turned his attention to the rest of the camp, where Omari, Zarya, and Kaijin lay near the ashy remains of the campfire.

Aidan sniffed once and turned his head. Outside the camp, he spotted shadowy movement.

"Oy, what a night," Nester mumbled from above.

Aidan half-watched from out of the corner of his eye as the brownie leapt nimbly from the branches and landed beside him. Aidan's attention stayed riveted on the shadows. "Strange. Aidan smells honeysuckle again."

"Aye? Well Zarya's sleepin' way over there. Your nose must be keener than a 'ound's, it is."

Aidan shook his head. "No, it is not Zarya—at least, Aidan does not think so."

The nearby bushes rustled, and Nester started. Aidan tensed. A figure emerged from the shadows and approached them, silhouetted by the morning sun. A tiny glint of light played over the steel edge of an arrowhead.

Startled, Nester reached into his boot and slowly withdrew a small shiv. "This ain't exactly what I wanted to wake up to this mornin', mate," he muttered.

Aidan grabbed Nester by the jerkin and tugged him backwards. "Wait," he whispered, frowning from the brownie's actions. Aidan snorted once and narrowed his eyes at the stranger. "The honeysuckle. That smell is coming from him."

"Wha—? The one who 'as an arrow aimed straight at us?"

"Yes. Now, stay your weapon, Nester."

"But—!"

The stranger, who kept his arrow nocked and aimed at them, stepped into the open light. The man's features were almost unnaturally perfect. His pure white skin looked silky and smooth, devoid of blemishes. On the breast of his worn, shoddy traveler's clothes was embroidered a stylized symbol of a Dragon.

His slanted, silvery eyes glittered in the light as he stared at Aidan. "*Darasv? Svabole wux tyrryr tenpiswo?*" His deep, gruff, throaty voice rolled every syllable in an animalistic way.

'*Half-Dragon*'? *Do they mean me?* Aidan blinked and tilted his head, somehow recognizing and understanding the language—a language that sounded so clear to him, much more than Common, and he didn't know why or how. "*Yugon ve?*" he replied. "'*Darasv*'?"

The stranger's eyes narrowed. "*Batybot ui svabole wux re, ui coiy ti?*"

Aidan opened his mouth to reply, but then closed it and glanced askance at Nester.

"What in th' soddin' 'ells is all that gibberish?" The brownie looked between the stranger and Aidan, bewildered. "Sounds like nothin' but growlin' an' snarlin'!"

"He is wondering why Aidan is here, Nester," Aidan muttered, not taking his gaze off the archer.

"You mean, you actually *understand* all that?"

Aidan ignored Nester's question. "*Nomexnoi resija thuryrli. Petrynas puxdout laraek mojka. Yth jatyli thric levniym.*"

The stranger's thin lips pursed, and he slowly lowered his weapon.

Aidan bowed his head. "Thank you, sir."

"So, my ears were not deceiving me before. You *can* speak Common," the man said.

Nester scoffed. "You call *that* 'Common'? It's 'ard enough tryin' to understand 'alf th' soddin' things 'e says!"

Aidan turned to the brownie. "Aidan speaks Common just fine."

"See! There you go again! For once, can't you just—" Nester stopped in mid-sentence.

Aidan turned back around to see what bothered Nester, and two more figures appeared behind the stranger. Steel glinted and magic shimmered from them.

"Look out!" Nester warned the archer. He flung his shiv toward one of the figures, who grunted.

The archer gasped. He re-aimed his bow at the brownie and loosed an arrow.

Aidan heard a grunt beside him and turned. Nester lay on the ground clutching an injury in his arm from which blood was already beginning to trickle.

* * *

Kaijin awoke to the sounds of a commotion. Opening his eyes, he discovered Aidan faced off against an armored swordsman and a woman wielding magic, while Nester lay pinned to the ground under the foot of an archer. Kaijin looked to Omari and Zarya, who had both sprung up, observed the fray a moment, then rushed to assist Aidan and Nester. Kaijin stood, about to follow, when he paused and looked to the orange-painted sky. He heard Miele shriek and saw her silhouette flutter out of sight.

"*What's going on? What do you see?*" Kaijin felt a sharp pang in his mind.

Groaning, he closed his eyes. He briefly saw the sky before whipping around to an aerial view of the camp. He could see the intruders—two men and one woman—bearing weapons and magic. The swordsman and mage flanked Aidan, while the archer towered over Nester, aiming an arrow at his face. The scene zoomed toward the archer, and Kaijin felt alarmed. The erratic images made him sick to his stomach, and he sensed Miele's panic.

The faster they descended, the harder his heart pounded, until they collided violently with the archer's face. The archer screamed in pain, and as they zoomed away, he saw blood dripping from a wound across the bridge of the archer's nose. Nester leaped up and fled, and the sky once again filled his vision.

"Miele? Where are you? Where am I? Am I flying? What's going on?" Kaijin heard a high-pitched screech in his mind in response, and suddenly he was plummeting again.

Again, they flew at the injured archer, his eyes wide with fright, who fumbled with his bow and took aim—that time in Kaijin's direction.

Kaijin saw the archer launch the arrow, and the scene immediately shifted back to the sky, climbing higher again, away from the danger. *"Miele! Was he aiming at you? What's happening?"*

Sharp pain lanced through his mind, followed by the sensation of his heart dropping into his stomach. The red-orange skies spun above, and then, everything went black.

* * *

Kaijin gasped and quickly opened his eyes. He clutched at his chest, instinctively gripping the glowing necklace beneath his robes. He gazed at the battle scene from where he lay and spotted the archer yanking an arrow from the soil. Kaijin groaned. The pain in his mind was unbearable. He tried to contact Miele, but he was unable to focus.

He saw Nester, Zarya, Omari, and Aidan lying lifelessly on the ground.

"Thank Celestra your magic stopped them in time, Sephiya," the archer said to the female mage.

Sephiya knelt down and picked up Miele's limp body from the ground, then locked her gaze on Kaijin.

The archer rubbed the open wound on his nose, stroking it until it magically mended. Turning, he assessed the unconscious bodies. "They didn't give us much of a choice, it seems. It's unfortunate that a half-Dragon and even one of our own had to get caught up in this bloodshed."

The male warrior limped over to Nester and prodded him gently with his foot. The brownie didn't move. The warrior glared at him for a moment, then gripped the hilt of a tiny dart that was lodged in an opening in the metal plating of his armor. With a groan, he yanked it out.

"Sigmund, are you all right?" the archer asked, approaching the warrior.

Sigmund nodded and examined the bloody shiv briefly before tossing it aside. "Nothing vital. I will survive." Placing his hand over the injury, he closed his eyes. A faint, blue light glowed from his fingers and suffused the wound, mending. "I don't see any Legion marks on the brownie. What about the others?"

The archer rolled Omari over, uncovering Percival, who lay beneath. The weasel was curled up in a tight ball, shivering. "We will probably have to strip them all down to find out."

"There's no time, Evan," Sephiya said. "They will only sleep for a short while. Our sister and the half-Dragon will awaken much sooner."

They are alive? Kaijin eyed his companions once more. Part of him was relieved, but it didn't counter his wariness of what their fate—and possibly his—would soon be.

"If they are not Legionnaires, then we must question them," Evan said. "They may know something about the recent killing."

Sigmund huffed. "And if they *are* Legionnaires, then this will not remain hidden from the Mistress."

The Mistress—do they mean the goddess?

Sephiya rubbed her chin. "I think it's best we let Her make that assessment."

"I'm still wary about bringing these people into Her lands," Evan said. "At this point, however, we've little choice. We can't just let them go now."

Sephiya approached Kaijin.

Kaijin lay on his side and didn't move. He stared helplessly at the slender woman who drew nearer and studied him. Her unnatural perfection gave her a strong resemblance to Zarya. He felt drawn to her beauty, yet something about her repelled him. In her hands lay Miele, bloody and with a fresh arrow wound in her chest.

Kaijin gasped softly. His mouth barely moved as he murmured, "Mi . . . mi . . . ele . . ." He shuddered and held his own chest again. Though he had no physical wounds, the pain felt real. *Why is this happening?*

As if in answer to his question, memories of his youth flooded in.

"She is your familiar—an extension of yourself. Any harm that befalls her will incur extremely painful consequences in you."

"What kind of consequences, Master?"

"Think of it like cutting off your own arm. Stabbing yourself in the chest. The shock is unbearable. You will feel her pain amplified. Words cannot explain the horrific sensation."

Kaijin blinked out of his trance and realized Sephiya was still staring at him. She tilted her head, her glittering, diamond-like eyes darting from him to Miele and back again.

"Yours, I presume?" she asked in a soft, yet commanding tone.

The throbbing pain that shot through Kaijin rendered him unable to speak, and he let out a loud groan in response.

"No matter. You're coming with us, as well."

Kaijin finally succumbed to the pain. His eyes shut, and he felt his body go limp.

The last thing Kaijin heard was the woman's distant voice uttering a single word: *"Teleporto."*

XIV

———

ⓒⓡⓢⓞ

Intense heat roused Kaijin. He stared up at the hazy, amber-hued sky, which flickered as if it were on fire. He turned his head, letting his cheek rest upon the flat ground. Flames danced all around his body, yet they didn't burn him. He felt alone, at peace.

The land, the same color as the sky, was barren and charred, yet it somehow burned constantly and stoked small fires that intermittently appeared and disappeared at random. Smoke made Kaijin's eyes burn. Strangely enough, he could taste ozone, its tangy bite in his throat as he breathed.

Kaijin looked back at the landscape. *Where am I?* The bed of fire he lay in was soothing and warm. Its comfort sparked memories of being in his mother's arms. Not wanting to leave the flames' heavenly embrace, Kaijin simply lay there, relishing the sounds of their crackles and snaps in his ears.

A sizzling sound grew louder.

Looking sideway, he saw a pair of burly inhuman legs, adorned with ornate golden cuffs, approaching him. The creature was barefoot, revealing a set of ashen-grey claws protruding from stubby toes. Its red-orange skin had a rough texture that blended with the surrounding flames. The creature's feet hissed when they touched the ground, and each step caught one of the fires, leaving a smoldering, extinguished spot.

Kaijin looked up the being's solid frame and was momentarily blinded by the shimmer of the brass scimitar it held in its clawed hand.

Wincing, Kaijin closed his eyes. When he reopened them, the creature stood over him, staring intently and snorting plumes of grey smoke from its nostrils. Its massive form, taller than any man and broader than a bull, overshadowed Kaijin, eclipsing him.

Kaijin heard the being's heavy breathing and felt its unsettling closeness. The strange ozone odor grew stronger. As Kaijin locked eyes with the creature, he shivered at the sight of its face. Its broad, flat snout wrinkled into a sneer to reveal a set of razor-sharp fangs. Two large black horns protruded from its head and curved upwards, and its frayed, pointed ears were adorned with brass rings.

The air around the creature shimmered from the heat of its body. It flexed its muscles, and Kaijin noticed a small mark branded on one of its bulging biceps. Recognizing the symbol, Kaijin's mouth slowly dropped open in shock. *Ignis!*

The creature's turquoise eyes bore into Kaijin as if they were staring into his very soul. Then, it spoke words that sounded like a series of hisses and crackles—like fire burning. "Why are you here?"

Kaijin furrowed his brow. Somehow, he could understand the fiery words. He replied in Common, "Where is 'here'?"

The creature snorted again and pointed its blade at Kaijin. "The Master has not yet summoned you. You have no business here. Begone, mortal."

Kaijin stared at the shining blade. "I . . . I don't know how I got here."

"Some other filthy mortal attempted to take something that does not belong to them," the creature replied. An image of the orb appeared before Kaijin in the thin air. The creature held up Kaijin's necklace. "This necklace's powers sent you here while your body slept. You have been asleep for precisely two and one-third mortal cycles."

Kaijin looked at the objects and gasped. The orb was grey and hazy. He focused on the necklace and, panicked, patted his chest. *It's gone!* His eyes widened. "That's mine! Why would the necklace save me?"

The creature held the necklace aloft and teasingly swung the charm like a pendulum. "Because the Master is not yet finished with you."

"Master?" Kaijin scrunched his brow. "I don't understand. What master?"

"The Master is He to whom you have vowed your soul."

Kaijin frowned. He assumed the creature spoke of Ignis, but its words were riddling. He could only assume that this was all a dream—a nightmare. "No, I don't believe you. Give me back my amulet!"

"You *dare* stand up to *me*?" the creature snarled. Its sword hand burst into flame, and fire traveled downwards and enveloped the weapon. It sliced through the transparent image of the orb, which disappeared.

Fear tingled down Kaijin's spine. He desperately tried to keep his composure, but he was failing fast. *This is madness. This is not real.*

The creature's eyes narrowed, its grim sneer twisting into an amused smirk. "No, Kaijin Sora. It is not madness. It is chaos—and it is very real."

This monster knows my name? My thoughts? Kaijin gaped.

A chuckle rumbled from the creature. "Yes, I can read your fragile thoughts like your kind reads books."

This couldn't be . . . Him . . . could it?

"No, Kaijin Sora. I am not He."

"Where . . . where am I? Who are you?"

"Who I am is none of your concern. You are trespassing in the Master's realm, and it is my duty to remove you." The monster inched the edge of the blade closer to Kaijin.

Kaijin swallowed a lump in his throat. He wriggled his body away from the flaming blade. "Spare me, please. I never meant to come here. I never meant to anger your master."

"Then awaken, and do not return."

"I don't know how to awaken. Perhaps I'm dead."

"You are not dead. Not yet. You reek of the same stench as mortals."

"Then show me how to awaken."

The creature chuckled again. It held its blazing scimitar at Kaijin's chest, pinning him in place. "With pleasure."

Kaijin felt a sharp pain in his chest.

There was pain beyond pain, and Kaijin wanted to cry out, but all he managed was a gurgling groan. His life flashed before his eyes.

Is this what death feels like?

The creature pulled Kaijin up to his knees, and Kaijin glimpsed the flaming blade piercing his heart. With a sinister grin, the creature lodged the sword deeper, until the cross guard was pressed against Kaijin's chest. Kaijin felt his body jerk and twitch from the monster's mishandling. He was certain that by now, the remainder of the blade protruded from his back.

The weapon's flames burned a hole through Kaijin's robes, revealing a gaping, bloodless wound beneath, reeking of scorched flesh.

Kaijin convulsed and went limp, held in place by the weapon.

The monster withdrew the sword. Fire cleansed the blade's edge, leaving it purified and shining like new again. "The Master sends His regards," the creature said as Kaijin slumped. It rumbled with laughter and tossed the necklace at him.

The necklace hit Kaijin's chest and landed in his lap. No longer could Kaijin feel pain. Instead, he felt numb, and the rest of his senses began to fail him. *So, it ends here.* He collapsed to the ground in a heap, breathing his last.

XV

ૠ

Kaijin's eyes shot open. He shuddered, vividly remembering that horrid creature's face. He traced his fiery charm, which hung securely around his neck.

He exhaled in relief. *Just a dream. That's all it was.*

Kaijin's body felt heavy as he stirred. He was lying on a smooth stone floor, and his back and neck were stiff and hurting. It took him several minutes to finally sit up and examine his surroundings, which were cloaked in darkness.

He soon realized that he was in a cave. The only source of light came dimly from the cave's massive mouth. Beyond the exit, the starry sky outlined a precipice. *This is not our camp. How did I get here?*

The ozone smell that he remembered from his dream hung heavily in the air. A shuffling sound diverted his attention to the back of the cave, where he spied two shadowy figures moving about.

"You sure this will be big enough?" a male asked in a whisper.

"Yes," another male replied. "Now, keep quiet and help me."

Still groggy, Kaijin squinted, trying to make out the two figures.

"I hope the others come soon," the first one said. "It was only luck we made it this far while she was away."

"Luck? If not for that spell I cast on you, you'd be clanking around louder than a golem."

He huffed. "I still don't understand why we don't just destroy this one. This is more trouble than it's worth, if you ask me."

"Do you realize how much money can be made in the black market for this? Some of the mages will pay top coin for just the eggshells alone!"

"Well, first, we need do get out of here. But I don't think that plan will go smoothly."

"Why do you say that?"

"Because it looks like the Celestials brought friends, this time."

"Reinforcements are on their way to deal with them. That's when we'll make our escape, understand?"

Confused by the pair's conversation, Kaijin looked around for his companions, but he saw no one. He listened carefully, but he heard only the light rustle of the two men nearby. Kaijin called out, "Nester? Aidan? Who's there?"

The rustling stopped abruptly. The air grew tense.

Kaijin felt a presence near him. He smelled the faint scent of brimstone.

A male voice uttered a phrase in Arcanic, and a soft white ball of light appeared in the hand of a stranger. He closed his fist slightly, dimming the light. The man wore a green cloak over his long black robes, upon which a symbol—two crossed swords over a Dragon's skull—was emblazoned on the chest. The light traced over the man's fair, weathered face as he studied Kaijin.

Kaijin looked back at the stranger and blinked. "Who are you? Where am I?"

Frowning, the cloaked man called to his companion, "Someone else is here—and he's alive."

"What?" The other man spoke in just above a whisper. He was dragging a very large bag across the cave floor, and Kaijin caught small glimpses of the man's shining armor. He stood before Kaijin, the dim light revealing the greenish skin and porcine features of an orc, whose face was beaded with sweat. Though donned in full plate, his movements were strangely muffled. He wore a dark green tabard, emblazoned with the same symbol as his cloaked comrade.

"I will crush him." The orc let go of the bag.

"Wait, there's no time." The cloaked man placed two fingers over his temple. "I've been contacted. Our brethren have come."

"But—!"

"Now! We must escape while we have the chance. Leave him. The others will finish him off once they have dealt with the Celestials' group."

Others? Kaijin tried to make sense of it all.

The orc grunted and reluctantly grabbed the bag.

The cloaked man clenched his fist, extinguishing the light, and went toward the mouth of the cave. "Hold on to me."

What's going on? Where are they headed?

The orc followed his companion and wrapped one arm around the man's waist while he tightly held the large bag. The cloaked man held up his hand and twisted a shining object on one of his fingers. The air surrounding the men wavered as they were enveloped in a translucent shield, and moments later, the two men disappeared.

Kaijin flinched. *Did they just . . .*

He lost his train of thought as he spied movement heading out of the cave. He rose slowly, approached the mouth of the cave, and peered out.

There was no one in sight. The precipice overlooked moonlit, craggy, and utterly empty lands below. Kaijin eyed a treacherous-looking rocky trail leading down the mountainside. Voices drifted up from further down the path, followed by screams and clashing metal.

Kaijin's head throbbed, and he grabbed it, groaning in pain. *Not again.* He heard his familiar's high-pitched call from above and behind him. Turning, he spied Miele hanging from the mouth of the cave. She flew at him, shrieking, and landed on his shoulder, her excitement easing the pain in his mind.

"Miele?" Kaijin asked aloud. *She's alive?* "Gods! Am I glad to see you! Are you okay?"

Miele stretched her wings, revealing her furry chest. Over her heart, a line of skin puckered with a faint scar.

She's alive! Kaijin studied the mark, but movement in the nearby brush interrupted him. Percival poked his head up from the small clumps of grass. Squeaking frantically, Percival ran to Kaijin.

"Percival? What are you doing here?" Kaijin asked the weasel aloud. "Did Omari send you?"

Percival fixed him with an intense gaze, then turned toward the rocky path that wound down the mountainside and began nervously weaving between Kaijin's ankles.

Kaijin studied the weasel's odd behavior, puzzled. "What's going on? Is Omari down there?"

Percival let out another whistle. He stopped pacing and stood on his hind legs, craning his neck and stretching his supple body to get a better view.

As Kaijin followed Percival's gaze, he heard a woman scream. *Zarya!*

The terror in that scream turned Kaijin's bitterness toward her into concern. He chewed his bottom lip and looked at Miele. *"What should I do? I don't know if I am strong enough to fight."*

Miele responded with a series of reassuring shrieks and flapped her wings once, sending him feelings of assurance and encouragement.

Kaijin remembered bits and pieces of what had happened a few days before. *"Wait, back at the camp . . . I was . . . part of you, wasn't I? What did you do then? How was I able to see what you saw?"*

She shrieked again, flew off his shoulder, and made small circles above his head.

Kaijin smiled. *"Can you show me what's going on down there? I want to know if everyone is safe. Please be careful. If anything should happen to you again, I—"*

Before he could finish, Miele soared into the air and followed the twisting mountain path.

He watched her carefully. Soon, he felt himself slip away into a trance.

Through Miele's eyes, Kaijin saw the moon-touched lands. He felt his stomach flip-flop as Miele soared through the night sky.

A battle raged at the base of the mountain. Despite the terrifying sensation, Kaijin also felt a sense of freedom, being so high above the chaos. *"I never realized how beautiful it was up here, Miele."*

Miele screeched, and the swooping sensation returned to Kaijin's stomach as she zoomed toward the heart of the fight, giving him a brief glimpse of the combatants before soaring back into the sky. Sigmund, Sephiya, and Evan—the same strangers he remembered from before—fought alongside his companions. The group faced seven armored assailants, who wielded swords, bows, and magic.

Raiders?

Omari slumped against a large rock, breathing heavily. The electrical sparks crackled dimly in his eyes. The ball of lightning he hurled at two archers who aimed at him faded, and the spell fizzled as it hit an invisible barrier surrounding the men. He unsecured his staff from behind him and stepped back into a defensive posture. His body swayed slightly. An armored raider lunged at him from behind, his broadsword poised to slice through the unsuspecting mage.

"Omari! Look out!" Evan yelled, aiming his bow at the raider. His arrow sliced through the air, punching through the attacker's exposed neck. The man collapsed, dropping his sword. Omari turned and jumped away, startled. With a sigh of relief, Evan scanned the rest of the battle.

Sigmund locked swords with an equally large armored man. He broke through the hold and head-butted his opponent. Momentarily dazed, the raider staggered backward, and Sigmund lunged in, driving his sword through the bottom opening of the man's breastplate and into his kidney. Sigmund withdrew his sword, and with a loud grunt, the raider collapsed.

Before the raider could hit the ground, Aidan grabbed him and pinned him against the cliff face. Blood flowed from the man's wound.

"Look at Aidan," the giant demanded, "and answer."

The man's eyelids fluttered. He convulsed and coughed blood.

Sigmund frowned. "Leave him, Aidan. This is no time for interrogations."

Ignoring Sigmund, Aidan remained focused on the dying raider, who coughed more violently.

Aidan bared his fangs and demanded in a low, beastly snarl, "Is Gaston here? You carry his scent. Where is he? Answer Aidan now!"

Blood dribbled out of the side of the raider's gaping mouth. His eyes rolled back, and his body went limp.

"Aidan!" Sigmund yelled again. "That's enough!" He ducked as two arrows zoomed by him. The two longbow archers, atop a large, flat rock, nocked fresh arrows.

Aidan grunted. The arrows had lodged deep into his back, just beneath the small protruding nubs. Aidan released the dead raider and stumbled forward, bracing himself against the rock face with a grimace. Blood trickled from the wound as he worked his muscles. While Aidan was distracted, two more raiders approached him.

"Finish the half-breed!" one of them ordered.

Aidan slumped to his knees and groaned.

"Aidan!" Zarya shouted, running to the giant. Two more arrows whistled by, halting her midstride. The arrows lodged in the ground just hairs behind her.

Miele soared toward the rock and hovered not far above where the archers stood. Behind the archers, a shadow moved.

Nester appeared in plain sight, like a ghost solidifying in thin air. He struck the two men from behind, driving his daggers through small openings between the flutes of their cuisses and into their thighs.

"That's no way to treat a lady." Nester twisted his blades deeper.

The two men cried out in pain and collapsed, firing their arrows toward the sky as they dropped their bows and grasped at their wounds.

Panicked, Miele zoomed away from the battle. Kaijin spoke softly. *"No, Miele. You're safe. They weren't aiming at you."*

A wave of relief spread through the bat, and she approached the battle again, more cautiously.

Nester pulled out his blades and gave them both a good, hard shake. As he did so, Sigmund approached from finishing off the other raider and drove his sword into the displaced archers' backs.

Nester blinked. "Remind me never to make you angry, mate."

Sigmund's face remained stony. "They must not live."

"I kinda figured that."

Sigmund rolled one of the dead raiders' corpses over with his foot and pointed at a small symbol etched on the breastplate.

"That symbol is the same one those two men in the cave were wearing. Who are they? What do they want?"

Confusion filled Miele, and she fluttered closer to Nester and Sigmund. They didn't seem to notice her.

"Do you see this, Nester?" Sigmund said. "It is the symbol of the Legion. They are slayers."

Nester scratched his head, his face scrunching with confusion. "I ain't seen a symbol like that before, but my

Uncle Nickle used to tell me scary bedtime stories about evil slayers. Gave me nightmares when I was a boy, they did. But I never saw one myself, so I figured they weren't real. I mean, 'e *did* used to pull my leg like that most of the time, despite 'im knowin' 'ow much I 'ated it."

Sigmund huffed. "Slayers are very much real. They are driven by cruelty and a blind faith heavily influenced by their dark god, Tydus. They have sinned beyond redemption and must die."

Nester gulped and nodded quickly. "A–aye! Of course!" He backed away slowly, then rushed off to join Omari, who was striking one of the enemy mages' ankles with his quarterstaff, sweeping her to the ground.

Miele followed the brownie.

The enemy mage's hands emitted a purple light as she tumbled backward, and she managed to utter the last phrase of her spell and unleash a fury of small hailstones at Omari.

Omari held his staff in front of him, hands shaking as he summoned small lightning bolts to block some of the hailstones. He fell hard on his back, knocking the wind out of him.

"'Old on, Omari!" Nester called. He dashed at the woman as she rose shakily to her feet.

The woman eyed him and frowned.

Nester mirrored her expression as he sheathed one of his daggers and slid his fingers into his belt pouch. "I ain't never 'it a lady before, an' I ain't about to do so now—no matter 'ow evil she might be." He pulled out a round, pea-sized object.

The woman glared. "*Evil*? How dare you!" She plucked a component from her pouch and grasped it in her fist.

Her hand began to glow again as she readied another spell.

Nester tossed the object at her. It exploded in her face in a small cloud of white powder. Coughing, she waved off the cloud, but moments later, she went into convulsions. The spell fizzled in her hands, and she gagged and collapsed. Her body continued twitching for a few moments and then lay still.

Omari gawked. "Nester, what in Malik's name was that?"

When the remnants of the white cloud dissipated, Nester approached the woman. He prodded her body with his foot. When she didn't move, he replied to Omari, "Datura. 'Ighly potent, it is."

"Datura?" Omari asked. "Those flowers grow wild in my home country. I did not realize they could be used like that."

"Aye. Poisons can be made from many types of flowers."

"How many more of those things do you have?"

"That was my last one. Need to make some more soon, I do. Ankhram traders are usually th' only ones who carry it, unless you're lucky to find some in th' black market, and they sell like 'otcakes. Ankhram traders are sneaky 'ustlin' types, they are, chargin' an arm, a leg—and sometimes a few fingers an' toes—for small amounts!"

Omari bristled. "Do *not* speak about my people in that manner."

Nester raised his nose at him. "It's th' truth, and everyone an' their mum knows it."

Omari swore under his breath and crawled over to the woman. He examined her corpse a moment, and then held his hand out to Nester. "Let me borrow your knife."

Nester's eyebrow rose. "For what?"

"There is something I must do."

"An' 'ow do I know you're not just gonna stab me with it?"

Omari scowled. "I am a mage, not an assassin."

"Don't it mean th' same thing, these days?"

"Enough, Nester. Give it to me!"

Frowning, Nester reluctantly handed him a dagger, then took a large step backward. Omari took the tiny weapon, cut off one of the woman's ring fingers, tore off a piece of cloth from her sleeve, and wrapped the finger inside.

He placed the wrapped finger in his bag. Looking at the woman again, he pursed his lips and repeatedly drove the blade into her throat.

"Death to all renegades," Omari muttered, staring at the bloodied blade. His eyes momentarily went white and pupilless, crackling with electricity, before returning to normal. "May you forever burn in the Abyss." He snarled and tossed the dagger at Nester's feet.

Nester grimaced, and retrieved the weapon. "Now what in th' soddin' 'ells did you do that for?" He wiped the blade on the woman's robe.

"I have my reasons. . . ." Omari's eyelids fluttered, and his body swayed. He sank to his knees and rubbed his temples.

Nester sheathed the dagger and rushed to Omari's side. "Oy! You don't look so 'ot, mate. Are you all right?"

"I am fine," Omari grumbled, waving the brownie away. "I exerted more energy than I should have. Go help the others."

Miele scanned the battleground. Only two raiders remained, and they both closed in on Aidan, who remained helpless and bleeding. Zarya uttered a prayer, and a shield of bright light formed around her and Aidan, momentarily blinding the raiders.

Sephiya approached the men slowly, her hand extended as she concentrated on something. "Leave him alone."

Two glowing yellow ropes appeared and bound the men. Her frown of concentration deepened as the men struggled.

Sigmund, Evan, and Nester surrounded the two raiders.

"Keep them restrained for as long as you can, Sephiya!" Evan shouted, aiming his bow.

Sigmund charged at the men, his sword poised to slice through them. Nester approached cautiously, his gaze darting nervously at the two men.

Sephiya trembled, and the ropes began to fade. "They are . . . strong—too strong. . . . These men have been enchanted somehow . . . Kill them quickly, before—"

One of the men broke free of the bonds and met Sigmund, force for force. Iron clanged on steel, and the raider managed to successfully deflect Sigmund's weapon and kneed him in the gut. Sigmund groaned and stumbled backward.

Sephiya's spell flickered and dissipated.

Evan launched his arrow at the other raider, but it plinked off the man's armor. The uninjured raider lunged at Sephiya, who still looked groggy from the loss of her spell. As he raised his sword, a throwing knife struck him in the underarm.

Amazingly, he barely faltered.

"Sephiya!" Evan yelled. He dropped his bow, pulled a dagger from a sheath hidden in his leathers, and rushed at the raider.

Sephiya made a desperate attempt to summon a spell to shield against the raider's incoming blow, but the man sliced through the spell with ease, and through the side of her neck. Sephiya collapsed.

Two more throwing knives pierced through the raider's neck, but he didn't slow. He spun around to face Evan.

Nester appeared behind the raider and stabbed behind his kneecap with a dagger dripping in a thick, greenish substance. "Soddin' 'ells! Why won't you die!" He drove the dagger down the leg, widening the wound.

The man went into a frenzy, then fell forward, the blade coming down on Evan. The blade skewered his chest, and the raider collapsed atop him, pushing the sword in until only the pommel was visible. Nester, with all his might, heaved the raider off of Evan.

"'Ey, wake up, mate," the brownie said, slapping Evan's cheek a few times. "We're not done yet."

Evan gurgled. His face was paling. "Sigmund . . ." he whispered. "Help him . . . please. . ."

Nester turned to the fight between Sigmund and the last raider standing. Sigmund swung low and struck the back of the raider's legs, but the man kept his feet.

"Defiler! Return to the Abyss from whence you came!" Sigmund's sword glowed white. The raider attacked again, and Sigmund struck his glowing blade underneath his arm, driving the raider to the ground. He placed his foot on his foe and stabbed again.

At first, the raider fought back, kicking and struggling, but his efforts quickly waned as blood oozed from the wound. Sigmund yanked his sword out, and the blade's glow faded.

Omari hobbled over to Nester and Sigmund. "I sense magic about him." He pointed. "There. His hand."

Nester, one hand pressing a small injury in his side, plucked a silver ring from the raider's finger. "This must be what made that bloke stronger than an ox."

Omari leaned most of his weight on his staff as he eyed the accessory. "It has been enchanted with a strength spell, which enhances the bearer's strength and resilience."

"Aye?" Nester looked at Omari.

Sigmund frowned. "Enchanted items. I should have known. They're nothing but useless junk now." As he spoke, the ring blackened and disintegrated in Nester's hand.

Nester blinked in surprise. "Aww. What a waste of good jewelry!"

Ignoring the brownie, Sigmund laid hands on himself and healed his injuries with a prayer, then went to Sephiya and Evan.

Omari scanned the sea of bodies and said coldly, "So, it seems that we have won."

Sigmund fell to his knees. "Sephiya . . . no . . ." He covered his face with his hand, and his body shuddered. Tears streamed down his cheek, and he quickly wiped them away.

Zarya dismissed the protective ward around her and Aidan and got up. Sweat poured down her cheeks. "You should be okay now, Aidan. I finally managed to mend the last portion of the wound."

Aidan turned to face her. He gingerly worked his back muscles, then flexed them more vigorously. A wide smile parted his lips. "You . . . you saved Aidan again!"

Zarya nodded slowly but said nothing. Her attention went to the corpses. She got up and approached Evan and Sephiya. "By the goddess," she whispered, her eyes widening. She clapped her hand over her mouth.

Nester stood beside her. "A little 'elp, beautiful?" he mumbled, showing her his wound.

Zarya faced Nester, then laid her hands over his injury. She prayed, and the small wound mended.

When she finished, Nester rubbed his ribs, stretched his side, and then smiled. "Much appreciated!"

"That is why Aidan does not like violence. Someone always gets hurt," Aidan said darkly, going to stand beside Nester.

Nester's brow wrinkled. "Aye? Well if I didn't know any better, I'd say you were ready to chew off that one bloke's 'ead, th' way you were goin' on like a mad beast!"

Aidan looked shocked and then rubbed the side of his head. "A–Aidan does not know what came over him. Something . . . made him very angry."

"You can say that again!"

"Aidan hopes it does not happen again."

Zarya knelt before Sephiya and Evan and examined them. "Maybe we're not too late. Maybe—"

Sigmund placed his hand on the priestess's shoulder, and she jumped. "No, there is nothing more that can be done. May the goddess take them."

Zarya looked at the guardian, eyes widening in horror. "But we cannot be so certain!"

Sigmund raised an eyebrow. "Once a Celestial dies, they cannot be returned to the mortal realm. Their bodies turn to dust. Surely you are aware of this, Zarya."

Zarya lowered her head. "It has been a long time since I've been around others of my kind. I have been told what happens, but I have never seen it for myself."

"A shame that you have been sheltered for so long, then." Sigmund pointed. "Witness it and embrace it, for they now return to the goddess, Celestra, our creator."

Nester shook his head. "I still can't believe you never told us about yourself, beautiful. Why th' big secret?"

Zarya bit her bottom lip. "I'm sorry, Nester, but as I said before, I have my reasons. Please know that I meant no ill intent by deceiving you like that."

"What are you gonna tell Kaijin when 'e wakes up?"

"*If* he wakes up, you mean," Omari interjected.

Zarya didn't respond.

Nester scowled at Omari. "'E ain't dead, I tell you!"

Omari crossed his arms. "How much longer are we going to wait for him to 'awaken', then, hm? Until we can smell his rotting corpse?"

Miele soared into the middle of the group, startling them a moment. She screeched and looked at each of them in turn.

"'Ey! Miele!" Nester said, beaming. "What're you doin' 'ere?"

"She looks healthy now," Aidan said. "Could it be that—"

"Aye! Kaijin must be awake. I ain't seen 'er this peppy in days."

Omari eyed Miele and huffed. "If that is true, then we should see him . . . or perhaps Miele is really Kaijin looking at us at this very moment."

"Eh? What do you mean?" Nester asked.

"Her eyes have a glow to them. She is possessed."

Flustered, Zarya turned back to the corpses. As she reached out toward the silk of Sephiya's robes, the mage's body disintegrated into a grey sand. Evan's body did the same.

Nester, Omari, Aidan and Zarya gasped in surprise. Sigmund simply lowered his head in prayer. "Celestra be praised."

While the others focused on that, Miele soared into the night sky back toward the mountain peak.

As Miele drew nearer to the top of the mountain, Kaijin saw himself standing alone at the cave's mouth, and he released his mental hold over her. He blinked a few times, feeling as though he were awakening from another long dream. He rubbed his eyes and looked at Miele, who fluttered to him, screeching happily. He couldn't believe what he'd seen and heard.

"Have you any idea what they were talking about?" Kaijin asked aloud.

Miele landed on his his shoulder. She batted her wings once and gave a low screech.

"Huh. Now I'm starting to wonder if that creature from my dream was right—that I really *was* asleep for almost three days. Nothing seems to make sense anymore."

A shadow suddenly swept across the ground from above, startling him from his musings.

Percival began chirping loudly, as if frightened. He stood on all fours, his supple body arched and trembling, his beady eyes turned to the sky.

Kaijin followed the weasel's gaze. A large shadow circled the mountain's apex. The great mass appeared to be a creature more than twice the size of the monster from his dream.

Kaijin heard the sound of large wings beating, and fear overtook him as the area reverberated with a terrible roar.

XVI

The monstrous silhouette descended from the sky, and a creature nimbly landed atop the mountain's crest. It reared and stretched its massive wings, which spanned almost twice its own length. The moonlight glistened on its scales.

Returning to all fours, the creature climbed down the crest and made its way to the cave's entrance. It poked its head inside, then jerked it back out and let out another mighty roar.

Kaijin stood paralyzed in fear. *A Dragon!* Sweat formed on his palms. *After all my reading and all of Master Jarial's stories, I never thought I would encounter such a majestic yet terrifying creature.*

Percival anxiously wove around Kaijin's ankles.

Kaijin turned his gaze to the weasel and then to Miele. "Am I . . . dreaming again?"

Percival shrilled, seemingly empathic to Kaijin's tension.

Miele shrieked, and a wave of warmth and assurance filled Kaijin.

The Dragon roared again, a thunderous sound that promised violence. A dazzling display of lightning streaked the starry sky.

Kaijin's heart pounded. *Dreaming or not, I'm not waiting to find out!* He fled down the winding mountain path as fast as his exhausted body would allow. Miele flew off his shoulder and soared above him, shrieking—though Kaijin did not sense fear from her. Percival followed in Kaijin's footsteps, frantically chirruping.

Kaijin's feet quickly grew heavy. His legs ached; his steps slowed to a stop. Miele landed on his shoulder, while Percival curled himself around Kaijin's ankles. Percival shivered and turned his ears backward, staring back at Kaijin.

Kaijin stopped for a moment, panting. "Don't . . . worry, Percival. I will make sure we . . . make it to the bottom safely."

Further down the mountain, his companions headed his way. Nester, leading the group, pointed at Kaijin and then broke into a sprint, leaving the others behind.

Is Nester mad? He continued trudging down the rocky path. "Stop, Nester!" he yelled, motioning for Nester to stop.

The brownie reached him. A bright, gap-toothed smile spread across his face. "Kaijin! I knew you'd wake up, mate!"

Kaijin huffed, catching his breath, and then reached to pull Nester with him down the trail. "Nester, we have to hurry before—"

Nester sidestepped away from Kaijin, and his gaze drifted toward the mountaintop. His face lit up. "She's back!"

"What? Who's back?" Confused, Kaijin spun around and watched Nester bolt up the path. The brownie stopped short of the Dragon, who sat near the cave's entrance. *This is madness! Can he not see that the Dragon is angry? Knowing our luck, it will take its anger out on us.*

Percival wound around Kaijin's feet, tickling his ankles. The weasel then skittered away, his stubbly legs a blur of motion as he went to meet Omari and the rest of the group. Miele flapped her wings and shrieked lightheartedly.

Kaijin received another warm, reassuring sensation from her, which piqued his curiosity. *"You're not afraid? The Dragon looks intimidating. Nester's liable to get himself squished like a bug if he keeps this up."*

Sigmund soon approached, along with Zarya, Omari, and Aidan. "It's a blessing that you're still alive, Kaijin." Sigmund carefully studied him. "I have seen enough death for one day." He peered up the mountain. "It looks like the Mistress has returned from her hunt." He beckoned the group to follow. "Come."

Zarya offered Kaijin a bright smile, and then ran to catch up with Sigmund.

"The Mistress?" Kaijin repeated, watching them ascend the path. "Wait, where are you going? Don't you realize—"

"The Dragon," Omari said, brushing past Kaijin. "Ker . . . Kah . . . Confound it! How in the hells do you pronounce it again, Aidan?" He looked back at the giant.

Aidan smiled. "Her name is Kyniythyria."

Kaijin furrowed his brow. He attempted to pronounce the name, as well, but only ended up getting tongue-tied. Aidan chuckled.

"Do not bother trying to pronounce it, Kaijin," Omari said. "It is a Draconic name, and Draconic is such an awkward language."

Kaijin hesitated. "Well, it doesn't seem so difficult for Aidan." He paused and glanced up the mountain. The Dragon was still occupied with Nester—and it seemed Nester was still alive. "She looks plenty mad. Are you certain she's on our side?"

Omari looked back at Kaijin and snorted. "Indeed. You have missed much while you were napping."

"Will you enlighten me, then?"

Omari picked up Percival, held him in his arms and stroked his tawny fur. "After our camp was attacked, we were captured and brought here atop this mountain."

Kaijin blinked. "We were? Captured by whom?"

"Them." Omari nodded toward Sigmund, who continued walking ahead of them. "There were two others, but they were slain."

Kaijin paused, thinking about the battle he'd witnessed. "Who are they?"

"They are an ageless race of creatures known as Celestials. Sigmund explained that Celestials are servants to the Dragons, and many believe they are descendants of the goddess."

Kaijin tilted his head. He recalled reading stories about the great Celestials as a child, and he'd thought them nothing more than just that: fanciful creatures in children's stories. "Descendants of the goddess?"

"Indeed." Omari nodded. "It is believed that their kind can live for almost a millennium."

"Really? There must be millions of them around, then."

"Not really, no. They are very slow to propagate. The Mistress went into great detail about it."

"Interesting. But how can they be descended from the goddess if they are mortal creatures? This all sounds a bit farfetched, don't you think?"

"It is cryptic, yes, I know. But it is not wise to question a Dragon's explanation. Take it for what it is, Kaijin. Look at any Celestial, and you will discover similar physical qualities that are linked to the goddess: perfectly proportioned, inherent healing powers, and they smell like honeysuckle, which is said to be Celestra's scent."

"They *all* smell like honeysuckle. Really." Kaijin quirked his eyebrow.

Omari urged Percival up onto his shoulder, and then scratched him behind the ears. "Well, to the Dragons, they smell like that, at least."

Kaijin sensed Aidan close behind him and he looked over his shoulder. "Aidan, I remember when we first met Zarya, you smelled honeysuckle, but Nester and I didn't."

Aidan raised his head to look at Kaijin.

That must mean Aidan is a—

"No, Kaijin," Omari said, as though he had read his thoughts. "Aidan is not a Dragon. At least, not fully."

Kaijin's eyes widened slightly, remembering Aidan's distinctive features. The scales, the size, the strength—the nubs on his back . . . *Wings?* "Is that true, Aidan?"

Aidan pursed his lips and stared at the ground again. "Aidan is who he is."

Kaijin looked between Aidan and Omari. "Who told you all this?"

Omari nodded toward the Dragon. "She did."

"Kyniythyria told Aidan wonderful story of Aidan's family," Aidan added with a smile.

Kaijin gawked at the giant. "What? You—you mean the Dragon actually *knows* your family?"

"No, but—"

"It was but a long-winded fairytale of princesses, demons, and Dragon kingdoms that ended up putting Nester and me to sleep." Omari rolled his eyes.

Kaijin smiled slightly at Aidan. "But still, if it really is true, it must be nice to know about your family."

Aidan shrugged but said nothing.

Looking ahead, Kaijin realized they were not far from the top of the mountain. He watched Zarya and Sigmund and noted the way the two of them walked: swift, graceful, and elegant.

Kaijin snapped out of his silent musings, turned back to Omari, and asked, "So Zarya really *has* been hiding her identity all this time?"

Omari smirked wickedly. "So that *was* you possessing Miele instead of helping us fend off those slayers. And to answer your question, yes, Zarya seems to be so ashamed of her race that she would hide her identity. Or perhaps there is some other reason."

Ashamed of herself. Kaijin frowned. He wondered what sort of darkness she masked.

"She is a woman, Kaijin," Omari continued. "Women tend to do strange, unexplainable things. Despite that, one cannot deny that she is an exceptional healer." Omari rubbed his temple and blinked a few times, looking amazed. "All that casting left me exhausted after the battle, but she somehow managed to strengthen my mind and body, and I have never felt better."

Kaijin recalled some of his master's lessons on the dangers of magic. Jarial's warnings frightened him as a child, and Kaijin had sworn he'd never cast magic on himself like that until he had truly mastered the Art. "It was most likely a temporary fix," Kaijin told Omari. "You should not become too dependent on that. A mage's mind is fragile. You need rest."

"Pah! I know that, you fool. Do not scold me like some confounded child! I am far more experienced than you will ever be."

I hope so, for your sake. Rather than press the issue, Kaijin looked at the ground.

Omari cleared his throat. "The fact of the matter is, Zarya helped me when I required it. It is none of my business, nor do I care to know why she has decided to disguise herself for so long. My only concern is finishing this confounded test."

"Test . . .?" Kaijin eyed Omari. "Ah, your staff? If I recall, you said you were trying to get it enchanted by a Dragon, right?"

"Correct." Omari nodded. "Unfortunately, however, the Dragon has done nothing for *me*. She refused to perform any enchantments until either *you* awoke or She was fully convinced that you were dead. Now that the former has occurred, She will waste more of my time wanting to interrogate you like She did us. She has been highly irritable and wary about slayers having moved into this area, which is also why we were brought here—the Celestials thought we were slayers."

Kaijin frowned. "How terrible." He cast another glance up the mountain. Nester, joined with Zarya and Sigmund, bowed before the Dragon, who regarded them with white, flashing eyes that crackled with lightning.

"The Celestials have not been so bad, since we convinced them otherwise. The Mistress allowed us to rest in Her cave and has offered us food. Mind you, it is not the most extravagant of accommodations, but only a fool—a dead fool—would outwardly complain to Her about it."

The mention of food made Kaijin's stomach rumble. He felt as though he hadn't eaten in days. He rubbed his stomach, slight embarrassment overcoming him when Omari looked amused. "I could go for a meal or two right about now," Kaijin said. He fantasized about his mother's mouthwatering apple porridge.

Omari huffed. "I am certain She will provide something once She has finished interrogating you."

"Right." Kaijin sighed. "These slayers sound like they're more trouble than they're worth."

"Quite an understatement, Kaijin."

Aidan growled. "Aidan does not like violence, but he will do what is necessary to deal with slayers."

Aidan's comment made Kaijin regard the giant with surprise. "This may end up bloody. Are you willing to . . . *kill*, as well?"

Aidan swallowed. His face paled, and he gave a small, reluctant nod. "If Aidan must . . . then yes. He feels very strongly about this. He does not know why."

"I do not think it is strange for you to feel that way, Aidan," Omari said. "Especially since most—if not all—Dragons regard slayers with such contempt."

Aidan's gaze shifted ahead. "Killing a Dragon is highest crime, the greatest dishonor one can bring to the goddess. One cannot continue to live with the blood of Her children on their hands."

"Listen to yourself, speaking like some priest," Omari said.

Aidan scowled at the elder mage. "Kyniythyria told Aidan!"

"I simply find it interesting—and amusing—that a pacifist like yourself has the potential to become as violent and threatening as a rabid beast."

"There are very few things Aidan will not tolerate. Killing the guardians of this world for one's personal gain is one of them."

Omari smirked. "I rather like that sinister side of you, Aidan."

Aidan bristled. "Aidan is not sinister. Slayers have no honor, and Aidan will not stand for it."

Kaijin kept quiet, so Omari couldn't switch to needling *him*.

The three of them walked the rest of the way in silence.

The fiery voice spoke in Kaijin's mind. *"Soon. Very soon."*

XVII

ᎧᏒᎬᎧ

The air at the apex of the mountain was dry enough to make Kaijin's face itch, and the back of his neck tickled as he felt the hairs stand on end. Still weak, he struggled to catch his breath in the thin air.

The stench of ozone had strengthened, making Kaijin feel queasy. He cupped his hand over his mouth and nose to shield the odor, and glanced upward.

Everything was dwarfed by the majestic beauty of a seemingly mythical creature come to life. The Dragon stood taller than fifteen men and half as wide, looming over him and his companions. Her body was streamlined, with powerful muscles visible in her upper torso and legs, though a small paunch indicated that she had fed well earlier that night.

Lightning darted angrily from her white, pupilless eyes and struck the dry brush around them, sending it up in flames. The firelight illuminated the area, revealing the dazzling hues of bronze, turquoise and emerald on her glistening scales. An aura of majesty emanated from her as she focused her intense gaze on them.

"My child! Where is my child?" she bellowed, her voice echoing off the cliffs. Her long tail violently whipped about.

Nester still stood before her, pale and shaking, his excitement replaced by fear. Sigmund and Zarya knelt before Kyniythyria, their heads lowered reverently. His expression stubborn and defiant, Omari kept looking in Kyniythyria's direction. Aidan stood beside Kaijin, arms crossed, regarding everyone with annoyance in his silver eyes.

Kaijin unintentionally looked into Kyniythyria's eyes and became caught up in her gaze. Her intense stare pierced him like ice. Kaijin tried to swallow the lump of fear rising in his throat, but his mouth was too dry, the air too thin. He licked his lips several times and considered speaking, but he thought better of it.

"Such incompetence! Such carelessness!" Kyniythyria's voice shook the ground. Her whipping tail stuck the side of the cave. Small rocks fell from the roof.

"Great Mistress," Sigmund said apologetically when Kyniythyria paused for breath. He kept his gaze lowered. "I take full responsibility for this tragedy. I will not rest until your child is found."

Kyniythyria growled and dug deep grooves into the rocky ground with her talons. "How could you allow this to happen, *guardian?*" Her voice boomed like thunder. Lightning flashed in her eyes.

Both Kaijin and Omari fell to their knees. Kaijin couldn't stop himself from trembling. *I knew it! She's going to kill us all!* Glancing at Aidan, Kaijin noticed the giant still stood stone-faced, seemingly unfazed by Kyniythyria's rage.

Miele fluttered around Kaijin's head, projecting reassurance in his mind, easing his fear.

"We encountered slayers at the base of the mountain, Mistress." Sigmund maintained his composure even in the face of the Dragon's fury. "We dispatched them. However . . ." He swallowed.

"However?" Kyniythyria repeated ominously, fixing her gaze on the guardian.

"I did not see any Dragon eggs in their possession. Moreover, Evan and Sephiya were among the slain." Sigmund licked his lips bitterly.

Kyniythyria's tail stopped its violent swishing. The electric sparks ebbed from her eyes, revealing a set of jade-colored orbs that were slitted like a cat's. A deep growl rumbled in her throat as she digested Sigmund's words. "Their deaths are most unfortunate, but they died doing their duty: duty to protect my child—a duty at which you all *failed*!" She snarled, addressing the group at large. "You *will* find my child—dead or alive—and bring justice to those responsible."

"Honored Mistress . . ." Zarya spoke meekly, keeping her head bowed. "I beseech Your Greatness for any wisdom that you may offer on where we should begin our search."

Kyniythyria lifted her head slightly and sniffed the air. She snorted. "The scent of my egg ends at the base of the mountain. I cannot smell anything else but blood of lesser creatures. From which direction did the intruders come?"

Nester slowly raised his hand. It trembled more violently the higher it went.

She narrowed her eyes at the brownie. "Speak quickly."

He gulped. "Th–th–th' south, m–methinks, Your Majesty! I w–was scoutin' th' area when I saw them comin' this way."

"They were agents of the Legion, Mistress," Sigmund added.

Kyniythyria's head swiveled back to the guardian, her eyes becoming a maelstrom of electric sparks. "If that is true, then it is imperative that my child be found *now*."

Omari lifted his gaze. "Now? Tonight? I beseech you, Mistress. I need to rest first. Can we not start our search in the morning?"

Kyniythyria reared her head high above the group, half-opening her mouth to reveal a set of dagger-like fangs. "Omari Batsuyou, if you do not find my child this instant, I will make sure you sleep and never awaken!"

Omari's eyes widened and he promptly lowered his head. "Y . . . Yes, Mistress. . . ."

"The Legion . . ." Zarya muttered, frowning. "One day, I would like to see them all eradicated."

"That day can't come soon enough, it seems," Sigmund said grimly. "But for now, we must deal with this one step at a time. The Legion has a long history—centuries' worth—of heinous crimes and misdeeds against the Dragons. They believe the Dragons are a threat to the world and want nothing more than to drive them to extinction. Most if not all slayers are, in some way, associated with The Legion. That is why we have been so vigilant in ensuring the safety of the Mistress and her home."

"And you have done a *deplorable* job!" Kyniythyria roared. "My child is *gone*!"

Daring to look at the Dragon once more, Kaijin was astounded to witness something that made his own inner rage seem mild. Considering the circumstances, however, Kaijin understood the reason for her anger. He recalled a bestiary book his master had made him read as a child. Very few things made an Exodean Dragon quick to anger, as it was believed that they were in direct connection with the goddess Celestra. To provoke a Dragon was like mocking the goddess herself.

Miele conveyed reassurance and calmness, allowing Kaijin to push aside some of his panic. He recalled waking up in the dark, dank cave and hearing voices—voices that were not his companions.

Kyniythyria gazed down at Kaijin. "You look like you know something, boy."

Kaijin glared and snapped, "I'm *not* a—!" He quickly stopped himself, realizing whom he was addressing. He clapped his hand over his mouth, his eyes wide. *She'll kill me, now.*

His companions—even Sigmund—gawked at him.

Kyniythyria hissed and then addressed the others sharply, "The rest of you, leave. Do not return until justice is served and my child is returned. Make haste! Now!" She gave a small jerk of her head toward the exit. Without hesitation or another word, the group left Kaijin to his fate.

Kaijin stood, petrified by the Dragon's gaze. *So this is how I die.* He swallowed. His hands shook. *Ignis, spare me—*

Miele shrieked nervously.

Kaijin shook his head. "*No, Miele. Go someplace safe. She will crush you. Go now!*"

Miele hesitated, then fluttered into the cave and hid herself in the shadows.

Kyniythyria snatched Kaijin up in her claws. She carried him inside the cave and tossed him to the ground. Kaijin grunted, dizzy, as he hit the cold, rocky floor.

The Dragon's eyes flashed, illuminating the entire cave as though a bolt of lightning had struck inside. Kaijin shielded his eyes from the blinding light.

When he uncovered them, he noticed a dim light lingered, casting eerie shadows that traced along Kyniythyria's scales. Her massive body nearly filled the entire mouth of the cave, blocking the only means of escape. She lowered her body to the ground and leaned her head closer to Kaijin, sniffing him.

Kaijin couldn't stop shaking, and the Dragon's cool breath against his face only made it worse. The sickeningly strong smell of ozone worsened his headache, and his stomach tied in knots. Trying to calm himself, he breathed deeply, attempting to get air—real air—into his lungs instead of her noxious scent. Slowly, he swallowed, willing himself to speak. "G—Great Mistress . . ." He whimpered, unable to finish.

Kyniythyria leaned back and snorted another draft of ozone in his face. "You are different from the others. Yes, very different."

Kaijin coughed. His head pounded. Her words sounded distant.

"Look at me, *boy!*" she snapped.

Kaijin flinched. Anger replaced the queasiness.

Kyniythyria seemed to notice the change; she looked down her nose at him, her eyes narrowing and flickering with electricity. "You have something to say? Then say it quickly before I destroy you as a damnable slayer."

Kaijin bit his tongue, holding back his anger. He gathered his words carefully. "No, Mistress, I am not a slayer. I swear it."

Kyniythyria flicked her long thin tongue at his face and gave him a mild static shock on his cheek. "No, *of course* you're not. Tell me who and what you are, then."

Kaijin winced in pain from the shock. "My name . . . is Kaijin. Kaijin Sora, Great Mistress."

"Yes, I know."

Kaijin blinked. *Is she toying with me? What does she wish to know?* "I, uh . . . I am a mage, Great Mistress."

"I have known many mages in my lifetime. You have yet to answer my second question. What are you?"

What does she want me to say? "I am a human."

"Do not mock my intelligence." She glowered at him.

Kaijin chewed on his bottom lip. His mind felt muddled. *What in the hells does she want from me?*

Kyniythyria snarled. The annoyance returned to her voice. "Answer me, *boy*!"

Kaijin's anger took over again, and he met the Dragon's gaze. "What am I? What *am* I? I am *not* a boy. I am a man!"

The Dragon didn't eat him or slash him to death for his outburst. Instead, she plucked him up off the ground by the back of his robe.

Kaijin's stomach sank as he was hauled up higher and higher. His legs dangled helplessly in the empty air. *Gods, what have I done to deserve this?*

She scrutinized him. "You may not be a boy, but you are a very foolish man. One that needs to be humbled. Interesting. I've had this same conversation with Omari—

that pompous fool. I put him in his place quickly, and he's behaving now."

Kaijin gulped, and the heat of the charm surged against the skin of his chest, echoing his pounding heart.

Kyniythyria meticulously hooked the cord with the tip of a talon and plucked the charm from beneath his robes. For a moment she gazed at the charm's mesmerizing play of swirling flames. Her eyes moved from the charm to Kaijin and back to the charm again. "Why are you wearing a cleric's holy symbol?"

Kaijin paused, confused by the unexpected change in subject. He swallowed several times as he tried to gather his thoughts. "I've . . . I've had it since I was a boy, Great Mistress. I encountered a drunken priest one night who was denouncing the gods, and he threw away this necklace."

"I see." Kyniythyria raised her nose at him. "I sense an extraplanar presence in you. You are obviously no Ignan priest, and yet this symbol burns with life." She paused.

Since the Dragon showed no inclination to either drop or eat him, Kaijin's fear eased into curiosity. "I don't understand, Great Mistress. Is something wrong?"

"No. Nothing is wrong. Everything is just right." She arched her neck and stared at him. "*I* know what you are now. You are a Firebrand."

Kaijin blinked. "Excuse me, Great Mistress?"

"How interesting it is to be holding an instrument of the Firelord himself. There are many names for those who are not inherently adept in the divine arts but can still be manipulated by extraplanar beings: the Horsemen of Tydus, the Champions of Celestra. In the case of Ignis . . . well. You can understand where the name came from."

Kaijin hung limply in her hold, staring at her. *What's a Firebrand?*

"That is what makes you different from the rest of your companions." Kyniythyria set him back down on the cave floor, more gently that time.

Relieved to be on solid ground again, Kaijin took a deep breath to calm his nerves. *I've never heard of Firebrands. Is it cleric magic?* "So, what does that mean, Great Mistress? I am a slayer?"

"I might have suspected that possibility if you served Tydus, but as you bear Ignis's symbol, that does not seem to be the case."

"So does that mean you . . . trust me?"

"For now. Do not give me a reason to reconsider."

"And that is why you wished to interrogate me alone?"

Kyniythyria huffed. "Among other things. You were asleep for three days; either Sephiya's sleep spell misfired, or you are highly sensitive to such enchantments. Either way, the spell should not have lasted for as long as it did. The strangeness made me wonder. You slept so deeply, in fact, that some of your friends presumed you dead at first, even though you were still breathing—albeit faintly."

Kaijin nodded, starting to understand what had happened. He stared toward the rear of the cave, remembering the two strangers and their odd burden.

"You know something, *Firebrand*. Tell me. Now."

He looked back at her. "I . . . uh . . ."

Kyniythyria flicked her tongue at him again, giving his cheek a more powerful static shock. A bead of sweat disappeared from the tip of his nose. "I can taste the apprehension on you. If you know something about my child, speak now, or else."

Kaijin fell onto his rear, and he rubbed the pained spot on his face. Gazing up at the Dragon, he meekly drew his knees to his chest. "I . . . I awoke in this cave and heard men's voices. I saw something—something big—being dragged. It was too dark to see much, Great Mistress." He looked behind him briefly, and then returned his attention to her. "One of the men used an item—a ring— and before I knew it, they were both gone—disappeared into thin air. I suspect it was a spell of some sort—like invisibility."

She growled. "They have gotten bolder and more foolish. They will pay dearly for this."

He lowered his head. "That is all I can remember, Great Mistress."

"Very well. I will allow you to join your companions. Use whatever gift the Firelord has entrusted you with to find my child."

Kaijin breathed a deep sigh of relief. *Thank you.* He relaxed. "Great Mistress, if I may just have a little food and water before I leave?"

Kyniythyria sneered. "Did you *not* hear what I told Omari?"

Kaijin cringed and slowly stood up. "Great Mistress, with all due respect, my mind and body are fatigued. I do not know how long—"

"I am done with you, and now you wish to try my patience." She let out an exasperated sigh and gestured sharply with her head toward a corner of the cave he hadn't noticed before, where a jumble of mundane items sat—a small sack, some waterskins, and miscellaneous weapons and camping gear. "Evan went hunting this morning. I'm sure you will find something there. Take what you can carry and leave quickly."

"Yes, Mistress." Kaijin rummaged through the items. Bags contained an assortment of nuts and berries, and the two waterskins were half full. Kaijin also dug his haversack from among the gear, and quickly stuffed a waterskin and some of the food into it.

Kyniythyria watched him for a moment before moving away from the mouth of the cave. She curled up in her empty nest and rested her head on the cool ground. Sparks flickered in her eyes and then subsided. "Evan and Sephiya's deaths were unfortunate but honorable. They protected my home and did their duty. As much as I would rather deal with the Legion myself, I fear I would only risk my child's safety. They would call for reinforcements. All this could very well be a trap for me, an attempt to draw me out of my home to search for my child."

"It sounds like a clever plan, Great Mistress," Kaijin replied. He finished packing and secured the straps on his haversack. "If it succeeded, they could kill both you and your child." He slung the bag across his shoulders.

Kyniythyria let out an irritated growl. "Indeed. I expect you to show them no mercy, Firebrand of Ignis. Now, go."

Without hesitation, Kaijin left, and Miele swooped down from the cave's shadowy ceiling and followed. He began his descent down the mountain path, walking quickly in hopes of catching up with his companions. Still, Kyniythyria's words echoed in his mind.

No mercy . . .

XVIII

‿❧‿

Nester and the rest of the group trekked swiftly through the Mallowyn Crags, the foothills that surrounded Kyniythyria's mountain. They stopped to rest, but only until the sky brightened with dawn, and then they were off again. They had found no clues of the Legion's whereabouts. Nester glanced behind him, seeing how everyone was faring.

"Gods, I am still tired," Omari grumbled as he straggled behind the group. "Why could we have not rested a little while longer?" Sitting comfortably on Omari's shoulder, Percival watched their surroundings.

Sigmund glanced over his shoulder. "I share your sentiments, Omari, but we must press on."

"Kyniythyria's child depends on it," Aidan added.

Omari scoffed. "If I am to be of any use in these endeavors, then I require ample rest, lest I risk clumsily mis-casting spells."

"Oh, quit your complain', mate." Nester said. "We're all tired. But that's what makes things interestin', eh? Besides, what's to say this ain't part of your Citadel test?"

"This is *not* part of my test. I was specifically instructed to have my staff enchanted, and that was all. I am only delaying these efforts by foolishly trudging through unfamiliar lands in search of an entire army."

Nester rolled his eyes. "Oy! You may think I'm not th' brightest light in th' 'arbor, but even *I* know that fiddlers are th' most convoluted blokes this side of Aransiya. They say one thing, but they really mean somethin' else. That's 'ow it goes, aye? Always keeps you thinkin' an' all that?"

"What?"

"It's a rather sneaky scheme, if you ask me. And I like it." Nester laughed.

"There is nothing 'sneaky' about this. I would have completed my task and *already* been on my way back to the Citadel if I had not encountered *you* people."

Nester shook his head. "Nay, if you 'adn't encountered us, you'd be lookin' for those slayers by your own soddin' self."

Omari swore under his breath.

"That's enough, you two." Zarya said. "The goddess has brought us together to work for a greater, common cause. These are Her children we are helping. It's a high honor and blessing that very few have the opportunity to experience."

Omari turned his head away, scowling bitterly.

"Aye, aye. I know, beautiful." Nester nodded.

Zarya looked away and lowered her head.

Aidan brought up the rear, walking a few paces behind Omari. "Aidan is hoping we finish this soon, as well. There has been too much violence—too much death."

Omari walked to the side, acknowledging the giant with a sneer. "You and your anti-violence fixation," he grumbled. "Do we even know where we are going, exactly?"

Nester halted and unfolded his large map. "We're 'eadin' south toward th' Carran Marches. And if we keep walkin' in this direction, we'll be in Ankhram in a few days."

"Ankhram!" Omari exclaimed, blinking.

Hearing everyone halt behind him, Nester faced them and nodded. "Aye, an' I don't know 'bout you guys, but I'd rather avoid those lands like th' plague. Nothin' worthwhile there, anyway—just sand everywhere."

"We are not going to Ankhram," Sigmund said. "We are going to search this area. Stay vigilant, everyone. We must work quickly."

Aidan turned to Zarya. "Is something wrong?"

The priestess snapped her head up. "Ah, no. Nothing," she said quickly. "Let's be off." She promptly resumed walking and brushed past the rest of the group.

Nester folded his map and looked behind him. In the distance, he could see the mountain that held Kyniythyria's cave. Its peak was almost completely shrouded in a thick, lingering haze, which made it look haunted, forbidding. "She was plenty mad at us, She was," Nester mused. "Acted like *we* were th' ones who prigged 'er egg!"

Omari rolled his eyes again. "Would you not feel threatened if someone stole *your* child, Nester?"

"Mmm . . . Well, I don't rightfully know. I ain't got any li'l ones."

Omari groaned. "Thank Malik."

Nester thoughtfully stroked his sideburns. "Say, you don't think She's gonna do somethin' to Kaijin, do you?"

Zarya sharply eyed Nester. "What?"

Nester froze. "I–I'm just sayin,' beautiful. I mean, She *did* kinda rush us all out. I didn't wanna leave, but, well . . . It ain't wise to anger a Dragon any more than they already are, aye?"

"I believe She merely wished to interrogate your friend before entrusting him with searching for Her child," Sigmund said. "There is no need for alarm."

Chewing her bottom lip, Zarya looked at the guardian. Sigmund frowned at her. "Zarya, do you doubt the guardians of Exodus—those chosen by the goddess?"

"No, I . . . I am just worried about Kaijin."

Nester raised his eyebrows. "Aye? And 'ere I thought you wanted nothin' to do with 'im."

Aidan smiled at Zarya. "Aidan is glad you do not hold any more ill feelings toward him."

"He is a disturbed man," Zarya replied. "But in these past few days, I've had the opportunity to pray to the goddess and meditate. I've come to realize that Kaijin holds the key to the many answers I seek."

Omari stared down his nose at her. "Kaijin is but one man. He does not hold all the answers to life's problems."

"I know, but—"

Oh, this is gettin' good. Nester smirked as he listened to his comrades.

He spotted movement in the distance behind the priestess and squinted. A lone figure trudged the rocky path, heading toward them. Even at that distance, Nester could see the glow of the figure's red hair. "Speakin' of that fiery sod . . ."

* * *

Kaijin, uncertain how long he'd been walking, continued following his instincts as he trudged through the rocky land. He wanted to stop, but his body refused, somehow. He felt something tugging at his mind, controlling his body.

Where am I going? My companions are all gone. I am a fool to be exploring these unfamiliar lands alone.

"*You are exactly where you need to be,*" the fiery voice replied.

"And where is that? Lost?" Kaijin said aloud. When the voice didn't respond, he continued lumbering along in silence. A sharp ping hit his mind, and he looked up just in time to see Miele fly off ahead.

"Miele! What's going on? What do you see?"

A mental link with his familiar allowed Kaijin to see his friends, who walked not far ahead. At his urging, Miele zoomed toward the group. His stomach sank as he felt himself diving down from the sky, only to stop just shy of impact from the ground. Startled, the group stopped in their tracks to acknowledge Miele.

"That is Kaijin's familiar, is it not?" Sigmund pointed.

Nester nodded. "Aye. She's a wee li'l thing, but she packs a wallop with those 'uge, pointy teeth o' hers. I bet she can eat a man in a single gulp!"

Zarya laughed. "She is a fruit bat, Nester. A *harmless* fruit bat."

"'Armless?' She soddin' near bit my ear off, she did!"

Omari cleared his throat, and said sharply, "Does it matter what she is? The fact that she is here means that Kaijin is not too far. Let us find him and get this confounded task over with."

Aidan peered behind him. "Aidan will get him."

Kaijin severed the mental link and rubbed his eyes, feeling slightly disoriented. He looked up; Miele flew in circles around him. A cool breeze swept across his face, and a large shadow nearly eclipsed him. Kaijin found himself staring at a large, silver-scaled chest.

Gods be damned, he's intimidating! "A–Aidan?" Kaijin blinked.

"Yes," the giant replied. "Aidan is glad to see you safe. The others are waiting ahead. Can you walk?"

"Uh . . ."

Aidan smiled and hefted him in his arms. Kaijin tensed, remembering Kyniythyria's manhandling.

"Come. Aidan will help." The giant held him securely in his arms, rendering Kaijin unable to escape. Having witnessed Aidan's wrath before, resisting him was the last thing Kaijin wanted to do. And Aidan could walk far more quickly than Kaijin.

They approached the group.

"Really, Aidan?" Omari scoffed, crossing his arms. "He could not just walk on his own like everyone else?"

"It's good to see you, too, Omari," Kaijin quipped, flashing half a smile.

Zarya frowned at Omari. "Who knows what terrible things the Mistress has done to him?" She then looked at Kaijin, her face softening.

"Nothing," Sigmund said, "else Kaijin would not be here now."

Aidan set Kaijin down and stood back. "Aidan was only helping."

"It's best we carry on." Sigmund set forth. "We can chat along the way."

Kaijin trailed behind his companions and watched them search their surroundings.

"Walk faster, lest we leave you behind." Omari broke Kaijin from his thoughts.

"I'm sorry. I didn't realize I was falling behind." Kaijin quickened his pace. "Why couldn't the Dragon let us all recuperate before setting out?"

Omari slowed until Kaijin caught up. "The only thing on her mind is her missing child, which is understandable, but annoying. I cannot function this way. I sincerely hope I do not end up mis-casting a spell. Anyway, Zarya's enchantments have allowed me— allowed all of us—to endure. But there is no telling how much longer she will be able to keep this up until she will need rest herself."

As Kaijin was about to reply, Miele shrieked. He winced, holding his head. "Ah . . ."

Omari raised an eyebrow. "What is it now?"

Kaijin lowered his hands from his head. "Miele has made me rather jumpy lately. Ever since . . ."

"What? Confound it, get to the point already!"

"My intermittent possession of Miele. It makes my stomach turn upside down every time it happens—hells, every time I think about it, for that matter."

Omari chuckled darkly. "You are frightened over *that*, Kaijin? How pathetic. And you call yourself a mage."

"I can sense Miele's feelings. But actually *flying* with her? Thank the gods I'm not afraid of heights."

"She is a bat. Moreover, possessing one's familiar is as normal as breathing. Surely, they taught you that in school."

"Yes, my master taught me about it, but this is the first time I'm actually experiencing it."

Omari watched him coolly. "So, as I suspected, your training was piss-poor, and here is proof of it. So now I suppose it is up to *me* to teach *you* something that a novice learns during their first year at the Citadel."

Kaijin stiffened. "Now, wait a minute. I—"

"Look, Kaijin. It is obvious that I am more advanced than you." He eyed Kaijin with pity. "Your 'experience' is one of the basic aspects of having a familiar. A mage is so attached to their familiar that they have the ability to possess them mentally. How could you possibly *not* have experienced this?"

Kaijin ignored the insults for a moment and thought about his experiences during his training and the first time he acquired Miele. "Miele and I have been together since I was ten, and it's never happened before. I guess my master was right. A mage never stops learning. Does this mean you can possess Percival at will, too?"

Omari inclined his head slightly. He scratched the weasel behind the ears, and Percival trilled softly. "Yes, though I do not exercise that skill unless I must. I prefer to give Percival his freedom."

"I see." Kaijin rubbed his chin. He laughed. "My master once said that familiars are an extension of your self. I didn't realize he was being so literal."

Omari huffed. "Your master was incompetent to not tell you about something so exceptionally basic. You *do* realize that such incompetence is not tolerated at the dignified schools?" He bore his gaze on Kaijn. "Schools like the one *I* attended, the most highly-esteemed school in all the lands: the Ghaeldorund Citadel."

Kaijin tensed and frowned slightly. "My master, Jarial, was an excellent teacher. I still have nothing but the utmost respect for him, and I would appreciate it if you would not speak about him in that manner."

Omari halted and spun around, wide-eyed and pale. "Jarial? As in Jarial Glace? He was your *master*?"

"Yes. Do you know him?" Kaijin drew up alongside him.

"*Know* him? What student of the Citadel does not know a member of the Council of Nine! The members of that council are the backbone of Ghaeldorund, overseers of the Citadel. Master Glace was the fifth-tier master of the Council, specializing in illusion."

"You two, don't fall behind!" Sigmund called, his gaze stern. He beckoned for them to catch up.

Kaijin quickened his pace, as did Omari. "Master Jarial mentioned that he was once part of the Citadel, but he never told me much more than that. What was it like for you, studying under him?"

Omari gazed up at the sky, thinking. "He was very strict. He pushed us to our limits, but only to bring out the best in all of us. He was admired by many, including me. He departed from the Citadel not long after I entered my third year there. I was almost seven years old at the time. His council seat was replaced by Master Faulk—who, though not as strict, was a master that a student learned quickly not to underestimate."

"Master Jarial came to Easthaven—my home—and sold books in the marketplace. That was where I first met him."

Omari grunted. "Well, confound it all. Never thought I would ever meet another one of his students outside the Citadel like this." He made a sour face. "I guess you cannot be *all* that bad."

"Thanks . . . I think."

"But it sounds like he has gotten soft in his years."

"Hardly. He's taught me so much about magic. I owe him my life."

Omari pursed his lips. "He has obviously not taught you enough."

"Would you dare say that if he were here?"

Omari fell silent and looked away. "Of course not," he grumbled.

Kaijin's gaze hardened. "He's a good teacher. Unfortunately, following the events in Easthaven, we parted ways. He said he would return to the Citadel to report to the Council about the tragedy."

Omari glanced ahead at the rest of the group and then inched closer to Kaijin until their shoulders almost brushed. He lowered his head and murmured, "So, were you there when it happened?"

The question made Kaijin scowl, and Omari's closeness unnerved him. He took a small side step away. "Why do you wish to know that?"

"Because I have heard a mix of stories and want to know the truth of the matter."

Kaijin hesitated. *Would he really understand?* He felt Miele soothe him. He looked up at her fluttering silhouette in the sky. *"He was one of Master Jarial's students, so he can't be all that bad, right?"*

"Kaijin?" Omari intently stared at him.

Kaijin's head snapped back to him. "I, ah . . ."

"So you *were* there." Omari's eyes glittered with curiosity. "Tell me what *really* happened. And spare me no details."

Kaijin sighed. "It . . . it began with monsters— undead—invading Easthaven. A man—a renegade former student of the Citadel, ironically—was behind it all. He was later killed, but the monsters afflicted many residents and threw the city into utter chaos."

Omari blinked. "The instigator was a Citadel student? Who? Who was it? Tell me."

Kaijin swallowed. *Xavorin.* The name continued to haunt him. Once a beloved friend of Jarial's, Xavorin had turned to the darker arts of magic—to necromancy. Kaijin had heard about him a few times from Jarial. He'd only seen Xavorin a few times, and each time was more grisly than the next until Xavorin had finally become just like the rest of his undead servants.

Kaijin took a deep breath, trying to dismiss the images from his mind. "Ah, I don't remember." He bit his tongue. "Anyway, does it matter who he was? He's dead, and that's all that matters, right?"

Omari peered at Kaijin and grumbled, "Yes, well . . . I guess you are right. All renegades must die."

Kaijin had a bad taste in his mouth and changed the subject. "So tell me about your homeland, Ankhram."

Omari's eyebrow slowly rose. "Have you been eavesdropping on my conversations?"

"Of course not. Uh . . . Nester mentioned it earlier." Kaijin nodded quickly. "Were your parents mages, as well?"

Omari shook his head. "Just my father. Not long after I was born, he traveled to Ghaeldorund to do some research, but left the city only a few months later due to a 'conflict of interest', as he put it. Upon returning to Ankhram a year later, he revived the Harran—a mage's circle started by my forefathers. He has remained there ever since and sent me off to the Citadel when I turned four."

Kaijin tilted his head. "Strange. Why didn't your father teach you magic, instead?"

Omari shrugged. "My father respects the Council of Nine very highly. His wish is for me to become one of them one day."

"Wouldn't that prove easier if he were a member of the Council?"

"Yes, he is good at what he does, but he is also a solitary man. And my being one of the Nine would bring a greater honor to not only him, but to the entire Batsuyou line, as our influence would then spread further."

"Very interesting."

"The Batsuyou are of Ankhram origin. We are a wealthy, highly esteemed family line of mages, seers, and enchanters."

"It's amazing that you know so much about your family line."

Omari raised an eyebrow. "And you do not, I assume?"

Kaijin stared at the ground. "Well, my parents did not speak much of anything. All I know is that my mother was from Ankhram."

"Was she, now?"

"My parents and younger brother were the only family I knew. They died during the attacks in Easthaven."

"I see," Omari said flatly.

"I feel so alone, you know? Like an outcast—like I've nothing else left." He stopped himself, realizing whom he was talking to and immediately anticipated insults.

Omari opened his mouth, then closed it, to Kaijin's surprise and relief. Omari exhaled through his nose. "There is nothing wrong with you, Kaijin. There is just something wrong with the world."

Kaijin considered Omari's words.

"Oy! I think I found somethin', I did!" Nester called. The brownie stood atop a boulder and looked down into a valley that lay a lengthy distance away from the crags. Wisps of smoke rose from a large camp.

"Do you think that might be them?" Zarya asked.

Aidan sniffed the air and then let out a low growl. "Gaston . . ."

"We need a plan of action before we attack," Sigmund said.

Omari huffed. "And what do you propose we do, Sigmund?" he asked coldly. "Simply walk up to them and ask them nicely for the egg?"

Nester smirked. "Say, that's not a bad idea, mate!"

Omari rolled his eyes. "I was being facetious, you fool."

"But think about it!" Nester gestured. "They won't expect us! They'll all be caught off guard and—"

"—They will either kill us, destroy the egg, or both." Omari finished with a scowl.

"No," Sigmund interjected. "We need to be careful. We don't know what we're going up against." He looked at Nester. "How skilled are you at reconnaissance?"

"Me? I'm as subtle as a fly on th' wall. Are you askin' me to scout th' place out?"

Sigmund nodded. "We will be close by while you do that."

"Perhaps Kaijin and I can assist, as well," Omari said. He lightly elbowed Kaijin, and smirked.

Kaijin blinked and looked to Omari, bewildered. "Uh . . . s–sure."

Zarya's brow furrowed. "What are you two going to do?"

"We will assist in Nester's reconnaissance. Do not ask how. We have our ways, do we not, Kaijin?"

Kaijin looked between Omari and Zarya and then nodded slowly. *Oh, I think I know where he's going with this.*

Sighing, Zarya regarded Kaijin, Nester, and Omari. "All right, be careful, you three." She approached each of them, laying her hands over them and speaking a brief prayer. "*By Celestra's grace, may you all be protected from the enemy.*" Her hands emitted a white glow.

The three of them bowed their heads, accepting the priestess's blessings. She stepped back.

"C'mon," Nester beckoned toward the camp. "Let's get closer." He led the way down to the valley, with Kaijin and Omari following.

The fiery voice returned as Kaijin walked, and its tone was savage. "*Show no mercy.*"

XIX

ৰৎ৪ৎ

Locating the egg within the camp wasn't too difficult for Omari, thanks to Percival's keen nose. The weasel searched each of the eleven tents, slinking stealthily amongst the packhorses and men of the Legion. Omari monitored his familiar closely, entering the weasel's mind while he searched.

Omari spied two men leaving a small tarpaulin tent. *"Try that one over there."*

Percival scampered over and poked his head under the entrance flap. All Omari saw were two bedrolls, a lantern, and some worn clothing thrown into one corner. A canteen perched on one bedroll, while a sheathed longsword lay on the other. The egg's scent was not as strong in there, so Percival backed out of the tent and went to another.

"Confound it!" Omari sighed, frustrated. *"Keep searching. Alert me as soon as you find something. Be careful."* He severed the link and allowed Percival to explore on his own.

Returning to his own senses, Omari nodded toward Zarya, Aidan, and Sigmund, who all stood watch nearby, then looked at Kaijin beside him. The younger mage's eyes were distant with concentration.

Omari peeked around the large boulder between them and the camp a short distance away. He saw faint, child-sized footsteps appear in the rocky dirt as Nester stealthily approached them. Omari narrowed his eyes and held his breath as he waited for Nester to reach them.

Nearby shadows coalesced around Nester as he slipped behind the rock and became visible. He acknowledged Omari and Kaijin with a wide grin.

"What did you find?" Omari asked.

"'Bout a 'alf-dozen lingerin' around." Nester rubbed his nose. "I'm sure more'll be wakin' up from their tents pretty soon. No sign of th' egg, though."

"Yes, Percival is still searching." Omari nudged Kaijin to gently break him from his trance. "Come, Kaijin. Let Miele alone. We should inform the others of our findings."

Kaijin's gaze snapped into focus. Startled, he shook his head and acknowledged Omari and Nester.

Nester pushed himself off the rock and ran off toward the others. With a small tilt of his head, Omari beckoned Kaijin to follow.

* * *

Gaston slammed his fist on the table in the middle of his tent, knocking over pawns and markers and sloshing ale from a tankard onto the tactical map. He glared scornfully at the two lackeys standing before him—Thokas and

Searil—who kept their heads bowed. Beside Gaston, Raban took a quick step backward.

Gaston tensed his neck. "I've thought things over since last night, and I've come to a conclusion. Your stories do not make much bloody sense! You can steal from a Dragon, but you cannot even fend off a small group of ruffians?"

Thokas and Searil remained silent.

Raban sidled around the table until he had his back against the tarpaulin wall and continued observing in silence.

Gaston reached across the table, grabbed Thokas by the collar and tugged him closer so that they met eye to eye. "Just as easily as I've obtained you, Raban can discard you." He sneered at the orc, and then glared at Searil. "If either of you have brought dishonor to the Legion, then it is my duty and my right to rectify the problem."

Thokas grunted and looked away from Gaston. "We speak the truth, my liege."

Gaston scowled and released the orc with a firm shove. "How many times are we going to go over this, Thokas? It is unacceptable. We are breaking camp soon, and I'll leave your corpses behind to rot if you do not give me a valid reason to spare you."

Searil protested, "We were outnumbered, at first. Reinforcements came as planned, sir, but they were killed too quickly. A large half-Dragon tore through our group like ragdolls. His friends finished off the rest."

From the corner of his eye, Gaston spied Raban smirk and cross his arms. Gaston's scowl deepened—the druid returned to his stone-faced expression—and his attention darted back to Searil. "You did not tell me this last night, Searil. Go on."

Searil shifted uncomfortably and brushed an unseen speck of dirt from his red robes. "He was a man with a body like armor. I saw him pick up two warriors at once and fling them as though they were straw men. The scouts shot arrows at him, but they hardly pierced his skin. He . . ."

Gaston quirked his eyebrow at Raban, then looked toward the rear corner of the tent, where a large sack lay. "So, my opponent has returned for a rematch," he murmured. He turned back to Thokas and Searil. "Leave."

Thokas grabbed his startled companion and quickly left the tent.

Raban looked coolly at Gaston. "I will dispose of them for you, sir."

Gaston ignored his comment. "The hard part of our job is complete, Raban. We will soon see a profit once we reach Ergoth. Our brethren there will be pleased."

"You are certain the egg will survive the five-day trek through the Ankhram desert?"

Gaston glanced back at the sack. "You would be amazed at the resilience of a Dragon's egg. The shell alone is almost as hard as adamantine. Whilst in my care, it will remain safe."

Raban sniffed and turned away from him, the hem of his black robes sweeping across the ground. "And what of our young recruit? I do not think he is ready to embark on such a journey."

Gaston brushed past the druid, toward the exit. "He is eager, and he has seen more in these few days than most recruits live to see in their lifetime. But I do like Carver. He is looking for guidance—to be molded into a warrior."

He glanced over his shoulder and smirked. "Stop worrying about the boy. Why don't you go deal with those two imbeciles, instead?"

Raban made a face, bowed, and swept out of the tent.

Moments later, Gaston followed him. As he passed through the tent flap, a crow swooped down from atop the exterior roof of the tent, cawing mockingly at him as it flapped toward the center of camp. Gaston could hear the bitter reluctance in the bird's squawks. *You will never achieve my success, Raban. That is why I lead.* He watched the bird's silhouette disappear in the camp.

* * *

Alone in his tent, Carver secured the last loop of his studded leather cuirass and checked himself. It fit snugly, but he was still able to move with ease. *I don't look half bad in this.* He grinned. It had only been a few days since he'd begun traveling with the Legion, and Carver had already felt their camaraderie; they accepted him—a complete stranger—as one of their own. *I could not ask for a better family than this.*

Hearing his tent flap open, he spun around. Gaston entered, his armor glinting from the sunlight outside. "Sir Gaston!" Carver beamed. "What do you think?" He showed the man the front and back of his armor.

Gaston observed him a moment, then smiled. "It looks good on you, boy. But with every defense, there must come a good offense. I trust your training with Kelvin has been fruitful?"

Carver nodded. "Yes, sir. He's a good teacher and an even greater fighter. Though not as good as you, sir."

Gaston bowed. "You do me honor. You'll need to learn how to wield a true warrior's weapons if you wish to fight alongside me."

A prickle of excitement ran down Carver's arms. "Oh, I do, sir! It would be such an honor to join you on the battlefield!"

"I like your enthusiasm, Carver. It will take you far. When we get to Ergoth in a few days, I will introduce you to one of the trainers there. I will also see that you are properly marked."

Carver tilted his head to the side and furrowed his brow. "'Marked', sir?"

"Indeed. Every member of the Legion is marked—a constant reminder of their eternal servitude." He turned his head slightly, revealing a symbol burned into his skin on his neck. "Once you are a Legionnaire, you are *always* a Legionnaire. Unless you bring dishonor on the Legion in some way—but I trust that will not be the case, now, will it?"

Carver shook his head quickly. "Oh, no, sir! Never!"

Gaston patted Carver's shoulder. "Good. Now pack up. We will be setting off in a few hours."

After Gaston left, Carver heard raised voices outside his tent. His curiosity piqued, he quietly trailed Gaston's footsteps, keeping out of the warrior's sight.

Gaston walked toward the center of camp, where a group of spectators stood in a small circle around the ashy remains of a campfire. Inside the circle was Raban, along with Thokas and Searil.

Carver hid behind a tent and watched in silence.

"The price of failure is death," Raban croaked.

Searil gasped. "What? But . . . we retrieved the egg as instructed."

"Too many of our brethren died. You could not perform a simple task without bleeding our forces with casualties. Our numbers have been reduced to fourteen because of your incompetence!" Raban glowered. "The Dragon was not even around! There is no excuse for this."

"Please, spare us, sir," Thokas pled. "We did not foresee—"

"Silence!" Raban raised his hand in front of his face and curled his fingers into a tight fist, which began to glow with an eerie green light.

Thokas and Searil whimpered and attempted to flee, but they halted as Gaston entered the circle of spectators.

"We will survive, with or without you two." Gaston unsheathed a dirk from his belt, and glided to Searil in a single step, looming over him like a shadow of Death. He cast a brief glance at Raban. "Restrain them."

Smirking, Raban unleashed his spell. Green light surged from his hand to hit the ground around Thokas and Searil's feet. The dirt crumbled, and several thorny green vines broke through. They wrapped around the frightened men's ankles and held them in place.

Thokas and Searil struggled and grunted, but their weak attempts at escaping the vines' hold proved futile.

"I should kill you both," Gaston sneered, his eyes glittering. "But I think I will offer you to our Ankhram brethren, instead. I am rather fond of their methods of punishment. However, your failure dishonors the mark of the Legion. Therefore . . ." He seized Searil first and tore off the right sleeve of his robe, revealing the brand on the man's shoulder. With the tip of his dirk, Gaston carved the brand out of Searil's skin.

A terrifying cry echoed throughout the camp. Searil paled, clutching the wound, and looked wide-eyed at Gaston.

Gaston tossed the severed skin to the ground and stomped it into the dirt. He nodded to Raban, and the druid waved the vines away from Searil's ankles. Gaston shoved Searil aside and moved on to Thokas.

The orc struggled against the vines' firm hold, but grunted as he was still held firm and bleeding from the thorns. "P—please, sir. I beg you . . ."

Gaston's expression remained stony. He kneed Thokas in the groin. The orc dropped to his knees with a howl. Gaston gave Raban another nod, to dismiss the entanglement spell.

He grabbed a tuft of Thokas's scraggly hair and yanked his head to one side. As he had done with Searil, Gaston carved the brand from Thokas's neck and shoved him into the dirt, where the orc lay gasping and bleeding.

Gaston wiped his bloody blade on Searil's robes, sheathed it, and then spun around and faced the ring of pale-faced onlookers. "Honor is not won through selfishly sacrificing others." His voice boomed, and he pointed at those who watched. "You would do well to remember that, all of you."

Carver gasped and ducked his head behind the tent to avoid Gaston's gaze. *I sure hope I don't get on his bad side.*

Something furry brushed against his leg. He jumped from his hiding spot with a yelp. A weasel was slinking away toward a tent. Carver exhaled and relaxed. *Ha! He must be looking for breakfast.*

*   *   *

Gaston faced the rest of his men. "Let this be a warning—to *all* of you." Gaston glanced at Raban—who answered with look of contempt—then turned to leave. "Now, let us break camp."

He took a step and felt a sharp pain in his lower back. Several of his comrades gasped.

Rattled, Gaston reached back for the source of the pain. He grabbed the hilt of a small throwing knife lodged in a gap in his cuirass and tugged, grunting. When he yanked the blade out and examined it, it was covered with blood—*his* blood.

* * *

Raban's eyes widened in astonishment. "We are under attack!"

The other warriors scrambled about in a panic, unsheathing their weapons. One of them ran to Gaston. "Sir!"

Gaston flung the dagger to the ground. "Warn everyone!" he ordered, returning to his tent as he held his injury. "Guard the egg! To arms!"

Raban looked around wildly for the attacker, then heard a faint squeaking sound above him. He snapped his gaze up to look at the red-orange sky. The small fruit bat he saw had an unnatural aura. Raban raised his fists, and called forth the spirits of nature. He transformed into a crow and flew off, chasing after the bat.

* * *

"They're scareder than a 'erd of deer!" Nester beamed proudly at Kaijin and Omari.

Maybe. Kaijin wasn't entirely convinced.

Omari frowned and carefully pushed a stray branch out of his line of sight. The three had posted themselves not far outside the camp's perimeter, with an ideal view of its center. "Thank Malik your little stunt did not expose us, Nester." He glared at the brownie.

"'Stunt'? Now look 'ere, mate. If I wanted to be seen, I'd 'ave done so."

"Enough, you two," Kaijin cut in. "Remember the plan?" *We attack from the south; Sigmund, Zarya, and Aidan flank from the north. Then we take advantage of the uproar.* He turned to Omari. "Did Percival find anything?"

Omari's gaze went distant. "He has tracked the scent of the egg. It will not be long before it is located. How is Miele faring?"

Kaijin shook his head slowly. "She's not found anything yet. She will alert me if—" Pain cut him off. He looked to the sky, hearing Miele's panicked fluttering, followed by a squawk and the sound of larger wings flapping.

"What is it, Kaijin?" Omari asked.

"Miele . . ." Kaijin muttered. "I must save her. I will catch up with you."

Omari gawked at him. "Are you mad? We have to do this together if we intend to succeed!"

"Oy! What are you two waitin' for?" Nester motioned for Omari and Kaijin to follow. "Let's go before th' blokes get themselves organized!"

Kaijin glared at Omari. "Miele is in trouble. I have to help her. Go, now!" Another surge of pain pounded in his head, and he winced, dropping to his knees. "Erg!"

"Kaijin!" Nester exclaimed.

Omari stuck out his arm and barred the brownie from stepping closer. "Wait." He scanned the sky briefly and withdrew his quarterstaff from behind him. A crackle of electrical energy leapt from his weapon hand.

Nester flinched. "Woah! Watch it! I don't feel like gettin' shocked again, aye!"

Omari uttered "*Fulgori*" toward the sky, summoning a bolt of lightning.

Gasping, Kaijin lunged at Omari, in his last attempt to break his concentration. "No! Don't hurt her!"

But it was too late.

Kaijin shut his eyes, preparing for the pain—perhaps for death itself. Several seconds went by, but he remained mentally unscathed. Instead of Miele's death cries, Kaijin heard something else—the raspy cries of a crow. He opened his eyes and gazed at the dawn sky. The bird soared unsteadily toward the camp, a portion of its tailfeathers ablaze. It didn't make it very far, though, and crash-landed in the brush several paces away from them.

"Soddin 'ells! Did you see that?" Nester stood on tiptoe to get a view of the smoking crow. "Strange, that was!"

Omari pushed Kaijin aside and approached the fallen bird cautiously. "Strange, indeed. All the more reason for me to shoot it down."

Kaijin was about to reply when he felt Miele approach. She landed on his shoulder, shrieking happily. He smiled and stroked her underbelly. *"Miele! Thank the gods you're safe."*

As they drew nearer, a strange transformation overtook the crow. It grew and reformed into a man, who rolled over and extinguished the fire that smoldered on the hem of his black robe.

Nester blinked. "A man?"

"Not just a man—a mage," Kaijin said.

The corner of Omari's lip curled. "Not just a mage. A renegade."

XX

ദ്ദ

The crow-turned-man drew himself up and glared at Kaijin, Nester, and Omari. "How *dare* you call me some filthy mage!" he spat. He got up and brushed himself off. "I am Raban, and my powers far exceed the unnatural scope of the arcane."

Kaijin raised an eyebrow. "How, exactly?"

Omari studied the dark-robed man a moment and then shook his head. "He is right. He is no mage. I do not feel an arcanic aura about him."

"What? Then how do you explain—" Kaijin stopped himself and realized Omari was right. Raban's aura radiated something unfamiliar. He'd never felt anything like it before, and it was certainly nothing he recalled from Jarial's teachings.

Nester sniffed at Raban and wrinkled his nose. "Nay, 'e ain't a fiddler. 'E's a foresty bloke. They always smell like old cabbage."

Omari confronted Raban, his hands clenching his quarterstaff. Lightning crackled from the tip of the staff. "You bear the symbol of the Legion on your robe." He scowled and spat at Raban's feet. "I will only ask you once. Where is the egg?"

The druid chuckled darkly. "You think I am intimidated by your magic?" He extended his glowing fists to the ground. Moments later, vines began to sprout from the soil.

Kaijin, Omari, and Nester jumped back. Miele flew off Kaijin's shoulder and hovered just above him.

Omari positioned his staff defensively. "Get going, you two! I will handle him."

Kaijin stepped forward, reaching for Omari's shoulder. Electricity arched from Omari's body to Kaijin's hand, and Kaijin yelped and jerked it away.

Kaijin's cry made Nester gasp and instinctively rest his hand on the hilt of one of the daggers sheathed at his belt.

With his eyes glowing white, Omari swept a quick, sidelong glance at Kaijin. "Confound it! I said 'Go!' You two must help the others!" The vines drew closer to Omari's feet and began twining around his ankles. Omari unleashed his lightning spell, searing the grasping vines to ash.

Kaijin started following Nester, then stopped to look over his shoulder.

Raban smirked. "So you want to play with lightning, do you, mage?" He stretched his hand toward the sky and began chanting in an unfamiliar language. His hand emanated a green glow, and he closed his fist. Grey clouds formed, blotting out the morning light and dimming the area. Raban quickly lowered his fist in front of his face. A bolt of lightning shot down from the sky toward Omari, but the mage raised his staff toward the bolt just as it struck him. A near-deafening crack of thunder followed.

White, blinding light encompassed Omari. His eyes lit up, pupilless, and his entire body jolted. He stumbled backward and redirected the lightning from his staff toward the druid.

The counter-attack knocked Raban off his feet. He stood back up. Omari went at him more swiftly than before with seemingly renewed energy. Raban called forth more spiraling vines to block the incoming mage, creating a tangled, thorny thicket of plants that seemed to move on their own.

Kaijin moved to assist Omari, but Nester grabbed his hand and tugged him away from the danger. "Nay, Kaijin. We should go before that foresty bloke starts shootin' lightnin' at us next!"

"But—!" In his gut, Kaijin knew Nester was right. He reluctantly followed Nester toward the southernmost part of the camp.

Men and women scrambled from their tents to fend off attacks from Sigmund, Aidan, and Zarya. Miele flew around above the camp, and then dove for one of the tents. As Aidan stood his ground, Kaijin could see the rage in his eyes. Aidan savagely attacked one of his opponents with his claws, effortlessly ripping through scale armor like paper. After his victim had fallen, an unknown caster unleashed a binding spell at Aidan, which trapped the giant in place.

Zarya rushed to his side. Her eyes darted back and forth, searching unsuccessfully for the spell's caster. She summoned a shield of blinding light around them both. Two attackers flanking them dropped to their knees, cried out, and covered their eyes.

"Goddess have mercy . . ." Sigmund drove his longsword through the back of one of the warrior's necks, severing the spinal cord. He impaled the other through the liver.

"Sigmund! Look out!" Zarya jumped to her feet.

As Sigmund withdrew his blade from one of the corpses, another warrior shoved him from behind. Sigmund grunted as he fell, and the warrior closed in, his weapon pointed at Sigmund's throat.

"You get Zarya. I'll get Sigmund." Nester told Kaijin, then ran out to help their comrades.

Kaijin began heading toward Zarya, but his steps slowed as he felt his feet grow heavy. He looked at the ground. Everything seemed normal, but somehow, he was unable to run.

What's going on? I feel like I'm walking through mud! As Kaijin struggled, someone grabbed his arms from behind, immobilizing him. Panic fluttered in Kaijin's chest as he desperately attempted to locate his assailant.

A man in a cloak materialized in front of Kaijin.

"Our brethren will be avenged—starting with you." The man raised a fist that glowed red.

Gritting his teeth, Kaijin struggled against his captor, but he was held fast. Kaijin felt the fire charm slip out from beneath his robe's collar as he struggled. "Your men attacked my companions. You stole a Dragon's egg!" Kaijin panted.

Not far away, Miele flew out of a tent, followed by Percival. The two animals dispersed, Miele returning to the sky, while Percival scampered out of the camp.

The cloaked man laughed. "The Legion does not steal, *boy*—they earn."

Kaijin's left eye twitched. The man's jeer ignited rage deep inside him. "I am *not* a boy!"

The man raised his fist, about to chant a spell, and his gaze focused on Kaijin's necklace. The man's eyes reflected the charm's pulsating, fiery glow. "What is this?" he whispered, lowering his hand.

Kaijin felt the heat of the charm, and he struggled to get out of the man's grip. *They must never have it.* "No! Stay away! Leave it alone!"

"Keep him still," the cloaked man ordered his armored comrade. "Amazing. Gaston would love to have something like this."

No! Kaijin attempted to kick the cloaked man, but his feet remained like stone. The more he struggled, the more his captor's iron grip tightened. His shoulders strained under the pressure.

The cloaked man grabbed the necklace. His face contorted in pain, and he quickly uttered a spell; an orange glow encompassed his grasping hand.

Kaijin wanted to burn him to death, but he was too distraught to concentrate on a single spell. *He can't . . . He won't have it!* He smelled burning flesh.

The cloaked man snapped the hemp cord from Kaijin's neck.

"What is that thing, Devyn?" the armored man asked.

Devyn grimaced and hissed, quickly prying the charm from his flesh and holding the necklace by the broken cord. He glanced at the imprint scalded into his palm. "I don't know, but I will find out soon enough. Find what other valuables he has on him, then kill him and go help the others deal with his friends." He turned and walked away.

"Yes, sir," the armored man responded.

Kaijin swallowed. The world around him blurred. He felt naked, as if a piece of him had been taken away. *"Ignis!"* his mind called out. But there was no response. Kaijin's heart raced.

So I am truly alone. I have finally lost everything I've ever loved. . . .

He went limp. He no longer had the strength or will to fight back. The armored man jostled him and shoved him to the ground. He ripped Kaijin's haversack from him and tossed it away. The orb spilled out through a gap in the top.

Kaijin curled up and awaited his fate. The last thing he saw before his eyes closed was the orb emitting a faint, fiery glow.

* * *

Aidan felt no pain, only rage and contempt. The sensation confused and frightened him. Was it instinct? *Slayers are your enemy,* he kept hearing in his mind. Though he was not a full Dragon, he shared their sentiments. It was time to bring those lowlifes to justice—for his blood's sake.

Zarya summoned a shield of light, shattering the spell that restrained his arms and legs.

Aidan sought the caster and then sniffed the air. The mage was well hidden, but his scent was strong. Aidan followed the trail, ignoring the two warriors closing in on Zarya and Sigmund.

"Aidan! Where are you going?" Zarya yelled after him.

Focused on his unseen enemy, he didn't respond.

"Zarya and I are being flanked, Aidan!" Sigmund called.

Another scent caught Aidan's attention. *Gaston.* Aidan ran. The trail was hot, and he would not let anything stop him.

He followed the trail to a large tent. His invisible assailant fizzled into view out of thin air, blocking his way.

Aidan narrowed his eyes and growled at the red-cloaked human, who quickly retrieved something small from his belt pouch. "Where is Kyniythyria's child?"

The mage stepped backwards, closing his hand over the dark-colored object. He uttered a phrase, and his hands glowed purple.

Aidan stepped forward. "Aidan asked you question!"

Something large and firm bashed him from behind. Aidan grunted and fell flat on his face.

Gaston secured a steel shield to his back and loomed over Aidan. "So, the half-breed pacifist has finally shown his true nature."

Aidan dug his claws into the ground and bared his fangs. His voice crossed from his own to an animal's growl. "Gaston . . ."

Gaston tilted his head. "My, what has incited such rage in you, my friend? It is something worth studying your corpse over. I have a few friends that would love to acquire you for their research—and they are willing to pay quite a large sum, too. But first . . . Devyn?" Gaston nodded to the mage behind him.

Devyn returned the nod and, smirking, unleashed two bands of purple light that extended toward Aidan.

Aidan roared and snarled, twisting, trying to get away, but the bonds restrained his hands and feet. He turned his head and glared at Gaston, vision going red.

What is this? The red scared Aidan, and yet he knew what he had to do. Something sharp prodded in the side of his neck; Aidan suspected it was Gaston's sword. He winced, closed his eyes, and took a deep breath.

"Carver, now begins your first test," Gaston said. "Come here and make your first kill."

Footsteps approached Aidan from the side. "Y . . . yes, sir."

Carver? Aidan exhaled and opened his eyes. Carver had donned scale armor that bore the Legion's symbol. The eagerness and enthusiasm Aidan remembered had left the boy's face; all that remained was fear and uncertainty.

Carver took the sword from Gaston and slowly aimed it at Aidan, but he did not attack.

"Hurry up, boy!" Gaston barked. "We must deal with the rest of his friends."

Aidan's rage ebbed, leaving a hollow sadness. "Carver . . ."

Carver swallowed and bit his bottom lip. "I can't believe I trusted you, Aidan. I had no idea you were so dangerous."

"No, Carver," Aidan said. "Gaston has deceived you."

"But your kind has killed innocent people!"

"No, that is not true."

Gaston scowled. "Enough. Give me that." He snatched the sword from Carver. "Hesitation means failure, Carver. You have failed this day. You are not worthy of joining us. You seem to still hold some feelings toward this stinking half-breed."

Carver gasped. "N–no, sir! I swear, I pledged my allegiance to you and the Legion!" He tried to grab the sword, but Gaston shoved him away. Carver stumbled and hit the ground hard.

Aidan's rage returned, and he fought the magical bonds. He dug down deep and tapped into something he had never touched before, something that felt strangely familiar.

He stared at Gaston. He recognized the man's scent, yet he didn't know how. It was blood—*Dragon* blood. Aidan deflated a little. "Aidan has question."

Gaston raised a curious brow and looked back at Aidan. "A final question before your death?" He smirked. "Very well, half-breed. Entertain me."

"Where did you get that armor?"

Gaston blinked. After a moment, he laughed. "My . . . armor? A rather odd but ironic question to ask. I suppose I can understand your curiosity. It's quite lovely, isn't it? I paid a hefty sum for it on the black market a few years ago. The armorsmith, also a brother of our cause, obtained the Dragon scales himself. The female he'd slain was rumored to have also been a descendant of a royal Dragon clan that has been extinct for over three hundred years. Amazing, is it not? My armor has history and purpose. That is why I wear it proudly. Now that I've answered your question, it's time for you to answer mine—in blood."

Aidan widened his eyes. *Royal clan?*

"I've smelled your type before," Kyniythyria had told him, the night after Aidan and his comrades were taken to her cave. "Long ago, there was a clan of silver kin, called the Koraseru, who were rulers of the Great North. Every Dragon of Exodus knew of the Koraseru Clan. It was believed that they possessed a power that was bestowed upon them by the goddess.

"Unfortunately, their reputation also gained the attention of slayers and fiends. The clan scattered, but they were uncovered, one by one, and killed. The clan was deemed extinct. You may be a descendant. If that is true, then you must find a way to restore your bloodline."

With Gaston about to kill him, Aidan jerked up, straining the purple bonds.

"He's strong, sir!" Devyn exclaimed, grimacing. "I don't know . . . where this strength has come from . . . but I can't . . ."

Aidan's blood boiled. He could feel the spell weakening the more he moved. With a ferocious growl, Aidan strained his arms and chest and tore through the magical bonds in a rage.

He lunged at Gaston, who stared.

Aidan smirked. Claws extended, he reached for Gaston's throat.

Out of the corner of his eye, Aidan glimpsed a flash of light just over the tops of the tents. Something large emerged from beyond them—something much larger than he was.

People screamed. Brimstone and blood scented the air.

A grotesque creature towered over the crowd of frightened men. Its crimson body burned like fire.

It easily dwarfed Aidan, and its body rippled with muscles. Its gruesome face sparked fear in Aidan. The cold fury in its turquoise eyes drove deep into his soul. For the moment, Aidan forgot Gaston, and his rage quickly subsided.

He heard a sword hit the ground with a muffled clang, as well as a whisper: "What in Tydus's name . . ."

Fire licked the monster's red body, but its flesh didn't burn. It smiled at the chaos around it—people screaming and fleeing for their lives, horses scrambling to get to safety—as parts of the camp went up in flames. The monster summoned balls of fire in its massive clawed hands and hurled them at tents and fleeing victims alike, until the entire camp became a raging inferno. A thick, choking smoke rose from the flames and blanketed the area.

That creature . . . So intriguing, yet so destructive! What on Exodus is it? Aidan almost didn't notice when Gaston wriggled away. He went to grab him again, but Gaston had grabbed his sword and kept it between them.

Gaston scrambled to his feet and yelled to his remaining comrades, "Retreat! Everyone retreat!" He fled, crashing into Carver as the boy ran by, knocking him down. Gaston stumbled, but remained on his feet.

Carver grunted. "Sorry, sir!"

Gaston kicked Carver in the ribs. "Stupid boy. Out of my way!"

Carver cried out, and his body folded in pain.

Gaston motioned to one of the fleeing men, who carried a large sack. Gaston snatched the sack from the man, kicked him aside, and fled.

When Gaston had gone, Aidan made his way to Carver, scooped him up into his arms, and followed the fleeing group.

* * *

Outside the camp, not far away, a fantastic display of elemental magic flashed across the sky and ground. Gratefully, Zarya's energy boost to Omari's mind and body still buoyed him. Without it, Omari knew he surely would've fallen prey to Raban's spells.

Raban's attacks with the thorny vines and briars were weakening. Omari quickly countered the attacks with destructive lightning bolts, which shot from his staff and singed the wild plants where they sprouted.

"Is that all you can do, mage?" Raban jeered. Sweat beaded over his face as he concentrated and chanted more phrases. A slight breeze whistled through the area. Thunder rumbled, and the wind quickly intensified, whirling into a powerful tempest. Hail fell from the sky and pelted Omari. The winds concentrated around him, lifting him, whipping through his clothing. Omari gripped his quarterstaff, his knuckles turning white as he tried to concentrate. "*Tueri . . . elementa . . .*" An invisible barrier surrounded him, shielding him from the tempest. He fell back to the ground.

The camp glowed, aflame, and a creature rose up from the inferno. Shocked, Omari dismissed his spell. The storm also dissipated.

"Enough of this stalling, mage," Raban spat. "I have more important things to deal with." He transformed into a crow and flapped his wings, cawing mockingly at Omari.

The sight of the camp—as well as Raban's sudden withdrawal—stunned Omari only briefly.

"*Tenae*," Omari said.

A small bolt of lightning shot from his finger toward Raban.

The bolt became an electrified shield that surrounded Raban and held him in place.

"Not so fast." Omari walked to the crow and disabled the shield to seize the shape-shifting druid. He held the bird with both hands and squeezed its body tight, crushing bones. "You challenged me—therefore, you will finish the fight."

Raban squawked as Omari squeezed more tightly. Omari could feel Raban attempting to shift back into a man, but Omari managed to break the druid's concentration.

An electric current surged through Omari's body and into Raban's, shooting thousands of volts into the bird until its feathers caught fire. Raban cawed loudly, his voice becoming more garbled as he burned.

The bird fell silent, and Omari smelled charred feathers and flesh. *Should have tried that sooner.*

* * *

Kaijin remained on his side, and he smiled darkly at the monster standing before him, a creature like the one in his dream.

A roaring blaze appeared around its bare, clawed foot, then traveled up the rest of its body. Kaijin closed his eyes to relish the flames' heat.

He felt himself be seized and set on his feet, and he opened his eyes again. Kaijin stared into the monster's soulless eyes.

It spoke to him, its voice hissing and crackling like fire. *"They must die. Show no mercy. Show them the true power of the Firelord."*

Kaijin's smile widened. The firm voice soothed his mind. The red-orange hue around him changed to pure white, flickering light.

His strength returned to him, ten-fold. He instinctively reached for the fiery charm around his neck, but it was gone. He gasped, remembering the theft, looked to the monster, and frowned.

The monster nodded once. *"Find it."*

Without hesitation, Kaijin set off into the blazing camp. He clenched his fists, and white fire blazed around them. The world appeared to burn before his eyes.

They took the one and only thing most precious to me. His blood boiled. *They dared steal my necklace.*

He hurled balls of white fire at two fleeing warriors, and their bodies were instantly consumed by the flames. Fire roared louder throughout the camp, echoing Kaijin's fury.

Kaijin spotted Devyn, the one who had stolen his charm, lagging behind his comrades who fled the burning camp. The man scrambled to keep up with his leader. Kaijin looked back at the creature. *"That is him."*

Grinning, the monster approached Devyn. With its massive claws, it scooped four people—Devyn, Carver, Gaston, and Aidan—lifting them up and holding them in front of its face.

It plucked Devyn from the group and held him in its other hand. Devyn screamed and wriggled about helplessly.

The monster paused, watching him, then closed its fist around Devyn, silencing his scream. The creature's fist blazed for a few moments and then went dark.

When the creature opened its fist, all that remained was the charm, buried in ashes that blew away in a passing wind.

Gaston's grip loosened on the sack he held, and it dropped.

Kaijin ran toward the creature, focused on the charm in its hand. He beamed, relief spreading through him, and he waited eagerly for the creature to give it to him.

"Kaijin! The egg!" Zarya yelled from behind him.

Kaijin turned and watched the priestess, who sprinted toward the falling sack, her hand extended, praying quickly, "*Almighty Goddess, I beseech your power to extend your gentle hand upon your endangered child to soften the fall.*"

A glow of white light streamed from Zarya's hand and encompassed the falling sack. The sack slowed its descent.

Disregarding the dangers around her, she lunged at the sack, catching it in her arms an instant before it hit the ground. She and the sack tumbled to the ground. The back of her breastplate crashed into the creature's massive foot; she gasped, winded.

The men Sigmund had been fighting had all fled in fear of the flaming creature. Sigmund turned to the monster, pointed his sword toward it, and shouted, "Creature of the flames, you have done enough damage to please your master. Now, by Celestra's holy light, return to the Realm of Fire, from whence you came!"

A beam of light, white and golden, shot forth from the blade. The attack penetrated the creature's burning skin, but it remained unharmed.

The monster's attention briefly shifted from Zarya to Sigmund. It stared, eyes narrowed, at the guardian, who frowned.

Nester sprinted past Sigmund, hiding himself in the shadows on the ground as he made his way to Zarya.

Kaijin focused on his necklace, but the creature paid him little mind. Instead, its attention returned to Zarya, who remained at its foot. It dropped the necklace, flung Aidan, Gaston, and Carver into the wilderness, and raised its foot over Zarya and Nester, eclipsing them in a large shadow.

Kaijin caught the necklace with both hands. A surge of warmth and assurance spread through every fiber of his being. *At last.*

He grinned. The charm pulsed, attuning itself to Kaijin's heartbeat. He donned the necklace, re-knotting the hemp cord around his neck. The charm heated his chest; it felt heavenly.

Reality set in once more, unusually clear. Nester and Zarya were about to be crushed beneath the creature's foot.

Kaijin blinked and then concentrated his mind on the creature. *"No! They are friends!"*

* * *

For a moment, Aidan was unsure where he was. His head still spun. He vaguely recalled being in the clutches of a gruesome creature.

He first thought he might be dead—but Carver and Gaston were regaining consciousness beside him. They'd some distance away from the Legion's camp, but the creature loomed over its burning remains.

Gaston stirred. He got up awkwardly and groaned in pain. His armor was battered. He stumbled forward a few steps, but managed to maintain his footing and stood upright. "I may have lost my men, but I will not lose my greatest prize," he growled, scowling at Aidan. His gaze then focused on the flaming creature. "That thing took my egg."

How dare he! Aidan sprang up and yelled, "That is *not* your egg!" but Gaston ignored him.

Carver slowly stood and moaned, clutching his shoulder. He recovered himself. "Sir, should we not leave? We have lost our men. There is no way we can face that thing alone!"

Gaston hissed and backhand Carver across the mouth. "You are no longer a Legionnaire, Carver! If you want to cower and run, then do so! I will not leave until that egg is once again mine!"

Aidan was about to intervene when he picked up the faintest scent of the egg amid a blanket of smoke and ash. His attention turned toward the burning camp. He remembered Kyniythyria's voice: "*Restore your bloodline.*"

Without another thought, Aidan sprinted back toward the camp.

*   *   *

The monster stopped short of stomping Zarya and Nester, and it glowered at Kaijin. "*The Firelord does not have 'friends,' mortal.*"

Kaijin met the monster's gaze and gulped.

Screaming and crying for help, Zarya and Nester scrambled away. White-knuckled, Zarya clutched the knot of the bag.

Sigmund drove his glowing sword up into the creature's foot and ripped it back out. Fire erupted from the wound, and Sigmund quickly summoned a protective shield around him to ward off the flame that rained down from above.

The monster roared and withdrew its foot. The wound quickly closed on its own. The monster locked its eyes on the guardian.

Sigmund raised his glowing sword, ready to strike again, expression determined. The monster advanced and raised its foot to stomp on Sigmund. The fire surrounding its body intensified.

Kaijin ran toward Sigmund. He got sideswiped by Aidan, who went barreling past.

Aidan grabbed Zarya with one hand and snatched the bag from her with the other, animalistic frenzy burning in his eyes.

Zarya grunted and struggled to get free of Aidan's grip. "Aidan! What are you doing? We must help the others!"

Aidan released her but clung to the bag and fled the burning camp.

Kaijin eyed the monster. *"The Firelord does not have friends, but he seems to have allies, for I am somehow His tool. These people have helped me in fulfilling the Firelord's tasks. Destroying them will not bode well for you, should your master find out."*

The monster halted and snarled at Kaijin. It reluctantly retracted its foot. *"They took your necklace too easily. Next time, your carelessness will not be spared, Kaijin Sora."*

The burning flames around the creature converged into its body, becoming smaller until only the orb remained.

The flames dissipated. The land was charred, covered with cooling embers and rising coils of white smoke, highlighting smoldering remains of debris. The air reeked of ash and death.

Kaijin froze in awe of the monster's departure. *Did he really listen to me out of fear? Or something else?*

It would be an answer he'd most likely not find out in his lifetime—if ever.

He slowly approached the orb, which still pulsated with its usual fiery glow. It was hot to the touch, yet soothing in Kaijin's hands. Energy rushed through him as he held the orb. He gazed upon it. *"So, it is you who lives in there."*

The fiery voice whispered, *"Do not attempt to fathom my power, mortal."*

Kaijin swallowed and tore his gaze from the orb. Sigmund and Zarya slowly drew nearer. Nester appeared from the shadows and followed the others.

"Inconceivable . . ." Sigmund's gaze was fixated on the orb.

Nester hid behind Sigmund, expression still shocked, his face devoid of all color. He was rendered speechless—for once.

Zarya was still trembling. She bowed her head and spoke a prayer of assurance and calmness. Her voice became firm and lent a much-needed tranquility to the scene.

Kaijin smiled, showered by the warmth and beauty of Zarya's prayer and the assurance of Miele, who settled on his shoulder and softly screeched.

Sigmund turned a hard gaze on Kaijin. "Are we dealing with afriti now?"

Kaijin blinked. "What?" The name sounded familiar.

"Has that monster been living inside that orb this entire time?" Sigmund asked.

"I . . . I don't know. This is the first time I've seen it come out."

"Afriti . . ." Zarya muttered. "Ferocious beings of fire. They have been known to level cities and towns with flames—kill entire populations. . . ."

Kaijin and Sigmund looked at the priestess.

"P-p-*populations*?" Nester repeated.

"I realize what it is, Zarya," Sigmund said. "What I want to know is what it's doing in that orb. And why." He looked back at Kaijin.

Kaijin locked his eyes at the guardian. "How in the hells am I supposed to know? I didn't tell it to come out!"

"You are the only one who can hold the orb like you do." Sigmund pointed at the orb in Kaijin's hands. "You obviously have some authority over it."

Kaijin fell silent and looked at what he held.

"Moreover," Sigmund continued, "I was unable to even harm it when I attacked. I sense rage and fury in the creature, and yet, I could also feel some sort of divine aura about it. It doesn't make sense."

Nester blinked at Sigmund. "Wha—what're you sayin,' mate? That . . . fiery thing's a god or somethin'?"

"No," Sigmund promptly replied, "I'm not saying that, but . . ."

"Perhaps not a god, but a manifestation of one? Or a servant?" Zarya suggested.

Kaijin swallowed. He continued staring at the orb, not wanting to face his companions.

"Afriti thrive in the Realm of Fire—not an orb," Sigmund said. "Unless, it is a beacon of some sort—a link from the mortal realm to the Realm of Fire. I don't know. But while this orb remains in our possession, I remain wary of that horrid creature paying us another visit."

Kaijin stuffed the orb back in the bag. "I don't think the creature will come out anymore."

Sigmund scoffed. "Are you certain, Kaijin?"

"No, but if I have authority over it like you say, then I can tell it to stay in the orb, right?"

"You think it's that simple?"

Kaijin scowled. "Do you have any better ideas?"

"... No, I suppose not."

"Let's just tread carefully from now on," Zarya broke in. "Let's avoid towns, cities, and any other densely-populated areas. We are still taking the orb to The Pyre, right?"

Kaijin nodded. "Yes. I think it belongs there. Maybe the clergy there can shed some light on some other things, as well." He'd hoped the suggestion would satisfy Sigmund, but the guardian still kept a narrow watch on Kaijin, as though he were a dangerous criminal.

Kaijin sighed. "Where's Aidan and—"

He spotted Omari approaching the camp, bloody and walking with a slight limp, with something in his hand. Percival walked alongside him.

The four of them rushed to meet Omari, relieved that he was still alive. Omari held up the cooked corpse of a crow and smiled thinly. "This is what happens when someone challenges me."

Zarya grimaced.

"Ugh! What in th' soddin' 'ells is *that?*" Nester asked, making a face.

The sight also revolted Kaijin, but he maintained his composure as best he could.

Sigmund crossed his arms and regarded Omari, stone-faced. "Your point has been proven, Omari. Now, get rid of that gruesome thing."

Frowning, Omari tossed the bird-corpse into a pile of ashes. "So this is what remains of the camp? To whom do we owe this glorious destruction?" He eyed Kaijin, smirking.

"This is no time for your little quips, Omari." Kaijin frowned. "We need to find Aidan and that egg."

"He took it right out of my hands and fled!" Zarya said. "To where, I don't know."

"Perhaps back to the Mistress?" Sigmund asked.

She slowly shook her head. "He's been acting strangely as of late."

Nester raised an eyebrow. "Aye? I didn't know 'e was actin' *normal* before."

"We must find him and the egg at all costs," Sigmund said. "Or we will *all* face Her wrath."

XXI

‿‿

Aidan fled until he was satisfied that the egg was far enough from the camp to be safe. He stopped to rest, and from where he stood, he watched light consume the camp. As the glow spread, he worried about his friends, but his urge to protect the egg and keep it safe was greater than his concern for them. He fidgeted with the knot on the bag while he mused.

I am not a coward. The sound of footsteps approaching snapped Aidan back to the present. He clutched the bag close to his body.

Gaston drew nearer with Carver slung over his shoulder. Gaston stopped in front of Aidan and dumped Carver at his feet.

Aidan's lip curled, and a growl of distaste rumbled in his throat.

"A trade," Gaston said coolly. "The boy for what's in that bag. No violence, no hard feelings."

Groaning, Carver lifted his face from the dirt, and he gazed at Aidan pleadingly.

Aidan glanced from Carver to Gaston and bared his fangs. "Do not take Aidan for fool."

Gaston lifted his eyebrow. "Of course not. I just thought you would have more feelings for this boy than you would for an egg. An advantageous trade, wouldn't you say?"

"Aidan, I'm sorry," Carver whimpered. "I should've listened to you. Please don't let him hurt me."

"Shut up, boy!" Gaston drove his heel into Carver's back, causing the boy to let out a yelp.

Aidan winced in sympathy. Seeing Carver being abused left a bad taste in his mouth.

"Well, Aidan?" Gaston asked. "Are you going to give me what is mine, or not?"

"This does not belong to you," Aidan retorted.

Gaston scowled. "So it seems you would rather do this the hard way." He drew his sword and slipped the blade under the top shoulder seams of Carver's armor, slicing them through.

Aidan swallowed. *No . . . but if I interfere . . . I must protect the egg.*

Gaston put the point of his blade against the tunic on Carver's back.

Carver froze. "No!" Gaston planted his boot on Carver's back, smashing him into the dirt.

Gaston looked coldly at Aidan. "I can keep going." He pushed ever so slightly on the sword and Carver cried.

Aidan gritted his teeth at Carver's reaction but did not let go of the bag. *I cannot. I . . . .* He barely repressed the fury. "Only a coward would kill helpless boy."

Gaston laughed and pressed the sword deeper. "What do you know about courage, Aidan? Half-breeds like you are the bane of this world: too lowly to be accepted by your own pure-blooded Dragonkind, and too repulsive to be accepted by the rest of society. Half-breeds are like festering wounds that won't heal. Now, give me that egg!"

No, I must stop Carver's suffering . . . but . . . Aidan clenched the bag's knotted top more tightly. "No. There is no need for death. It solves nothing."

"You're insane, Gaston!" Carver shouted. "Get off me! Aidan, help!"

Aidan shut out Carver's voice and said to Gaston, "You will not kill him."

"Oh, no?" Gaston lifted his foot and drove his blade into the small of Carver's back. Carver screamed in agony.

Aidan froze. *This man really is evil.*

Gaston smirked. "All I have to do is give it a little twist and he will die a slow and painful death."

Aidan gently set the bag down.

"Good," Gaston nodded at Aidan. "Now, give it to me."

He frowned. He had a feeling he'd lose both Carver and the egg if he continued playing Gaston's game. "Aidan is no fool."

Gaston tilted his head. "Did you not hear me, Aidan? I am going to kill him."

"You will kill him regardless of what Aidan does."

"And what if I do? It's not like you can do anything about it. You are too much of a pacifist. You will not kill me. You've never killed."

You've never killed. . . . He *had* killed—only once in his life, true—but he still regretted it. He wanted to forget, but he couldn't. Would he be forced to add more darkness to his shame?

The more Aidan dwelled on his thoughts, the more Carver suffered.

"This is unnecessary," Aidan said softly. "Please do not force Aidan to do something he will regret."

"No, you will not kill me," Gaston jeered. "Because if you do, it will haunt you forever. You will have a huge bounty on your head. The Legion will find you and avenge my death. You will always be a fugitive. No one will trust you—not even your own kind. You will be forever shamed. As if you weren't already alone, half-breed."

"No, Aidan will not be shamed. He will have saved Dragon's child from evil slayers like you."

Gaston's smile quickly faded, and he slowly twisted his hand. Carver began screaming more loudly.

These weren't screams of pain—they were dying screams.

Aidan snapped.

He lunged at Gaston and tackled the Legionnaire to the ground, knocking the sword out of his hand. He tore at Gaston's armor, tearing the scales away and puncturing skin with his claws.

"You . . . you won't kill me," Gaston sputtered, blood running down the sides of his mouth. "You *can't* kill me . . . pacifist."

Aidan felt as though he'd entered a nightmare—his greatest fear. But he couldn't stop. He felt like he had to do this—he had to finish the job.

Gaston gagged and weakly looked up at Aidan. "My death . . . will only prove everyone right. That Dragons are a dangerous threat to society and must be . . . exterminated."

Aidan gritted his teeth, frustrated. His eyelids fluttered, feeling as though something had possessed him, he drove his claws into Gaston's neck and severed his windpipe and jugular.

Blood spurted; Gaston writhed, then went still. Blood dribbled on the ground beneath the jagged wound, coalescing between Aidan's fingers.

Aidan lowered his head and slowly withdrew his hand. He watched the warm, crimson liquid drip from his fingers, staining the ground. Gaston died looking right at him, the way Aidan's first victim had died, so long ago.

The image had etched into Aidan's mind, and he remained on his knees, staring at his shaking hand.

Carver stirred nearby and groaned in pain. "Aidan . . . Aidan . . ."

Aidan's gaze turned to the boy, but he did not respond. *There has been too much death already, and the day is not yet over.*

Carver's body twitched. He was barely able to swivel his head to gaze at Aidan. "Aidan, I . . . I can't feel my legs!"

Aidan focused on the burlap sack. He undid the knot, uncovered the egg, and examined its speckled surface. The urge to protect his kin was so strong that it frightened him. He rubbed his bloodstained hand over the egg's shell, checking it for cracks or other damage.

Blood smeared onto the surface. Aidan attempted to wipe it off, with little success. To his relief, the egg overall appeared safe and sound. Aidan tenderly nestled it back into the sack, re-knotted the top, and carried it over his shoulder. His feral urges subsided.

He went to Carver, who looked up at him with a face drawn with pain.

"Aidan," Carver whimpered. "My back . . . I can't move . . ."

Aidan carefully scooped Carver up with one arm and slung him over his other shoulder. He sniffed the air and caught the scent of Kaijin and the rest of his comrades not far away, faint amid the reek of smoke.

Slowly, Aidan began his trek back toward the camp's smoldering remains.

* * *

"Look! There 'e is!" Nester pointed toward Aidan in the distance amid large rocks and boulders that dotted the landscape. He ran ahead of the group to greet him.

"Nester, wait!" Kaijin flung his hand out, but the brownie was gone. *He couldn't even wait for us?* Kaijin sighed.

The group eventually caught up with Nester, who had stopped in his tracks and gawked at Aidan, who carried a boy in his arms. Aidan was bloody and looked exhausted. He barely acknowledged them.

Zarya gasped and rushed forward. "Aidan! What happened to you? Who is that?"

Aidan didn't respond. Instead, he laid the boy on the ground in front of Zarya. There was sadness in Aidan's eyes—and regret.

"Please, help me," the boy said weakly. He turned his head, trying to see everyone. His gaze settled on Zarya, who knelt beside him.

Zarya laid her hands lightly on him and spoke a prayer. The healing light came in answer. She released him.

"Your spine was almost severed. You are lucky to still be alive. What on Exodus happened?"

The boy stirred, and his face lit up. "Oh! I can move again! Thank you! Thank you!" He leaned on an elbow and slowly eased himself up to a sitting position.

"Will someone explain what in Celestra's name happened here?" Sigmund demanded.

Nester narrowed his eyes at the boy, scrutinizing him. "Wait, I think I've seen you before. Somewhere in Faywald, methinks, aye?"

The boy's gaze leaped from Sigmund to Nester. "I used to live in Faywald, yes. My name is Carver. I was recently recruited by Sir Gaston to join the Legion. I thought it would be a great opportunity to finally get off the streets and make something of myself. Gaston had me convinced that Aidan was evil, like all the other Dragonfolk. But Gaston hurt me and tried to hurt Aidan." He sighed and lowered his head. "I was such a fool. Aidan got injured because of me. I'm sorry, Aidan."

Aidan's gaze fixed blankly on the camp.

Zarya mended some minor scratches on Aidan's back, chest, and arms. "Something has happened. Aidan is in shock." She looked at him closely. "Can you hear me, Aidan?"

Aidan's gaze flicked to her briefly, then away again. They watered, but no tears came.

Nester stood before the giant and jumped up and down, waving his hands to get his attention, but Aidan didn't seem to notice. "Nope! 'E ain't 'ere."

Tension kept Kaijin on edge. The sensation came from Miele, who fluttered not far above him. He had her attention, and she beckoned him to follow.

He left the others, following the sounds of her flapping wings for a short distance, until he noticed a small mound further away. It looked like a human body.

Kaijin approached it but stopped when he was a few steps away. The armored man's face and body was maimed to the point of being almost unrecognizable. A large gaping hole replaced his throat.

"Looks dead to me," Omari said from behind him.

Kaijin jumped. *Did he follow me the entire time?* He exhaled and turned to the other mage. "Aidan could've not done this, could he? I mean, he doesn't like violence."

Omari studied the body. "Perhaps the afriti did it? . . . No, the claw marks are much too small. Perhaps it was a bear."

"These lands seem too sparse for bears." Kaijin paused. *Claws. Could it have been Aidan after all?*

Percival approached the corpse, sniffed it once, and then retreated back between Omari's ankles, shuddering.

Omari picked up his familiar and set Percival on his shoulder. "It is all right, my friend," he said aloud. "He is the way he should be: dead." He cast a dark look at Kaijin.

Nester skidded to a halt beside them. His eyes widened, and his jaw dropped. "Soddin 'ells! Is that . . ."

Nester tilted his head and squinted at the mutilated remains. "Aye. I remember that armor. Scalier than a fish! 'E was a big bloke, too! What *'appened* to 'im?"

"I don't know," Kaijin replied. "We found him this way. Omari suspects he was attacked by an animal of some kind."

Nester blinked. "Aye? Well it must've been a pretty big animal!"

"Did you know this man, Nester?" Omari eyed the brownie.

"If it's who I think it is, then aye. I remember 'im from back in Faywald. 'E was crazy enough to challenge Aidan to a fight! Aidan beat 'im, of course . . ." Nester suddenly scowled. "And that's when we won all that money and . . . Arg! Aidan was a soddin' fool and gave it all away to some orphanage. . . . Oh, all that money . . ."

Leaving the brownie to wallow, Kaijin and Omari joined the rest of the group.

"Find something?" Sigmund asked.

Kaijin and Omari exchanged glances.

"There's a . . . corpse back there," Kaijin said.

"A corpse?" Sigmund craned his head to see past Kaijin's shoulder toward the stretch of rocks and boulders beyond.

"Oh, Goddess . . ." Zarya whispered, rushing in the direction of the small mound in the distance.

Aidan had not moved from his spot, though his face had lost its usual silvery sheen and gone dull. He blinked once—the first time he'd blinked since he brought them Carver.

"Aidan, are you all right?" Sigmund asked.

Aidan clutched the knotted top of the bag. His mouth slowly opened.

"That corpse . . ." Carver said suddenly. "It's Gaston."

Sigmund's attention snapped to Carver. "Gaston? I've heard that name mentioned recently in my travels. He is a slayer." He scowled at the boy. "And you are working for him?"

Carver lowered his head. "Not anymore, sir."

"I am a Celestial guardian, appointed to protect the Dragons from slayers and other evil. Give me one reason why I should believe you."

Carver gasped. "A Celestial? A guardian of the Dragons? Oh, hells, I . . . I didn't realize—"

"Answer me this instant, boy."

"I—I swear it, sir! I swear I won't have anything to do with the Legion anymore! I will return home to my life on the streets and learn to enjoy it."

Sigmund observed the boy for a long moment and then rubbed his chin. "I have a better idea. But first, we need to return to the Mistress."

A tear rolled down Aidan's cheek, and he rubbed it away with the back of his fist. "Leave Carver alone. He had nothing to do with it. It is Aidan's fault that Gaston is dead."

All eyes turned to the giant.

"Wait . . . So you *did* kill him?" Kaijin asked.

Omari smiled thinly. "I knew that sinister side of you would be of use to us, Aidan."

"No, Aidan regrets what he has done," Aidan continued. "That is why Aidan does not like violence. Someone—"

"—always gets 'urt. Aye, aye, we know, Aidan," Nester finished with a roll of his eyes and a shrug.

"Unfortunately, violence was necessary this time." Kaijin said.

Aidan shook his head. "Violence is never 'necessary'. It is just convenient way to resolve problem."

Kaijin opened his mouth but closed it again quickly and thought about his response. "Sometimes, some of us do not have control over how we resolve problems," he said finally. "Sometimes we cannot change fate."

"Defeating him was part of the mission, Aidan," Sigmund explained. "He committed a crime—no, a *sin* against the goddess—by doing what he did. Not even I could detect any aura of goodness in that man's heart."

"But Aidan does not like killing," Aidan said.

"Not everyone likes killing, but justice must be served. Would you have let him live so that he could steal more eggs? Kill more Dragons? Sell their corpses for his own fame and monetary gain?"

Aidan hung his head.

"He was going to kill me, Aidan," Carver broke in. "And you, too!"

"There are black markets all over the world selling Dragon scales and body parts," Sigmund explained. "I would not be surprised if they were going to do the same to you, too, Aidan."

Omari's lip curled. "Despicable."

"Indeed, it is." Sigmund's expression mirrored Omari's distaste. "They care nothing for the well-being of others and care only about filling their pockets with gold. The death of this one man has saved the lives of countless others."

Kaijin nodded. "Take it for what it's worth, Aidan. You saved a baby Dragon. The Mistress will be very happy."

Aidan managed a small smile, but he looked back over his shoulder at Gaston's corpse. Zarya returned, her head hung low.

Omari huffed. "What are you so sad about?" he asked her.

Zarya looked up, regarding everyone solemnly. "I prayed for the goddess to take him."

"What? So you even pray over the corpses of enemies? I thought Celestials despised slayers?"

"We do," Sigmund broke in. "But as servants of the goddess, born of Her breath, we must ask Her to take their souls away and pronounce on them the final judgment that only She can give."

Zarya sighed. "I am ready."

Aidan slung the bag lightly over his shoulder and led the way back to Kyniythyria's mountain.

XXII

⳩

The return trip to Mallowyn Crags was a swift one. As the group began scaling Kyniythyria's mountain, Aidan, who had lagged behind, stopped. *Did the egg just move by itself?*

He waited to see if it would happen again. It did.

Startled, Aidan held the bag in front of him. He waited a few moments and saw the bag jerk.

"Aidan! What are you doing?" Sigmund called from up ahead, where the rest of the group had paused.

Aidan peered inside the bag to examine the egg. Its smooth, speckled surface twitched. The movement was too slight for most beings' eyes to notice, but he felt it, too.

He waved to his companions and smiled. "Aidan thinks egg may hatch very soon!"

The group stared, evidently stunned, as he approached.

"We must hurry, then," Zarya said.

*   *   *

The sun began setting by the time Kaijin and the others reached the mountain's peak. Kyniythyria poked her head out of her cave and greeted them. She hissed at the group, and then her cat-like eyes moved to Aidan. "Czylenemaraad! Oh! My child is safe!" She let out a low growl and eyed the rest of the group. "Who is that?"

Sigmund shoved Carver. "She means you, boy."

Carver gulped and cowered at the Dragon. "Ah . . . M–M–My n–name is Carver."

Aidan dropped to one knee, bowed his head, and carefully took the egg out of the bag, cradling it in his hands. He and Kyniythyria started speaking in a series of what sounded like growls and snarls to Kaijin.

Beside Kaijin, Nester was the first to mirror Aidan's actions and kneel. Everyone else followed suit until Kaijin was the last one left standing.

Miele landed on his shoulder and huddled her furry body against his neck. Kaijin bowed his head slightly, and glanced sidelong at Omari, who appeared to be in deep meditation. From the set of his shoulders, Omari had to be exhausted, and Kaijin could only assume that Zarya's spell was finally beginning to wear off. Percival nestled against Omari, his beady eyes drawn to the Dragon.

Kaijin quietly called to Zarya, trying to get her attention, but she remained focused on the conversation, so instead, he lightly nudged Nester. "Do you know what Aidan and the Mistress are saying?"

Nester kept a cautious eye on the two Dragonkin, and whispered, "Ah, not really, mate. But methinks she's 'appy to 'ave 'er child back, at least. Whether or not she's gonna kill us now? I've no soddin' idea."

Kaijin blinked. "What? But why would she kill us? We saved her child like she told us to."

"Aye, but . . . well, Dragons can be funny about that kinda stuff sometimes, y'know? She might think we took too long or somethin'."

"I sincerely hope not."

"Shh!" Zarya hushed, eyeing the two of them sternly.

Kyniythyria took the egg from Aidan and disappeared into the cave. Afterwards, Aidan stood, beamed at the others, and followed.

Kaijin stood and called, "Aidan, wait—" But it was too late.

"Follow me." Sigmund beckoned everyone who remained.

They followed the guardian inside to find Kyniythyria curled up in her nest, cradling the egg in her claws. Her tail was curled close to her body, and her wings were draped about her like a cloak. Aidan sat cross-legged before her, reverently staring at the egg as if his mere gaze alone would make it hatch.

Miele flew from Kaijin's shoulder and found a comfortable spot in a small shadowy alcove above. The rest of his companions gathered before the two Dragonkin and stood in silence.

The menacing cast to Kyniythyria's eyes had vanished; she seemed much more soft and generous—motherly. "Friends, I must thank you for rescuing my child. May the goddess bless you for your courageous effort."

Sigmund and Zarya promptly bowed their heads and each fell to one knee. Nester, Omari, and Carver followed suit. Kaijin shifted his gaze left and right, watching his companions, then—slowly—also knelt.

"We are truly honored to have been given this opportunity to do this for you, Great Mistress," Sigmund said. "Only a few of Gaston's men managed to escape, but I do not think they will cause any more trouble in this area for now. Justice has been served upon Gaston, the head of that small band of Legionnaires."

Sigmund grabbed Carver by the back of his tunic and shoved him forward. "Great Mistress, we found Carver with Aidan. He was apparently in the service of Gaston for a short period of time."

"Very short," Carver muttered, giving Sigmund a dirty look.

Kyniythyria's gaze hardened. Her muscles tensed slightly, and she drew the egg against her body. "Why have you brought him here?"

"Because, Great Mistress," Sigmund said respectfully, "he has seen the error of his ways and has chosen to cease his journey upon the evil path he had begun to follow. I would like your permission for him to accompany me so that I may train him to become a guardian."

Kyniythyria's claws loosened from the egg and her body relaxed. "A guardian? Really, now?"

Carver blinked, and he looked askance at the two of them.

Zarya furrowed her brow. "I thought only Celestials could be guardians."

"Technically, yes," Sigmund replied, "but that does not mean Carver can't help by other means. He can be a liaison for us, searching for slayers in places we may be unable to go. No one would suspect someone like Carver to be in the service of the Celestials and Dragons."

Nester tapped his chin. "Oh, I see. 'E can act as a spy for you folks, aye?"

Sigmund cleared his throat. "Yes, something like that."

"Wait, don't I have a say in anything?" Carver blurted. When all gazes turned on him, he cringed. ". . . Uh, never mind."

Kyniythyria let out a soft hiss at Carver, and then acknowledged Sigmund. "I think it is an acceptable idea. But be warned, guardian. His failure will mean your failure."

Sigmund bowed his head. "Of course, Great Mistress. Thank you." He yanked Carver back to him. "We will begin tomorrow."

"Tomorrow," Omari repeated. "Yes, tomorrow sounds good right about now." He yawned and scooted away from the group. He sat with his back against the wall and closed his eyes. Percival curled up in his lap and fell asleep.

"Not a bad idea, mate," Nester said, stretching. "I could go for a few winks." He, too, found a secluded spot and lay down.

Sigmund exchanged glances with Zarya, then the priestess left to find her own place to sleep. "Great Mistress, is that all for tonight, then?" Sigmund inquired of Kyniythyria.

Kyniythyria nodded. "Yes, please rest. We will speak more in the morning."

Watching everyone get comfortable made Kaijn's eyelids grow heavy. He found an unoccupied spot in the cave, sprawled on his back, and immediately fell asleep.

* * *

Aidan was exhausted, and yet, he had trouble sleeping. Even after the rest of his companions had retired for the night, he never left Kyniythyria's side.

Her egg cradled in her arms, she allowed him to sleep beside her—a privilege that he certainly did not decline. He lay with his back against her smooth, scaly belly and closed his eyes. He reveled in her ozone scent, less strong as it had been when she was enraged. Beneath that sharp odor, he smelled something more homely—familiar yet undiscernable.

He turned his head, his cheek pressing against her scales, and stared at the egg. He was certain he had detected movement before, and yet it still had not hatched. He couldn't sleep, not remembering the way Gaston's corpse had stared at him.

"What ails you, Aidan?" Her low rumble vibrated against his cheek, startling him. He looked up and saw she had half-opened one eye.

He settled back into her side, not wanting to disturb her. "Nothing, Mistress," he replied softly in Draconic. "I am just having trouble sleeping."

"It was you who killed Gaston, wasn't it?"

Aidan paused, and then looked at her. "How did you know?"

Her body shook as she let out a soft chuckle. "I can smell his blood on you."

"Did you know him?"

"Not personally. Though I knew one of the victims he'd slain. He carried Gaston's same bloody scent."

Aidan sighed and lowered his head. "I hate killing, Mistress."

Kyniythyria opened her other eye. "So do I. So do most Dragons who serve the goddess, unlike many misconceptions. But your actions are forgiven."

Aidan swallowed. Memories flooded his mind again. "I . . . I have killed once before and swore I would never do it again."

"Sometimes death must occur in order for life to continue. Who was this unfortunate soul?"

She would understand what the rest of his companions would not have. "He was a slayer. He and his small army killed many of my brethren, as well as the civilians we were helping. . . ." He lowered his gaze, horror preventing him from saying more.

Kyniythyria half-lowered her eyelids. "The goddess forgives you."

Aidan looked at her, surprised. *Is it truly that easy for Her to forgive?* He pursed his lips. *Maybe I am just tired.*

He nestled more comfortably against her. He sighed, closed his eyes, and began drifting into a troubled sleep.

Only minutes later, a sharp sound interrupted his dream—a forceful crack. Aidan's eyes shot open, and he saw Kyniythyria fully awake and staring intently at her egg, which bore a tiny crack near the top. Aidan sprang up and whispered, "Is it time?"

Kyniythyria gave a solemn nod. She gently ran her claws along the first cracks, which slowly lengthened.

Aidan huddled near the egg. He looked to his companions, tempted to wake them.

"No, Aidan, let them sleep. This is a moment worthy for kin to witness."

Aidan beamed at her. *'Kin'—she accepts me as family?*

More cracks appeared, and the egg looked ready to break. Clear liquid oozed from the cracks. Kyniythyria didn't help her baby along, which puzzled Aidan.

Kyniythyria glanced at Aidan, then back to the egg. "You have not witnessed a hatching before, have you?"

"No, Mistress," Aidan shook his head, still gazing at the egg. Pieces of speckled eggshell broke and littered the ground.

He leaned closer and glimpsed the baby's yellow-green scales. There was movement inside, and the baby suddenly broke free.

Aidan's body went warm with delight. *What a beautiful, strong child it is.* He couldn't stop grinning, and his eyes burned from joyful tears that streamed down his face. He rubbed the tears away, and he gazed at the baby Dragon, which was as small as a human toddler.

Its eyes still closed, it let out soft chirps.

"It chirps like . . . a bird?" Aidan furrowed his brow.

Chuckling, Kyniythyria pulled her child closer. She flicked her tongue over its slick back, and the baby ceased its small cries. "Of course," she said. "It is a temporary defensive mechanism since he is so tiny. After about a week, however, he will get a little bigger, and his vocal cords will begin to develop."

"I see . . ." Aidan glanced around the cave. His companions were still fast asleep. "So it is a boy, then? You knew all this time?" He tilted his head slightly, attempting to get a peek at the baby's underside.

Kyniythyria wrapped her claws around her child, cutting off Aidan's view. "Indeed. He tastes and smells like a male," she said simply.

Aidan pulled back and decided not to continue the conversation. The day's events had caught up with him. He tried to remain awake, but his eyes grew heavy, and he nodded off briefly.

Jerking himself awake, he lay back against her belly. As soon as the back of his head touched her scales, he fell asleep.

XXIII

⎯⎯⎯⎯⎯⎯⎯

∞❦∞

'**E** looks just like 'is mum, 'e does!"
Kaijin awoke the following morning to the sound of an excited Nester. He sat up slowly and rubbed his lower back, feeling old and new cramps and agitating the stiffness in his bones from from the days of being comatose. *Ugh, that's the last time I sleep on a cave floor.*

His comrades clustered around Kyniythyria. He heard a chirp. *Birds? In a cave?* Curious, Kaijin craned his head, trying to catch a glimpse of the center of the group. He saw movement faint enough that he thought it was his imagination at first, until he saw Zarya kneel down.

A bright smile stretched across the priestess's face. "He is absolutely adorable, Mistress! Truly a beautiful creature blessed by the goddess."

Kaijin raised an eyebrow then made his way over to join them. What he beheld made his jaw drop. Another Dragon—a *baby* Dragon. Its big, green eyes were open wide, swiveling around, taking in its surroundings. It chirped and crawled over to Zarya.

"I think 'e likes you already, beautiful!" Nester laughed.

Zarya cradled the wyrmling in her arms, though it seemed to prefer walking around on its own, by the way it attempted to squirm away. "It is such an honor to hold such a precious creature. How could anyone want to bring harm to him?"

Kyniythyria snorted. "It happens. And that is why we must remain ever vigilant."

"So, did you pick out a name for 'im yet, Your Majesty?" Nester asked eagerly.

Kyniythyria chuckled. "I'd decided on his name long before he hatched. His name is Czylenemaraad."

Nester blinked. "Uh . . . you're excused?"

Aidan rumbled with laughter. "That is his name, Nester."

"'Ow in th' soddin' 'ells do you even *say* that?" Nester scratched his head.

"You should know by now that Draconic is the world's most mind-boggling language, Nester," Omari said. He stood a small distance away from the rest of the group, feeding Percival some berries from his rations pouch.

"Actually, the Celestial language is," Kyniythyria interjected, somewhat amused. "But who's counting?" Her tail swished, and her eyelids lowered.

Nester looked at Zarya. "So all that strange mumblin' you do in your prayers is just you talkin' in your secret language?"

Zarya smiled. "It is not a 'secret language'. It is a very old language."

The baby crawled to Sigmund and rubbed its cheek against him, much like a cat marking its territory.

Sigmund smiled faintly at the wyrmling and rubbed under its chin but did nothing more.

"'E seems to like you, too," Nester said, grinning at the guardian.

Sigmund bristled. "Yes, well. I have seen many births. The Mistress and Her child are very dear to me, but I cannot develop an attachment. I must go where and when my duty calls."

"Your 'duty' is with me until I say otherwise, Sigmund," Kyniythyria said sharply, glowering at him.

Sigmund bowed his head. "But of course, Great Mistress."

"Now then, why don't you take Carver outside and start him on his training, hmm?"

Carver looked up from the baby. Terror lingered in his eyes, but he said nothing.

"Yes, right away, Great Mistress." Sigmund bent at his waist, giving a more formal bow, and then grabbed Carver's arm and tugged him outside the cave.

Kyniythyria nudged her child back into the nest, where it sprawled out on its belly and fell asleep.

"Now, then." Kyniythyria turned to the rest of the group, "I believe there are a few matters that need to be addressed before I send you all on your way, yes?"

Omari bolted upright. "Indeed, Great Mistress," he said quickly. He retrieved his staff and presented it to her. "I have traveled all the way from the Citadel in hopes of fulfilling the requirements of my test by having you enchant my staff. If you would do me this honor, Great Mistress . . ."

"Mmm. Of course." Her eyes flickered in a dazzling array of electric sparks as she gazed at him. Bolts of lighting shot from her eyes and into the tip of the staff.

Omari jumped back, still holding fast to his staff as it crackled with intense energy. The force sent Percival flying off Omari's shoulder and slamming into the cave wall. Percival yelped in pain, and Omari echoed him. The group drew back, leaving Omari and Kyniythyria together in the center.

Zarya took a step forward, about to help Omari, but Aidan stuck out his massive forearm, barring her from continuing. She gave the giant a pleading look, but when he ignored it, she reluctantly stepped back.

Omari gritted his teeth and closed his eyes; Percival's pain had obviously affected him. Streaks of lightning encompassed Omari, before disappearing within him. The tip of his staff crackled with energy.

Kyniythyria reared and then dismissed the magic. Her eyes returned to normal, and her body relaxed.

"It is done," she said sharply.

Kaijin, Nester, Zarya, and Aidan gawked at Omari.

Omari fixated on the dancing bolts of lightning, and it seemed as if his eyes now possessed a similar energy within them. Even Percival miraculously revived and rushed to Omari's side as if nothing happened, seemingly drawn to the staff's aura.

Omari tore his gaze away from the glowing staff. "My thanks, Mistress."

Nester's eyes had gone wider than wide. "If I ain't seen th' most craziest fiddlin' before . . ."

"That was amazing," Kaijin agreed. Then he asked Omari, "Are you all right? How do you feel?"

Omari shifted his gaze to Kaijin, and grinned. "'All right'? I am more than just 'all right'. I am rejuvenated! This is the greatest feeling I have ever felt."

"Well, what does it feel like, mate?" Nester asked.

Omari shook his head slowly. "I . . . I cannot explain it. The power of the Dragons, perhaps?"

"Hardly," Kyniythyria said flatly. "The enchantment I placed on your staff binds to you mentally, and enhances your innate abilities."

"Permanently?" Kaijin gaped.

Kyniythyria laughed. "Of course not, Kaijin. The enchantment will last only long enough for Omari to show his teachers proof of the completion of his test. By the way, Omari, I attached a message for Na'val on the enchantment."

Omari blinked. "A message? Where? How do I deliver it to him?"

"It will be delivered as soon as he sees you."

"You sound like you've done this many times, Great Mistress," Kaijin said.

"So far, in my lifespan, Omari has been the fourth mage." She glanced at Omari. "You are one of Na'val's students, yes? He is the only one who sends his students to me. It is his way of checking up on me, I suppose. After all, he did rescue me from slayers long ago."

Everyone gasped. Aidan stiffened, his biceps tensing.

"*You*, Great Mistress?" Zarya exclaimed. "You were a victim of slayers?"

"My parents were, but I managed to escape. A generous young man named Na'val Faulk found me and took me someplace safe."

"Oh, Great Mistress, I am so sorry . . ." Zarya lowered her head solemnly.

Kyniythyria snorted. "Save your pity, priestess. Dwelling on the past solves nothing. Only the future matters."

Zarya lifted her head. Her eyes had gone glassy.

Such a sad story, indeed, Kaijin thought. *I wasn't aware of the constant dangers and perils that Dragons have to go through, despite their being the guardians of the world. Their lives seemed to be in an ironic state of affairs.*

"Master Faulk has only sent four of his students to you?" Omari quirked his brow. "But he has hundreds of students. I do not understand."

"Perhaps he only sent the ones he deemed worthy and capable of surviving the trip?" Kaijin suggested.

Omari shot a cool gaze at Kaijin and huffed. "Yes . . . yes, perhaps that is it, then." He secured his glowing staff to his back.

"His reasons are his own," Kyniythyria said. "I saw nothing interesting about the other three he sent. You are no different, Omari. . . . Well, except that you and Kaijin strangely carry the same scent." Her eyes shifted to the cave's entrance, and she appeared deep in thought.

Omari made an appalled face. "What?" He glanced at Kaijin.

"Uh . . . Should I be worried about that?" Kaijin asked the Dragon.

Nester snickered. "Of course they would smell alike, Your Majesty—them both bein' fiddlers, an' all."

Kaijin rolled his eyes. Whatever the Dragon meant, he was not in the mood to dwell on it.

Kyniythyria chuckled and then looked at Zarya next. "Zarya. Your willingness and determination to please the goddess is admirable, but do not become blinded by your own aspirations—that is your greatest weakness."

Zarya gulped. "But . . . is it not my duty to help protect Her world and Her creatures?"

"Of course. But as a priestess, it is your duty to spread Her truths to those who may doubt. Prevent the Legion from strengthening in numbers. There is more to serving the goddess than simply pleasing Her. We, the Dragons, are your advisors to ensure you do not stray from the prime objective."

Zarya bowed her head again. "Y—yes, Great Mistress. I understand."

Kyniythyria looked at Aidan next, but Nester jumped up and down, waving his arms, yelling, "Me next, Your Majesty! Me next!"

"Nester!" Zarya retorted, shooting a sharp gaze at the brownie.

Kyniythyria snickered, tiny sparks of lightning escaping her nose. She held up her claw to silence the priestess. "It's all right. I'm rather fond of brownies, actually. They make me laugh."

A guffaw suddenly burst out of Omari, but as all eyes turned to him, he quickly caught himself and brushed his hand down his robes, as though removing some specks of dirt.

"Aye?" Nester's gap-toothed grin brightened. "Well, 'ow 'bout a joke? I know plenty. . . . So, a Dragon and an orc walk into a pub and . . ." He went on for several minutes with bizarre joke-telling that left Kyniythyria reeling in laughter and the rest of them scratching their heads.

"I don't get it," Kaijin muttered.

Frowning, Omari nudged him and muttered, "His jokes are obviously not meant for intellectual minds."

Kyniythyria stopped in mid-laugh and glowered at Omari. "What was that?" she growled.

Omari's head snapped up. There was obvious apprehension in his eyes. "Ah . . . I meant to say, Great Mistress, that the rest of us lack your outstanding intelligence to comprehend such complex forms of humor." He dropped his head.

Kaijin looked sidelong at him. He hadn't often seen Omari so submissive; it was a refreshing change.

Kyniythyria looked down her nose at Omari. "Indeed." She returned her attention to Nester. "Excellent, Nester. You should be a traveling entertainer."

"Aww, y'think so? I ain't as good as my cousin Nellie. She's th' queen of jokes, she is! She'll make you snort lightnin' through your nose before she even gets to th' punchline! I think she almost killed a man before, she did. 'E laughed so 'ard 'e couldn't breathe! She called it 'th' killer joke'!"

"Death by laughter. A most dangerous weapon, indeed." Kyniythyria chortled.

Omari turned around and grumbled, with a dramatic roll of his eyes, "Great. More of Nester's senseless rambling."

Kaijin half-smiled at Omari. "That's what Nester does best."

"Right. Have fun listening to that blithering idiot. As I am finished with my business here, I am leaving." Omari rummaged through the pile of rations, then filled up small pouches and retrieved a waterskin.

Should I stop him?

No, Omari was right. Their journeys had been separate all along.

But Kaijin was concerned about Omari surviving his trip back. He hoped Kyniythyria would take notice of

Omari's actions, but the Dragon appeared preoccupied with Nester. Aidan and Zarya continued staring. Perhaps they were still attempting to decipher Nester's joke.

Nester's bright smile faded slightly. "By the way, Your Majesty, can I ask for a little favor?"

"You need not ask for favors, Nester. Just ask."

Nester blinked, surprised at her response. "Well, in *that* case . . ." He rubbed his chin. "I'd like to be a great merchant like my Uncle Nickle someday, but . . . well . . . I can't seem to get my big break, y'know what I mean? Maybe you can 'elp? You can make somethin' extraordinary with all that fiddlin' you did before, aye? I mean, with a Dragon on my side, I can't lose!"

Kyniythyria beared her fangs. "That is your way of saying you want one of my priceless, shiny trinkets from me? There is nothing more precious to a Dragon than its hoard."

Nester's eyes lit up at the mention of a treasure hoard. "Uh . . . O–of course not, Your Majesty! I wouldn't even *think* of askin' you for a beautiful . . . sparklin' . . . shiny . . ." Kaijin was certain he saw a stream of drool ooze from the side of Nester's mouth as he began talking in slurred speech.

Kyniythyria's tail twitched. "Good. Because I had no intentions of giving you any of my treasures, anyway."

Nester deflated a little.

"There is one trait I find most admirable amongst brownies," she continued. "Their strong sense of determination. Why be as good as your uncle? Why not be better than him? Become a great explorer, instead. You will not only be rewarded with useless trinkets, but you will also gain fame and notoriety. Encounter new and exciting places around the world and make the most unlikely of friends as you've begun to do." She gestured to Kaijin, Aidan, Zarya, and Omari, who paused from packing his bag and looked up guiltily. "Surpass your uncle, the merchant, and become Nester, the great explorer."

"'Nester th' Great Explorer' . . ." He thought for a moment, and then his eyes lit up with delight. "'Ey! I like th' sound of that! Thank you, Your Majesty!" He happily bounced over to Omari. "Did you 'ear that, mate? I got a new title, I did! Straight from th' Dragon's mouth! Nester th' Great Explorer!"

Omari cringed at the brownie's boisterious speech and brushed past him, heading toward the entrance. "Is that synonymous to 'Nester the Thief'? 'Nester the Confounded Brownie that Does Not Know When to Be Quiet'?"

Nester frowned. "'Ey, now!"

Kyniythyria narrowed her eyes, which crackled with electric sparks, and she exhaled a small bolt of lightning toward the cave's high ceiling. A large rock fell from the shadows. Nester leapt out of the way just in time as it crashed on the back hem of Omari's robes and pinned him in place. Percival squeaked and skittered away from the danger.

Omari yelped and tried to free himself. He pressed his back against the stone and looked behind him fearfully. "What in the—"

"I did *not* dismiss you yet, Omari Batsuyou!" Kyniythyria growled.

Omari made no further attempts to leave. Percival poked his head out from behind the sacks of footstuffs.

Convinced that the danger had passed, he returned to Omari.

When the tension in the air died down, Aidan implored Kyniythyria, "Mistress, Aidan has small question."

"You want to know where to find your ancestors," Kyniythyria said, as though reading his mind, "I cannot tell you where to begin your search—if any still live, that is."

Aidan pursed his lips. Rage filled his eyes for a moment, as if the Dragon had said something offensive. But he stayed his tongue.

"I understand your frustration, Aidan," Kyniythyria continued, "but what happened was in the past—long before you were even a spark in your father's eye. You cannot change what has happened. However, you can work toward forging a new future and restoring honor to your clan. If any of your kin are still alive, then they are most likely disguised and living amongst society. Use your senses—learn to study people—and you will find what you are seeking."

Aidan bowed his head in thanks. He backtracked to the cave wall, slid down, and drew his knees to his chest. He rested his forehead on his knees.

Zarya looked from Aidan to Kyniythyria, confused.

Kaijin considered his own situation. The last time he'd encountered the Dragon, she'd seemed too flustered to give him a straight answer. He wanted to know who he was—*what* he was.

He knew he was no ordinary man who just happened to have an affinity for fire. He was *different*. Aidan's situation reminded Kaijin of his own family. Regret wrenched his heart.

". . . And last, the Firebrand." Kyniythyria said caustically, breaking Kaijin's concentration.

Kaijin met her gaze. *What great things am I really destined for?* He made a sour face. *I'm a murderer—a* monster.

"Oh! Ask 'er about th' orb, Kaijin! Th' *orb!*" Nester exclaimed.

"Yes, about the orb . . ." Kyniythyria began. "I've sensed its presence ever since you first arrived with it, Kaijin."

The orb. Yes, that's all I really have of importance, isn't it? He looked at the Dragon curiously. "You knew I had the orb here? And you didn't touch it?"

Kyniythyria chuckled darkly. "After witnessing what happened to Omari when he tried to touch it? Dear boy, even *I* am aware of the painful consequences of attempting to handle something that a deity has reserved exclusively for someone else."

Surprised, he glanced at Omari, who tried to hide a frown. Kaijin recalled the last nightmare he had. *The necklace protected me . . . from Omari?* That didn't make sense. "Omari? Did you try to steal the orb from me while I was unconscious?"

After a few moments' silence, Omari said, "I was not trying to 'steal' it. I simply wanted to study it."

"An' it burned 'im pretty bad, it did." Nester added. "Took Zarya almost an 'our to patch 'im up again."

"Well, tell him my whole life story while you're at it, Nester!" Omari snapped.

"That's what you get for thinkin' you're a better prigger than me!"

"Why, you—"

Zarya stepped forward. "Enough. Omari has already learned his lesson, and we have already talked about this and moved on. Let's not dwell on past issues." She glanced at Kyniythyria. "Forgive us, Great Mistress."

Kyniythyria waved her claw dismissively. "I found it very amusing, actually." She focused on Kaijin again. "Show me what you have there."

Kaijin slowly retrieved the orb from his haversack and held it up to her. He clutched it tightly.

Kyniythyria's gaze was glued to the swirling flames. She hissed irritably and made no move to grab it. She sidled closer to the nest, blocking the path to her sleeping child with her body. She tensed; her eyes narrowed. "Where did you get that?"

Kaijin, sensing the Dragon's displeasure, pulled the orb close to his chest. It felt warm and soothing, much like his necklace's continuous pulsating heat. "Nester and I found it amongst some druids' ruins in Houndstooth Marsh."

"I knew I could count on you, mate, for givin' me credit!" Nester beamed.

Kaijin gave him an odd look, then asked the Dragon, "Do you . . . know what it is, Great Mistress?"

She growled and dug her claws into the cave floor, creating deep gashes in the stone. "That is a *bruane* in Druidic: a fire orb. Druids craft items like those to contain essences of the elements, for use in rituals. The fact that you happened to find one still intact is quite . . . shocking."

"Aye?" Nester blurted out, standing beside Kaijin and focused on the orb. "So what's it worth?"

Kyniythyria chuckled. "It's as useless as a ball of lint to someone who is not a druid. It is, quite literally, fire trapped inside a glass ball. Even a novice mage can emulate such a trick."

Kaijin ran his hands over the orb's smooth, glassy surface, mulling over his thoughts. "How can something so beautiful—so powerful—be worthless? I don't understand."

"Sometimes true beauty does not have a price."

Kaijin chewed on his bottom lip. "What about the afriti? It lives in the orb."

Kyniythyria's gaze hardened. "An afriti . . . interesting. You saw it? Spoke to it?"

Kaijin nodded. "It spoke to me, rather. It consumed Gaston's camp with fire and killed almost everyone. Why would an afriti live inside this druidic item?"

"Because it is a being of fire. It can 'live' anywhere it wishes, whenever it wishes, so long as there is fire for it to consume. It could live in your necklace, if it so chose. But it seems more content being inside the orb as opposed to its home plane, the Realm of Fire. Do not question the creature's motives. You cannot stop it from doing whatever it does."

"What?" Zarya blinked. "What do you mean, Great Mistress? We cannot prevent it from killing innocent people?"

"Afriti are not chaotic beings." Kyniythyria touted a claw at them. "They do not kill for the sake of killing. They *do* have a sense of order among themselves, as they *always* serve a master."

A master . . . Kaijin felt his heart pound. The orb grew hotter in his hands for a moment, before cooling back to its normal comforting temperature. *Perhaps the afriti is growing irritable.*

"Ignis . . ." Zarya mumbled. "It makes sense. Afriti are fire beings. Of course, they would serve the Firelord, right, Kaijin?" She looked to him for comfirmation.

"I would think so, yes." Kaijin nodded to Zarya, then his gaze swiveled back to Kyniythyria. "Despite this orb's . . . *strangeness,* I am rather fond of it."

"As you should be." The Dragon nodded. "For anyone who reveres the Firelord, that orb is worth more than diamonds."

Kaijin's jaw dropped. "Really?"

"*Really?*" Nester repeated more enthusiastically, inching closer to him. "'Ey now, mate, we might 'ave somethin' 'ere!"

Kaijin glared at the brownie. "What are you talking about?"

"Think about it! We go to th' Pyre an' sell that to th' weird fiery blokes there, an' we'll be rich in no time!"

Kaijin felt his left eye twitch. *Blasphemy.* "No, I will not do that." He licked his lips, tasting bitterness in his words.

Nester opened his mouth to argue but frowned and shook his head, then dragged himself over to where Aidan sat.

Kaijin returned the orb back to the haversack and acknowledged Kyniythyria. "What else do you know about me, Great Mistress?" he asked. "What other advice can you offer?"

Kyniythyria hissed. "I know that you enjoy fire. And I know that despite your unlikely power as a Firebrand, you regret something that happened in the past." She eyed him sternly.

Kaijin cringed. Regret wasn't the right word to describe how he felt. He crossed his arms and rubbed his biceps, dwelling on his thoughts. He could feel the gaze of his companions bearing down on him. As it stood, they all admitted to his difference from them; would his admitting to his crimes only make things worse?

Who cares at this point? It seems I've nothing more to live for. He looked at Kyniythyria, eye-to-eye. "I regret everything I've done and more. No one had to die, Great Mistress."

He didn't care who listened. He could see Zarya out of the corner of his eye. Omari stared at him, intrigued. Aidan remained sitting but seemed to intently listen to the conversation. Nester stood next to Aidan, bearing a look of uncertainty on his face.

Kyniythyria tilted her head to the side. "*Who* died?"

Kaijin swallowed. "Everyone, including my parents and younger brother. My whole family is dead, Great Mistress. So many innocents are dead because of me." He lowered his head. His eyes burned with tears. "I . . . I did it. I killed them all. . . ."

Zarya looked shocked.

Kyniythyria tilted her head back. She stared at him coolly.

"I wish I could have controlled it," Kaijin continued. "But I am a dangerous threat to society. I am a monster— I am a mage."

Omari scowled.

"You rescued my child," Kyniythyria replied. "You are hardly a monster."

Kaijin frowned bitterly. "My former master said that I was different—that he'd never seen magic quite like mine. He said my magic was 'tainted' in some way. And I still don't know how. I'm an abomination, Great Mistress. I should be dead! I hear voices. I . . . . I feel things that are beyond my power. I—"

"You dare doubt my words, boy?" Kyniythyria growled. "Cease this senseless talk. If you were truly as evil as you claim to be, then I would've not entrusted you to find my child—in fact, I would've killed you myself while you slept in *my* cave. I sense there is more to your story than you let on, Kaijin. But alas, the goddess forgives those pure in heart. If it were not so, then you would not be standing here telling me your woes."

Zarya bit her lip. "Forgive me, Great Mistress, for not offering that comfort and assurance that Kaijin needed during his times of trouble. I've said and done terrible things—I failed. . . ."

Kyniythyria snorted. "Then fix those failures, learn from them, and do not make them again, lest you are determined to fall from grace."

Zarya nodded quickly and stood beside Kaijin. She touched his shoulder—soft, soothing. He shivered, disinclined to shake her off. She bowed her head and said almost inaudibly, "Forgive me, Kaijin."

Her soft words surprised him, and yet, they seemed to be just enough to ease his troubled heart. *Forgive me, as well.*

"Now, then, Kaijin," Kyniythyria continued, "tell me about the voices you mentioned you heard."

Kaijin sighed. The last thing he wanted to do was recall that sinister voice.

He heard the Flames. He *always* heard the Flames. "It crackles. It tells me to destroy. It tells me to punish. It demands my obedience. Then, I feel like I'm dreaming and someone else is controlling my body. Recently, I've found myself able to cast any fire-based spell without the use of components. My fire . . . sometimes it turns white and burns so hot, I'm certain it can melt the skin off a person. And yet, it feels wonderful."

"White fire? Interesting." Kyniythyria pondered.

With the bottom of his robe still pinned under the rock, Omari sat down cross-legged. "You act as though that is strange, Kaijin? Even *you* should know that fire is at its hottest state when it burns white."

"White fire is what encompasses Celestra's sword," Zarya interjected. "As it states in holy texts, 'The fire is whiter than purity, burns brighter and hotter than the heavens; it has the power to bring destruction to the darkest evil . . .'"

"Yes, pretty much," Kyniythyria nodded to the priestess, then looked back to Kaijin. "That is the essence of what makes you a Firebrand. What you are seeking cannot be found here. You must travel to the Pyre in the east. That is where you truly belong."

Truly belong. Kaijin had to smile at that. Would the Pyre finally grant him a sense of belonging, something he'd forgotten for so long? Zarya's hand slid off his shoulder. He bowed his head to the Dragon and stepped back. "Thank you, Great Mistress."

Kyniythyria observed each of them in turn. "You have all done a great service, to not only me, but to the goddess. May She continue to give you strength during your travels."

Aidan stood, and that was everyone's cue to leave. Kyniythyria plucked the large rock off Omari's robe, freeing him. With Percival perched on his shoulder, Omari headed outside. The rest of the group took a minute to pack enough rations and water to last them for a few days.

"Thank you, Great Mistress," Zarya said as she followed the rest of the group out.

"Safe travels, all of you." Kyniythyria returned to her nest and curled up with her child.

After saying their good-byes to Carver and Sigmund, who were engaged in swordplay outside the cave, the group descended the winding mountain path for the last time.

XXIV

೫೩೮

Kaijin and his friends had walked for less than an hour when they arrived at a swiftly flowing river. Nester, leading the way, halted at the rocky edge of the riverbank.

"Now what?" Omari grumbled.

"Dead end, mates." Nester pointed to the rocks, dead trees, and sparse wilderness across the way. "It's a long way to th' other side."

Kaijin eyed the rushing rapids and cringed. Miele, who soared above them, briefly flew to the other side of the river, then returned.

"Is there no other way around?" Zarya asked.

Nester shook his head. "Nay. The Valdell River runs a long way north and south."

Aidan, remaining silent, walked to the bank and waded in. The rushing waters crashed against him, but he stood as firm as a rock. "Aidan can swim across."

"*Swim*?" Kaijin repeated, eyeing the giant with awe. "Aidan, are you mad? The current is too strong!"

Aidan shook his head. "Aidan can handle it. Besides, water feels nice."

"Well, that's all well an' good, Aidan, but what about th' rest of us?" Nester asked.

"Aidan will carry as many as he can on back."

Zarya blinked. "What? No, Aidan! That's ludicrous! Do not risk your or anyone else's safety like that. Please, get out of the water."

But Aidan remained where he was. He looked across the river to the other side, then turned back and nodded curtly. "Aidan can do it."

"Well," Omari began, "unless someone else has a better idea, it looks like that is your best bet in getting across. As for me, I think this is where I will take my leave." When all eyes fell on him, he bristled. "You did not honestly think that I would be accompanying you to the Pyre, did you? I have accomplished what I came here for. I must return to the Citadel now."

He can't be serious. "You can't *possibly* survive the rest of the way on your own, Omari," Kaijin said.

Omari huffed. "Says you. I feel more powerful now than ever before. No one had better challenge me. You heard the Dragon—my powers have been enhanced."

"Kaijin's right, you know." Zarya waved her finger at Omari. "These lands are no place for people to travel alone."

Omari gave her a cool gaze. "I am sorry, priestess, but I have made up my mind. And no one will change it—not even you."

"This is foolish, and you know it," Kaijin said.

"Do not tell me what to do, Kaijin." Omari scowled.

"I'm not. You are your own man. Why do you have to always be so damn obnoxious?"

Omari narrowed his eyes. Percival snarled on his shoulder, echoing his master's fury. Omari stormed over to Kaijin and thrust his face so close to Kaijin's that their noses almost touched. "What did you say?"

"'Ey! 'Ey!" Nester moved between them and broke them up. Soddin' 'ells! You two bicker worse than two brothers!"

Omari reluctantly stepped back, still glaring at Kaijin. "I do not give a rat's ass who he is or *what* he is. The day I am related to him is the day I drink poison."

Kaijin scowled. *That day can't come soon enough.*

Omari spun on his heels. "I am leaving, and that is final. Do not try to stop me, or else." He held up his staff and shook it threateningly. He secured it to his back and began walking along the riverbank, upstream.

He'd only made it a few steps, however, when he was grabbed from behind by Aidan. The lower half of Aidan's body was soaked, and he left a trail of large footprints in the mud leading down into the river. The giant held Omari by the back collar and lifted him a few inches off the ground. Percival leaped from Omari's shoulder, to the ground, and wildly chirped at Aidan.

Omari thrashed. "Put . . . put me down, Aidan!" he demanded. He tried reaching for his staff, but he couldn't get his hand past Aidan's big arm.

Kaijin, Nester, and Zarya watched, not daring to intervene.

Percival nipped at Aidan's ankle, trying futilely to sink his teeth into the giant's tough skin.

"As Zarya said." Aidan ignored the weasel. "These lands are no place for people to travel alone."

Omari gritted his teeth. "This is none of your business, Aidan. You—none of you understand the importance of my test. I must not stall any longer than I already have. Now, confound it, put me down this instant!"

Ignoring Omari's pleas, Aidan carried him into the river and waded back in until the water reached his waist. "Trust Aidan for once."

Terror filled Omari's eyes. "No! Stop!"

Aidan took a deep breath and lunged into the water.

Omari scrambled atop Aidan's back, pushing the giant's head down and grasping handfuls of his hair as he clung for dear life. He shivered. Percival ran after his master and hopped upon his shoulder from a large rock, only seconds before Aidan swam off.

Aidan, still seemingly calm in the wake of Omari's panic, swam like a fish across the river, his head and body submerged just below the surface as if swimming came naturally to him. The rushing current crashed against the giant's massive frame, veering him only slightly off his path. Kaijin, Zarya, and Nester watched as Aidan went from one side of the river to the other in mere minutes.

"Wow! I didn't know Aidan could swim like that!" Nester gawked.

"You and me both," Kaijin agreed.

Zarya smiled at them. "Aidan is just full of surprises, isn't he?"

When Aidan reached the riverbank, he flung Omari off his back and returned to the rest of the group. He carried each member one by one across the river, not looking in the least bit exhausted when he had finished.

He grabbed Kaijin last. *Hells, I don't think I'm ready for this.* Kaijin was hesitant to enter the water, but like Omari, he had little choice in the matter. He held onto

Aidan as the cold water soaked his body and face, making him shiver uncontrollably. His heart raced, but something seemed to keep him calm. His necklace pulsated intensely, warming his body. Miele flew overhead as Aidan swam to the other side with ease.

After setting Kaijin down on the bank, Aidan stretched his arms and legs. "That was good exercise."

Zarya laughed as she finished wiping water from her weapon. "It was! I'm glad you enjoyed yourself. Please forgive me for doubting you before."

"Aye!" Nester grinned, sheathing his many blades, which he'd thoroughly dried. "You make a great boat, Aidan!" He shook water off his face like a dog, getting droplets on Zarya, who gave him a playful pout. Nester wrung out parts of his clothes, and slicked his hair back.

Aidan smiled sheepishly at them.

Kaijin, soaked and still shaken from the ordeal, warily eyed the rapids. He opened his haversack and checked its contents. The dagger was dry, but parts of his spellbook were not. He frowned, fearing some of the pages might have been damaged.

Zarya knelt beside him and held out her hands. "May I?"

Kaijin glanced at the priestess. He clutched his spellbook, at first reluctant to surrender it to her, then finally did so, slowly.

Zarya gently ran her hand along the spellbook's outer surface while she spoke a soft prayer. A faint, blue glow emitted from her fingertips, and moments later, the spellbook was restored to its former state. Zarya handed the book back to Kaijin with a smile. "There. Much better."

He skimmed the crisp pages. "Thank you." He beamed.

He glimpsed Omari nearby, and his happiness faded. The other mage sat with his knees to his chest, his face pale. He rocked back and forth, staring blankly at the river. Percival ran in circles around him.

"Omari? Are you all right?" Kaijin approached, head tilted in curiosity. Omari said nothing. He looked more scared than someone who'd seen a ghost. He breathed slowly. Percival chirped.

"Omari!" Kaijin grabbed the other mage's shoulders and shook him. "What's wrong? Get a hold of yourself!" Aidan, Zarya, and Nester started toward them, but Kaijin gave them a look over his shoulder, stopping them. "No, let me handle it. Stay back, please."

Concern showing on their faces, the three halted and remained silent.

Kaijin turned back to Omari. The older mage's eyes were hazy. "Omari!"

Omari gasped, blinked a few times, and looked around frantically before his gaze settled upon Kaijin. His breathing was ragged. "Where . . . I . . . I am still . . . alive?"

Kaijin was taken aback. *Is he actually afraid?* He replied, voice low, "What? Of course you're alive. We all are. What happened to you?"

Omari bit his bottom lip. "I thought . . . I thought I drowned. No, I was *certain* I drowned."

"Aidan carried us all across the river, safe and sound."

Omari's expression hardened, and he wriggled out of Kaijin's grip. "Right, of course I am alive. Why would you think I would drown, idiot? I know how to—" He stopped abruptly and shifted his gaze.

"Swim?" Kaijin finished, raising an eyebrow.

Omari glowered at him. "Yes. *Swim.*"

Kaijin leaned back and mulled over the other mage's actions. "Don't worry, I won't tell anyone. I don't know how to swim, either."

Omari's eyes widened. He looked behind Kaijin, perhaps to see if any of the others had heard. "Idiot!" he snapped in a loud whisper. "Of *course* I know how to swim! I just . . . I just forgot, all right?"

Kaijin sighed. "Why can't you just swallow your foolish pride?"

Omari crossed his arms and growled in his throat. "Fine." He sprang up. "*Fine!* I do not know how to swim!" He froze.

The others stared at Omari.

"Don't know 'ow to swim?" Nester repeated in a sarcastic tone. "You? Th' Great Unstoppable Omari?"

"Nester!" Kaijin glared. He turned back to Omari. "Look, it's all right. No one is perfect. I'll make sure they keep their lips sealed about it if you agree to come with us to the Pyre."

Omari's eyes widened. "What! You are blackmailing me, now?"

"Of course not. You seriously don't expect to still travel alone after this, do you?"

"Well? Why not? I will brave the rest of the way myself."

"And what will happen if you are thrown in a lake? Or forced to cross a river to escape danger?"

"That will not happen."

Kaijin slapped his forehead. *This is getting nowhere.* "Didn't we have this conversation before? Surely, I don't think your master would be so foolish as to send you out alone on such a treacherous journey without help."

Omari fidgeted with his hands. "Sometimes I believe he underestimates me. Some of the other masters did not even assume I could successfully get my staff enchanted. Look, Kaijin. Your help is noted, but not needed. I must prove to the masters that I am worthy to ascend as a full-fledged mage."

"But what if part of your 'test' was seeking help from others? There is no shame in that."

Omari slowly shook his head. "You do not understand. You will never understand. You are an outsider; you do not understand the inner workings of the Citadel."

Kaijin opened his mouth to respond but quickly closed it. He remembered the time Jarial had abandoned him during his field training—or at the very least, had made Kaijin feel as though he was abandoned. "This could simply be a test of your pride. I may not know the Council of Nine like you do, but I would think that even *they* would call on each other for help when needed. What makes you so different from them?" He paused. "Or are you simply afraid to ask for help?"

"I am not afraid of anything." Omari scowled.

Kaijin rolled his eyes. "You would've not gotten your staff enchanted in the first place if it hadn't been for all of us working together."

Omari lowered his head and thought. He looked up from Kaijin to the rest of the group, then sighed deeply. "Fine. We will do it your way, Kaijin. But if I am punished in any way for delaying my assignment, you will be the first one I lay blame to."

Kaijin nodded. Part of him was relieved to have finally gotten through Omari's thick skull. "Feel free to blame me for everything. I don't care. I've nothing to lose anymore. I'm only here on this journey because I am heeding the call of the Firelord. If I'm to be punished for obeying a deity, then so be it. I will take it willingly." *And maybe the voice will stop torturing me.*

Omari raised an eyebrow at Kaijin's rambling. "Either you are very serious or very stupid."

"Or perhaps I am both." Kaijin chuckled softly and then motioned to the rest of the group. "To the Pyre."

XXV

C3⊛80

Kaijin and his friends trekked through the Wilds for two days. While the rest of his group talked amongst themselves to pass the time, Kaijin lagged a short distance behind. He feared and anticipated what he expected to find at the Pyre.

Nester stopped just short of a rocky path that ascended, leading into a mountainous landscape. The others nearly tripped over him.

Zarya frowned. "Nester, will you please not stop so abruptly like that?"

Nester smirked. "Sorry, beautiful. Look over there!" He pointed toward a massive golden structure far in the distance that sat high in the mountains and was encircled by a thick blanket of smoke.

Kaijin gaped. *What a magnificent sight.* He beamed at Miele, who screeched happily as she soared above him. Kaijin could smell charcoal in the breeze and hear a faint crackle of flames that nobody else noted. A soothing, welcoming heat bedazzled his mind, calling out to him.

"Come closer," the fiery voice beckoned.

Kaijin slid his foot forward. Rocks scattered under his boot. *"Is this why you harassed my mind for so long? Is this why you've made me do such terrible things?"*

When he received no response, he brushed past his companions and continued along the path. His heart pounded in anticipation. His necklace pulsed with an urgent intensity.

"Kaijin? Are you all right?" Zarya approached and placed her hand on his shoulder.

Kaijin shivered at her touch, and then shrugged her hand off. "I . . . I'm fine, Zarya. Really. I'm just . . . curious as to what I might find there."

Zarya smiled. "We all are."

"I did not come all this way with you for you to hesitate now," Omari grumbled.

Kaijin glared at Omari. "I may adore the Firelord, but I am still a mage. I might not even get past the front door." He continued climbing the path, a little more confident than before.

Omari snorted. "Let us hope not."

"Oy! Those fiery warders are a buncha strange blokes," Nester added. "They shooed me off last time I came 'ere.'

"Why? Were you annoying them?"

"Omari, enough!" Zarya snapped, the first one to react to Omari picking on Nester yet again.

"If they are true believers of Ignis, then they should accept you no matter who or what you are, Kaijin," Aidan said.

Kaijin glanced over his shoulder at the giant.

Zarya nodded. "Aidan is right, you know. Besides. The Mistress called you a Firebrand. The words of a Dragon should be reason enough for them to accept you. Dare I ask, Kaijin, if you have ever considered becoming an Ignan priest?"

Kaijin stared at the plumes of distant smoke that rose gently into the sky. "Maybe once. But I don't hold the same interest in the divine arts as I do magic." *At least, I don't think I do.*

After some time of hiking, the smoke began to hinder Kaijin's visibility, and he could barely see the rest of his group. The smell of burning wood bit at his senses. The temperature increased, and the air became drier the higher they ascended.

Suddenly, the smoke parted for Kaijin, revealing the golden structure not far away.

He heard a faint rumble and halted. He tried to pinpoint the sound. "Did you hear that?" he asked.

Zarya, Omari, and Nester looked around curiously.

"Was that thunder?" Zarya asked.

"Ugh! I 'ope not!" Nester put his hands over his head, anticipating rain.

Omari narrowed his eyes suspiciously and slowly turned his head, looking behind him. "No . . . that sounds like a—"

"Sorry, Aidan is hungry." Smiling sheepishly, Aidan patted his stomach. It rumbled again.

Omari rolled his eyes; Zarya twisted her lips, trying to hide her smile; Kaijin and Nester simultaneously sighed in relief.

The group resumed their trek and soon reached the end of the smoke-lined path. The smoke lifted, and Kaijin stood before a shallow staircase that led up to two massive, ornately carved shining brass doors. A tall, burning brazier sat on each side of the doors and lit up the entire entrance with dancing flames.

"It's more amazin' than when I was 'ere last!" Nester rubbed his eyes and blinked several times. "It's like . . . everything's even *more* shiny!"

Kaijin called to Miele, and she swooped down to land on his shoulder. He slowly ascended the stairs and examined the doors. A pattern of flames was etched along the frame. Looking closely, Kaijin could also make out what looked like runes engraved in the door, but he was uncertain of what they said. He ran his fingers along the warm etchings, admiring every intricate detail.

"Are you in there, Ignis?"

There was no answer.

Kaijin pressed his ear to the door and listened. While he heard nothing on the other side, the door itself felt very warm. A ripple of white fire trailed up the length of the doors and disappeared. Kaijin pulled away and tilted his head back, staring up at the massive doors in amazement.

Zarya approached Kaijin and stood beside him. "This is truly a work of art, Kaijin," she said, tone hushed.

Nester squeezed his way between them and scrutinized the door. "This was as far as I got before some of th' warders discovered me an' shooed me off. I still ain't figured out 'ow to open this soddin' door. No keyholes or even a 'andle! There ain't no easy way we're gonna get this open."

"Do not tell me we came all this way for nothing," Omari grumbled. He held Percival in his arms and stroked his back.

While the rest of the group chatted, Aidan approached the door. He gave three firm knocks. "Hello? Is anyone home?"

Everyone immediately stopped talking and gawked at the giant. Aidan looked back at them and smiled politely.

Omari slapped his forehead. "Great. Just what we need: A bunch of Ignan priests angry at us for disturbing them! Great going, Aidan!"

Aidan's smile faded. "Well, how else will they know we are here?"

Before anyone could answer, unlocking sounds came from within. The chattering of two voices rose. Moments later, one of the doors opened a crack, and a robed, middle-aged, bearded man peeked out. The scent of burning charcoal wafted from inside.

"Yes?" the man asked gruffly.

Aidan tensed and expectantly looked over his shoulder at Kaijin.

Kaijin swallowed and stepped forward. He could feel the man's gaze piercing him. "Ah . . . m—my name is Kaijin. Kaijin Sora. I am . . . a follower of the Firelord, and have come here—at His behest, I think."

The man flinched. He opened the door a little wider, and another man, shorter, but dressed similarly, appeared beside him. The bright colors of the shorter man's robe gave off the illusion of fire. He scrutinized the group curiously.

"'E's a *Firebrand*, your majesties!" Nester blurted. "A Dragon said so!" He nodded sagely.

"Nester!" Zarya elbowed him in his chest, glaring at him.

"Ow! What? It's true, ain't it? An' maybe they won't shoo us off like they did me!"

The two robed men briefly sneered at the brownie, evidently remembering him.

"If you would give me the honor, sirs," Kaijin said, lowering his head and revealing his necklace to them from under his robes, "I simply seek answers. May my companions and I enter?"

The men's eyes widened slightly. The shorter man pulled the door all the way open. "Yes, brother. You and your companions may. I bid you welcome. I am Canicus. That is Brett."

Beaming, Kaijin stepped across the threshold. He beckoned his friends to follow.

Brett stopped Nester. "Not so fast, brownie. Are you *really* with him?"

"I swear on my Pa's grave that I'm with Kaijin, aye! 'E's my best mate! We've gone on adventures together, 'aven't we, Kaijin?"

"Yes, uh, of course," Kaijin said absently, his attention drawn to the brass-colored interior of the building. The yellow and orange high-ceilinged chamber stretched upward for several stories. Large red and gold tapestries embroidered with Ignis's holy symbol hung along the walls of the main hall. The tall arched stained-glass windows tinted the light a bright orange. The polished black obsidian floor reflected the dancing flames of the numerous braziers and torches lining the walls and aisles.

At the center of the main hall was a raised platform with twenty shallow stairs leading up on all four sides. Atop the platform was a massive burning brazier—which, though not as ornate as the rest of the interior, contained beautiful white flames that leapt from within, and plumes of white smoke rose up the main atrium. The brazier gave off the brightest light and a heat so soothing that Kaijin didn't want to leave. Robed priests stood around the brazier, appearing to be in deep meditation.

"This way," Brett called, leading the group. Canicus brought up the rear, to ensure no one in the group strayed.

Kaijin followed a few steps behind Brett. As he took in his surroundings, too lost for words at the sheer beauty of this place, he pulled out his necklace from beneath his robes and prominently sported it. Robed men and women bustled throughout the main hall, whispering amongst themselves while their hardened gazes focused primarily on Kaijin.

The group was escorted to the foot of one of the stairs leading to the platform. Kaijin gazed upward at a group of priests who stood in a circle and realized they were praying. One of the priests, an elderly man, paused, and looked toward him curiously.

"Stay here, Kaijin," Brett ordered, holding his arm out, barring him from continuing.

Kaijin obeyed, not taking his gaze off the circle of priests. Brett gathered the skirts of his robes and climbed the stairs to speak with one priest. They spoke in hushed tones for several minutes before Brett gestured for Kaijin to come join them. Kaijin did so without question, not even looking back at his companions. He now knew what he needed to do—it was clear to him while he treaded these holy grounds. There were no voices speaking in his mind, nor were there unknown presences possessing his body. He was, once again, at peace with himself. He stood before the two priests, then bowed his head. The other priests in the circle paused their prayers for a moment to acknowledge Kaijin.

"Kaijin, this is Vargas, high cleric of the Vein," Brett explained.

Kaijin furrowed his brow. *Vein?* He politely bowed, hoping to hide his confusion.

"Greetings, Brother of the Flame," Vargas said with a nod. "You have piqued my interest. I sense you have come a great distance."

"Oh yes, sir, I have." Kaijin nodded firmly.

"Indeed, the Firelord has deemed you worthy to be here."

Kaijin glanced at the other priests, then looked behind him at his companions. Some of the other robed clergy had stopped their daily chores and gathered around the platform to listen.

He turned back around and cleared his throat. "Honorable priest, I've come here seeking answers—about myself, about the Firelord, and about my purpose. I don't know what I can offer you in exchange for this knowledge, but I will do my best to repay whatever debt you deem worthy. . . ." He sighed softly. "I must warn you that I am . . . a mage." *They must know. And hopefully they will understand.*

Vargas's eyebrows rose. Several clergymembers murmured to each other. "Are you, now? Well, you are not the first mage who has walked in here, nor will you be the last. But you . . . There is something different about you than other mages." He made a small gesture with his head. "Come with me, Kaijin. Let us talk in private." He called forth Brett and a few of the clergymembers lingering nearby. "See to it that Kaijin's companions are given ample hospitality."

"Yes, Honored One." Brett gave the elderly man a respectable bow, nodded to Kaijin, and then descended the stairs. There was hesitation in their steps as he and the other clergymembers quietly escorted Kaijin's group to a corridor that branched off to a room to the left of the main atrium.

Yes! Thank you, Ignis! Kaijin smiled at them until the last person left, then followed Vargas. He was led to the rear of the main hall, to a separate corridor that was lighted by rows of brightly burning braziers and decorated by hanging tapestries and portraits.

He glanced at one of the portraits as they passed. It depicted a regal man in flaming armor, posing victoriously with a spiked chain in one hand. Fire burned in his soulless-looking eyes. The background was washed with gradients of oranges, reds and yellows, which gave the illusion that the man was practically made of fire.

Kaijin felt some familiarity with the being in the portrait. He stayed silent and relished the warmth of the corridor they walked through.

Vargas opened ornate brass double doors that led into a secluded room at the far end of the corridor—an extravagant two-story library, or perhaps it was simply a pristine office. A cozy sitting area of plush, red velvet couches and chairs was in one corner. A desk sat in another corner of the room, while two floors' worth of bookshelves stuffed with old, thick tomes lined the walls and extended to the ceiling.

Miele flew to the ceiling and remained there, watching Kaijin and Vargas.

The smell of old and fresh parchment made Kaijin salivate in delight. He breathed in the papery scents and closed his eyes, briefly remembering the days he spent studying magic and visiting the booksellers in Easthaven's marketplace during his early childhood. His daydreaming came to a halt when he heard Vargas's voice. Kaijin opened his eyes.

"I thought someone like you would find solace in a place like this." Vargas indicated for Kaijin to sit.

"That's an understatement, sir." Kaijin sat on one of the couches. The plush velvet almost completely swallowed him; it was more comfortable than anything he'd ever felt. "So many books. . . . This—all of this—is truly amazing!"

Vargas laughed. "These books are just a few of many. Below us is another library: the largest Ignan library in all of Exodus. It is our sacred vault of recorded events, extending almost as far back as the days when the gods walked Exodus."

Kaijin gasped. "An entire *vault* dedicated to Ignis? I can't believe it! I am honored that you have entrusted me with such valuable information."

"Of course, Kaijin. You are a Firebrand and a chosen of Ignis. It is your right to know. The Celestials have been the primary contributors to many of the older works in the sacred vault. They have been known to be the race of creatures, second to the Dragons, to have the closest connection with the goddess. Through Her, they are provided essential information about the other gods, as well—like Ignis."

"I think I've found my new home."

"Perhaps you have, Kaijin. Do you wish to stay here? Though I do not think your companions would feel the same way."

"My companions have their own purposes in life. And I now seemed to have found mine. I can finally learn the answers to the many questions that have been plaguing my mind for so long. Before, I thought I had lost everything. But here . . . I feel as though I've gained the world. I came to know Ignis when I was very young. Strange things have happened ever since I acquired this necklace." He indicated his holy symbol. "I see things. Feel things. My magic behaves oddly."

"In what way?" Vargas raised a curious brow, eying the necklace.

"Sometimes I feel as though something has a hold of me, making me cast fire-based spells that I know are beyond my level of study. Sometimes my magic feels stronger than it usually is. Many times, I cannot control my own power. My former master says my magic is 'tainted' somehow—manipulated by a divine power. My companions and I met a Dragon recently, and She spoke of Ignis most likely being behind it all."

Vargas looked surprised. "You met a Dragon, you say? The Dragon was, indeed, correct. A divine presence has made its way in you, leaving behind a powerful aura. The Firelord feeds on strength, not weakness."

Kaijin pursed his lips. "A voice speaks to me, Honored Priest. A strange voice that sounds like fire. It toys with me—with my mind. It is very destructive. I've been labelled 'mad' and 'strange' and 'a threat to society' because of what happened in Easthaven. . . ." He bit his tongue. The memory burned.

Vargas's eyes narrowed slightly. "We have heard that people blamed magic as the cause of Easthaven's destruction. What impact did you have on that city?"

"Undead invaded the city, afflicting many people and creating utter chaos. I helped fight back the creatures with my magic, and something took over. My magic was much stronger—so much so, I lost control. The next thing I knew, I woke up and found the city completely destroyed."

"The power of Ignis manifested in you, giving you the ability to cleanse the city of its evil," Vargas whispered, as if to himself.

Kaijin scowled. "'Cleanse'? You mean 'destroy'! I lost my entire family! They were not evil!"

"And how do you know the undead did not afflict them, as well?"

Kaijin's stomach lurched. His parents had been mutilated beyond recognition. Kaijin tried consulting the presence in his mind, but no one answered.

"Kaijin?" Vargas called.

Kaijin suddenly broke from his trance and blinked several times. "I . . . I don't know what happened prior to discovering their corpses. I just know what I . . . *felt*. If Ignis favors me, then why has He allowed me to witness the death of my family? Why has he used me to destroy?"

"You cannot question His actions, Kaijin. It is in His nature to destroy, in order to purify the world. You have my condolences for the loss of your family. You must understand, however: You, as a Firebrand, are being used by Ignis for His agenda."

Kaijin looked up helplessly. "And what is His agenda?"

"That is something only He can reveal to you. But know this: All that you have experienced and endured has not been a mistake." Vargas placed his hand on Kaijin's shoulder.

Kaijin shivered. The touch was comforting but confusing. *It was not a mistake to lose my family?* His blood boiled. The world around him shifted to a red-orange hue. Feeling the presence manifest within him, he gritted his teeth.

Vargas gently squeezed Kaijin's shoulder. "Kaijin. Calm yourself."

Kaijin saw a reflection of two glowing fiery orbs in Vargas's eyes, and he mentally gasped. *Are my eyes glowing? Have I been possessed?*

"Kaijin!"

"Kaijin."

"No," Kaijin responded aloud to the fiery voice. "What do you want? Have I not done what you asked?"

"Kaijin!" Vargas barked.

The two voices around Kaijin become a jumble of words. "No, I don't want to lose control . . . Not again . . ."

He saw Easthaven burning; his brother's pale, bloody face as he died; his parents' mutilated bodies; his master, Jarial's disgust in the aftermath of the city's destruction.

Death. Too much death.

Kaijin's breathing went ragged, and he slumped. *Please, put me out of my misery. Take me out of this nightmare.*

Vargas lay hands on Kaijin's head. "Almighty Ignis, we beseech your holy flames for guidance."

Energy surged through Kaijin. The sensation was both familiar and impossible to resist. *"It's you."*

Another voice, hissing and crackling like flames, spoke from Kaijin's lips. "I have brought this boy to this sanctuary to fulfill My work. He is My disciple."

Vargas promptly released Kaijin and fell to his knees, fear washing over his face. "Y—yes, Almighty Ignis! Your will be done! Your holy flames shall burn brighter and stronger than ever!"

Kaijin's head canted, and his eyes narrowed, staring at the priest. Kaijin saw a glimpse into Vargas's heart—it seemed unsettled, perhaps from his fear. "See that it is so. Fail in this task, and you will be consumed in my raging whitefire; your life will be forever forgotten in the blaze of death." Kaijin's lips curled into a smirk.

A small part of Kaijin's subconscious spoke out to the possessor. *"Was that a threat? A forewarning? Do you see something in him that he does not?"*

But Kaijin received no response.

"By your holy flames, I will see to it that he is educated and trained," Vargas groveled.

Kaijin regarded Vargas without sympathy. "There is no room for failure—there is no room for weakness."

The divine presence left Kaijin. He slumped back into the couch and exhaled, feeling something let go inside.

He gazed up at the pristine ceiling and the walls of portraits and tapestries. In the corner of his eye, he noticed the bookshelves and soon remembered where he was. The hazy world around him reacquired its natural colors. Somehow, he managed to decipher Ignis's strange context, and it made him feel stronger than before.

"Part of the process of learning your seventh, eighth, and ninth-tiered spells is seeking the knowledge yourself," Jarial once told Kaijin.

Was this what he meant? Have I finally reached that point in my understanding? Kaijin felt alive, renewed, beyond anything he thought himself capable of.

Vargas slowly looked up, his hands still shaking. He took slow breaths to regain his composure. "K . . . Kaijin?"

Kaijin mumbled. "He said—"

"Yes, I know what He said."

Kaijin frowned. "Does this mean I must join the clergy? Do I have to give up my magic in order to do so?"

"No, Kaijin. Your abilities are heavily influenced by Ignis's divine flames, and you must be shown how to harness it. You must also be further educated about His ways, to better understand both yourself as a Firebrand and this power you've been blessed with."

Kaijin nodded slowly, still rattled.

Vargas helped Kaijin to his feet. "Why don't we speak more later? You must be exhausted. Come. You need some food and rest."

Momentary light-headedness made Kaijin groan as he stood. He fingered the flap on his haversack. "A moment, Honored Priest. There is one other important matter."

Kaijin retrieved the fire orb, which pulsated with life.

XXVI

ॐ

Zarya, Nester, Aidan, and Omari sat at the long dining table of the refectory, where they had been offered an exquisite meal, fit for nobility. The immaculate brass tableware shone brightly enough that it appeared to be reserved for special guests only.

Zarya ate slowly while she took in the place, which seemed large enough to easily hold a hundred people, despite the single long center table that only accommodated fifty seats. A plush red carpet ran down the center of the room to the massive fireplace in the rear. Flames danced, and the popping and crackling light provided a coziness, comfort, and warmth. Torches lined the walls, amply lighting the refectory.

"Aidan, 'ow many more of those are you going to eat?" Nester asked.

Ignoring his question, Aidan filled his plate with samples of everything except the sweets. He didn't seem to have a sweet tooth, most likely due in part to his Dragon heritage. He guzzled his third goblet of almond milk, which Zarya assumed was his favorite beverage.

"Enough to fill that bottomless pit of a stomach he has." Omari feasted on helpings of mutton, cabbage, bread, and custard tart, and he washed it all down with spiced apple cider. Next to his chair, Percival happily feasted on a plate piled high with meat.

Zarya hid her smile behind the rose wine-filled goblet she brought to her lips. She'd found the soup, cheese, and bread more to her liking. "Oh, leave him alone, you two. Aidan can eat as much as he wants. He's earned it."

"Hmph! Easy for you to say," Nester grumbled. He sat back in his chair and crossed his arms, staring at his own two plates he emptied faster than he'd put food on them. "That's 'is third 'elping. You do realize 'e intends to eat everythin' in sight?"

The rear doors creaked open, and two silhouettes strolled in.

In the firelight, Kaijin looked refreshed and renewed. Miele flew off his shoulder and latched onto the ceiling above.

Zarya grinned. "Kaijin!" She scrambled out of her chair and ran over to him. "Have you found what you were looking for?"

"I have and more." Kaijin gestured to the man beside him. "Vargas and I were talking."

Vargas nodded to the group in greeting.

Omari rose from his chair. "Great, now we can finally get out of here."

Kaijin shook his head. "No, Omari, I can't leave. There's just too much for me to do here. This is where I belong."

"Well this is where *I* do *not* belong. I am not a follower of Ignis. Besides, I still have my own business to take care of. Now. I am leaving."

"Wait." Kaijin retrieved the fire orb from the haversack. "Remember this?"

Omari glared at the object. "Of course I do."

"So 'ow much is it worth, Kaijin?" Nester rubbed his hands together in anticipation.

"Have you learned more about it?" Zarya inquired.

Kaijin nodded to her. "I have. This fire orb is used in specialized druidic and cleric rituals dedicated to the Firelord. One of the rituals involves transport from one place to another."

"'Ow much?" Nester asked again.

Kaijin looked at Omari. "I can use this orb to transport you to the Citadel, Omari. The holy flames will carry you there."

"The what?" Omari raised an eyebrow. "No, I will not—"

"It's a form of magic that is both arcanic and divine in nature—like the elements," Kaijin explained. "And the Threads of Magic are comprised of the elements that make up the base of our spells—like my fire and your lightning."

Nester cleared his throat. "'Ow much?" When all eyes turned to him, he huffed and crossed his arms, waiting for an answer.

"It's worthless to you," Kaijin said.

The brownie scowled.

Kaijin acknowledged the rest of his comrades. "I must thank you, everyone. Coming here was the best thing that could ever happen to me." He graciously bowed his head.

Omari threw his hands up. "Great. I have helped you, now what about me?"

Zarya sighed. "Did you not hear Kaijin? He said he would send you home. Does it really matter how it's done?"

"Yes, actually. I would like to be certain I get back in one piece."

"Don't worry. You will," Kaijin said, then he and Vargas exchanged a glance. Vargas nodded to Kaijin, then turned and left.

*   *   *

After the doors closed, Kaijin slid into a seat next to Aidan, who was still eating quietly. Aidan looked too into his meal to be listening to the conversation, but one could never tell for certain.

Kaijin smiled at Zarya, Omari, and Nester. "I'm going to use the orb to send you all back to Ghaeldorund. That was our original destination, was it not?"

Omari raised an eyebrow skeptically. "How will the orb do that? What if that afriti comes out and torments us again instead?"

"That won't happen," Kaijin assured him.

"Are you sure this is going to work, Kaijin?" Zarya asked. "Do you . . . *really* want to stay here?"

Kaijin nodded. "My magic is influenced by Ignis. He has manipulated my powers so I feel stronger every time I use them. What I must learn now is something only these people can teach me. I feel like I belong here. I must stay."

Nester made a face. "Eh . . . Not like we 'ave much of a choice, do we? Though, I don't know where in th' soddin' 'ells we can stay in a city like Ghaeldorund. You realize 'ow expensive it is?"

"Maybe Omari can vouch for us, yes?" Zarya suggested with a smile. "After all, we *did* help him with his test. Perhaps someone there will be generous enough to offer us room and board for a night."

Omari bristled. "Hmph! If you think for one minute that I am going to help you people—" A loud clank interrupted him.

Aidan had dropped his fork against the edge of his empty plate. He glared at Omari. "Aidan thinks that you should stop being so selfish. It is least you can do—if not for us, then for Evan and Sephiya, who died honorably in battle so that you could successfully finish test." He took the large soup container from the center of the table and drank the rest of its contents.

"Do not scold *me* about selfishness, you big oaf! *You,* who has not even the decency to leave Kaijin anything worthwhile to eat!" Omari gestured to the empty plates and pitchers of food and drink. Only the sweets remained.

"I will be fine, Omari," Kaijin assured. "Besides, I've been so excited about coming here I've not been very hungry. Are you ready to go back now? We will need to gather around the altar in the main hall so that I can properly perform the spell."

"Yes, let us get this over with," Omari grumbled, brushing past Kaijin as he headed toward the door. Percival scampered after him, a hunk of pheasant in his mouth. Nester and Aidan followed, and only Kaijin and Zarya remained.

Zarya stared at the doorway a moment before facing Kaijin. Her cheeks flushed red. "Kaijin, I just . . . I just wanted to say that despite the problems we might have had, I am glad to have been able to travel with you." She paused. "I will . . . miss you."

Kaijin raised an eyebrow, taken aback. "Miss me? For what? You are a priestess. You will always be busy with duties to fulfill. Don't worry about me."

He felt amusement from Miele. She swooped down from the ceiling and out the door.

Zarya tilted her head to the side. "I am never too busy, Kaijin. I do hope I can see you again someday."

Kaijin gathered his thoughts. "Uh, I will be here, Zarya. I've no intentions of leaving anytime soon."

Zarya looked away a moment, then stared at the floor. She slowly raised her gaze, leaned closer to him, and planted a gentle kiss on his cheek.

Kaijin froze. *She kissed me?*

His first kiss. His heart thumped, and a tingle ran through his body. He felt his face heat, and Zarya chuckled.

He covered his cheek with his hand. "What . . . What was that for?"

"In case I never see you again."

"But I told you that—" Before Kaijin could finish, Zarya had already left.

What did she mean by that? He swallowed and followed after the others.

* * *

When Kaijin and his friends arrived in the main hall, he found the other Ignan priests gathered around the altar waiting for them. At the top of the stairs on the raised platform, Vargas stood beside a tall, lean woman dressed in a ravishing satin flame-colored gown with sequins. Her red belt was likely trimmed in gold metal. Around her neck, she wore a golden holy symbol. She had dark skin, big brown eyes, and soft, full lips. Her dark hair was braided back into two twin plaits.

Kaijin stopped before the foot of the stairs and the two priests. His gaze settled on the woman. Her beauty rivaled Zarya's, more natural than the Celestials' beauty. Something about the woman drew his eye, made him notice her, and made him hope she noticed him. *Surely someone so beautiful must be important.*

He sensed Miele hiding not far away, watching. She eased his pounding heart with a feeling of assurance. He took a deep breath and relaxed.

He'd been so fixed on the beautiful woman. When he finally tore his gaze away from her, he noticed more clergy had gathered and stood on either side of him and his companions, creating an aisle that ran from the base of the stairs to the top step. Kaijin knelt before the stairs and lowered his head. He heard his companions draw closer. Zarya knelt down beside him and bowed her head. He smiled. He would miss her.

"Have your companions decided?" Vargas asked.

Kaijin raised his head slightly. "Yes, honorable one. They will return to Ghaeldorund."

Vargas nodded and whispered something to the woman beside him. Afterwards, she smiled to Kaijin, revealing a set of pearly-white teeth. Her smile was beautiful and perfect, much like Zarya's.

"Arise, Firebrand and allies, and stand before the altar of holy flames," The woman spoke regally.

Without hesitation, Kaijin stood and ascended the stairs, his companions not far behind. As he drew closer to Vargas and the woman, his steps slowed. His gaze remained drawn to the woman. *I can't stop looking at her. Her face . . . so stunningly beautiful. . . .* He realized he'd been staring for far too long and finally managed to tear his gaze from her and look at Vargas.

Smiling, Vargas gestured to her. "Kaijin, this is Ranaiah. She is the high priestess—the Eternal Flame—of the Pyre."

Ranaiah bowed her head. "An honor to meet you, Firebrand."

Kaijin gulped. *The Eternal Flame—the highest religious authority in the Ignan clergy!* "The honor is all mine, great priestess." He was about to kneel down when she placed her hand on his shoulder. He froze. Her touch was perfect—like Zarya's. *Is she a Celestial, too?* He couldn't find a flaw about her. He took a deep breath and straightened. "Forgive me."

Ranaiah graciously nodded and removed her hand. She stepped to one side and gestured to the large brazier before Kaijin. "Are your friends ready?"

Kaijin looked back at his companions. Nester slowly raised his shaky hand.

"What is it?" Kaijin asked.

Nester bit his bottom lip. "Ah . . . it . . . it's not gonna 'urt, is it?"

Vargas chuckled, then responded for Kaijin, "Of course not. The holy flames of the Firelord will take you to your destination. The trip will be faster than a blink of an eye."

When there we no more questions, Kaijin drew closer to the brazier. The heat invigorated him. He peered inside, and the white fire nearly blinded him. He took the orb from his haversack and held it aloft. The swirling fires within it flickered and moved in various patterns; it became more alive. The heat traveled down his arms and to his chest, where it warmed the necklace.

"Come closer," called a voice from the flames.

The brazier's white fire no longer blinded him. The dancing flames entranced him. *"So beautiful."*

Kaijin wanted to feel the holy flames of the Firelord. He wanted to touch Him. He leaned over the brazier, the orb in his hands. His necklace burned, as if in response to the heat of the white fire.

In the heart of the flame, where it burned the brightest, Kaijin glimpsed a faint outline of a figure. Its shape varied.

As Kaijin saw it, it disappeared.

"You belong to me, Kaijin Sora."

"I belong to . . . you. . . ." Kaijn whispered under his breath. The world around him became a blur, and all he saw were the flames. He smiled.

He felt Ranaiah's gentle touch on his shoulder.

"Kaijin, it is time," she said softly.

Her warm breath on the back of his neck eased his tension. He blinked a few times, and the white fire blinded him once again. He had to turn away. "I'm ready, priestess."

Ranaiah's hand slowly slid off his shoulder and down his back, and he shuddered.

He heard a gasp behind him—Zarya. He glanced over his shoulder. Zarya had turned her head away from him. Ranaiah commenced the ritual before he could ponder her behavior.

She folded her hands and bowed her head in prayer. Vargas and the rest of the clergy followed suit. "The Firelord has blessed this day by bringing to us one of His servants. Kaijin Sora has been deemed worthy as His disciple. May His holy flames forever burn."

"May His holy flames forever burn," repeated the rest of the clergymembers, and then Kaijin.

Something took hold of Kaijin again. His vision blurred, and the world gained a red-orange hue. He heard his chanting slur until it became hissing that resembled the crackling flames of the brazier. He couldn't even understand his own speech.

He lowered the orb into the brazier. The flames licked his arms and felt wonderful, softer than silk. It cleansed him, burning away the dirt and dust from his travels. As he leaned forward, the holy symbol hung above the flames.

"I am your Master."

Kaijin whispered, "Master, I beseech your great power. Please send my companions back to Ghaeldorund safely."

There was a series of irritated hisses and crackles before the voice finally replied, *"Know that they will always fear and respect me."*

"Of course, Master."

Kaijin stared at the white fire one more time, and everything went black.

*   *   *

Zarya watched as Kaijin began to glow and flicker like the flames around him. He closed his eyes, and a fiery essence surged through him, igniting every vein in his body. The heat and brightness intensified, making everyone in the main hall cringe.

Zarya's heart pounded furiously. The heat intensified, and she drew back, uttering a prayer of protection from the goddess. A protective ward appeared around her, Omari, Aidan, and Nester.

Nester ducked behind Aidan, who grimaced and shielded his face. Omari stood firm, invoking a translucent shield of his own. Percival hid between Omari's ankles, chirring frantically.

Kaijin released the orb into the brazier. The flames roared, blazing into the atrium. Ranaiah and Vargas jumped back, gawking.

Zarya's invisible shield dampened the heat around them, but as she strained to concentrate, she had a feeling it wouldn't last for long.

Kaijin turned away from the brazier and regarded everyone with a blank stare. His usually sienna eyes glowed with possession. He extended his hands toward his friends and chanted.

Flames leapt from the brazier and engulfed the group. Omari and Zarya's shields collapsed. Aidan fell to his knees, cringing in fear. Nester huddled himself into a ball, screaming.

Zarya no longer saw Kaijin or the other clergymembers—only living, swirling white and orange fire. But the image of Kaijin remained embedded in her mind—as did the sadness. She had seen him for the last time, and her heart sank with the realization that her feelings for him had not seemed reciprocated.

That is where he belongs. He is happy now, that is all that matters. And she is . . . perfect for him.

And then she saw black.

* * *

Omari screamed and thrashed, feeling himself burn, but when he opened his eyes and didn't see fire on him, he calmed down. *How? It feels so real.* His eyes watered, and his vision wavered.

The flames were gone. He wasn't sure if he were alive or dead—last he remembered, he and his companions were encompassed in the flames.

Cool night air kissed his skin. The moon was nearing its apex. He heard crickets, the rustle of grass, and the scurry of small nocturnal animals. Percival, coiled and shivering, sat in his lap.

Omari sniffed the air. It was fresh and crisp—nothing like the pungent coal and brimstone from the Pyre. *Have I been dreaming? Did I even pass the test?* His staff lay in the tall grass beside him, the tip glowing with an electrical shimmer.

Passed. He smiled.

He looked at the grassy fields and realized they were familiar. To the north, a path snaked at the base of a mountain pass. Gryphon Pass. Ghaeldorund wasn't too far away.

Weary, Omari slowly stood. He set Percival on his shoulder, relieved that the adventure was over and he could resume a more stable life. "Hmph. For once you managed to do something right, Kaijin," he muttered.

Someone groaned nearby. He turned toward the sound and spied the rest of his companions laying in the grass. Omari approached them and nudged each one gently with his foot, attempting to rouse them.

Zarya stirred. She groggily opened her eyes. "Mmm . . . Omari?"

"Yes, yes, it is me." Omari helped her to her feet and assisted Nester and Aidan.

Nester rubbed the back of his head. "You mean . . . that li'l trick worked? Kaijin did it?"

"Seems so," Omari said. "Kaiijn got what he wanted, and so did I. Now, I must return to the Citadel. Ghaeldorund lies just beyond the mountains there, through Gryphon's Pass."

Aidan stretched, making his knuckles and his neck pop. Omari cringed at the sounds.

"So, Kaijin is still at the Pyre. . . ." Zarya said wistfully.

Omari huffed. "He is where he belongs. I am just glad to be home." He paused and added reluctantly, "I will see what I can do, for you all to be given some accommodations for the night. Afterwards, however, I must finish my business."

"Of course." Zarya nodded curtly. "It was an honor to have traveled with you."

The group walked the majority of the way in silence. Omari couldn't help but stare off toward the southwest, toward the Pyre.

He is really gone. Omari found himself wondering how Kaijin was faring.

XXVII

ॐ

The essence of Ignis left Kaijin. He sank to his knees, feeling empty, as though his body had been used and discarded just as quickly.

Kaijin leaned his back against the bottom of the braizer and groaned. He stared blankly at the polished obsidian floor.

"Kaijin?"

"Let him be, Vargas." Ranaiah shuffled beside Kaijin and knelt down.

She smelled sweet, flowery. He focused on her. His gaze traced the hem of her robe, then trailed upward, noticing the faint outline of feminine curves. He finally looked into her eyes. Much of her reminded him of Zarya, except she had imperfections. Miniscule dark blemishes dotted her cheeks, and yet, it did not detract from her beauty. It was the only thing he saw about her that assured him that she was, indeed, human. Her natural beauty did not jar him, as Zarya's seemingly unnatural one had. Ranaiah's imperfections were what truly attracted him. He couldn't help but smile at her.

Ranaiah's expression softened. She placed her hand on his and whispered, "Don't try to move around too much. The Firelord has demonstrated his power—and we were all honored to have witnessed it." She gestured to the rest of the hall where the clergymembers stood awe-struck.

Kaijin's smile faded. His companions were gone. *Did the spell work?*

"How do you feel, Kaijin?" Ranaiah asked.

His tension eased. He looked down at her silky smooth hand upon his.

His experience had been far more powerful than what he experienced at Easthaven. "Words can't explain how I feel right now. I'm a Firebrand. I still don't think I am worthy of such an honor. I am a mage. Why has Ignis chosen *me*, of all people? Why has He not chosen you, Ranaiah? You are the Eternal Flame." *And you are beautiful,* he wanted to add.

The priestess tensed. "He has chosen me to do other duties as the Eternal Flame. Ignis has chosen you as His disciple and a conductor of His power. One cannot argue the ways of the gods. Don't worry, Kaijin. I will help you in any way I can." She helped Kaijin to his feet.

Kaijin slowly stood up and braced himself against the edge of the braizer. "Is this going to keep happening to me for the rest of my life?" he asked Ranaiah and Vargas wearily.

Vargas shook his head. "It will happen for as long as Ignis allows. This is something beyond the control of mortals."

"For now, it seems you have completed His task," Ranaiah added. "But that does not mean He is done with you. He is never done with any of us. The Firelord constantly finds new uses for us and tests us through life. We must always be prepared. The way of the Flames are unpredictable; they soothe; they hurt; and they heal."

Kaijin stared at the ground blankly. "People have died because of me. I lost my city—I lost my family."

Ranaiah tilted Kaijin's chin toward the direction of the braizer. "You cannot blame yourself for what happened. Look deep into the brazier and listen to Him. Call out to Him for these answers and listen. He will tell you everything you need to know."

Kaijin had no choice but to look. Old memories—old wounds—reopened in his mind. Easthaven, his family, his friends, his enemies, his master—he saw them all. Sighing softly, he stared into the white flames, looking for that strange figure he had seen before.

The flickering entranced him.

Everything turned hazy, grey and barren.

"Why?" Kaijin called out in his mind. *"Why must there be so much destruction?"* He trekked within the endless, yet familiar barren, grey void of his mind until he encountered a bright light. He shielded his eyes.

The light shimmered into an image of burning white flames that no longer blinded him. *"Purity cannot come without destruction. Destiny cannot be made without purpose."*

Kaijin asked, *"What about my companions? What has become of them?"*

"They are where they desired to be. They are alive and no longer concerned about you."

"Why did you allow my family to die?"

"Their deaths were necessary, for you to begin your path to where you truly belong."

Kaijin's gaze wavered. Tears formed and quickly evaporated, leaving a dry, salty crust on his cheeks. *"No . . . I loved them."*

The flames chuckled. *"They would never understand you, Kaijin Sora. They would forever deem you 'strange.' They have always doubted you."*

"No, they loved me."

"Magic runs deep in your lineage, Kaijin Sora. Your mother knew what mages were capable of and was determined to break that line of Ankhram tradition by distancing herself from the rest of her family. She always worried about your love for magic.

"She also knew she couldn't stop the inevitable, so she gave into Ramon's decision for you to study magic. But even after you had become adept at the art, you would never have been welcomed back home."

Kaijin's eyes burned. He wanted to cry, but the tears wouldn't come. *Is it true?*

"Rorick was always jealous of you," the flames continued. *"He wanted to learn magic, something he could never understand. He shunned you for being different. Your family regretted this path you have chosen, but your undying servitude shall be rewarded soon enough."*

Kaijin cringed. He missed his brother dearly, and he could not begin to believe that he had been unwanted by his family. But the Firelord had always seemed to speak nothing but truth. A lump formed in his throat.

The light brightened, blinding Kaijin again. He groaned, shielding his face and dropping to his knees. His hands slid from his face, and he opened his eyes and discovered he was consumed in darkness.

Kaijin awoke with a gasp. *Where am I?*

A fireplace in the corner and several strategically placed candles lit the room. It was cozy like a bedroom, with a bed, a desk, and a bookshelf. Miele stirred in the shadows of the ceiling above, screeching in an echo to Kaijin's surprise. Ranaiah stood at his bedside.

Kaijin relaxed when he saw the priestess. "Ranaiah?"

"Yes, it's me, Kaijin," she replied softly.

"Where . . . Where am I?"

"One of the recovery rooms in the Pyre. You fell unconscious shortly after the ritual and have been asleep for about two hours."

Kaijin blinked. He let his hand slip off hers. "Have you been here all this time?"

Ranaiah smiled. "Of course. I wanted to ensure that you were all right."

"But—"

She placed her finger over his lips, silencing him. "You are important to all of us here. It is my duty to see to your needs." She lifted her finger.

He licked his lips, tasting a hint that was sweeter than the sweetest honey. *What is happening to me? Why do I feel this way?* The necklace pulsated steadily, but his heart fluttered. He took a deep breath. "Please, Priestess. Don't . . . Don't worry so much about me. You should tend to your other duties."

She chuckled. "You *are* part of my 'other duties', Kaijin. In fact, you are my highest priority."

"You have done far more than you should. I am eternally grateful. Please don't trouble yourself any more than you have."

Ranaiah paused, slowly leaned forward, and kissed his forehead. "You are anything but a bother, Kaijin, but I will respect your wishes and leave you be. Rest some more.

We will talk in the morning. Don't move around too much."

Kaijin stared up at her, feeling lost in her beauty. He swallowed the small lump in his throat. *Should I be feeling like this?* "R–Ranaiah . . ."

She gazed at him, her eyes glittering. "I am always here for you, Kaijin." As she stood, Kaijin gently grasped her hand.

So enamored he was by her, Kaijin hadn't realized he'd done something possibly wrong until he saw the surprise on her face. He quickly released her hand. "Ah . . . forgive me," he mumbled, lowering his head in shame.

Damn it. What's come over me? "I . . . I think you're right. I need more rest. Thank you, Priestess. Thank you for everything." He lay back in bed, and stared up at the ceiling, feeling content. He noticed Miele fluttering happily.

To his relief, Ranaiah was not upset. She smiled at him, her cheeks flushing, and then quietly left.

*   *   *

After shutting the door behind her, Ranaiah rested her back against it and sighed. *So, he is the one I have been seeking. At last, I have found him.*

ABOUT THE AUTHOR

R.M. PRIOLEAU is a game designer by day and dangerous writer by night. Since childhood, she's continued discovering new ways to expand her skills and creativity as she delves into the realm of literary abandon. When R.M. is not leveling up, RPing, or indulged in the latest old school fighting games and RPGs, she is hard at work advocating for great non-profit literacy movements and organizations. Find out more about the author at www.rmprioleau.com.

www.ingramcontent.com/pod-product-compliance
Lightning Source LLC
Chambersburg PA
CBHW021345130726

47899CB00018B/2950